VENGEANCE—BUT AT WHAT COST?

If you were given the chance to right wrongs done to you, to those you care about, or to completely innocent victims, would you claim this "justified" vengeance? Would revenge give you the ultimate satisfaction—or would you discover that, given a choice, you would follow a different path? When these questions were posed to seventeen of today's most imaginative explorers of the fantastic, they come up with such different, original, and compelling answers as:

"The Astral Outrage"—Someone—or something—was preying on the innocent young ladies of a private academy. Could a psychic investigator not only find the culprits but make the punishment fit the crime?

"Even Tempo"—Robbed of his master creation, a young bard is only too willing to face the music to gain his revenge. . . .

"Listen to the Cat"—When her ex-husband would not stop tormenting her, she found a four-footed champion ready to bound to her defense. . . .

VENGEANCE
FANTASTIC

VENGEANCE
FANTASTIC

edited by
Denise Little

DAW BOOKS, INC.
DONALD A. WOLLHEIM, FOUNDER
375 Hudson Street, New York, NY 10014

ELIZABETH R. WOLLHEIM
SHEILA E. GILBERT
PUBLISHERS
www.dawbooks.com

First Printing, October 2002
1 2 3 4 5 6 7 8 9

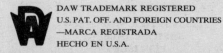

ACKNOWLEDGMENTS

Introduction © 2002 by Denise Little.
Devil Drums © 2002 by Mickey Zucker Reichert.
A Quiet Justice © 2002 by Michelle West.
Knotwork © 2002 by Nina Kiriki Hoffman.
The Capo of Darkness © 2002 by Laura Resnick.
The Astral Outrage © 2002 by P. N. Elrod.
MarySue at Forty © 2002 by Alan Rodgers.
Even Tempo © 2002 by Jody Lynn Nye.
Nothing Says 'I Love You' Like the Kiss of Cold Steel
© 2002 by Yvonne Jocks.
Listen to the Cat © 2002 by Janet Pack.
Boon Companion © 2002 by Elizabeth Ann Scarborough.
Punkinella © 2002 by Deb Stover.
Smoker © 2002 by Mel Odom.
Matchbook Magic © 2002 by Bill McCay.
Sometimes It's Sweet © 2002 by Susan Sizemore.
The Wedding Present © 2002 by Kristine Kathryn Rusch.
Have a Drink On Me © 2002 by Gary A. Braunbeck.
Exits and Entrances © 2002 by Tim Waggoner.

CONTENTS

INTRODUCTION

by Denise Little

WE all know the feeling. You've been wronged, life's unjust, and the urge is boiling in your blood to make the person responsible pay, and pay big. It's a natural feeling, even if civilized constraints and the threat of criminal prosecution keep most of us from acting on our desires. But what if we had the power to strike back without the risk of getting caught? What if we had fantastic powers or magical means of retribution available to us? What would happen then?

Think of it. You're ready to even the score with someone who wronged you, and the opportunity to bring a magical, even a fantastic, twist to your revenge presents itself. Will you take it? What will it do to you and/or your victim if you do? Was the wrong done to you sufficient that the universe has handed you this chance to even the score? What price will you have to pay? Will the consequences be worth the risk? And how does it change you to loose larger-than-life forces on the world for selfish reasons?

It raises a few interesting possibilities, doesn't it? So this is what I asked of the writers who contributed original stories to this collection: Take a look at the fantastic possibilities inherent in revenge in this world and many others, with special emphasis on keeping cosmic forces in balance. Every action, after all, has an equal and opposite reaction. And then take revenge!

Collected here are the results of that challenge to the writers. The stories cover the spectrum from contemporary to ancient, from divine intervention to divine retribution, from bouncy fairy-tale revenge to the darkest of dark arts, and just about everything in between. The taste for revenge comes in all flavors and styles, as the stories in this book demonstrate—but all of them have one thing in common: the revenge is fantastic in more ways than one.

Here's to getting even in fantastic style!

DEVIL DRUMS

by Mickey Zucker Reichert

Mickey Zucker Reichert is a pediatrician whose fantasy and science fiction novels include *The Legend of Nightfall*, *The Bifrost Guardians* series, *The Last of the Renshai* trilogy, *The Renshai Chronicles* trilogy, *Flightless Falcon*, *The Beasts of Barakhai*, *The Lost Dragons of Barakhai*, and *The Unknown Soldier*, all available from DAW Books. Her short fiction has appeared in numerous anthologies, including *Assassin Fantastic*, *Knight Fantastic*, and *Apprentice Fantastic*. Her claims to fame: she *has* performed brain surgery, and her parents *really are* rocket scientists.

FIRE leaped from cottage to barn to cottage, scattering men and women, and leaving a trail of smoking timbers. From the church window, I signed the cross ceaselessly, until it became a mindless, desperate gesture. I remembered my father and brothers and withdrew; but I could still hear the screams of my people. The wolf howls of the Norse invaders were as sharp as the swords that fed ravenously upon our Christian blood. The Norsemen impaled themselves on our spears and axes, as eager for death as to deal it.

Sister Meghan took my head in her hands and caught me to her breast. "Don't cry, Sister Enid. Our Christ will take vengeance against their heathen gods, and they'll trouble good Christians no longer." That trite promise no longer soothed me, but I let her hold me because she was all I had.

The darkness deepened. Soon, the war would end, one way or another. The baying of the Norsemen as they hounded and slew out fleeing warriors drowned the lap of the surf around our island. I knew the survivors would run here for sanctuary; they had no place else to go. Our

strongholds stood on the mainland, beyond the reach of
the dragon boats of the invaders.

Defended by the spiritual and physical fortifications of
the church, we could hold the Norsemen at bay with
arrows, spears, and boulders until we depleted our stores
of food. Then we would have to send our men out at
them again, and the blond barbarians would slay them,
rape and murder us, plunder and despoil the sanctity of
our temple. And, I thought with drooping conscience,
God would allow it, just as He had before. Although I
had been taught never to doubt, I questioned the pur-
poses of a deity who would allow infidels to slaughter
his worshipers. Fearing my own faithlessness, I clutched
my cross, whispered a fervent prayer, and followed
Meghan to the main gate.

As night enclosed us in darkness, the stragglers arrived, men and women I had known and loved since
childhood: Garbhan the cooper, just now without his
smile. Odhran the blacksmith clung to a notched sword
with the same love he had lavished upon his old lame
stallion until its death. Nuallan, the son of our chief,
cried without shame. Days before, we had laughed,
traded, sung in the cobbled streets, and shared beer. I
tried to forget the others, companions who, I thanked
the Lord, I could not imagine as gruesome corpses.

My father came, bearing the message that Mother and
five of my seven brothers had been killed. Brian staggered in later, my youngest brother Corbin in his arms.
The child clung to life, eyes tight, breaths shallow. Blood
stained the crudely wrapped bandages around his chest.

I did not have the strength to cry. Overwhelmed by
too many tragedies, I reacted to none of them. They all
blended into one numbing demon that had forced its
way into God's home.

Brian carried Corbin to the loft where Meghan and I
had spread straw for the wounded. Last night, I had
sneaked from my hard pallet and rested in the thick
straw. It had once smelled sweetly of meadows and summer. Now, it was tainted with the blood of injured Christians, and fouled by those too weak to stand. It muffled
the moans of dying men and the cries of my dear, handsome brother, cradled like a baby in Brian's arms. The

memory of hay-smell was overpowered by the all-too-present acrid reek of fire and death.

Sister Meghan tended the wounded. While she set to her task, my father presented me with a prisoner. When the raids began, I had helped my brother Annant learn the language of the Norsemen so that we could parley and perhaps avoid bloodshed. A peaceful man, Annant loved God and His works and wrote ballads as beautiful as nature. He'd convinced me to join the convent; his death in this raid made me doubt the Lord. When Annant had come forward to parley, the Norsemen tore out his throat like a pack of starved curs.

Because I spoke his tongue, he was now mine to deal with. My father had placed the bound prisoner in a small prayer room. As I entered the chamber, I stared at the tall, pale Viking, my heart filled with loathing and my mind with the memory of Annant's last words:

> *"A Norseman's heart*
> *Is an icicle in a fire pit.*
> *His marching feet are devil drums*
> *In the hollow caverns of hell.*
> *But hate them not, sweet sister.*
> *They are pagans who will one day find*
> *Our Christ*
> *And forget their barbaric, one-eyed god."*

I stared at the Norseman. "What do you want from my people?" I demanded. "We will give you your gold, gems, and jewels. What must we do that you leave us in peace? What is it you want?"

The Viking's mouth curled into a smile. "We will take your treasures as we win them. You can't give us what we want peacefully. We seek war! Death in glory and a place in Valhalla! The rhythms of swinging swords and the chiming melody of steel! The berserker frenzy that displays death in vivid clarity . . ."

I silenced him with a wave and translated his answer into a single sentence for those listening. "They will not bargain; they enjoy war."

"Blond beast." I hissed at the prisoner and slammed the door on his laughter.

It followed me. I wondered if the man who had injured Corbin had laughed, and looking upon my little brother became far more difficult for the thought. Meghan washed and rebandaged his wound, then attended the other six patients. It surprised me we had any wounded at all. Only a brave and skillful man could carry another victim away while horsemen harried his retreat and hacked down his escaping troop.

It grew quiet. The lazy lap of water against the shore became like the last trickling sands from an hourglass. All our windows and gates remained barred. The shuffling of weary bowmen and spear wielders on the ramparts seemed as eerie as the Norseman's laugh. With the church so crowded with people, I could only stretch out among the wounded or near the prayer rooms. The dying gasps of those we tended would bring me nightmares, and I did not wish to share their fever dreams. So, I slept instead in front of the door to the prisoner's cell.

I was awakened before dawn by a harsh, singsong voice chanting in the language of the Norsemen. Curious, I listened to my captive through the door, rose, and straightened my wrinkled white robes.

"Ye Odin!" he called to his heathen god in our church prayer room. "May daylight bring the battle tide and Norsemen reap enemies like ripe crops. May the madness you inspire fill our people. May Norsemen find Valhalla and our foes find Hel!"

I fled. I could not listen to the ramblings of a bloodthirsty animal. I found my brother Brian and my father and begged news.

"We shot two Norsemen who came within range of our walls this daybreak. The others linger, performing foul rites with fire and blood." Brian shook with anger.

My father handed me a mug of water and a piece of bread with a thin smear of honey. He nodded toward the prayer rooms. At my appalled stare, he lowered his head. "You don't want to feed him?" His curled, dark hair and close-cropped beard sagged with weariness. For the first time, his eyes had lost their hopeful sparkle.

"I don't want anyone to feed him," I replied vehemently. "He may have killed Annant or Alain or any of our brothers. He may have stabbed Corbin. He calls heathen gods into our temple."

"His heathen gods can't enter the home of God," insisted Brian. Tall and broad-shouldered like Father, he had Mother's sharp cheekbones and wide-set eyes. "But his words may still give us information. I've heard he's one of the chieftain's sons. Faiiing that, maybe you can convert him to Christianity so he can find heaven and Christ."

With misgivings, I took the food to the prisoner. Since we had shackled his arms, I held the bread to his bearded face and let him gnaw it. His eyes glowed with cold, blue fires, and his braided hair stank of dried sweat. He ate slowly, savoring every morsel. When he swallowed the last bite and I turned to leave, he spoke, "I am Ivar Thordarson. My father owns the flagship *Servant of Aegir*."

I suppressed the urge to run and recalled Brian's words. I faced him. "Enid," I said simply. "Perhaps your father will bargain for your return."

His smile was tolerant, like a priest trying to explain the Trinity to an ignorant savage. "My father has Sivard, my eldest brother whom they call Raven. He's the finest swordsman I know. Ketil lived last I knew, and Asmund is home tending the farm. He'll see me soon in Valhalla, if Odin grants me the honor to die in his name in battle." He paused with obvious discomfort. "It is far more humiliating that you captured me alive."

I squatted in front of him. "What are these rituals your people are performing?"

"They're preparing our dead for Valhalla," Ivar explained. "And making blood sacrifices to our gods— Thor and Tyr and Freyja . . ."

". . . and Odin," I said sullenly.

"No," replied the Viking matter-of-factly. "We prefer to hang victims to Odin."

With a gasp, I drew the cross and rushed from the room.

I spent most of my time with Corbin. I changed his bandage far more often than necessary, moved him to prevent sores from the straw, and chased mice from his wounds. Most of my people prayed to God for deliverance from the Norsemen who waited impatiently as we ran low on food. Some begged for everlasting food stores or for swift death and the joys of heaven. I prayed only for Corbin, who grew uglier as fever ravaged him.

Gradually, Corbin began to recover. His fever fell, and his speech became coherent. Then, on the fourth day of our imprisonment, as food and hope dwindled, Corbin died. He screamed once in his sleep, a pained howl that haunted me. "God!" His dying plea went as unanswered as my own. At that moment, I vowed my last brother would not die in the coming battle, the one I knew must begin tomorrow before our warriors grew too weak to fight.

I needed an escape from the pitying glances of friends who had loved Corbin, and from the hopeless trances of my companions. I visited Ivar often. As time had passed, his eyes still held their wolfish gleam, but his hawklike face had grown hollow and his skin dry from lack of water. We spoke often, about his family, about mine, about his parade of deities, and about God. I never converted him to Christianity, but that may have been because I was so unsure of my own faith.

"My brother died," I announced flatly. I did not care if he answered.

"That's sad for you," he said softly. "But he did succumb to battle wounds, in glory. Had he been a believer, he would have reached Valhalla."

I smiled weakly. I knew he gave Corbin a great compliment.

After a respectful silence, he asked a different question. "The war begins tomorrow?"

I nodded.

"I don't hear the storming of Thor the Thunderer. How does the day look?"

"A gray cloud stalks the horizon," I replied. "It is death come to claim many good men."

"And evil men as well, Enid," added Ivar.

A tense silence passed between us. Apparently, he pondered his past victories. I thought of despairing matters.

"Do your gods answer your prayers?" I asked, scarcely audibly.

"Odin?" Ivar laughed. "Almost always if it's for battle. He likes nothing more than watching men tear one another to pieces."

I shuddered and signed the cross methodically. "How can your people be so cruel?" I quivered with impotent rage. "How can you rape and murder without remorse? What sort of religion demands the blood of men?"

Ivar smiled. "All religions, Enid."

"No!" I screamed. "Not mine. My God is merciful. My God . . ."

". . . lets his own followers die," he finished. "And he demands the conversion of infidels. Their conversion, or their death. Your people do and will kill in the name of your God. They will sweep across happy lands they call pagan and slaughter in the name of mercy. You watch, Enid."

"No!" I gaped. I had no energy to argue. The strange idea that writhed through my mind frightened me. "I hope our armies oust your berserkers. I hope we trample you the way you trampled us. I hope . . ." My voice became a hysterical shriek. Quickly, I left the room and Ivar with his arrogant smile, no longer certain whose will I served.

I scarcely slept that night as I lay in the straw with the four wounded still left alive. Sister Meghan came to comfort me when my tossing awakened her, but I would not let her touch me. Tomorrow would see the end of our men, the end of our people, and the end of an age. Eventually, I knew fate had determined our White Christ would end the reign of the grim Father of Warriors, Odin the Gray, but that would bring scant comfort when I watched my father and the last of my brothers die. Should I remember this when Ivar and his savages raped me and Meghan and the church? According to God, men must help themselves, and I would aid my people.

When our soldiers marched toward death, I draped the huge stone crucifix in our altar room with ropes and did not allow myself the time to think. But when I trot-

ted down the bleak white corridors to Ivar, I knew it
was my decision, and I could still change it.

His wrists blistered from bonds tied too long in place,
Ivar followed me curiously, with quiet patience. Proudly,
I displayed the wooden crucifix, towering to nearly twice
a man's height, its carved Christ looking thin and helpless, silently judgmental despite His closed eyes. Ivar regarded me quizzically. "Are you planning to crucify
me?" He laughed, mocking my religion, but he
laughed alone.

Before he could think to move, I had flicked the noose
around his neck, and there was no way left for him to
fight. Quickly, using the ropes as a triple pulley, I hauled
him from the ground with a strength I never knew I had.

Ivar could not speak, but his sea-colored eyes widened
in amazement and horror.

I hanged him, calling upon his own god. "Lord Odin!
Grant my people the battle madness to slice down your
Norsemen like scythes among wheat. Claim the souls of
your men, dark with blood. Let us reap the carnage you
love, gray god!" Irony seared me. This pagan god might
aid my people while my own God would only assure the
Northmen their victory. And Ivar got his wish, to die in
Odin's name.

Thunder boomed like the toppling of a mighty fortress. A chill wind tore open the door in front of me.
I fainted.

"Enid! Enid!" Brian stood over me. Terrified, I
glanced at the wooden cross. Ivar's body was gone, as
well as the rope I had used to perform the sacrilege. I
dared not wonder who had done my cleaning.

"Did you hear me?" Brian nearly wept. "We won.
We fought like a well-trained army. We chased away the
conquerors. Naturally, we took our own losses.
Father . . ."

I tried to reply, but could not. My body burned, hot as
dragon breath. Destined to lose whichever side I chose, I
knew the pounding I heard was not thunder. It was too
steady, without lightning nor rain. It echoed like devil
drums.

A QUIET JUSTICE

by Michelle West

Michelle West is the author of a number of novels, including *The Sacred Hunt* duology and *The Broken Crown, The Uncrowned King, The Shining Court,* and *Sea of Sorrows,* the first four novels of *The Sun Sword* series, all available from DAW Books. She reviews books for the online column *First Contacts,* and less frequently for *The Magazine of Fantasy & Science Fiction.* Other short fiction by her appears in *Knight Fantastic, Familiars, Assassin Fantastic,* and *Villains Victorious.*

I wash the dishes without wearing rubber gloves, while the radio blares in the background, its announcer's voice smooth and curiously flat. My hands are shaking. The police have issued an advisory warning for women living in the Greenwood Danforth area; a serial rapist is on the loose. There is a phone number that follows this announcement. They want information.

I have one sink. I put the dirty dishes into it, glasses first, a precarious sculpture, while I run hot water in a thin stream from the tap. That's a miracle, that tap, the stainless steel faucet, rim crusted with minerals. Each glass comes out of the white suds, smelling like lemon, and rests a minute under the passing stream before I move it to the dish rack to dry. I love this part best, and I extend it, watching as fingerprints, old wine, dried milk, all evidence of the necessity of sustenance, are washed away; the glass is made new, for a moment, beneath the sheen of water.

Not so my hands; they pale in the water, and when I am finished with this simple task, they are wrinkled and heavy, nails soft and white. I have old hands. All that early exposure to sun, I suspect.

It has been a long time since I last saw my husband,

and I will see him again soon; it is why I am absorbed
in the ordinariness of these daily tasks.

When I was young, I had servants. I lived upon the
heights, for I loved the view, and while these servants
toiled and slaved, I would step out and gaze down, and
down again, into the green of valleys and fields, the
white of clouds, the blue—deep and endless—of the tur-
bulent, living sea. And my hands were pale and pink
with youth; no lines gathered above the knuckles,
around the joints. I wore gold as if it were wool, and
indeed wool was considered an inferior fabric; what need
had I of warmth? The sun was there, and it rode the
skies on command.

I was the daughter of important people, although their
names are forgotten now, and their achievements—if
they achieved anything at all beyond power and
wealth—have long been forgotten. Nonetheless, that importance was their inheritance, and I bore it with pride
and with an inevitable sense of duty.

I think of that, sometimes, in the small apartment I
now call home. I do not live upon the heights; I cannot
afford it. I was raised to be beautiful and dutiful, and in
this day and age, if one is prized, the other has fallen
out of fashion.

I dry the dishes, and watch as the towels grow wrinkled and damp. Like my hands.

I like the cleanliness of this small space, the neatness
I force upon it, day by day. I like the small television in
my spare living room. Its crisp color images, framed by
faux wood, are all the art I can afford; its voices, its
moving blur, its stream of information both solace and
company for much of the evening.

I seek no other.

Ah, I am so bad at telling stories. Even my own. Especially my own. They are tangled up in *him,* all of them.
My half brother was given the gift of poetry, of the passion of the spoken word, the written word. My half
brother was given song, and his fingers, his hands, found
no employ in the simple tasks of washing dishes, cleaning an apartment, making a meal.

I miss him. But he is gone. Gone.

What have I done?

* * *

Let me start in a different place. My apartment has two rooms. The bedroom is small enough that it fits only a narrow bed, and I spend little time there. But the single room that serves as living and dining room, capped on one end by a small kitchenette and on the other by an even smaller bathroom, has windows from one wall to the other.

From here, I watch the sun rise; I watch it set. I watch the changing face of the moon, silver and cool as it rests in the evening sky. I learn the names of the constellations in a hundred different languages, although I pronounce them all incorrectly. They don't seem to mind.

In the windows, I have planters. They are made of green plastic or rust-colored ceramic, and they are filled with a dark, rich earth. Into that earth, I plant seeds, and from it, I coax life, but the process is slow and almost thankless; so many of my seedlings die. I have learned that yellow is the color of drowning, and brown the color of dehydration; in some ways, I pay attention to these more than the colors of the blossoms themselves.

My sister had my grandmother's blood, through and through. She was given the gift of the gardener; there was no earth from which she could not cajole life, no plant that she could not cause to grow. Whole fields would ripen and quicken when she bent her mind to the task, singing wordlessly as she labored with a deep and quiet joy.

I remember when she lost her beloved child: the winter that followed, the first winter, was bitterly cold. I remember the surprise and horror we felt when the snows at the peaks of our distant mountains descended upon the earth, crushing and withering the life of the land with its bitter cold.

I remember pleading with her.

Do the right thing. Your daughter will learn how to be happy, I added—and the words torment me now—*because she has found a husband and started a life of her own. Oh, I know he's not a perfect husband, but who is? He is well-off, and he will take care of your girl.*

And my sister said, *She doesn't want him.*

*What does that have to do with anything? She is old
enough now that she should accept the responsibility of
adulthood with grace. And who else would have her now,
after what's happened?*

Aie, sister, wherever you are, forgive me. Forgive me.
She doesn't answer.

She, too, is gone. But the snows lay across the concrete of the city, and the ice gleams unrepentant in the
bitter winter sun, a reminder of her ancient wrath, her
ancient loss. I should have listened to her. Who better
to understand the laws of the living than the woman to
whom life itself was almost everything?

Her daughter was queen, in her right; she paid for her
power with her happiness. Who better than I to understand that? I saw her youth leeched from her face, year
after year, until nothing of the child remained in her. Or
to her mother.

But enough, now. Enough.

I have learned, sister. I wish I could go back; I wish
I could undo all the damage I did. I wish that I had had
the courage to let the winter reign until your injured
child was at your side forever; had we stood together
then, she would be the bright, curious girl that you so
loved.

I did not love her enough, not then.

How could I?

But no, let me take responsibility for my actions. I
was foolish. I was hurt. And as is so often the case,
others paid the price.

In winter, in this world, life does not stop.

In winter, in this world, no one would have come to
you, weeping, threatening, or mocking your loss, because
in this world, you are not the source of the harvest. Food
comes from places where winter does not reign. The
season is not considered a judgment; the mortals who
live within it do not hear the echoes of your frenzied
grief and your bitter withdrawal.

I walk among them, drawing my coat tight around my
shoulders while salt stains my boots, and wind, caught
by buildings vaster than the homes of old gods, pulls at
my hair, reddens my cheeks.

There are cars—I do not own one—that roar like angry beasts as they traverse the impossible length and breadth of this great city, leaving their plumes of smoke trailing across the air, some hint of their internal fires. I walk to work.

Work, for me, exists below ground.

Once that might have conjured images of dark caverns, whose heights, untroubled by meager torchlight or the all-seeing rays of the sun, were miniature nights, devoid of moon and star. In such a place, your daughter existed.

But here, in this time, there are no caverns. Light exists by some miracle of electricity, some spark that the gods did not own and did not invent. It comes in all manner of colors, phosphorescent, neon, other things I do not have the words for. A young man once explained to me how it worked; how it had something to do with the burning of coal or the fall of tons of water; I understood it only for as long as his words and his attention lasted. It is gone again.

Our niece, I think, would have understood it better.

And had I harkened to her, I, too, would have had some glimmer of that understanding. But she was so pure, so focused, so *driven;* I was afraid of her. I was afraid that she despised me.

I do not think she did; I do not think that I was worthy of even that much of her attention. Do you know that I envied her? For to her was granted the things I lacked: Reason. Intellect. Logic. Had she been ugly, I think I could have borne this with grace; she was not ugly. Although she was not graceful, not delicate, although she was not feminine, she was beautiful.

She did not use her beauty.

Men fought and died for her; whole cities raised her standard. Heroes were driven to her, and by her, and they, too, fell under her spell. And she never once chose to invoke the allure of her beauty; she abjured the only power that *I* had. Did you understand her? Did you understand that a life could have power that was not bestowed, and was not granted, by men?

I am trying to understand that now.

This is my battlefield.

I work in a small store that makes frames. I do not
own it, of course; I owned little in my own right, and
that has not changed. I am content to let ownership de-
volve to others.

The owner of this shop is a round, robust woman who
calls herself Carol unless she is angry. In anger she draws
out her family's name and places it, like a wall, between
herself and the outside world. But today, as on most
days, anger is not even hinted at in the youthful cast of
her features.

Things slender and starved are in fashion in this age
of plenty. I have seen it myself, countless times, and I
have fallen under the dictate of its tyranny. It is why I
like Carol; she has not. Her skin is smooth and free of
blemish, but the sun and the constant laughter that un-
derlies her expression have worked lines into the corners
of her eyes and mouth.

Only my hands look like that.

She smiles when she sees me, and rushes toward the
locked doors to grant me entrance, leaving the vacuum
cleaner whirring at her back. I step in, pulling away scarf,
gloves, hat, coat, layer by layer revealing how thin I am
in comparison, how joyless.

Her smile doesn't falter, but it does change; she places
a hand upon my arm. How many people dared to touch
me when I was young? Only one. One.

"You're seeing your ex today?"

I nod, wordless. I do not want to think of him now. I
look at her hand and I try to smile.

How many people dared to offer, without thought,
such a simple gesture of comfort? How many could conceive of the notion that I might desire comfort, who
had everything?

Why did it take scientists, with their clear cold eyes,
to understand that the farther away from the earth you
get, the colder you become?

I cut glass for a living.

Carol cuts glass as well, but it is not the whole of her
life: she enjoys talking with the people who come, day
by day, though the open doors. Men and women bring
their paintings, their slick, curled posters, their words

and their photographs, determined to preserve them
from the harm of simple air, simple sun. Glass will do
that, held by metal or wood, frames that serve to high-
light what they value.

It is seldom that I choose to speak with the customers.
But sometimes I can't help myself.

Today, just after Carol left for lunch, two people came
in. A woman much younger than I, with a child. She
was not remarkable in any way, although her dark hair
was silvered with streaks of early gray. But he? Five
years old, maybe six, and confined to a heavy, mechani-
cal chair. She waited for him; he pushed the small lever
on the armrest of his moving throne.

Her smile did not falter.

I think I forgot to breathe. I could barely look away
from her face to see the face of the boy.

She caught me staring.

Met my eyes, her own losing none of the warmth that
she offered her son. But I saw the exhaustion beneath
the smile, understood why her hair was so gray. I could
almost read the plea—and the warning—that moved beneath the surface of her unchanging expression. I set the
glass aside and stepped away from the protection and
safety of the counter.

"I'm sorry, Carol isn't here at the moment; she's just
left for lunch."

She frowned slightly. "Carol?"

"The—the owner." I realized that I'd make a mistake.
"I—Carol is usually the one who deals with customers.
I—I build the frames." This was not entirely true.

And she must have known it. She must have ascribed
the awkwardness to my lack of comfort. "Oh."

"But if it's not too difficult, I'm sure I can help you."

She walked over to her son's chair, and I saw that a
bag was hanging from the handles that jutted out of its
back. Pulling out a manila envelope, she walked toward
me. "I was hoping to have a couple of pictures framed."

I held out a hand; I took what she offered. I forgot
to put the counter between us again. A mistake.

There were three pictures in the envelope.

The first was of her, with her son in her lap. Her arms
were wrapped around his chest, as if she could absorb

him whole by simply drawing him tightly against her. His face was serious, studious; he had caught one of her fingers and was examining it carefully.

In the second picture, they were joined by a man in a suit, his hair grayer than hers. The boy sat between them in a chair, and they each stood with a hand on his shoulder, smiling into the camera as if posed that way by the person behind the lens. Mother. Father. Son.

But it was the third picture that was painful to me, that is still painful now. Of the three, it was the least polished; the focus was off, and the lighting was poor. The man, free from the confines of his suit, was in motion, his face lifted toward the ceiling, his eyes closed, his mouth open. Photographs are silent, robbed of the life of motion, but I could feel his; I could hear the low, deep tones of his laughter.

His son was high above him, arms draped over the backs of his hands as he was lifted in the air, a blur, a child laughing as he was tossed and spun against the whims of gravity. No wheelchair bound him, no reminder of the fact that his legs could not—and would never—carry his weight; he existed, as any child exists, who is both a source of love and joy.

"I know it's not really in focus," the woman broke in self-consciously. "But it's my favorite picture. I took it. My husband is the camera whiz. And he doesn't like the picture because his eyes are closed." She grinned. "We each got to choose a picture. That's mine. My husband chose the one of me and my son; my son chose the picture of the three of us.

"I know they're different sizes, but we'd like them to be in the same frame."

"Your husband seems . . . happy here."

"He's the cheerful one," she replied. "He's always been the cheerful one. My and my son have the dour genes in our family."

I knew I shouldn't ask. I *knew* it. But the words wouldn't stop. "When did you meet him?" I kept my eyes on the picture because I could not look away.

"My husband? Just over ten years ago."

I wanted to ask her if she loved him. I wanted to ask her what he said when she delivered herself of this child, this crippled child. I wanted to ask her if the child had ever doubted, for a moment, that he was loved.

I wanted to ask her if her husband lied to her, raped her, and then blamed her when the progeny of that union did not live up to his image of himself.

But the picture was enough of an answer. That picture, that wife, that child.

"Your boy," I told her softly, "is very lucky."

When I was young, I was taught how to be beautiful. I was taught how to be a perfect wife. I believed that the sum of my value was in those two things, provided I remained untouched. Pure.

There were good girls. There were bad girls.

Men were simply men.

Funny, that.

My husband was a man's man. I did not desire him, if the truth be known. He was rough, and lewd, and although he was handsome—we were all handsome—his eyes had an edge to them, and his words were a little too well honed. He wanted me, though. That was enough, back then; he wanted me, and I hadn't the means to protect myself.

Afterward, wet and sticky and in terrible pain, I knew that I had only one choice: to marry him, or to be beneath that holy state for the rest of my miserable existence. He had already let it be known to any who would listen that he had me; that I had fallen.

If I had been braver, if I had had any other skills, perhaps my life would have been different. Had I sword, had I shield, had I the ability to inspire and lead, I might have become a warrior and set myself upon another path.

But I had none of those things.

I married him.

And on the eve of our wedding, he in his triumph and I in my Pyrrhic victory, he was bedding the handmaidens; I could hear their piteous screams, their terrible wails. I hated him then, and I hated his victims, for it was clear to me that what he had taken from me—my freedom, my youth—had meant *nothing* to him. I was no different from any other woman who happened to

catch his attention, except for one little thing: my rank.
And what that rank would mean to him.

I could not accept that.

That is the truth.

I could not accept that I meant *so little*.

I could not hurt him, and I could not stop him, but I
could vent my pain and my anger upon the women he
desired, as he had desired me. Aie, the wrongs that we
do in our pain and our terrible pride. I pay my penance
now. I atone.

I remember the night that my eldest was born. I remember it clearly. I know what he told the others, my
husband; he had, after all, fathered other children, and
those children had been born whole. I was to blame. I
was the one who had, in my resistance, my hubris, borne
him this weakling son, this terrible stain, this accusation.

And I? Did I love the child?

No. He was proof of everything I had lost, and he was
not even a pretty cage, a pretty chain; he was what I
was: crippled. Unable to leave. Ugly. And yet . . .

He repudiated the child.

I did not wish to lose my husband. He was all that
was left me; he was all that I had. What he said, I accepted. But I watched my child from a distance.

Had my husband ever taken joy from him, had he
ever shown him the love that this stranger's husband
showed her son, things might have been different.

But things change.

You've no doubt heard many things about my son's
wife. That she was beautiful goes without saying. She
was no fool; she was aware of her beauty. Had she been
born today, she would still be made of plentiful, soft
curves; she has no desire to be mistaken for a child or
a scrawny maiden.

Everywhere she went, men desired her. Everything
she did drew the eye; every word she whispered was an
invitation. But it was an artless invitation; I understand
that now. She was unskilled at lying; everything that
came to her came as it comes to a child, absorbing the
whole of her attention and her focus.

Was she a bad girl?

Was I good?

In the terms of that day, yes. She was born to be loved because it was so easy to love her; she offered everything she hard, time and again, with a wiliness and an openness that I have never shown. I hated her.

That is the truth; a harsh truth. I denied myself the pleasure of her company because I knew that I would be judged against it, and found wanting, always wanting, in the comparison. Where I could undercut her, I did, whispering softly about the looseness of her morals, while safe in the lofty abode of mine. Because no matter how hard I worked, I could never have what she possessed by nature.

And so I remained, safe and alone, and she wandered in the world, meeting, taming, conquering and being conquered, by the beauty she saw in everything. She was a gentle mirror.

I see her now; I welcome her when she calls. She isn't tentative with me; her smile is generous. She opens her ample arms and sweeps me into them as if I'm the one who is frail and in need of comfort. I speak of my work, and she speaks of hers. She will take me on her long walks, if the day is clear and bright; if it is not, she will join me among my potted plants, speaking to them as if they were her natural audience. I enjoy her company; there is no rivalry between us now. But it is after she leaves that I watch her most carefully, from my balcony, or from the steps that lead to my apartment.

I see her when she stops to speak to the children, her face dimpling in pleasure at their antics, their desire to please her. I see her when she reaches out a hand to help the elderly, the infirm, the blind; I watch as she carries odd parcels, opens doors, listens to the awkward confessions of total strangers as if those confessions were sacred and personal.

She does not judge what she hears. Sometimes I envy these passing strangers; I feel a pang of jealousy that starts from the very center of my being and spreads, like ripples in a still pond into which she has fallen whole.

I let it. I am not proud of jealousy, but it is part of

my nature; I can no more help feeling it than you can pain when the fire laps at your feet. But I do not act on it. I do not respond to it. I accept it, and it passes.

I could lie, but what is the point? Why twist words into a weave that holds no truth? I could say that I do not remember when my hatred of her passed into acceptance and the uncomfortable longing of love, but I *do* know.

I am a mother.

I have children, several children.

Of the four that I bore, two boys and two girls, three survive. The younger son was swallowed by technology, his mysteries dissipated by study and scholarship and the science that knows no mysticism. Although he would be pleased at the state of the world beyond the continent I have chosen as my home, he has not part to play in it; he is silent.

I will not speak of him further.

But I will speak of my oldest, my first, my crippled, frightened, angry boy.

When my husband first saw him, he was angered into a terrible silence. I was weak from the pain and the shock of a first childbirth, and in my delirium I gave my son to his father tearfully. He carried him to the mountain's craggiest face and left him, exposed him to the elements.

He could not understand, not then, and not later, that these elements, in their season, had nursed and nurtured me in the isolation of my childhood; that they would recognize my blood. The child was carried by the winter winds, his cries thin and weak, and delivered into the spring.

There, by the warmth of the ocean in a country that no longer exists even in legend, he found a home with two women—always, women—who took pity upon his deformity and raised him.

I could not leave my home immediately; I did not suckle him. I regret that loss more than I regret any other loss I have suffered: these arms did not hold him, these breasts did not provide him the nourishment he required. There is a terrible emptiness within me at the lack.

But I did not hate the two women whose love he had gained before he could even smile. Perhaps it was because they were plain. Perhaps it was because they were gentle. Perhaps it was because they were free of pretension. I do not know. But although they had what I desired, although they kept my son from me, I felt only gratitude toward them.

No, that is not quite true. I felt envy as well, but for the first time that envy was a thing of shame. I did what I could to help them.

When they came to me to tell me that my son could speak, I sent my nephew to them, with his honeyed voice, his gift with words, his passion for stories. When they came to tell me that he could think, that he could question—and did—all that he saw from their simple home, I sent them toys, heavy things of gold, with wheels and bells and secret compartments. I sent him a pony that spoke the language of men, and upon that pony I placed a saddle in which even a child with useless legs might sit.

And when they told me that he had taken the toys of gold to the smithy in the distant village, and had them melted and set with the smooth, beaten stones of the grotto, to create beautiful pieces of jewelry, I sent him other tools besides.

He was happiest when he was engaged in acts of creation. He saw himself, and knew that he was ugly, but until he left the side of the two women who loved him, he did not truly understand what a sin that was.

Is this the story that is told of me and my son?

No. Of course, no.

In the stories, I, jealous wife, cold perfectionist, tossed him from heaven's seat to the oceans below in the hope that he would drown.

But these stories were created after my son came to meet his father. His father, proud and cold, had seen for himself what the boy's gift was, and desired to own it, as he owned all else. *I? I would never have sent you away; you are not a mere daughter; you are my son, my flesh and blood. It was your mother, child, your mother who was weak. Women are weak. You must know that.*

My son said nothing; he might have believed his

father, for his desire for a father was so visceral it was almost a visible aura. But he had been raised by women, and they had been kind, and if there was weakness in them, it was the weakness and fear that comes only with a great love. He kept his own counsel, but he did not accuse his father of lying. Not then.

Instead, welcomed home, he wandered the halls of his father's great villa, his legs in braces, his stride a broken thump, like stuttering heartbeat, beneath the open skies. There he saw his aunts, his uncles, his brother and his sisters, his cousins; he saw their slaves, their lovers, their captives; he saw, with his own yes, that they were all perfect of form and figure, unblemished, unscarred. Whole.

He was not quick to understand people. But he was quick to learn of their cruelty. His youngest sister was not kind, although she was not deliberately malicious, but the others were remote and cold; they came to him for what he could produce and they left him just as quickly.

I know that he wanted their company. I watched him, when I could do so in safety, and I shed tears every time he was rejected, for he could not understand what he had done that made him so unworthy of their affection.

He was impossible for two months, and after that, in turmoil, he returned to the smithy that was his delight.

There are stories that he made women of gold in the smithy of his father—for that was a place in which the magic was old and deep—and that these women could speak and think and keep him company in the small hours of the night. I know that he did create such companions, but I do not know if he loved them, or if they loved him in such a fashion, for I never ventured into the privacy of his domain; it was there that he gave birth to his creations, and the act of creating, like lovemaking when it exists, is a private act; I did not wish to intrude upon it.

But where I could not intrude, *she* did, daughter of my husband. She was like a child; she could not conceive of a place in which she was not to be welcomed should she desire entry. I have already said I hated her, and it was true—but I think there was little then that I did not hate. I was prepared to feel anger; I was prepared to plan vengeance on behalf of my child for the damage she would do him.

I nursed these things that coiled within me; I treasured them as if they were lovers' obscenities. I could not conceive of any other outcome but his desire and her brutal rejection of it.

The first came to pass—and how could it not? There was not a male in the pantheon who did not desire her, did not scheme to bed her, did not demand, from her father, the right to possess her. As wife, of course. But he had his own plans for her, and she eluded all of her suitors, as I had failed to elude my husband, and she remained free.

And it was freely that she walked into the den my son called home, and freely that she left. I thought that would be the end of it, and I waited to hear my son's tears, but I waited in vain. She returned the next day, and the day after, and if she caused him pain, he kept it hidden.

Then one day he came to me after one of these visits, and he was much vexed, and angered.

I put my arms around what little of his shoulders I could; working the smithy had made his chest swell with the muscles that his legs would never possess. He shook free of me.

"I had—I had a visitor today," he said,

"Did you?"

He trusted me, of course. He did not know that I spied upon him, and so simply nodded.

"And did your visitor anger you? You seem upset."

He struggled with words, for words did not come easily to him, then or ever. At last he turned to me. "Mother, you are so beautiful. My father is so handsome. Why am I so ugly? What crime did I commit? What judgment am I prey to?"

"You committed no crime," I said, too quickly and with too much heat. "And you are *not* ugly. You are—"

"I *am*. I am ugly, and I am crippled."

I should have had comfort to offer him. I was his mother. But I gave him silence instead, and pity, which he did not need.

"Is there no way to fix it?" His palms were open in supplication. "Is there no way to make me what you—what you all—are?"

I tried to offer him kind words, but they were empty, and I knew it. "No," I told him. I drew myself up to my full height, leaving the curve of my throne, the smallness of its confines. "But would you have it, if there were? You have called your father handsome. And he is. To look at, he is fire and glory. When I fist saw him as a man, I could not breathe for the sheer exhilaration of the experience."

His expression darkened.

"But when that had passed, nothing remained. He was not kind. He has never been kind. I did not love him, and I did not desire him. When he came to me, I refused him as gently as I could. I knew that if I accepted him, I would sit at his side for eternity, and I knew that I would sit as Queen to his King, but . . . he was so cold and so terrible, I knew that I would never have a moment's happiness if I chose to do so.

"Healthy, whole, he did not care. He took what he wanted and left me no choice. I am here, I sit on the smaller throne. And I watch this *beautiful* man destroy the lives of almost every woman he touches.

"Is that what you want?"

He had stepped back, the gold of his braces catching the crimson of sunset. I had never said this to him before. I do not know if others had told him of his father's duplicity, but hearing it from me wounded him.

"Mother . . ."

"I am sorry. I speak out of turn. It is not my place."

"Don't speak of place," he whispered. "It's your life, and you've as much right to speak of it as anyone." He turned away from me. "I do not wish to be such a man, no. I hope that I could never be that. But I wish—I want—to be able to touch . . ."

There are some things, even then, that could not be shared with one's mother. He left. But that was not to be the end of the story.

She came to me.
I do not know how many days it has been, for the

passage of time had little meaning; I was young, and in
the way of young, immortal. But days had passed; the
sun had risen and fallen at the whim of Helios; exposing
the clarity of night, the cold light of moon, the darkness.

She chose the evening to pay me court. She came
hooded and unannounced to my presence, as if by doing
so she could hide her nature. Or perhaps, even then, she
understood *my* nature, and she wished to avoid my envy.
It is one of the few things I have never asked her.

There was no throne to separate us, and little distance.
My husband had failed to find a maiden to dally with,
and he had chosen to spend some part of the evening
with me. He had finished long before she arrived, and I
was therefore not at my best.

But I knew who she was. She could hide her face, but
the grace of her movement never left her. I was therefore on my guard. I do not know what I had expected
her to say.

"If you have time, I would consider myself forever in
your debt if you chose to answer a few of my questions."

I shrugged. "Perhaps. But I cannot make that decision
until I hear the questions."

She was silent for a long time, as if courage had
brought her this far, and had failed her at the last moment. And I was suddenly desperately curious.

Or perhaps I was, in my fashion, no more immune to
her nature than anyone else who lived upon the mountain. "I will answer your questions to the best of my
ability."

"I—" She chose silence again, and then she straightened her shoulders and gained height, stature. A goddess. "Your son came to see you the other day."

I frowned "You have me watched?"

"You?" Her eyes widened in genuine surprise, as if
the thought had never occurred to her. "No. I have no
one watched. But I went to visit him, and he was on the
way out. I asked him if I could wait, and he gave his
assent; he said he had to speak with you, but would be
back shortly."

"I see. And?"

"He did not come back. Not that afternoon. Not that
evening. I left before sunrise, and when I returned, his

doors were locked. He did not answer them. I waited outside for the afternoon and the evening, and at last one of his . . . servants . . . took pity on me. She came to greet me, and she was polite, but distant."

"His servants? He has none."

"He has the ones that he made, and that he makes. They are lovely, in their fashion, and they always smile; they speak with gentle voices; they smell of the ocean." For a moment she, too, smiled, and then the smile faded. It would not return for me that day. "She told me that he could not be brought away from his forge. They fear it, the golden maids; they fear its heat. I asked her why he could not be moved, and she told me that she did not know. But I waited, and at last she said, 'He feels that he will never be worthy of you, lady; he fears to make your life a misery.' " She pulled her hood from her face; her skin was pale and perfect, her hair the color of gold so pure that not even my son could make it. "Do you feel that I am unworthy of your son?"

I looked away because I could not bear to look upon her. The question was between us, and it was not a question that I had ever conceived of asking, or of hearing.

"Why would I feel so?"

"Perhaps because you have loved only one man in all of your life, and I have loved many."

I would have sat, but I was too far from my throne, and the floor was beneath my dignity. "You—you think I have loved only one man?"

"Are you not the Queen of Heaven?"

"What is Heaven?" I asked her bitterly. "This? This land of ice and cold, cold sun? This throne room, these great, empty halls? Do you see my husband? It is evening; do you hear his voice? Do you feel his presence?"

Her eyes widened again; she shook her head. No.

"What do you want from my son?"

She did not answer.

"What could you possibly want from my son? Can you not see him? Can you not feel the depth of his anger? Can you not understand that he alone, of all his kin, is flawed?"

"Is this what you told him?"

"He is no fool. I did not have to *tell* him anything. If

you seek sport, seek it below, in the lands of the mortals.
Among them there are many who are scarred and broken, and each of them would willingly die for your time
and your attention. He has been hurt enough in his life;
he needs no other pain."

"So," she said quietly. Just that. She left me.

But she did not seek solace in the mortal lands, nor
among her brethren. She flew at once to my son's side.
It was within her power to make him love her; that was
her gift. And he knew it, but so did she. Yet abjured it;
she divested herself of the power that made her the most
envied of the goddesses; she sought to take nothing by
force, no matter how gentle that force was.

I followed her.

She returned to his home, and she sought entrance
there. The golden maidens sought to deny her, and instead of commanding them, as was her right, instead of
binding them in the glory of her gift, she spoke. Her
voice was not so soft and not so sweet as it was in the
presence of her siblings, but it held a strength that I had
never heard before.

"You have said your master refuses me entry because
he fears to make my life a misery. Because he fears that
he is unworthy. Do you believe this?"

The tallest of the maidens stepped forward while the
others waited in silence. "No," she said gravely and
coolly. "No more than you believe it."

"Then you must believe that I am unworthy, that I
will make his life a misery."

"No, lady," she replied.

"Then you must fear him, if you believe neither of
these to be true and yet are still willing to deny me."

"No, lady."

"Then do not let him sit, alone, with his fears; do not
let fear be his only guide. I have come to you with nothing; I cannot coerce, I cannot compel. I can only beg,
and I am not so proud that I will not beg: Let me enter."

"Do you understand what it is that you ask, daughter
of the King of Heaven? Do you understand what must
come to pass, if we grant what you ask?"

"Yes."

"This is Heaven. Will you see it destroyed?"

She paused a moment, weighing her words, and at last, she said softly, "I have never touched you. I have never compelled you. Had I been asked, I would have said that you were like the legs that bear him; tools of his making; cold companions.

"But I would be wrong. What you feel for him is real. And it is not made of this place."

"The gods will ridicule you."

"Yes."

"They will deny him his due, out of envy.'

"They deny it now out of ignorance. And denied it, he has created a life for himself. He could have been like his brother, bent only on destruction, on displays of brutish power and incalculable cruelty. But he, who has been so wronged, has chosen instead to create.

"Are you his creations? Yes. But you feel things that he never intended you to feel. And when I look at you, when I look at the things, living and dead, that grace his halls, I see a beauty that impoverishes the whole of Olympus; you are his dreams and his visions. Where are his swords? Where are his spears? Where are his graves and his implements of war?

"I see women. And beyond, dogs, cats, miniature dragons that he scolds for destroying his precious metals. I see flowers, I see fountains, I see whole worlds that are different, and better, than this one.

"I will not be like the Queen of Heaven, raped and abused and worn like trophy. And I cannot be like the Goddess of Wisdom, separate, and alone, in eternity; I will not be the Huntress.

"I have dallied, yes. I have played at games of love, and I have *learned*. I have been raised on nectar and ambrosia; I have listened to the music of Apollo; I have walked in the wake of Hermes, and lived under the eye of Zeus. I have sought pleasure, and I have found it, but it is not a lasting thing. Should I while away eternity in empty praise of the unworthy? Should I wait until one or another of the gods is clever enough to bind me to his will and desire, and make me just another of his conquests?

"Do you think I care what the gods will say of me?"

"And of him?"

"I will let him decide. But I have made my decision. Make yours."

They did not take long to decide; they moved out of her way, and stood, like sentries, as she passed between them. But she paused once, and turned back, and she ran to the tallest of the golden maids and threw her arms around her shoulders. "I will make you proud," she whispered.

"Make him happy," the maid replied, "and we will laugh while Heaven itself erodes."

She ran past them, into the long hall that led to his fires, his forge.

And the golden maidens turned, as one, to me.

They had my son's eyes. As one, they bowed. I knew, then, that they would grant me no such entry, should I ask; they knew that I would never beg. But I was drawn to them because she had seen in them what I had never seen.

"She does not have to walk with her eyes closed to see beauty in this place," the tallest of the maidens said. "What will you do, Queen of Heaven?"

"Do? Wait."

"You know what will happen."

But I didn't. Not then. Guardian of the old order, I had no way of understanding the subtle birth of a new one.

I was the Goddess of Marriage. That was what was left me. Queen only by custom, and at that a queen whom men ignored in safety, and whom women obeyed because they feared my vengeful nature. When my son came to me again, he came with his wife by his side. Oh, the wedding itself had not been celebrated; no wine had been poured, no bridal gift paid. But there was, about these two, a quiet determination, and something else that I could not name. His large hands clenched and unclenched; hers, perfect and delicate, touched them, quieting the motion.

She said, "We have chosen each other, and we have come for your blessing. Will you give it?"

I said, before I could stop myself, "What blessing can I offer you?"

He flinched; she did not. She saw deeply, this woman that I had hated, and would never hate again. "The blessing of a mother; the blessing of a god whose will defines marriage."

"I am married," I told her softly; it was a confession.

"You are captive," she replied. "And the cage is gilded, but it is not pretty; it is not warm." Her husband looked down at her golden hair as she bowed her head.

"I would not wish upon you what I have."

She met my eyes and said, "Let that be your blessing."

I understood her, then. I envied her. I feared her.

For a moment I wanted to deny her her happiness. But the moment passed. Because she loved my son, and I had feared, worse, had been certain, that no one would.

"You could have chosen anyone."

"No," she said softly. "*He* could have. But he chose me, and I am profoundly grateful." She looked up at my son, and my son turned to me, straightening out his shoulders, standing as tall as a crippled man could.

He was much, much taller than my husband had ever been.

"We plan to leave Olympus," he said quietly.

"L–leave?"

"There is no place here for us. But there—there, in the world below, where all of life changes and grows, we will make a place together."

Could he, maker of all manner of things, make that?

"It will be hard."

"Yes. The hardest thing I have ever created. But . . . things that come easily are never things that we value."

"And if you would, we would be happy if you would join us," she added.

'Let me give you my answer later," I whispered. "After the wedding."

As weddings go, it was a painful affair.

My husband was beside himself with rage and thwarted lust, for although he had never touched her, he had desired her; she was his. My younger son was in a black and bitter fury, and my brothers cursed and spit behind the placid smiles they chose to turn outward. They were insulted, of course; they had each made their offers and vowed their undying love to my son's bride, and although she had often bowed to the whim of their lust, she had never given them what she openly gave to Heaven's Smith.

My sisters were quiet, however. If they felt envy, anger, revulsion, if they pitied her, it did not show. Athene surprised us all; she offered the couple the rings by which they might exchange their vows.

And Diana gave them not spear or bow, not furs or the meat of the hunt, but rather, a single blemished apple. She was unusually quiet as she did, and she has never been a talkative person. But it was to me she turned, when the gift had left her hands; to me that she said, "There have only been two ways, two paths by which we can walk. Until now, only two."

Demeter gave them seeds. Not seedlings, for she said she did not know which terrain they would make their own when at last they chose to settle. "Some will die," she added, "when you plant them, for in any soil, in any environment, there are plants which will not grow. Remember that; accept it. Look forward."

These were the notes of grave in the ceremony; the skies were stormy, the music off-key; even the wine seemed sour, as if it had stood too long in the warmth of the sun. And yet I would say of all ceremonies held on those lofty mountains, it was the most moving, the most beautiful.

Afterward, the stories began, but I ignored them, for when I watched my son and his wife exchange their vows, when I saw the gentle way in which they spoke, the smiles, devoid of glee or lust, that they exchanged, the heat of a passion that had everything to do with dedication, nothing with possession, something inside of me broke.

My own marriage, my own wedding came back to me, like a ghost, like a slain creature intent on justice or vengeance. I had been told, in my childhood, that he who married me was fated to be the ruler of the Heavens, and it made me proud and vain. But while I was dreaming—as children dream—of romance, and love, and safety, my husband was dreaming of other things, and in the end, when he raised me, he raised me as crown, no more; an emblem of his place in the universe. He offered me no kindness, then or since; paid no heed to my dreams and my desires.

I kept my counsel until the moon ruled the skies, and then I went to Demeter's daughter, in the darkness, where the dead dwelled. I bowed before her, this woman whom I had wronged in my pain and anger, and I apologized for what I had done.

"I should have understood your fear and your desire," I whispered, while the dead listened. "I should have stood beside you, because I understood your loss—but I felt that if you returned to your childhood and your happiness, it would diminish my life. I am sorry, Persephone."

Her skin was white with lack of sun, her eyes dark. But she rose, and came to me. "Why have you traveled here?"

"I need your advice. You rule the dead. You understand what dying means."

"Do you wish to die, Queen of Heaven?"

"No," I whispered. "I wish to live."

"And what would you have of me, trapped among the dead?"

"I wish to know how to kill a god."

She bowed her head a moment. "So," she finally answered. "It has come to pass. I cannot tell you what you need to know; I am forbidden the knowledge. But if you would gain it—and pay its price—you must visit the weavers at their loom."

And so I traveled to the Three. They were old, bent with knowledge, adorned by it; their skin was wrinkled and textured, like the surface of a rough parchment, and their eyes were white as ivory. Yet they turned as one when I entered into their home

"Ah, I told you, sisters, she is here. The weaving is almost done."

It seemed endless to me, their loom and their spindles, their tapestries, their depictions of mortal life.

"Shall we rise? Shall we rise and pay our respect to the Queen of the Heavens?"

"Why should you, when no one else does?" I answered. "It is not respect that I seek, but knowledge, and I am not of a mind to care how it is delivered."

The woman who had spoken first chuckled. "What do you wish to know, daughter?"

"I wish to know how to kill a god."

I expected horror, or shock, but they had seen everything, would see everything, until there was literally nothing to see. "If you wait, daughter, you will see gods die. The time is coming when the natural world will assert itself in the face of faith and belief, and it will whittle away the power of the gods until only those gods whose power resides in affairs of the heart remain." She fell silent, but she did not turn away; she knew that I had not yet finished.

"What must I do?"

"If you wish to destroy the King of Heaven? Do what the mortals do; uncover the truth. Reveal it. That is all."

I turned to leave her, little understanding her words, but she stopped me; the looms fell silent. "Daughter, we promised you that the man you married would rule us all. But we did not tell you what would happen if he lost you." She bowed. "Understand that your course is hard, and you will lose everything that you have valued; when he falls, so, too, must you. Be prepared, if you will travel this path, for you must stay your course."

I thought of my son. His wife.

I nodded.

It is time to leave. The story is almost at an end, and I have told it, to remind myself that the smallness of my life, the loneliness of it, is no less bitter than the life I led then.

When my son and his wife left Olympus, I left with them. My niece gave me the names of the followers she most admired. *"These are your scientists,"* she whispered. *"These are the men who gaze boldly into the unknown and demand answers. They are half-mad, divine in their obsession, but they will bring you the peace that you seek."*

I asked her why she chose to help me, when her life was so full, and her gifts so plentiful, when she had so much to *do.*

And she said, wise woman, *"I believe in Heaven. I believe that we have never truly seen it.*

"But if the words of the Fates are true, you will never see it; your followers will forget you in their drive to gain mastery over the natural world.

"It is that," she said quietly, *"or this, this empty pleasure, this pointless passion, for eternity."*

And I took the names and fled the wrath of my husband.

The early years were hard.

Many of the men who followed her were killed for their beliefs, or forced—as if thought can be contained and destroyed—to recant those beliefs; they were fed to the fires of my youngest son, devoured and consumed.

But their words lingered, and their beliefs took hold, slowly and certainly.

The names of my oldest son and his wife were forgotten, but he found a home everywhere we traveled, and she—she had no need of a home. She spoke all languages with ease, and saw to the heart of every culture through which we passed, spreading the seeds of our own deaths.

My name?

It was forgotten as well. I do not remember it now; I do not remember the texture of it in the air, or on the tongue. I answer to the name that is convenient in the life I have chosen, when I choose.

I was the Goddess of Marriage. There is no Goddess of Divorce, but if there were, she would be a vastly more powerful deity than I, now. What was once unthinkable, and punishable in so many places by torture or death, has become the fabric of everyday life.

And it was my choosing, my sacrifice, my desire.

Do you judge me? Do you yearn for other days, when things were simpler? I have lived in those simple times. Yes, my heart sickens and my anger flares when I see a good man, a good woman, left on a whim after years of devotion. But it gladdens when I see that a battered and bruised girl is not consigned to the hell of marriage with a man who is little more than a common criminal.

I will leave my apartment, and I will travel to the eastern center of the city; there I will watch, and wait.

The police are hunting my husband; their nets are closing. Men who would have once fought under his banner, without thinking, fight against him, aware of the threat he represents. Is he a god, now?

No.

Is his behavior, is his cruelty, laughed at, approved of, ignored? No.

Have I killed him, king of gods? No.

I was a cruel woman, and a proud one, and if I cannot now remember my own name, I choose not to speak his. But I want him to understand what we have made of him, in this world, what his place is:

Serial rapist with a pretty face.

No more.

KNOTWORK

by *Nina Kiriki Hoffman*

Nina Kiriki Hoffman has been writing for almost twenty years and had sold almost two hundred stories, two short story collections, novels (*The Thread That Binds The Bones, The Silent Strength of Stones, A Red Heart of Memories, Past the Size of Dreaming* and *A Fistful of Sky,* forthcoming in November 2002), a young adult novel with Tad Williams (*Child of an Ancient City*), a Star Trek novel with Kristine Kathryn Rusch and Dean Wesley Smith (*Star Trek Voyager 15: Echoes*), three R.L. Stine's *Ghosts of Fear Street* books, and one *Sweet Valley Junior High* book. She has cats.

WHEN we married, my husband and I tied knots in ourselves and in each other.

I am not from around here, and to me all knots mean special things. Where I come from, one moves through a lacework of knots; one learns to tie one's own knots; one learns how knots limit one. I came here to get away from knotwork, and yet, four years after I arrived, I consciously brought my skills into play, and crafted a tangle to bind two people together, as local custom seemed to dictate.

I thought the knots meant the same things to my husband that they meant to me. We had been seven years married, and somewhere along the way our wild mutual madness faded into something I found comfortable in its complex sameness. To me, the knots remained, even though the passion had died. To my husband . . .

"So, Nuala, what's this we hear about your husband?" Marie asked me when I joined my three best friends for our weekly Tuesday lunch at Le Chevre et Les Trois Framboises. This week Marie's hair was purple and shellacked into a fountain of lazy curls. She was a live mannequin in the window of the largest department store in town, and this week the clothing she advertised was severe in pink and black. Everyone in the restaurant stared at her, which gave the rest of us a measure of anonymity.

I put my beaded purse on the table beside my place setting. "So what is it you hear?"

Anika, who worked in the same corporate office as my husband—in fact, she was the person who had introduced me to my husband—said, "We hear he takes Jacy Hines, one of the associates, everywhere with him."

"He took her shopping in my store," Marie said. " 'I saw them come in together from my window, and later I asked the clerks where they went. To fishing equipment. When's the last time a man asked a woman to look at fishing equipment?"

"Perhaps she knows something about it." I had met Jacy at one of the firm's office parties. She was a small pigeon woman, comforting and round, with short brown hair and bright brown eyes, ruddy of complexion and neat of hand, and I had liked her. She hadn't borne any of the marks of threat one learns to look for when one leases her husband to a job for the bulk of the day. Jacy and I had discussed knotwork and the mysteries of coffee. If she had had the energy of a spouse-taker, wouldn't I have felt it? I had given up several of my special senses when I bound myself, but not that one.

"He took her out to buy you a birthday present last week," Anika said. "Last year he sent his secretary. This year he took Jacy, and they shopped together."

My birthday celebration would happen on Saturday. It was something Hugh and I had always did alone together. I hadn't realized that selecting my gift was a task he delegated; the gifts I have received from him had been sensitive and thoughtful, and I had been touched.

I had not smelled them closely enough. The stink of someone else must have been on them. I used my eyes too much these days; I had lost some of the vital information streams I used to fish.

"He took her to coffee yesterday in my restaurant," said Polly, who owned a diner two blocks from Le Chevre. We never met at Polly's for lunch; she liked to get away and eat somebody else's food once in a while. "They sat on the same side of the booth instead of across from each other."

Hugh had taken Jacy to Polly's restaurant? Then he intended me to know; he knew about my friendship with Polly, certainly knew she would tell me what she had seen. Perhaps the other things could be explained somehow; Jacy had special knowledge of fishing; Jacy had a woman's feel for a gift. But to have coffee with her in Polly's place. Why?

I had signed up for three new classes through community education this term, but I always signed up for classes. Hugh hadn't wanted me to work when we married, and I was satisfied not to. Instead I taught myself the intricacies of housekeeping and mankeeping and cooking, which were not overnight things to learn, but now I had them mastered and had time for other things. I took classes: two of them this term were night classes, which meant I left him to sketchy dinners and his own company twice a week. Was that enough reason for him to slip my knots?

I waited for him to come home that evening, even though I should have packed my portfolio for life drawing class and left before he pressed the garage door opener.

Hugh came into the kitchen from the garage. I studied his dark suit; his strong, square hand around the handle of his briefcase, his dark hair disarrayed because he pulled it when stuck in traffic, the shadows under his blue-gray eyes: my first thought was fondness.

"Oh! Nu! Still here?" he said.

He must have seen my car in the garage. "Why pretend surprise?" I asked, more direct then usual. I did not want to take the time for our usual dance.

"I know you have class tonight. I thought maybe one of your friends picked you up."

"This is only the second week. I have no friends in class yet. I understand you've been more friendly than you should be, though."

A flush of red touched his cheeks and was gone. "We said long ago that we would keep our old friends."

"And make new ones? The rule was we could keep

our old friends, but the new ones we would make together or not at all."

"That was the rule," he said. "You break it every time
you take one of these classes."

"Those aren't real friends. Those are driving-together-
and-discussing-class-material friends. Any of them I want
to keep, I introduce to you. And you always say no. And
I always listen." On occasion, I had listened with regret.
I liked a boy from madrigals class. Hugh nixed him, and
I unknotted him; not the easiest unlove I had ever done,
either, since the origin of his attraction was natural
rather than induced.

"I've known Jacy longer than I've known you." Hugh
set his briefcase on the kitchen table and ran his hand
through his hair.

"Have you?"

"We went to grade school together."

I twisted my hands in my lap. He had never told me.
We told each other things of this sort; it was part of
our pact.

Our pact. Established in passion, a heat I thought
would never die. Where had it run to? It had drained
from us both as surely as snowmelt leaves mountains
in summer.

Eventually, I said, "If you have something to say to
me, I wish you would just say it, rather than sending my
friends as your messengers."

"I have nothing to say to you except what's for
supper?"

A chill lodged in my heart. I opened the freezer com-
partment of the fridge. "You decide." I grabbed my
portfolio and left.

That night at life drawing class we had a male model,
a man who drove city buses during the day. He was an
older man, in his fifties at a guess, with a black beard
streaked with white, his hair thinning on top. He had
folds of fat at his waist and kind eyes, and I liked drawing him much more than I had liked drawing the model
last week, a Greek god who could not hold a pose more
than a minute without wavering, and when I complained,
he moved even more to spite me.

I laid down line with my darkest, fastest pencil, trying

to be pleased with the exercise, the model, everyone else in class looking at skewed views of this same pose, our instructor walking around to stand behind us for a while, then leaning forward to discuss technique with us when she sensed an opening.

I laid down line. I could not stop thinking about the early days with my husband, how we had pledged our lives to each other, so deeply had we felt our love, how we had bound ourselves tight, thinking that what we wanted at the time was what we would want always.

Now a small brown woman whom my husband had known before he had met me inched between us, though truth to tell there was a big enough gap between us that anyone could have fitted into it.

"Ouch," said the model, dropping out of pose and clapping a hand to his buttocks.

I looked at my picture, realized I had laid down the line of his buttocks with too much heat in my hand. Smoke rose from the page. My face burned. I touched the paper with my ice hand.

This should not have happened. I had locked all these touch powers away when I had woven the vows that bound me to Hugh. Something had broken, and now my vows were coming unthreaded.

I had done nothing. Hugh. It was Hugh.

"Cramp?" the teacher asked the model.

The model nodded. What else could he say? Or maybe he had experienced it as a cramp. He wouldn't have a mental opening to experience a line of fire along his buttocks; what couldn't happen couldn't be called by its true name, a human law that allowed me to operate within this realm without too much risk of discovery.

I set down my pencil and clasped one hand in the other, letting my hands speak to each other until both were in the middle of their range.

I came here to find friends I could not discover where I lived before, and I had made these friends: Marie, Anika, Polly at college, young, naked, trusting as un-fledged birds who opened their mouths for whatever a parent would put inside. I had shaped myself by learning what had shaped them, and how they operated in their worlds. Anything they did that produced a reaction I liked, I learned to do. They fed me a human character. I learned from the other people we spent time with, as well. The dorm, the cafeteria, classes, fraternity parties, football games, bars, the student union, road trips over the breaks. It was my perfect nursery.

I watched my three friends fall in and out of love, and practiced a little myself. I met boys and enjoyed them, but none touched my heart.

It was four years later, after we had left college for the world, that Anika introduced me to Hugh. When I first saw him, I felt a flare of heat that surprised me, and I judged I had waited long enough to try the rest of the accoutrements of love. I dropped some of my walls and let love consume me.

It seemed to me that Hugh, too, lost himself in love. We were both mad in the best ways.

"Nuala? Something the matter?" asked my art teacher.

"My hands hurt."

She rubbed my shoulder. "Maybe you were holding the pencil too tight."

I smiled at her and picked up my pencil, then flipped to a fresh page. The model had dropped into a new pose, and I hadn't drawn a line of it. These were five-minute poses, and I had no idea how much longer I had with this pose, so I scrawled lines quickly, flowed in the outline of where the model was. Pencilwork was one form of knotwork, though I had not let myself play with that before. I tried to keep these parts separate: knotwork from what everyone else did here. One of my vows to myself when I bound myself to Hugh had been that I would remain undiscovered.

"Wow," said the teacher. "I've never seen you work so fast and well."

I glanced over my shoulder at her, then looked at my drawing. I had let some of the other world out of my fingers, the merest caress of that which speaks touchpower. I set down my pencil again.

"Don't stop," said the teacher. "I didn't mean to interrupt your process."

"I'm sorry," I said. "I'm having trouble concentrating."

The madness had seeped out of our marriage so slowly
I hadn't noticed it leaving. One day I woke up after
Hugh left for work, and I knew I didn't care if I saw
Hugh again that day. I couldn't remember the last time
joy leaped into my heart at the sight of him. I still had
my vows and agreements, though, which I must honor,
or I feared I would dissolve. So I looked around for
other things here that could excite me. Classes woke up
a sleeping part of me for moments at a time. Friends
helped, too. I settled into an existence that was gray with
small spikes of color here and there. It was enough.

So I thought. Eventually, Hugh would die; my vows
would end, and I could choose where to go next,
whether back to my home where I could live as myself,
to a new world, or somewhere else in this world, perhaps
to find someone else, perhaps to try a different kind of
sharing, a shorter one, or a more intricate one, or a more
unbalanced one. The possibility of finding joy again
existed. I had found it once.

Waiting has always been one of my skills.

I was not willing to wait while my husband betrayed
me in public. Perhaps I could have let it go if he had
been discreet. If he had been discreet, and our vows
dissolved because of his actions, I could have moved
on. But to do it so all my friends knew. This seemed a
deliberate act.

If he had nothing to say about it, I wondered if perhaps Jacy would tell me something.

"Maybe you should always draw when you're having
trouble concentrating," the art teach told me. "This is
wonderful."

"It's a mistake." I ripped the page off my easel and
tore it to bits, severing the lines and their touch-power.
Who knew what they had already carried to the model?
At least he didn't seem to be suffering.

Or did he? He had held the pose surprisingly well for
a long time while I thought things over. When I ripped
up the page, he collapsed and breathed hard for a moment. He shook his head like a bull shaking off a bee,
then slapped his face.

"You okay?" the teacher asked.

"I think I'm coming down with something," the model

answered. "Hot flashes, then this weird paralysis. Maybe I better take a break."

The teacher checked the clock. Half an hour earlier than the model's scheduled break. "All right," she said. "Everybody take ten minutes and then come back. Nuala?"

I closed my pad. "I better go home," I said. "I'm not feeling well either."

Hugh would not be expecting me home for forty-five minutes or an hour. I couldn't decide if I would rather surprise him or wait. In the end, I stopped for coffee at the twenty-four-hour coffee shop and sat in a booth, thinking about what to do.

I went to a phone booth and checked the listings, found Jacy Hines. I called her number and she answered.

"This is Nuala. May I come and see you?"

She hesitated. I waited.

"Let me meet you somewhere," she said at last. I wondered if Hugh were there with her now.

I told her where I was, and she came fifteen minutes later. She wore a brown jacket over a dark orange dress, and black tights and shoes. She looked small and comforting, like someone I would like for a friend.

We both got coffee and sat across from each other in the booth. I waited.

She had drunk half of her coffee when she finally spoke. "What do you want?"

"What are you doing with my husband?"

She stared into her cup. "He said you wouldn't mind."

"You have been misinformed."

She glanced up then, and I drew that look on the tabletop with my darkest pencil, letting touch-power enter her outline.

"You see," I whispered when I knew I had her attention, that her gaze would not waver, "I made promises when I married him, and he gave me promises in return. Are his promises mist? Does that make mine water, to melt and flow instead of staying hard as ice?"

"He said you were no longer sexual with each other." Her whisper was strained.

"I don't remember by whose desire." I rubbed my fingertips over my forehead.

"Do you want him still? I didn't know."

"I am bound to him by vows I hold sacred."

For a moment she said nothing. "I'm sorry."

"He has drawn you in. Does that mean I pull you farther into our vows, or that I let go of our vows?" I got a different pencil out of my box and drew carefully on the portrait of Jacy, added lines of warmth where I had learned they would most affect a human. She twitched and shuddered as I worked, and red flowed across her face.

"What are you doing?" she asked in an agonized whisper.

Another touch there. Three tweaks. I slid my eyes sideways, watched her shudder again.

"Whatever I like." I watched her for a while, left her suspended almost all the way to where she would find release, not quite there, just the itchy anxious side short of it. Then I touched my drawing, and she shook and shuddered, her breath panting in and out of her. Finally she melted back against her bench.

I traced the lines of my picture with summon power until the picture released the tabletop. It eased into my hand. Jacy's shoulders lifted. "What are you doing?" she whispered again. A tear leaked from one of her eyes.

"Knotwork." I tied the lines of her drawing in several complicated knots and slipped it into my pocket. This was so easy for me that I knew my vows had indeed melted. Since I had not stepped outside them, I knew Hugh had destroyed them.

Did I want to reinstate them? Or should I leave him now? I ran my fingers over the small knot of lines in the bottom of my pocket. Jacy jumped and twitched.

"Please," she said. "Please don't do that."

I rubbed the warm places in my knots with the ball of my thumb. She leaned back, eyes closed, mouth open. Low gasps rang from her. I rubbed slower, then faster, until she melted down under the table. People at nearby tables watched her when her gasps grew loud enough. "Stop," she moaned. I gave her lines one last rub, and she cried out, loud enough for everyone in the restaurant to hear.

I took my hand out of my pocket. I finished my coffee.

I glanced at the waitress, who came over to me after a couple of minutes.

"Is your friend all right?" she asked as she refilled my cup.

"She's fine." I pointed to Jacy's cup and the waitress refilled that, too, and went away. I poured two creams into Jacy's coffee, as I had seen her do when she first sat down. I sipped my coffee. Then I leaned down and spoke under the table. "You can come out now."

She had curled into a ball. "I'm never coming out." Tears streaked her face.

"You can come out, or I can make you come out."

She rubbed her eyes. A little later she crept out from under the table and settled herself in her seat. People stared. She looked toward the wall, her cheeks flushed.

"Drink your coffee."

She drank. "What do you want?" she asked.

"I don't know yet."

"I'm sorry. I'm so sorry. He said—"

I nodded. I dropped money on the table to cover our coffees and a tip. "Let's go."

She collected her purse and her jacket from the bench and tried to stand. Staggered.

I slipped my hand into my pocket and stroked strength into her lines. She straightened, took a deep breath, and followed me out of the restaurant.

"Are you a witch?" she asked in the parking lot.

"Not exactly."

"But you can make me feel things." She blushed again.

"Did you like it?"

She stared at the ground. She shook her head. She smiled a tiny smile, the smile one smiles for oneself. "I can never go into that restaurant again."

"Let's go back right now."

She touched my arm. "Please. Don't."

I stared at her hand until she dropped it. "Please," she whispered.

I cupped her knotwork in my hand. She tensed.

"Let's go to your apartment."

She relaxed.

I let her drive us in her car.

My husband's scent was in her living room.

It was a small and comforting place. I sat on her brown velvet couch, and she dropped into a red armchair across a walnut coffee table from me. Bookshelves lined one wall, most of the books hardcovers and well-worn. A plant stand held a number of leggy, healthy plants. A red and blue Persian carpet the size of a bathroom stall in a hotel covered a patch of floor between furniture.

Brown velvet smelled of my husband, his satisfied scent.

"I bound myself to him, and he to me," I told Jacy.

"I'm sorry. I didn't realize. He acted as if there were nothing between you anymore."

"When I met you, you didn't smell like a threat."

She shook her head. "I never thought of it. I was surprised when he came into my office and asked me to help him evaluate a portfolio. He's my senior. I thought perhaps he was grooming me for a higher-level position. I thought it was because of my merits. Then he kept asking for my help. Things that seemed natural at first, and then things that seemed outside our jobs. Step by step he walked me away from what I thought was right, and I did not notice. Until one night we were up here together. I thought we were talking about work. And then it was different somehow. He sat close to me. I've been alone a long time. People don't see me that way, and I—I'm so sorry, Mrs. Breton."

"I don't know if that's my name anymore."

She covered her face with her hands. "I never meant—I don't know how it happened. I should have listened to Barry. He told me to stay away from Hugh. But it seemed like nothing at first, so innocent. I am such a fool. I am deeply sorry."

"Was he here tonight?"

She lowered her head. Her lips tightened.

"Why did he make your relationship public?" I wondered. "If he doesn't mind my taking classes—if he knows it means he can see you—why let me find out about it?"

"I don't think that's right," she said in a low voice. "I think he minds."

I slipped my hand into my pocket, cradled her lines inside it. "Does he speak to you of me?"

Her gaze fixed on my and in my pocket. She was frightened. "Sometimes," she whispered.

"What does he tell you?"

"He says you don't care about him anymore. That you're gone a lot. That he's a passionate man and you no longer want him."

I tried to view this as Hugh did. Had he told Jacy his own truth? I was not gone a lot. Perhaps twice a week seemed like a lot. Perhaps he resented the time I spent with my friends while he was at the office. Did I signal Hugh that I no longer wanted him? We climbed into bed and went to sleep. We never turned to each other anymore.

All the knotwork I had made with Hugh was what we had woven together; in my vows I had decided that I would not hold him in my hand the way I held Jacy now. That was part of the risk and wonder of our marriage for me. Where I came from, one wove knots on knots. That was what one knew: the skill of the knotmaker determined who ruled the connection between any two people. I had come here to find something new.

No knots but first knots. Shelve that skill and try something new. So I had new skills, but it was time, past time, to reclaim the old ones.

I took Jacy's knotwork out of my pocket and sat with it in my hand. She shivered and leaned forward to look. "Is that me?" she asked.

"It is not you, but what I use on you. We spoke of this when we first met."

"We did?" She reached out a hand, touched the edge of her knot, jerked the hand back, her eyes widening. "I felt that."

I smiled at her and drew a finger along an edge, watched as she straightened. This was a stroke up her side. She stared at me. I stroked down her other side. She glanced at her side, then at me.

"It's not fair," she said. "How can you do that to me?"

"Fair has nothing to do with it." I had woven myself

tight in a lace of rules, played at being one of them. All of that was gone.

I set Jacy's knotwork on the table between us and leaned back against her couch. Again I smelled my husband's satisfaction.

All his actions told me that he wanted everything to change. Did he want to go back to what we were? Did he want to move on, join with Jacy and abandon me? He was no longer the person I had married; nor was I the person who had married him any longer.

What did I want?

I thought of my friends, the knots we had tied in our lives where they intersected, our weekly lunches, our telephone conversations, our movie dates, the occasional friend emergency where we met one or two or three or four together, to comfort someone in trouble. I thought of my studies, the greatest of which was my study of how to mimic a human, all the rest subsidiary. I thought of the pleasures Hugh and I had shared, how they had swallowed every other consideration until I had thought nothing else mattered.

I took a pencil out of my purse, pulled out my grocery list, flipped to a blank page, and drew Hugh.

I had never knotted him in this way before. I had knotted spirit in him, but never body. I had abdicated that power after our marriage.

This time I drew on all my memories of our days and nights, on how I had touched him everywhere, and how he had touched me. I drew his spark points and his dull points, the parts of himself he groomed and those small spaces that escaped him.

I left these lines blank, open to whichever power I would choose to pour into them when I was ready. I took out the other two pencils and laid lines on top, the warmth lines, the pain lines. I turned my husband from equal to object.

I dropped the pad on the table beside Jacy's knotwork.

"What is it a picture of?" she asked.

I startled. I had forgotten she was there.

I turned the pad so she could see it better and looked at her, my eyebrows up. How well did she know Hugh?

Her eyes shifted as she studied the knotwork. Slowly a frown pulled the edges of her mouth down. "Is it—" She sat back suddenly, eyes wide, cheeks pale. "This is Hugh?"

I smiled.

"What are you going to do?" she whispered.

"I don't know yet." I leaned forward and picked up her lines. She hunched her shoulders, then relaxed them, but bit her lower lip. I set her knotwork on top of the picture of Hugh's, wondering what would happen. Hugh's work was not active yet; I had not powered it; but Jacy knew what it was.

Her lines curled away from the image of Hugh's. No attempt to tangle.

Jacy and I stared at one another.

"You renounce him?" I asked.

"I never meant . . . I can't stay with someone who betrays someone else that way. I trusted what he told me, that you wouldn't mind. He lied to me. I don't want a person who does that."

I lifted her knotwork, held it between my hands and talked the knots into dissolving, let the power loose. Some of it came back to me, and some went into the air.

I rubbed my hands against each other, then took a napkin from my purse and wiped off the stain.

"What?" Jacy said. She patted her chest, her face. "What?"

I showed her my empty hands.

She heaved a big sigh and smiled at me. "Thank you." Then she frowned. "What do you want me to do?"

"I have let go of wanting to dictate your actions."

"But with Hugh—"

I picked up my pad and looked at my knotwork. "I don't know what I want." I lifted a finger of my fire hand and held it just above the knotwork, ready to charge the picture with power. "What would you do if you were me?"

She shook her head.

"What is the human response?" I asked.

She swallowed. "There is no one answer. Some wives look the other way and nurse their pain. Some talk it over with the husbands and decide that they can work it out. Some leave. Some kill their husbands." She covered her mouth with her hand. "Forget I said that!"

"Among my people, killing another is a sign of lack of imagination. So many other things are more satisfying, and hurt more."

She dropped her hand from her mouth, clasped her other hand in it. "Where do you come from?"

"Somewhere else."

She frowned, then crossed her arms, hiding her hands in her armpits. "Why did you come here?" she whispered.

"To learn."

She stared down at her feet for a moment, then gazed at me again. "Does Hugh know what you are?"

"No." I had let him bind me, but had not told him what powers I gave him, what powers I gave up. I knew, and that was enough.

"He's an idiot," Jacy said.

I cocked my head and stared at her.

"Did you try to keep what you were a secret from him?"

"I became something else in the framework of our marriage. I gave up my powers. How could he know what I was when I wasn't myself?"

"You said we talked about the pictures—the strings? —when we first met?"

"Knotwork," I said.

"Knotwork. Like macramé?"

"I don't know that word."

"What do you remember about the conversation?"

I thought back to the party. So many drunk people. I don't like talking to drunken people. They don't make sense, and they don't remember what they said later. It's as though the conversation never took place. So why have it take place?

Only if I want information, and by that time I was not looking for information about my husband's daytime environment. I was content to own the sphere of home.

At the party, Jacy had held up a glass, but she only took little sips. So I talked to her. She spoke to me about coffee grinders in supermarkets, which ones had the best blends and which blends were not good; and we spoke of knotwork. "You told me who everyone in the room was, and how they were knotted to each other."

"Oh." She frowned. "I didn't call it that, though, did I?"

"I don't remember. That's how it made sense to me, so that's how I remember it."

"Knots are—" she began.

The phone rang. It sat beside the couch. I looked at it, then at Jacy. She licked her lip and picked up the phone. "Hello?"

She listened a moment, then said, "I don't think—"

She put her hand over the mouthpiece and whispered, "Hugh."

"What does he want?" I whispered back.

"To come over."

Strange feelings eeled through me. I picked up my drawing of my husband and nodded to Jacy.

"I don't think that's a good idea," she said into the mouthpiece, "but if you really want to—"

She listened a little longer. "All right." She hung up the phone and looked at me. "He said you should be home by now. He said you should have a little of your own medicine. If you're going to make him wait, he will make you wait."

"He'll make me wait while he's with you."

She nodded. "I don't think he would have heard me even if I said no. I've never heard him talk like this before. If I had—"

I waited.

She twisted one hand in the other, shook her head. "I would suspect that there was something else going on, something I wouldn't like. Obviously there's still an emotional charge. He still cares, or he wouldn't want you home on time."

"I heard you went shopping for my birthday present together," I said.

Her face went crimson. "He told me you liked silver," she whispered, "and that if I picked it, it would be better. Something delicate, Celtic knots, he thought, but he said he didn't know what looked good."

"Did you find me something good?"

She ducked her head, twisted her hands. After a moment, she nodded.

"Thank you."

A knock on Jacy's door, then the sound of a key in the lock. I lifted my knotwork from the table and touched both ice and fire to it.

"Jacy?" Hugh said. All he saw was her. He came across the room, stooped beside her armchair, and kissed her. Her hands clenched on the arms of the chair. "Honey?"

She lifted one hand and pushed his face away until he could not help but see me. He straightened. "Nuala."

"Hugh." I stroked summoning power into my drawing until it pulled free of the page, and then I knotted it. The knot for power over another's body. The knot for power over another's speech. I hesitated a moment, thinking of other knots: power over another's heart, power over another's mind, power over another's spirit. Without the knots, I could still stroke the pain and pleasure lines, manipulate the knotwork and cause strong but temporary effects, as I had with Jacy. With the knots, my power would be absolute, unless the person I knotted had his own knot power. I did not think Hugh had such power.

I looked at my husband. Great sadness struck me. I still loved him. Just the sight of him made me soft and fond, even here in the apartment where he had taken another woman in the way he had promised he would only take me.

I did not put the other three knots into my work. There was always time for that if I needed it.

"Nuala, what are you doing?" Hugh asked, an uneasy edge to his voice. He gripped Jacy's shoulder.

"I am choosing a future for us, my love."

"What do you mean?"

I looked at the knotwork I held, the complex and the simple parts, a diagram of my husband, by necessity flat where he had depths, no true image of all there was about him, but true enough that I could capture him in it.

"By betraying me, you have set me free. I don't know what I want from this freedom. I will discover it."

"Honey—"

"Don't call me by the same name you use for her."

He glanced down, saw that he had his hand on Jacy's shoulder, that she glared up at him. He sucked air in and released her.

Jacy rose and came to sit beside me on the couch. "You told me she didn't care anymore, Hugh," she said. "You lied."

"Do you care?" Hugh sat in the chair Jacy had left.

I said, "I do. I would never have left you as long as you lived."

"But we had nothing left."

"We have everything. Some parts of it were asleep. Why didn't you tell me you wanted to wake them?"

"Didn't I? All those nights I reached for you, and you turned your back."

Had he reached for me? I remembered his touch on my shoulder, on my back. I had cherished that touch, but hadn't thought it meant anything more. Had it been a request? We were speaking different languages with our bodies, after those years when we had known without words what would please the other and ourselves. When had we lost our language?

"I thought you just wanted to touch my back. I didn't know it was a request for something else. Why didn't you say something?"

"I thought you were telling me it was over."

"That's so strange," Jacy said. "You don't talk with words?"

"Everything with him is a dance," I said. "He approaches what he wants, but he never says it out loud. This is not my first or second or even third language. Sometimes I know what he wants, and sometimes I get tired of trying to figure it out and give up."

"I can't talk about these things," Hugh said.

I looked at the knotwork in my hands. There was the knot I had put on his speech. If I twisted it one way, words would spill out of him. If I kinked it with skill, they would be words I was interested in hearing.

"Do you know what she's holding?" Jacy asked Hugh.

"Knitting?" Hugh guessed.

Jacy reached into my hand and stroked the knotwork. Hugh jerked, clapped a hand to his side. Jacy pressed a different place, and Hugh clapped his knees together. "What are you doing?" he asked in a choked voice.

"You don't know what you're touching," I told Jacy.

"Yes, but this is fun." She touched the knot for speech.

"I am so confused and scared," Hugh said. "I wanted something to happen, but I didn't know how to direct it, so I flailed around and tried things, and this is what happened, but what is it? I don't understand it, and I'm terrified."

Jacy lifted her finger and looked at me, then frowned at Hugh. "What do you feel for Nuala?" she asked, and touched the speech knot again.

"She frightens me and I love her. I know she has a secret life she will never share, and I'm jealous. I think she's leaving me. I think she's found someone else. I think she no longer likes me. I want to hurt her. I want to wake her up and make her remember what she's losing. I want her to come back. I want her to notice that I've left. I don't know what's going on in her head."

"Why don't you ask her?"

"I can't ask questions like that. I'll get smacked."

"Smacked by who?"

"My mother will hit me if I ask for anything. She always says no questions, no wishes. Every answer is a smack." Hugh writhed in the chair, covered his mouth with his hands. Sweat beaded on his forehead.

Jacy jerked her finger off the knot.

Hugh collapsed, breathing hard. "What are you doing to me?"

I closed my hand around my knotwork, then opened my hand again and stroked lines. Hugh settled back. His breathing eased.

"Whatever I want," I whispered.

After a moment he opened his eyes. A tear ran across his cheek. "Nuala, what is this?"

"Ah, husband, this is my secret side, the side I gave up to be with you, but since you left me, I reclaimed it."

"I haven't left you."

"You broke our vows. You left me."

"I wanted to stir things up. I wanted things to change between us."

"You got your wish." I glanced at Jacy, who had been used like an instrument. My husband had made her an object and a weapon, just as I had made him. Once you make a person an object, everything changes between you. The climb back up to person is much harder than the first climb.

Jacy had made that climb.

I studied the knotwork. I could use it to bend Hugh any way I liked.

If I bent Hugh, would I want to go home with him? If all that he was was what I chose—I could choose good things. I could tie knots to make him trustworthy and loyal. But I would always know that I chose it, and in time would not be able to tell what was left of who he had really been.

"Nuala," he said.

"Hugh. Now that you've changed everything, what do you want?"

He groaned. "I want to go back to when things were good between us."

I glanced at Jacy. She frowned.

"What do you want?" I asked.

She slumped back against the couch and sighed. "It doesn't matter," she said.

Cupping Hugh's knotwork in my left hand, I sketched another Jacy with my right. She straightened as she watched. Her tongue darted out to lick her upper lip.

I charged the work with both hands to encompass her complexity.

"What do you want?" I asked her again.

"Not to be lonely," she whispered, and then, "I want to learn what you know."

Happiness heated my chest. I began to see work I could do, a direction I could go; stay here, keep Hugh, learn new things. The old vows were gone. I was through playing fair.

I set aside the knotwork of Jacy. "Watch carefully," I told her. She bent her head over my hands as I manipulated Hugh's knotwork. "This is the knot for power over another's heart. This is how you stroke it when you want him to be true." We both studied what I had done, then looked across the table at Hugh.

Heat had kindled in his eyes. He leaned forward, his gaze fixed on my face, and I felt my own heat rise within. He wanted me, and that excited me.

We couldn't go back, but we could go forward into a second love. I could add Jacy into the mix, and make Hugh like it.

I would bend him in increments. I might lose who he had been, it was true; but who he had been had chosen to betray me.

I could always bend him back.

THE CAPO OF DARKNESS

by Laura Resnick

Laura Resnick, a *cum laude* graduate of Georgetown University, won the 1993 John W. Campbell Award for best new science fiction/fantasy writer. Since then she has never looked back, having written the best-selling novels *In Legend Born* and *In Fire Forged,* with more on the way. She has also written award-winning nonfiction, an account of her journey across Africa, entitled *A Blonde in Africa*. She has written several short travel pieces, as well as numerous arti-cles about the publishing business. She also writes a monthly opinion column for *Nink,* the newsletter of Novelists, Inc. You can find her on the web at *www.sff.net./people/laresnick*.

THE day them two polenta-eating bums from Eden came to the Underworld began like any day down here. Just another Eternity of hellfire and brimstone, nothing special. Business as usual. I checked in on the wailing of the damned, acknowledged blood sacrifices from 17,459 politicians, brokered the souls of a few no-talent international movie stars, called in a marker on Wall Street, culled some vig from a shipment of virtue headed for Our Lady of Perpetual Chastity School for Girls in Yonkers, and made sure that every IRS agent who'd ever lived and died was still engulfed in the in-ferno of Everlasting Suffering where they belonged.

Like I said, nothing special.

Then *they* showed up.

I knew who they was right away, of course. Who else in all of Creation wears fig leaves, for Chrissake? (I can say that name down here. It's *upstairs* that you gotta be careful about taking it in vain.) Okay, fine, the two of them screwed up and had to be thrown outta the outfit. I get that. A boss can't go soft and let his crew get away with disobeying orders. But Mister Yaweh went too far, giving them nothing but fig leaves to wear when He kicked them out of Eden. And don't think   didn't say so to His face back when I used to work for Him.

Yeah, that's right. I used to be an enforcer for the Big Guy, Yaweh, Jehovah, the Lord of Hosts, the Head Honcho, the *capo di tutti capi* in all of Creation. The Supreme Being who started the whole show. And although we had a pretty serious falling out when He damned me for all Eternity and sent me to Hell, you won't never catch me making no disrespectful remarks about Mister Yaweh. What He done to me was business. Nothing personal. And whatever I done back to Him since then ain't personal neither.

Sure, I had a rough time after being kicked outta Heaven, but things worked out pretty good for me in the end. Mister Lucifer saw my potential and offered me a little work. Next thing you knew, I was a made guy on his crew. Didn't take me long, neither, to work up to the job I held the day *they* arrived.

It was the woman who spoke to me first. Of *course*. Hey, she was the one who ate the forbidden fruit first, too, you know what I'm saying? She had a rep as a sassy broad, and she seemed like she was still living up to it after all these millennia; but I knew the Dark Prince had fond memories of her, from way back when they was all in Eden, so I figured I could let the attitude roll off me when she demanded, kinda snooty-like, "Who's in charge here?"

"The Boss," I said. "Who'd ya think?"

She frowned. "Who are you?"

"I'm his *consigliere*. You want a favor from Mister Lucifer, you gotta talk to me."

"*Consigliere?*" the guy with her asked.

"Yeah," I said. "I'm the *capo*'s right-hand soul around here now."

"*You're* seated at the right hand of the father?" he asked, looking sorta stupid.

"No, you're thinking of a different boss, kid." *The* boss, if truth be known; but, hey, I knew it wasn't smart to say so down here. Then, because people made this kind of mistake all the time, I asked, "Are you sure you're in the right place? Heaven's way up—"

"We're not going to Heaven. We *can't* go." The broad straightened her fig leaf and added, "But you already know that, don't you?"

"Yeah," I said, maybe seeing a little of what Lucifer had liked about her back when they was both in Paradise, "I do. I used to be with that outfit." I shrugged. "Cherubim talk. I heard things."

She looked startled. "You used to be in Heaven? And now you're working for the Lord of Flies?"

"He don't go by that title no more. He didn't like the novel, thought it showed him in a bad light. And don't call him 'Beelzebub,' neither," I advised, figuring it wouldn't hurt to give these underdressed kids a little help. "He's gotten real sensitive about it. He thinks it makes him sound like a character in an English comedy."

I shouldn't have wasted my breath. She rolled her eyes and said, "I told him that more than five thousand years ago."

"Yeah, right, sweetheart. Hell is full of women who say 'I told you so.' We keep 'em here to torment the men who welshed on bets and ratted to the Feds."

"We're wasting time," she said.

"You're right," I agreed. "What business you got down here?"

"That's for us to discuss with the Dark Lord."

"You're asking for a sit-down with Satan?"

"Yes."

"This goes against protocol," I warned her.

"It's important," she insisted.

"It better be. He gets cranky if I waste his time. And when the boss gets cranky, *I* get mean, sister. You understand what I'm saying?"

She leaned closer—*real* close—and suddenly the fig leaves kinda appealed to me, being so skimpy. "I didn't back down when Yaweh got in my face in Eden, so I'm certainly not going to let the likes of you scare me, buster."

I grinned. "You can call me Vito."

Okay, so I like a broad with huevos. So sue me.

"Vito?" The guy went a little pale. "Not . . . Vito 'The Knuckles' Giacalone?"

"The very same." So they'd heard of me. Well, lotsa people have, I don't deny it.

"You were pretty high up in the Heavenly Choir," he said.

I shrugged. "I don't sing. Never did."

The broad looked a little impressed now. "They say Yaweh didn't make a move without consulting you."

"No, no, He was His own deity," I insisted modestly. "Always. Sometimes He just, you know, liked a little feedback, that's all."

"They say you're the one who cleaned up the Road of Good Intentions for Him."

"They?"

She shrugged. "Like you said, cherubim talk."

"So I guess they talked about why I left, too."

The two of them exchanged a glance, then she said, "You were sending Lucifer a cut of the souls on the Road to Salvation. When Yaweh found out you'd been skimming off the top and not giving Him any vig, He condemned you to Eternal Damnation."

I nodded. "The Big Guy's got a hell of a temper."

"Hey, you don't need to tell *us*," the guy said.

"In fact," the woman added, "that's why we're here."

"Oh?"

She met my eyes, square and direct. In that moment, she didn't look like she was made from Adam's rib. She looked like razor-sharp steel. "We want take out a contract on Yaweh."

"Adam and Eve to see you, boss," I said to Lucifer.

Old Nick had had a thing for Eve millennia ago, as everyone knows, so I wasn't surprised to see his eyes shoot flames of hellfire when she and Adam entered his diabolical presence.

"You're looking well," the Dark Prince said to her.

"Thanks," Adam said.

We all looked at him. After a moment, he turned red and fumbled for a chair.

"You don't sit until the devil invites you to, kid," I advised him.

"Oh! Um .. " Adam got even redder. "Sorry. We've been, you know, outcast and exiled for so long, I've forgotten . . ."

"Your manners?" Lucifer murmured, making the air quiver hotly with his terrible voice.

"He's just nervous," Eve said, giving the boss a pointed look. "Leave him alone."

What *is* it about women? The Prince of Darkness, the only *capo* in Creation who's ever given Yaweh a run for His money, apologized to her and invited them both to take a seat.

Being a very busy omnipotent archdemon, Lucifer decided to get right down to business. "Vito tells me you want my help whacking out Yaweh."

"That's right."

"Out of the question."

"We're ready to pay whatever price you demand," Eve said, looking steely again.

"No."

"Our eternal souls are yours for the asking."

"Are you listening to me, Eve? I said—"

"It's not as if you haven't killed others."

"No!" Lucifer thundered, getting impatient.

Adam bleated, "It was all her idea! I had nothing to do with it!"

"Yeah?" I said. "That's just the excuse I'd expect from the guy who said, when Yaweh asked why he ate the fruit, 'The woman made me do it.' " What a pansy the Supreme Deity had picked to be the father of all mankind.

Adam got hot under the fig leaf. "I couldn't lie to *God*!"

"Some stand-up guy you are," I said. "Back when I was still alive, you know what we did to guys like you? First we cut off their—"

"This is really beside the point, Vito," Lucifer said.

"Yes, boss."

"And we can't whack Yaweh," he added to Eve, "regardless of what happened in Eden."

"I would have thought," Eve said, "that you, of all entities, would have the guts—"

"He's an eternal being," Lucifer said. "'*The* eternal being. I could whack Him out all day every day from now until the end of time, and He wouldn't die. It just doesn't work that way." He sighed and added morosely, "Trust me on this."

Eve gasped. "You mean you've already tried it?"

"*Hull-o-o-o!*" Lucifer said. "Did the whole war between Good and Evil which has existed ever since I got cast out of Heaven completely escape your attention?"

"I got the memo," she snapped back. "I guess I just missed the footnote about you trying to bump off the Maker of All Things."

"Yaweh kept it quiet," I said. "Getting whacked out gave Him a terrible migraine, and He didn't want anyone else getting ideas and following Mister Lucifer's example."

"So you're saying it can't be done?" Eve asked, looking sort of despairing.

"That's what I'm saying," Lucifer confirmed.

"But . . . But . . . We want vengeance!" Eve cried.

"My dear girl," Lucifer said, "if you've got grievances with Yaweh, I suggest you go lay them at His feet, not at my hooves."

"Grievances? You can call what He did to us a mere grievance?"

"We disobey one little order," Adam added. "We taste one little piece of fruit, which didn't taste good anyhow, and—"

"Ingrates!" Lucifer said, steamed now. "That wasn't just a 'little piece of fruit' that I gave you! That was the fruit of the tree of knowledge!"

"It was sort of sour," Adam insisted.

"More like bitter," Eve opined.

"Didn't care for it at all," Adam added.

"And the aftertaste," Eve said. "Yech."

The two of them made identical faces. I seen Carmine Corvino make a face like that just before he keeled over from the strychnine a hit man from the Matera family put in his minestrone.

"It wasn't intended to be a gastronomic experience."

His satanic majesty sounded real grumpy. "The fruit of knowledge made you self-aware and gave you the freedom to choose between Good and Evil."

"I was burping for hours," Adam confided.

"Choice! Self-determination! Free will!" the boss shouted, making the halls of Hell quiver. "I told Yaweh that you, His greatest and finest Creation, were worthy of these gifts! But did He listen to me? Noooooo! He knew best. He *always* knew best." Lucifer sneered. "He had no need to listen to a mere archangel."

"So why was the tree there in the first place?" I asked. "I always did wonder."

"Yaweh and I were playing poker, and—"

"He used to play poker?" Adam asked.

"Don't interrupt the devil, kid," I said.

"Sorry."

"He was *terrible* at it," Lucifer said. "Vito, you never saw anyone so bad at a bluff. It was almost tragic." He shrugged the magnificent red-and-black wings whose feathers had been singed off eons ago in his fiery descent from Heaven. "I probably could have gambled my way back into Heaven long ago—as if anyone would want to—except that He quit cards altogether after what happened in Eden."

"I get it, boss. You're saying that He lost a pot to you that had the tree of knowledge in it."

"Seven card stud. He was trying to make me think He had pulled to an inside straight. Like even being the Supreme Deity could make *that* happen." The boss snorted with ribald amusement. Adam jumped out of his chair a second before Satan's fiery breath singed it. "When He called my hand, I showed Him my four aces. I thought He'd burst into tears."

Eve guessed, "You cheated."

"That's such a low word. Let's just say I employed certain skills which are not necessarily observed within the strictest canon of the game."

"And the result," Eve said, "was that you tempted me—"

"And then *she* tempted *me*," Adam added.

"Petulance is so unbecoming to the father of mankind," Lucifer chided.

"And we've been outcasts ever since!"

"So have I," the boss pointed out, "but I've made something of myself. You two, on the other hand, appear to have been moping around ever since Eden."

"Yaweh threw us into Limbo!" Eve looked pretty pissed off.

"Limbo?" I frowned. "No way. I'd have known."

"Oh, yes, you were skimming off Limbo, too, I know that." Now she sounded pretty pissed off, too.

"Just making sure certain people who didn't really belong there got out before too many millennia passed." I said to the boss, "Boy, and people thought Purgatory was bad. Did I ever tell you what a mess Limbo was until the Big Guy finally closed it down?"

"Let me guess," Lucifer said to Eve. "Yaweh imprisoned you there, but He kept it off the books—even the second set of books."

"You know Him so well," Eve said coldly.

"So *that's* why I didn't know you was there." I didn't mention that I'd never even known there'd been a second set of books. I got a rep to maintain, after all.

"So when they closed Limbo . . ." Lucifer prodded.

"We tried the Road to Redemption," Eve said, "but Yaweh's heart was still hard. So laying our grievances at His feet, as you suggest, Mephisto, won't do any good."

I took a quick look at the boss. Using that old pet name . . . Oh, yeah. I could see it had just the effect Eve wanted it to have. This broad knew how to play *her* cards, even if Yaweh didn't.

But Lucifer had a rep to think about, too, so the *capo* of Darkness merely raised one terrible claw to his toothy mouth, faked a yawn, and said, "Ho-hum, so Yaweh condemned you unfairly, locked you up in the most boring place in Creation without telling anyone, and now He won't let you back on His—if I may be excused for saying so—notoriously dull team. Why should I care?"

"Because it's your fault!" Eve shouted.

"Don't shout at the devil," I said.

"My dear girl," the Evil One said, "*you're* the one who ate the fruit of knowledge. I merely suggested you might be a trifle hungry."

"You did more than that, and you damn well know

it," she said between gritted teeth. "You coaxed me. You convinced me. You cajoled me."

Adam added, "Yeah!" Such a help.

"You *seduced* me!" Eve accused.

"Yeah!" Adam paused. "Um . . ." He looked at Eve. "Seduced? You never told me that."

"You owe me, Lucifer," she said.

"Seduced?" Adam repeated. "How exactly?"

"I still wouldn't know what that damn tree was for, if you hadn't told me," Eve continued.

"You told me he 'talked' you into it, Eve. Seduced? No, you never said *that*. I would remember."

"And as for my voluntarily biting into a fruit that smelled the way that one did . . . It never would have happened if not for you." Eve said.

"Eve, you want to explain to me about the *seduction* you forgot to mention the five million other times we've discussed this?"

"Jesus H. Christ, Adam!" Eve suddenly caught herself and looked at us. "Uh, can I say that here?"

We both nodded.

"Jesus H. Christ, Adam! It was eons ago! Could we please focus on the problem at hand?"

"Oh, excuse me if I'm just a little sensitive about this, but as I recall, Yaweh made you for *me*. Me! *My* companion. *My* partner. *My* mate. And now I find out that the first time another entity came along—"

"This is why I never told you! I knew this is exactly how you'd react! 'Mine, mine, mine!' "

"Oh, as if *you* didn't get jealous about Lilith!"

The infernal temperature suddenly seemed to drop a few hundred degrees.

"I told you," Eve said to Adam, in a voice I'd never even heard a federal judge use, *"never to say that name in my presence again."*

"I'm glad you advised this sit-down, Vito," Lucifer said to me. "This is getting interesting."

Adam went all red again. Eve was as white as the Pearly Gates.

"Do go on," the Prince of Darkness urged them.

"We'll discuss this later," Eve said to Adam.

"We certainly will," he replied.

She faced the monarch of Hell. "Even if you don't feel you're at all responsible for what happened—"

"No, no, I take full credit," he said. "I just don't feel guilty about it."

"Yes, well, rumor has it that no one with the capacity to feel guilt winds up here," she said.

"No, we've got some Jews here." A moment later I admitted, "Well, okay, only the ones who were lawyers."

"Mephisto," she said, pouring it on now. "You've had your differences with Yaweh, too. Don't you want to help us for your own sake?"

"For evil's sake?" He sighed. "Hmmm . . ."

"Or just," she said, moving in for the kill, "for the fun of it?"

"The fun of it? Ah, it *would* be fun," he admitted, "but since He can't be whacked out—"

"So let's torment Him instead of killing Him."

"Do you happen to have a plan?"

She nodded. "What would send Yaweh into a depression for centuries?"

"A growth in Hinduism," Lucifer said promptly. "That whole nirvana thing always bugged the shit out of Him. He said Eternal Paradise was a waste if people were going to strive for sheer nothingness, and he got really—"

"No." Eve sounded impatient. "Not Hinduism. Let's try this another way. What does He value most?"

"Mankind?" Lucifer guessed.

Eve rolled her eyes, then said to me. "I'll bet you know."

"His rep," I said without hesitation. "Mister Yaweh's very big on His rep. Doesn't like it messed with."

"Exactly!" Eve smiled.

"So you want us to mess with His rep?" I asked, stunned.

"That's what I want."

Wow. I was right, this broad had huevos.

"He'll take it hard," I told Lucifer, "that's for sure."

"Oooh! This does sound like fun," the Dark One said, rubbing his claws together.

"How we gonna do it?" I asked.

Eve explained, "Lucifer will endow thoroughly un-principled and morally bankrupt men with tremendous powers of charisma and persuasion, then provide them with opportunities to humiliate Yaweh before millions of people and thoroughly undermine His credibility in their eyes."

"What an interesting concept," Lucifer said. "I'm in."

And that's how televangelism was born.

It went exactly the way we planned. Guys you wouldn't loan five bucks to or leave alone with your daughter were going on TV every week and convincing millions of people to send them charitable donations in Yaweh's name. Next thing you knew, these goombata would be caught using the money to pay for their mansions, their private jets, their underage girlfriends in hotel rooms with jacuzzis, their personal playgrounds, their booze, their drugs. Whatever.

It was brilliant, and we was incredibly pleased with how good it was going. We figured that any minute, Yaweh would have a nervous breakdown.

Of course, you've probably already figured out what we overlooked. When trying to smear Yaweh's rep, we completely forgot one of the things He's best known for: giving people second chances. It's a trait He passed on to his favorite creation, mankind, and they emulated His endless benevolence by forgiving a bunch of these goons, go figure. And these bums getting forgiven, well, it made them come to love Yaweh, which in turn made everyone else love Yaweh even more, too. And next thing we knew, Yaweh's polls were at an all-time high, and He was feeling so benevolent that He decided He'd been too hard on Adam and Eve—whom He forgave and let into Heaven.

"Which," Lucifer said grimly to me, "was probably Eve's plan all along." He sighed, wafting fire and smoke through the halls of Hell. "I'd forgotten how damn clever that woman is. I'll bet you anything she nibbled on the fruit of knowledge before I ever came along."

"You think, boss?"

"I'll bet she only pretended I'm the one who talked her into it, so she could blame me when Yaweh asked her about it."

"Guess it backfired," I said, thinking of her millennia in Limbo.

Lucifer nodded. "She didn't know about the poker game. He was always so sensitive about little things like that."

We sat in silence for a while, both feeling pretty gloomy.

Finally he said, "You know what this means now, don't you?"

"Yeah, I think so, boss." I was the one who'd advised the sit-down with Adam and Eve. So now I was the one who had to take the fall for it.

"It's not personal, Vito."

I nodded. "I know. Just business."

"I'd bump you off if I could," he assured me.

"I appreciate the thought, Mister Lucifer."

"But, seeing as how you're already dead . . ."

"Guess I'm exiled?"

"I'm afraid so, Vito."

"Well . . . No point in hanging around then. It's been a privilege working for you, boss."

"I know," he said.

And that's how I wound up leaving Hell, all on account of Yaweh's rep being the best deserved rep in Creation, and Lucifer being maybe a little too overconfident.

I ain't bitter, though. Like the boss said, it was business, nothing personal. And I'm sure Mister Yaweh will be businesslike about it, too, when I go to Him now and explain about how I helped invent televangelists all in an attempt to earn my way back into Heaven.

I think it'll work. After all, Yaweh's very big on giving people second chances.

THE ASTRAL OUTRAGE

by P. N. Elrod

P. N. "Pat" Elrod has written over sixteen novels, including the ongoing *Vampire Files* series, the *I, Strahd* novels, and the *Quincey Morris, Vampire Dracula* adventure book. She has coedited two anthologies with Martin H. Greenberg and is working on more toothy titles in the mystery and fantasy genres, including a third Richard Dun novel with Nigel Bennett.

ONE morning in the fall of 188–, Mr. Jones, a man with a rare psychic talent and a very high-level initiate in the Aetheric Sciences, sent a telegram requesting I come 'round to his London lodgings as soon as might be convenient. This sounds irregular, but his lodgings are also where he conducts his business in much the same way the great consulting detective Mr. Holmes sees to his own remarkable trade.

As I had no plans for the day, I donned my hat, gloves, and walking coat and set off at a brisk pace, reticule and umbrella in hand. Mr. Jones lived but ten streets away and a good constitutional, even in the foggy air of the city, was just the thing to clear my head in preparation for whatever might lie in store.

At this point I must introduce myself to you, the patient reader. My name is Catherine Elizabeth Pendergast, and I am a psychical investigator. Being both psychically and magically gifted, I have lately trained to develop such supernatural faculties as I possess so as to be of service to others. How I came to this situation is a complicated story which I will share in full at some future point, but for now let it suffice that I first met Mr. Jones at a séance.

I'd been recently widowed and was there in a misguided attempt to speak with my dear husband Bernard.

I've learned wiser ways since, but was very much the
innocent then, though not utterly devoid of sense.

I shall not indulge in details to spare the feelings of
the other witnesses, but the instant the medium deepened her voice to a hoarse whisper and claimed to be
Bernard, I knew her for a cruel charlatan and thief.

Possessing a mighty temper that wanted expression, I
broke the medium's nose along with several items of
furniture when she fell into them in the course of my
angry assault. I was prevented from inflicting further violence upon her by one of the attendees, a certain Mr.
Jones, who seized my arms and with some effort, gently
persuaded me to a less violent strategy of reckoning
against the offender.

He himself was present for the purpose of determining
if the medium was an honest one, but I spoiled his own
revelation of her deceit with my fierce reaction. Thank-
fully, this caused no setback for his investigation; indeed,
it helped to galvanize other angry witnesses to appear
in court against the person who would have continued
defrauding them with her odious deception. Mr. Jones
later contacted me, and after lengthy interviews and in-
troductions to other members of his Aetheric Sciences
circle, he convinced me that I had a talent worthy of
development. He said I had dormant psychic and magical abilities and these, apparently, coupled with my
strong memories of dear Bernard helped me see through
the sham.

Since that fateful day I have striven to explore and
develop my talents, putting them to constructive and
positive use. Lest you wink and say that Mr. Jones is
but another swindler out to profit himself, I state that
he is an honest gentleman with considerable private
means who takes not one penny from those within our
Sciences circle or from those he helps. In fact, few if any
of the public are aware of our existence. It is his prefer-
ence, asserting that it keeps our Aetheric delvings
above reproach.

I rang the bell of his house, a modest structure in a
quiet cul-de-sac not far from the far richer homes of
Grosvenor Square. On the door was a brass plate, still
shining from that morning's polish, with the name *Jones*

etched in Roman letters much the same as for a Harley Street physician. As the household was small and somewhat informal, a young page boy rather than a butler opened the door, and I was straightway escorted to the study. I entered with a firm step and much curiosity. Our little society holds meetings twice a month, during which anything of note is introduced for discussion, study, and perhaps investigation. Occasionally, one or two of us might venture forth under Mr. Jones' instructions to look into various oddities, and I hoped that this summoning might portend such an adventure.

Mr. Jones, a strongly built young man who looks more Irish than Welsh, rose from his chair by the fire, setting aside a leather-bound volume with a Latin title. "Mrs. Pendergast, how delightful. I hope you did not think you had to rush right over." He bowed slightly over my extended hand, then led me to a sofa opposite, indicating I should sit.

"Not at all. I had nothing to impede my immediate departure."·

"As you know I do not believe in coincidence, so I shall take that as a sign of good fortune for what might come."

"And pray, what would that be?"

He smiled and tapped the side of his nose. "Mystical events that want looking into. As it happens, I believe you are perfect for the task."

I composed myself to give him my full attention and thus learned of some strange goings-on taking place just north of London.

It seemed that a finishing academy for young ladies of good family had a disturbing shadow overhanging its very respectable walls. A number of the girls there, once vivacious and in the bloom of health were suffering from some debilitation that no doctor could remedy. Each complained of unsettling dreams that, once wakened from slumber, they could not or would not recall.

I snorted. "Perhaps they are raiding the kitchen pantry for a midnight feast. That would account for any reluctance in admitting to a dream that never happened."

"Admittedly, that was my first thought, too," said Mr.

Jones. "As a lad, my mates and I had all manner of
excuses to offer the headmaster on those times when we
were caught red-handed in the kitchens. But after an
extensive consultation with the headmistress of this
school I believe there is more than youthful high jinks
at work here. I was only allowed into her office and must
admit to feeling a decided weight in the atmosphere of
the place. It might have been the gloomy surroundings,
for the original architect was obviously a cheerless sort,
but I trust my psychical impressions even within such
a framing."

"Were you able to interview any of the students?"

"That was not permitted. The headmistress is most
concerned with the welfare of those under her charge
and preserving the reputation of her school. She is a
sensible woman, and understands that if she puts too
much stock in their stories it might create an atmosphere
of communal hysteria."

"Hysteria? That's a rather strong word."

"She *is* decidedly worried, Mrs. Pendergast. Being
quite experienced in the behavior of young ladies, she
is well aware of the possibility of how quickly a small
prank can get out of hand if given too much attention.
But she has emphasized to me, in very clear-cut terms,
her impression that the girls are truly in the grasp of
some acute malady. Many fear to sleep, and some are
in such a depleted state that she may be compelled to
remove them from the environs. By the way, the headmistress is a friend of Mrs. Eldershins, who brought the
situation to my attention once she caught wind of it."

Mrs. Eldershins was a most level-headed member of
our scientific circle, a kindly lady of sharp mind and
balanced judgment. If she suspected untoward mischief
afoot on a supernatural level, then we could trust it to
be serious enough to warrant an inquiry.

"Am I to involve myself in this?" I asked. "And if
so, how?"

"You make me suspect you use your gifts to read my
very thoughts."

The twinkle in his eye forestalled any denial on my
part for taking such a liberty, so I merely smiled back.
Besides, he knew I was not gifted in that particular abil-

ity, for which I was humbly grateful. Useful as it might be for the investigator, it struck me as a terrible faculty to possess. Few people hear much good by eavesdropping, how much worse would life be if some were able to take in the innermost reflections of their fellows?

Mr. Jones continued. "If you are free, I should like you to go up to the school for a day or two, perhaps longer, and see what's at the bottom of their murky pond. From what I've gathered, the headmistress, a Mrs. Mallory, is out of her depth on psychical matters. She's strictly C. of E. and holds no truck with what you and I accept as commonplace. You shall have to be discreet."

"That won't be difficult, but if she is not aware of psychical matters, how do you explain my being there?"

"She believes you to be the daughter of a doctor who has traveled extensively and gained much knowledge about exotic diseases. I said I'd send someone down who might be able to identify what troubles her students. Don't let her think otherwise."

"Of course."

"Mrs. Mallory doesn't want her girls upset by even the hint of another doctor, though, so I have worked out an acceptable story to tell them. It will provide you the freedom of the school and grounds and put you in contact with the students in such a way as to encourage them to speak—you are to be a novelist researching your next book."

I nearly gasped in a mixture of surprise and mortification. "You cannot be serious, sir. I know nothing about the writing of books."

"You are an avid reader, though."

"I also ride trains, but that doesn't qualify me to impersonate the engineer."

"True, but it's not what you know, but what others think you know. I have on occasion convinced a number of people that I was a gas-fitter, a groom to Her Majesty's stables, and—in one stretch—an American millionaire. It is not as difficult as you would imagine. If Mrs. Mallory introduces you to her charges as a novelist, why should they suspect otherwise since the information comes from a trusted mentor?"

"But what if they want to know what I've written?"

"Come up with some title and say that it's at the type-setters and not yet in the shops."

"And if I'm asked how to go about writing a book?"

"Tell them to find pencil and paper and write. I have heard that exact same answer from an acquaintance who has dozens of books published. The briefer your reply, the more they will accept it as truth."

That made sense. Being curious about the goings-on at this school, I was willing to try. "What sort of novel would you suggest I research?"

"Something along the lines of *Tom Brown's School Days,* but about a girls' school. Since you wish it to be as accurate as possible, you will be there to ascertain how things are done today at a typical academy. Your walking about at all hours in all places asking questions will be taken as normal."

"Indeed, I may find myself overwhelmed with much that is useless." I dreaded the idea of hearing giddy, giggling confidences. "You are aware that what is of life-and-death importance to youth is more often than not minutiae to be disregarded by a more experienced adult."

"Perhaps, but it is within the minutiae of living that heroic discoveries are made. A certain Dr. Pasteur I know spends his time peering through a microscope re-searching the crimes committed in a drop of tainted water. The results of his attention to detail have earned him the gratitude of connoisseurs the world over when his work saved the French wine trade."

"I doubt my delvings will turn up anything on that level of import, but I shall do my best."

"Excellent. I have every faith in your abilities—all of them."

"You think I will have to exercise my magical gifts?"

"I suspect it might be necessary, else I should ask Mrs. Eldershins to go instead. She, alas, does not have your natural—perhaps I should say—supernatural strengths in magic, though. Also, you are much closer in age to the young ladies there than she, so they may find it easier to confide in you."

Mr. Jones advanced me sufficient funds for my trip, dispatching a telegram to Mrs. Mallory so she would know when to expect me. I quickly packed to make my train, and that afternoon I found myself at the Mallory Academy. It was indeed grim of aspect, and I felt a chill as I crossed its threshold.

Mrs. Mallory was rather warmer, but seemed caught between relief and misgiving. Apparently she'd been expecting a somewhat older person. But I presented a confident face, inviting her to recount to me all that she'd told Mr. Jones and asking if the afflicted girls showed any improvement.

"Bless me, but that is my only prayer day after day," she said as we took tea in her private drawing room. "My poor girls are so pale and drawn as to draw rumors of consumption. To put a short end to the gossip I called in the village physician who found nothing and advised that they get a good night's sleep. Silly man, if only they could! He had the chemist make up a number of sleeping draughts, but it only made matters worse. The girls slept, rather too deeply, and woke late and even more exhausted than when they retired. They complain bitterly of dreams, but are unable to say aught of them."

"Are all the girls so distressed?"

"Some dozen of my fifty charges have been aggrieved by this odd malady, but three in particular seem to suffer more than the rest."

"Are these three close friends?"

"I see you might think them joining together as though for a prank, for that occurred to me right away, but no. All the girls are acquainted, but not especial friends with each other. Violet is a quiet, studious type, Winifred interested in sports, and Anna the sort of butterfly who will do well in society. They have a circle of friends within their own areas of interest and little overlap. Being of different ages and academic skills they don't have any classes together. The only commonality is their restless sleep and dreams they cannot remember."

"I should like to be introduced to them as soon as may be. One at a time would be best."

"Of course."

"It would also be helpful if you could find yourself called away for an extended period that I might speak to them alone."

Mrs. Mallory gave me a shrewd look. "That can be easily managed, provided you keep me informed of any conclusions you make."

"Certainly."

Arrangements were made and, in the guise of a rising young novelist, I was able to interview all three before it was time for them to retire.

What struck me upon meeting each was the seeming gauntness of their physical appearance. I say seeming, for upon close examination their limbs were not thin as with a chronic disease. The impression of waste came rather from their hesitancy of speech, the circles under their dull eyes, and a general lassitude of manner. They ranged in age from sixteen to eighteen, but lacked the sparkle and energy of their years. What could be stealing it away? If not for this malady, the girls would be most striking in their looks. When the fullness of womanhood came to them, they would be outstandingly beautiful. That was the only other commonality I could find besides their ill health.

Whenever Mrs. Mallory withdrew on feigned business, I encouraged her charges to speak as freely as they'd like about their life at the academy. Most girls would delight in an invitation to gossip or confide. Not these. Their monosyllabic replies to my leading queries fell short of my expectations.

Thus was I forced to apply other means to gain information. Under the tutelage of Mr. Jones and others in our Atheric Sciences circle I'd learned the art of perceiving and interpreting the aura, that colorful corona of light that all things possess, both animal and vegetable. Even certain geographic locations are capable of radiating an aura to those with eyes to see.

I was quite shocked at my first attempt with Violet, less so on Winifred, and decidedly grim with Anna. Their auras were all but invisible, even to me. Where there should have vigorous bands of color and energy were instead rootless pale hazes, like a watercolor sketch that's been dipped in a bath basin. Even as I watched, they seemed to fade. This could not be borne. If I could not find some way to check this decline, the girls would become more physically ill, perhaps even die. I'd read of similar events in Mr. Jones' archives and knew the gravity of the matter. They were under some kind of psychic attack.

Unfortunately, I could say nothing to Mrs. Mallory. Were I to even hint at the truth she would dismiss me as a lunatic and prevent my having further contact with her girls.

Instead, I told her I'd require more time to study the situation and asked if she could provide accommodations for the night. She'd anticipated that and had had a small, comfortable room readied for me. After dinner I gratefully retired there to compose myself for the next step in my inquiry.

My Aetheric instruction included forms of meditation that allow my mind and body to relax into a state that makes it possible to travel outside of myself. I strongly warn novices never to attempt this unless under the close supervision of an adept teacher, for travel on the Astral Plane is rife with dangers. One does not enter the deeps of an unknown jungle without a guide to point out deadly perils and how to protect oneself from them.

I had excellent teachers, and thus with little effort was able to drift up from my body where it lay on the bed and hover near the ceiling. From there I was free to roam as I pleased, for the restrictions of normal reality do not apply to the Astral. There are exceptions, but most of the time a wall is no more a barrier to an Astral explorer than a patch of river mist is to a train.

Traveling through the school I located young Violet, who was tucked away in her own bed, along with three other girls with whom she shared the room. For now all was peaceful, but her Astral form was very wasted and sickly. I looked in on Winifred, who shared quarters with only one other girl. Both slept soundly. Anna, however, was not so lucky.

Mr. Jones remarked on the gloomy atmosphere of the school. Here, I was able to see it for myself. As I approached Anna's room, I sensed a darkness ahead that grew thicker and more difficult to pass, like trudging through ever-deepening snow. This did not put me off, rather was I all the more anxious to hurry forward to discover its source.

When I finally did push past the worst of it I was
hardly prepared for the shock. Poor Anna was quite
prostrate on her bed, eyes sealed shut, her limbs
twitching as though in the throes of a terrible dream.
Pressing close upon her I perceived three distinct forms
as black as a coal mine. They seemed so solid as to be
corporeal, until I realized their extreme opacity on this
place was due to untoward strength, strength they were
very obviously stealing from Anna.

At first I thought them to be some Darkside creatures
unknown to me. Those tend to be small, though, and
easily routed, these were fully man-sized. And with that
thought I— with much horror of spirit—realized the
truth.

My heart flooded with both fury and sorrow, fury for
these wicked, wicked villains and sorrow for their hap-
less victims. Merciful it was that the girls had no memory
of what was being done to them.

The things below were Astral travelers like myself,
male, and brutally indifferent to any shred of decency
and honor. For the last several weeks they had been
invading the academy, insinuating themselves, feeding
from and ravishing the poor girls like the Vandals of old.

There was little I could do until these projections returned to their bodies. How that rankled. If I could have
fallen upon them like an avenging angel with a sword of
fire, I'd have cut them to ribbons and suffered no pang
of conscience.

But I had to wait until their hideous outrage was
finished.

It could not have taken long, yet seemed an eternity.
Still, it was far worse for the poor child below, even if
her waking memory was clouded. I waited them out,
righteous anger building in me like lava trapped within
an ancient volcano. This was unwise, for there are beings
on the Astral Plane that are attracted to such negativi-
ties, but I could not help myself.

At long last the three were done with her and withdrew. Like myself, each had a thin cord that tied them to
their earthly bodies, and they used this thread to guide
themselves back. Were I to cut that cord, their projec-

tions would be adrift, their bodies left forever in a cataleptic state unless by chance the owners found their way home again. I considered, but decided against that action. Satisfying it might be to me, but it could create problems for other innocents.

Careful not to reveal my presence, I followed the black forms across miles of countryside, taking the crow's path to their nest. This proved to be a manor house of vast size, the final destination an upstairs room. There, in its shrouded center, they lay on the bare floor, three middle-aged men, fat and lewd as satyrs on a Greek vase. Inscribed on the floor in chalk was a great circle, large enough for them to lie in, heads in the center and feet out like wheel spokes. The circle was embellished with various arcane signs and sigils meant to help them get to the Astral Plane. Such workings were obviously those of novices who had just enough knowledge to abuse it. No true adept with an honorable thirst for wisdom would stoop to so base a purpose. To do so invites reprisal.

Obviously, these cravens thought themselves immune.

They woke from their trance, grinned at each other and stood, bowing, and waving wands about like band leaders. The ritual complete, they removed from the circle and celebrated their latest offense with brandy. Their laughter made my blood boil.

I listened to the disgusting recount of their assault, and discovered they planned another outing later on. From the description of the girl they chose, it would be young Violet for the next attack.

As I said, it could not be borne.

I tore back to the school, reuniting my own projection with my physical body rather too suddenly, sitting bolt upright, gasping for breath and chilled to the bone. Action would remedy the chill, though. Those damnable would-be adepts were in for a terrible lesson if I could ready everything in time.

From my earlier excursion, I knew the location of Violet's room in the great house and thence took myself, stealing along on tiptoe. Now did my magical skills serve me well as I cast a protective barricade around that chamber stronger than any suit of armor. Such work should have exhausted me, but I was yet fired by anger, which made me only more robust.

The casting had a second purpose: to lead the intruders to my room.

Their unclean desire and hunger overcame them sooner than I expected. I'd just locked my door when I sensed their bafflement at encountering the barrier surrounding Violet. From a distance I felt it as they tried again and again to break through, evoking an image of bloated flies bumping against a malarial net. I sensed their surge of frustration as they searched for the source of the block.

I barely had time to compose myself, gathering about me such magical force as I could muster. Much that is referred to as magic is simply a form of energy that can be used for good or ill. The same steam that drives a train engine can also scald one to death. Much of the power for magic comes from the worker's emotions. One learns to take care and beware. But I was so very, very angry. It is one of my worst faults and, at times, my greatest strength—as these three discovered.

Anyone else would have been unaware of their sudden entry into my room. I sensed them instantly, yet forced myself to lie still on the bed, appearing to be as defenseless as any of the other girls they'd taken. It was very difficult to remain in place as they hovered over me, then came lower and lower. Through my eyelashes I marked their progress, the black shapes closing in like the pall of death.

If one of them hadn't laughed, things might have turned out differently.

At that horrid, sniggery sound, so full of greed and lust, my self-control broke. I'd prepared to send them packing back to their bodies with an illusion of a fiery Darkside creature ten times the normal size. Then later Mr. Jones would find some way to deal with the abuses, but it didn't come out like that at all.

My rage gave substance to the illusion of a kind that could interact with their projections. And I lost control of it.

As I lay flat, a dark red *thing* filled the small room

and seized the three interlopers as easily as a starving dog snaps up a tossed scrap of meat. Their screams beat upon the air of the Plane. Now did I cower as they were flung about and worried, thrown high and caught again like toys. Each tried to escape. Each failed. As I watched in horror and awe, the black strength they'd acquired from their misdeeds faded to deep gray, then became more and more pale. Long streaky shimmers of color were flung from the projections, to vanish through the shuddering walls. It was the strength they'd stolen, returning to their victims.

What a terrible thing to behold, but within me burned the knowledge that the outrages they'd committed were being avenged a hundred times over.

Just as I thought the whole house would come down about my ears sudden silence reigned. I thought myself deaf, until I sat up and heard the reassuring creak of bedsprings. Throwing on a wrap, I ventured forth, pacing the long halls and listening most carefully with *all* my senses. Not one sign of the projections could I find. The great thing my anger had empowered had taken them away I knew not where.

It was difficult the next morning to rise and appear normal, and I failed at it, for Mrs. Mallory inquired with some sympathy whether or not I had slept well. We broke our fast in her sitting room, and though the repast was splendid I was only able to drink a bit of tea and nibble a crust of toast. She asked if I'd drawn any conclusions from my interviews with the girls.

"I rather think this creeping malaise has run its course," I ventured.

"How can you assume that?"

"I've seen this sort of thing before, though never so focused a case." Remembering the background Mr. Jones had created for me, I spun a fanciful tale of my father's sojourn to India (he had never traveled farther than Dover) where such maladies were not unheard of. "Sometimes whole villages are brought down by it. The natives in their ignorance prayed to their gods for relief from the nightmares and exhaustion, and sooner or later they would recover with no harm done."

Mrs. Mallory was not a woman to be easily fooled, but before the end of the meal I had her convinced of the reality of my lies. I must have a very trustworthy face.

I was spared from further sins by one of the teachers, who knocked hard upon the door, then burst upon us like a breathless rocket.

"Oh, Mrs. Mallory, it's just in from the village! There was a fire last night at Lord Wexter's house!"

"Good heavens. Was anyone hurt?"

"Lord Wexter himself was killed along with two of his guests."

I felt the blood drain from my face and had to grip the edge of the table hard to keep from falling.

"Oh, no! How awful!" cried Mrs. Mallory.

"It's all very mysterious, for the fire was confined to an upper room of the house. Constable Bets said it was a miracle it did not spread to the rest of the place, else everyone would have been burned in their beds. Uncanny is what I'd call it."

"A miracle, indeed. But poor Lord Wexter—and his friends. This is a dreadful, dreadful day."

"Constable said to pass the word to you that there was to be a special prayer service for their souls at noon today in the village church."

"Then I must attend. Please see to organizing a similar service here for the girls."

"Yes, ma'am." She darted out.

"Lord Wexter?" I asked, breaking in on her shock.

"One of our patrons. The fees we collect are sufficient to see to the academy's support, but his regular endowments enabled us to do more. He frequently gifted us with funds for parties and treats. Often did he say there was nothing sweeter in life than to see a young girl's face lighting with a smile. He was like a second father to some of them."

Dear God, but I felt ill. Mrs. Mallory was too lost in praise for her dead patron to notice.

MARYSUE AT FORTY

by Alan Rodgers

Alan Rodgers' short fiction has appeared in such anthologies as *Miskatonic University, Tales from the Great
Turtle, Masques #3,* and *The Conspiracy Files.* His first
published short story, "The Boy Who Came Back
from The Dead," won the Horror Writer Associa-
tion's Stoker Award for Best Novelette. He lives in
Hollywood, California.

OVERHEARD AT A STAR TREK CONVENTION

"SHE'S such a MarySue," Fran says.

Jill scowls. "No," she says, "she only thinks she
is."

Your reporter leans in close, feeling a little stupid. "I
don't understand," he says. "Who's MarySue?"

Fran laughs.

"MarySue is the term for a type of fan fiction character," Jill says. "You see MarySue in *Trek* fanfic all the
time."

Trek fanfic is what dedicated *Star Trek* fans call the
stories fans write and publish in their amateur publica-
tions, generally without the knowledge or even tacit con-
sent of Paramount, the studio that owns the *Star Trek*
copyrights.

Fran shakes her head. "You're missing it," she says.
"MarySue is a girl who's fourteen or so, and totally brilliant—usually she's Lieutenant MarySue when it's *Trek*
fic."

"She's fourteen, she's already a lieutenant, and she's
got the Captain's attention because she's so completely
brilliant," Jill reiterates.

As the women speak, your reporter hears something
unsaid in their voices.

It's in their eyes, too.

It's as if the women see themselves in MarySue even as they scorn the stereotype.

As if, perhaps, all the young women who write and read these stories see themselves in MarySue.

And perhaps they do.

When MarySue was fourteen years old, she was totally brilliant. Everyone who knew her loved MarySue, and all of them respected her.

But none of them knew the revenge she would take on the man she loved more than anyone else in the world; or why; or how she came to love that man; and if they knew those things, they'd never make the sense of them that you and I can. In the end, and no matter how brilliant she was, that revenge is the thing we really need to know about MarySue.

It started that year, when she was still fourteen—that was the year MarySue graduated from Yale with a Ph.D. in micron physics and went to work in the bowels of a secret government project solving all the world's problems. After a few months she'd solved world hunger, poverty, prejudice, illiteracy, and child welfare, and she knew she'd made a terrible mistake.

"This is *boring*!" MarySue said. She meant it, too.

Her administrator frowned. "Boring?" she asked. "Oh, MarySue, please tell me you aren't thinking about leaving us!"

"I need to live my life," MarySue said. "I need romance! I need intrigue and heartbreak and adventure!" She saw a tear come to her administrator's eye, but she didn't let that stop her. "I need to experience the seven natural delights of the universe! I need a happy ending!"

Her administrator sobbed. "But we need *you*, MarySue!"

"I'm sorry," MarySue said, "but this is the way it has to be." (She never explained why, but that was MarySue for you: sometimes the hardest things were so obvious to her that she never bothered to explain them.)

"I understand," said the administrator, though of course she didn't. "We'll miss you, MarySue."

MarySue went back to her desk, gathered up her notes, and left without saying another word.

On her way home she stopped by the stock market to make her fortune, stopped by the travel office to find her destiny, and called her parents to let them know she was okay.

"I'm going to find my love, Mom," MarySue said. "Ill let you know where I find him."

"Aren't you a little young for that, dear?"

MarySue sighed. "Oh, Mom," she said. "Don't you know? You can never be too young, too thin, or have too much money."

Her mother didn't answer right away. "Well, stay in touch, dear. And remember that we love you."

"Of course I will," MarySue said.

Mothers say the silliest things sometimes, don't they?

MarySue spread the papers she'd got from the travel agency across her kitchen table and tried to figure out where she was going to find love. She thought about everywhere—Aspen, Vail, California, Florida, Texas, Maine, Hawaii, but finally she decided on Las Vegas. *Lucky in love,* she thought, without bothering to remember the other half of the saying. *And Vegas is just the place to find someone lucky.*

But Las Vegas isn't a good place for fourteen-year-old girls to go wandering alone, and MarySue knew it. She thought about that for a while, and finally decided that (being totally brilliant) she was a special case.

And maybe she was.

So she fudged the age of majority on her papers (reatomizing ink and photo-plastic molecules is no big trick for a girl with a Ph.D. in micron physics from Yale), put on makeup, and spent three hours practicing Acting Older. By the time she was done, anyone who met her would have mistaken her for a young woman in her late twenties.

She got to bed early and took the first plane out to Vegas in the morning. When she got to town, she rented the flashiest car they had and drove up and down the strip, looking for the biggest, ritziest casino she could find. She finally settled on the Araby Mirable. She chose a room with an extravagantly deep carpet, an in-room Jacuzzi, and a fully stocked wet bar. When she got inside her room, she fell to the floor, luxuriating in the plush-ness of the carpet and the coolness of the climate-controlled air. She thought, *There is so much to do!* And got up, went to the bathroom, filled the Jacuzzi, and took the sort of lingering rich bath that she'd read about in romantic novels.

When the Jacuzzi had unwound every muscle in her body, MarySue eased out of the extravagantly warm water, dried herself, and dressed to kill. Which meant she dressed (as she had on the plane) to make folks think she was an Older Woman—and mostly she succeeded. But not entirely. The long hot bath had put a deep flush in her cheeks—the sort of bright healthy glow that only comes to the very young. MarySue did what she could to mask it with cosmetics—but she couldn't hide it entirely. So she made herself a highball and drank it down quickly, thinking that the scent of liquor on her breath would make her youthful glow seem like a drunkard's fever.

That thinking was right, mostly. Certainly no one challenged her on her way downstairs to the casino. The dealer at the blackjack table didn't deny her access to his table, either— not even after the twenty or so rounds it took her to win an enormous pile of cash, a sum so large that it put his table deep in the red for that entire month.

As she played, as she won, the house plied MarySue with free drinks and expensive cigarettes, but those things didn't faze her. They faze ordinary people easily enough— there's a reason that the winners at the tables drink for free, and the biggest part of that reason is that drunkards have lousy gambling judgment—but MarySue was much too smart to lose her knack for numbers in the haze of alcohol.

And that only makes sense, doesn't it? Mastering blackjack couldn't be a chore for the totally brilliant girl who solved world hunger, poverty, prejudice, illiteracy, and child welfare in the course of a few months' government employment. If she'd kept at it for another hour, MarySue could have come away owning the casino. But it didn't even occur to her to break the house's bank. MarySue wasn't into *power* back then; she went to Las Vegas looking for love. Forty minutes at the blackjack

table left her even more extravagantly wealthy, totally
bored, and no closer to love than she'd been when she
gave notice to her boss at the secret government project.

"I'm bored," said MarySue, catching the dealer un-
awares. "Deal me out."

The dealer cocked an eyebrow. "You've got twenty
on the table," she said. "Are you sure you want to
fold now?"

MarySue sighed. "Don't you people ever listen?" she
asked. "I told you to deal me out."

The dealer shrugged, and turned over MarySue's
cards. MarySue pushed her winnings into her purse and
wandered away from the table.

She didn't know where to go at first. She felt pensive
and unsatisfied, hungry as though there were something
she needed but didn't know how to name. It was love
she was missing, she thought. Later she decided that was
wrong, but that night she wandered the casino, woozy
from alcohol and jet lag, totally brilliant and entirely
possessed of a drunkard's bad judgment. Oh, not all her
judgment was bad; she could've gone back to the tables
and broken the house at any moment that she chose.
But where it came to knowing about people, MarySue
was still fourteen, and there were many things she
thought she knew that she only imagined understanding.

Later, years later, experience brought her to terms
with those things, the same way it brings all of us to
terms. But that night, that year in Las Vegas, MarySue
was fourteen and she'd analyzed the world, and though
her analysis was flawlessly consistent it misspoke the
truth. It's like that for all of us, isn't it? When we're
young, we look out at the world, look deep into the
hearts of those around us, and we think we understand
the things we see. But the things we know when we are
young are never what we think they are.

And so with MarySue: she stood for a long moment
resting against a pillar where the tables gave way to
banks of slot machines, watching the men and women
pulling levers and push buttons and piddle away their
money at a game no strategy can win, and in the blush
of youth and alcohol she saw the one true love of all
her days.

She knew him the moment that she saw him. She really did. He was perfect; he was beautiful; he was everything she'd ever decided that she wanted in her one true love. Because he met her needs (and then some), she resolved to get his attention, and keep it, by damn. She went to the machine beside his, and gambled at it frugally—she didn't mind spending a bit to get her love's attention, but she wasn't about to pour anything down the rat-hole slot machine that she didn't have to—giggling and preening as she went along. It only cost her a few dollars to get her man's attention, and once she had it, she reeled him in as quickly as she could.

"I never win," she said when she knew that he was listening. "You ever notice that, how you never win this game?" She stole a glance at him as she asked that question, taking her eyes just that moment away from the slots, away from the spinning fruits and numbered prizes.

Her one true love cocked an eyebrow. "Oh, I don't know," he said. "I find my luck comes and goes. There are days the slots pay very well."

"Oh, pshaw," said MarySue. Because she'd learned it reading books, she pronounced the word just like it's spelled. She didn't realize her error. "The slots are a losing game. Just blind chance, always stacked against you. If you spend a thousand dollars in this thing, you won't even get back nine hundred ninety-nine."

As the wheeling images spun 'round and 'round before her, she did not watch.

"It's the luck of the draw," her love said. "Sometimes the odds come for you; sometimes they don't. The statistics won't always carry you away."

"Pshaw again—" said MarySue, as the wheels stopped and the bells went off and the lights started flashing and the money started pouring out the basin at the low end of the machine.

Stopping her suddenly, right in the middle of her harangue.

"Luck is a lady," the beautiful young man told Mary-Sue, nodding at the fortune piling up before her. "Sometimes she loves you. Sometimes she doesn't."

"That's silly," said MarySue, ignoring the fortune that

had come to her. "Even when you win a game like this, you lose. It's a negative-sum game—the house doesn't return everything you put in the pot, and no scheme could ever give you an advantage of the odds. If you play it long enough, you'll lose—that's a certainty."

MarySue's one true love grinned ruefully. "Tell that to your winnings," he said.

And he laughed.

MarySue got so frustrated. "You just don't understand," she said. "Men!"

The beautiful man shrugged.

"I guess I don't," he said. "Buy you a drink?"

MarySue gathered up her winnings—no matter what her opinion of the game, she wasn't about to abandon her good fortune—and took the invitation by the horns.

"Let me buy," she said, kneeling, scooping the silver dollars into her purse. She had a very large purse, but even so there was hardly room for all of them. "Better yet, let me serve you myself—there's a bar in my suite."

"If you like," said MarySue's one true love. He sounded just a little wary, but what would you expect?

MarySue wasn't sure what to expect. For a moment she thought he would put words to his unease—but he didn't. He didn't say another word as he followed her to the elevator; didn't say a word as they rode the elevator high into the farthest penthouse reaches of the Araby Mirable. When they got off, he hesitated in the corridor, near a window that looked spectacularly out onto the desert mountains southwest of Las Vegas.

"It's beautiful, isn't it?" he asked.

MarySue stopped, turned back; stepped toward the window until she stood electrically close to the man she'd set her mind upon. "Nice enough, if you like deserts," she said. "But I prefer my landscapes thriving."

Her true love frowned.

"I don't even know your name," he said. "Tell me what it is."

"I'm MarySue," said MarySue. "Everyone knows that."

Her true love looked surprised. "Is that so?" he asked, but he didn't wait for her to answer the question. "Mary-

Sue, you ought to know the desert's more living than it looks. It thrives just like the rest of us, but it does it quietly."

"I know that," MarySue said. "I know everything there is to say about arid biodiversity. I know what's out there. But anyone can see it's mostly barren."

A shrug.

"Not if you look at the parts that are alive."

MarySue let out an exasperated sigh. *What a stupid conversation,* she thought. *Is the cup mostly empty or is it mostly full?* It could go forever and never reach an answer.

"You didn't say your own name," she said, changing the subject. "Don't you think you should?"

"My name is Ray," he said. "Ray Thomas Thomason."

He ignored the second question.

"Ray Thomas Thomason, do you want that drink or not?"

He didn't answer right away, and MarySue thought that might be just as well. This wasn't going like she'd planned. At all! This man was a mistake, she thought, he only looked like he was her one true love. An impostor—that was what he was! She owed him for that, she really did.

And in time, he paid. Handsomely.

He said, "I guess I do," and the rest became inevitable.

Ray Thomas Thomason took a seat in the plush recliner near the room's wide window and stared quietly out at the desert as MarySue went behind the bar.

"What'll you have?" she asked. "The bar is fully stocked."

Her love smiled quietly. When he answered, he almost sounded sad. "What have you got for Scotch?" he asked. "If you've got it, pour me a Glenlivet, neat."

There was Glenlivet, naturally. The Araby stocked every luxury imaginable. She poured his drink and hers, carried them out from behind the bar, and smiled hungrily.

"Here you go," she said. "I serve nothing but the best."

Ray Thomas Thomason looked distracted and displeased.

"I'm sure you always do," he said. "You impress me as a young woman of distinction."

MarySue smiled again. "And you're a perceptive man," she said. "Why don't you tell me about love?"

Ray Thomas Thomason sputtered in his Scotch.

"There's nothing I could tell you," he said. "I'm no savant in the mysteries of life."

"I'll bet you're not," said MarySue. But that wasn't what she thought at all. She trifled impatiently with the buttons of her blouse.

"Will you join me on the couch?" she asked.

"I'd rather not," he said.

MarySue harrumphed. "Don't be so coy!" she said. "It's not like we have world enough, or time."

Ray Thomas Thomason frowned. "How old are you?" he asked.

"I bet you'd like to know," said MarySue. "But it's none of your damn business."

"You're wrong," he said, and that was when MarySue knew he really was her one true love. "You're very young. Much younger than you look."

"What does that matter?" asked MarySue. "I love you," she said. "I want you. Age isn't part of that equation."

"Not true," he said. "Men go to jail when they get too close to girls as young as you."

"What are you insinuating?" MarySue demanded. "I'll have you know I've got a Ph.D. in micron physics—from Yale, no less. I've done work for the government! I have solved world hunger, poverty, prejudice, illiteracy, and child welfare! You don't know who you're trifling with, mister. I warn you—as my name is MarySue, I'll make you rue the day you treat me like a child."

As she spoke, MarySue's voice grew more and more hysterical; by the time she uttered the world *child,* she was reduced to sobbing racking tears.

"I guess I will," said Ray Thomas Thomason. "But I

still know right from wrong. And it isn't right to get involved with a girl who's still got growing up to do."

"Get out!" screamed MarySue. "Get out this very moment and never speak to me again!"

Ray Thomas Thomason did exactly as she told him, but that didn't make things one bit better. MarySue cried and cried into the big plush pillow that lay upon the couch, cried for hours as the sun went down and the desert night enveloped the Araby Mirable. After a while she fell asleep that way, still leaking tears into her pillow.

"I'll make him pay," she whispered in her sleep. "I swear I'll make him pay."

She woke in the small hours of the morning, feeling miserable, angry and sad and rejected and betrayed, insulted, too. Didn't that man know a woman of quality genius when he met one? And why was love to be denied to her so young, anyway?

She showered and dressed and packed her bags, intending to slink home defeated to her mother. But she stopped before she even reached the hotel room door.

I'm going to give that man a piece of my mind, MarySue thought. She dropped her bags onto the plush carpet and strode out into the hotel, looking for her man. She searched the bar, the casino; marched up and down the gleaming blinking rows of one-armed bandits. She kept thinking that she'd find him any moment now, just around that corner, just beyond that balustrade.

But she never did.

Not until she gave up and wandered defeated toward the hotel's all-night cappuccino bar and sandwich mongery, looking for chocolate truffles to salve the wound that was her broken heart.

And there he was, sitting sadly at a tiny table by the window, staring out into the desert night. Before him were a tepid cup of plain black coffee and an overflowing ashtray.

"You!" she said when she saw him. She didn't wait to be invited, but rather took the seat across from him unbidden, maybe even before he saw her coming. "I've been looking for you, Ray Thomas Thomason."

He looked up at her sadly, vacantly, as though from

an enormous distance. "I'm sorry," he said. "I never meant to make you cry."

And somewhere down inside MarySue thought that that was exactly right, that it was exactly the thing he should say if he were her one true love. But she knew it was all wrong, too, because it wasn't a part of The Plan.

"You don't love me because I'm smart!" she cried, but they both knew that wasn't true.

"That isn't true," her one true beau said.

"Is, too," said MarySue. She wanted romance! She wanted intrigue and heartbreak and adventure and the seven natural delights of the universe, but all she got was heartbreak. "I love *you*," she said accusingly. The accusation was a lie.

"You're too young, MarySue. It isn't right."

MarySue got so mad! But this time it was different, because it came on her so intensely that she never had the time to scream at him, just fell to crying, weepy tears all down her cheeks no matter how she tried to stop them.

And then she had an inspiration.

"Will you wait for me" she asked. "Will you wait until I'm older?"

He didn't answer that right away. His face got quiet, and the sadness of his expression receded a little—and then it returned.

"Would you believe me if I said I would?" he asked.

MarySue felt all cold inside. She gave him a hard, hard look, like her eyes could pin him the way an etymologist would pin a bug.

"You didn't answer my question," she said. "Don't try to be evasive."

He hesitated again. Longer and harder this time, and MarySue knew that there was something that he wasn't saying.

"Say it," she said. "Say it now."

Her true love shook his head. "You're still young, MarySue. The things you think you want now aren't what you'll want five years from now. If I told you that I'd be there, it wouldn't matter worth a damn, because your life will take you places neither one of us imagines.

It won't matter where I am when you get older, because you won't be here anymore."

MarySue wasn't having any of that, not for a moment. "You're wrong," she said. "You've got to promise me, you hear? I want to hear you promise me you'll wait."

Ray Thomas Thomason sighed. "I promise you I'll try," he said. But there was something in his voice—something MarySue didn't like at all.

"You're just saying that," she said. "You just don't want to hear me cry."

"You're wrong," he said. "I'd never lie to you."

MarySue laughed derisively. "I bet you wouldn't," she said, and even though she was being sarcastic, even though she meant to mock him with her words, she would have been right if she'd bet that way.

"Bet any way you like," he said. "I'm not about to bet against you."

"You," said MarySue. And got up, and left without saying another word.

MarySue was never the same after that. Oh, she was still totally brilliant, and everything to which she ever turned her hand flourished with a vengeance. But it just wasn't fun anymore. How could it be? Before she lost her heart in Las Vegas, life was a promise waiting to fulfill itself; after she'd lost it, every romance was a hollow echo of the love she'd never known.

Even worse, the way it turned out, Ray Thomas Thomason was right about the way things happened when she got older. She hated him for that! When she was sixteen, she was all wrapped up in numerology, which, by an odd convocation of circumstances, led her into an obsession with numismatics. When she was eighteen, she got bored with coins and numbers and fell into a life of idle luxury. Sometimes that year she drank too much, and sometimes she did other things. But even though she was older then, she never thought of Ray Thomas Thomason.

She didn't think of him when she was in her twenties, either. That was when MarySue decided that Love wasn't about romance, but power, and she went out and found herself the most powerful lover she could imagine. He had a wife who lived in a community property state, which meant MarySue had to be the other woman, but MarySue didn't mind. Love was power, and Power was love, and *God* he was good in bed.

One day her lover said, "I'm going to corner the market."

MarySue delighted in the spirit of the moment. "Which market?" she asked him hungrily from across the pillow.

Her lover smiled. "Capital goods," he said.

MarySue raised an eyebrow. "No mean trick," she said. "That represents an awful lot of capital."

"I can do it," her powerful lover said. "Arbitrage, leverage, warranties, and proxies. I'm going to bring it down this week."

"What about the SEC?"

"I've got them in my pocket. They know which side of their bread gets buttered, heh heh heh."

"I like it," MarySue told him. "Let's make it happen."

"It's happening today," he said masterfully. "Right now, right here."

MarySue groped for the remote control, found it, switched on the financial channel.

And saw a talking head on TV, stammering words like *catastrophic movement* and the *futures indices*.

"Oh," she said. "I love it. I love you—such *power*."

Later it seemed to her that what she felt that day wasn't Love at all, but something more immediate and ephemeral. But that day it was so good, like rockets in the air, like, like candy made from diamonds and liquor made of life.

Two days after that the President came to their private penthouse manse to kiss her lover's—*ring*. That was the best of all, the power come to them, answering to them, the whole world supplicating before them as they sold short through ten thousand untraceable intermediaries into a market that panicked suddenly, dropping like a rock.

"The *President*," MarySue said when he was gone. "The President."

Her lover smiled.

"He was in on the deal," he said. "He could buy Nevada with his cut."

"I bet he could," purred MarySue. "We ought to pick it up before he can." And they both laughed and laughed. God, it was so good that day.

But it didn't last. These things never do, do they? After a while, MarySue got unhappy and he did, too, and her power lover dumped her for a *girl* of a girl who couldn't've been twenty-one and might've been younger than eighteen, and MarySue hated her even if she did have to admit (grudgingly) that she was totally brilliant.

MarySue didn't care. She was turning thirty anyway, and every week she found herself thinking about babies.

Babies.

MarySue knew all about babies. You ever notice that? People always know all about babies until they have them, and then they move constantly through doubts, hopes, praying and fretting and knowing that they're going to screw something up but good, hoping like hell they can get it right but knowing all the while they can only do it as best they can.

Life is like that for a lot of people. It was like that for MarySue, too, but there were days when she was too brilliant to realize how deep she was in.

She planned out marriage and motherhood just like she planned so much else about her life—made a list of what she wanted in a father (good genes, a good salary, a pleasant way with children, a sense of family values, and of course he also had to be the love of her life if she was going to marry him); made a list of places the father of her children was likely to be found, and began searching those places methodically. She started at the top of her list and worked her way to the bottom one by one. As she went, she made a scorecard and kept it carefully, secreting it in her purse so that no one else could see her tally.

MarySue spent years searching, counting and recording and discreetly interviewing those she considered potential candidates—but the methodical process didn't work out at all. Hardly surprising; that kind of studied attention to detail is at odds with true romance, and neither is it especially disposed toward the kind of bonding that grows out of romance to build a family. When MarySue had narrowed her suitors to a list of three, she paused a moment, stepped back, and looked into her heart—and found herself consumed with ennui.

I don't love them, she thought, sitting at a sunny table on a beautifully cloudless day. She was at her favorite Marin County country club, sipping a mint julep and watching the three of them play golf. She wondered, not for the first time, if they suspected what she was about. *I don't care,* she thought. *None of them are right.*

And for the first time in her life she wondered what *was* right, and realized that she didn't have a clue. How could she ever find it if she didn't have a way to search?

She reexamined her plan, trying to find the place it'd gone wrong. But no matter how she cogitated, understanding eluded her.

When she saw the three men reach the eighteenth hole, she pushed her seat away from the table and crept away from the golf course. Into the clubhouse, out through the front door, into the parking lot. She took the keys to her Mercedes from the valet and ran for it— found the car in the valet lot where he'd parked it, got in and sped away.

And she didn't look back.

Didn't go back to that country club, either, for the longest time, no matter how it once had been her favorite.

When MarySue finally slowed the car she found herself in San Francisco, not far from the discotheque she'd frequented in the first wild years of her majority.

She didn't really think about that place. Didn't really even decide to go there. It was more like, like—like something that happened by force of reflex. She saw where she was, and the old habit surrounded her. A turn here, another and another there; and now she was pulling into the lot, leaving her car with the discotheque's valet; now she was wandering casually in through the wide dark hall. The door behind her; the bar to her left; the dance floor to her right.

As the music of her lost youth pounded all around her, its hard constant beat seducing her, drawing her in—

She got a double bourbon from the bar, found a place along the wall, and stood there for the longest time, watching the dance floor. There wasn't much to watch at first, but by and by the disco filled with people, and the bourbon-glow enveloped her, and MarySue found her heart veering back into the place it'd found in her wild days.

When the gaunt young man invited her to dance, she followed him; when the music took her, she didn't resist.

She drank a lot that night. Too much, probably. She should have regretted that consumption—she was thirty-seven, for God's sake, not twenty-two—but she didn't dare. If she'd stopped a moment for regret, it all would have overtaken her—the love, the children, the romance she'd always lived for, her biological clock ringing long and hard and slow like a time bomb just before it blows; all the things she'd lost and twisted in the years, all the things her plans had neglected, misunderstood, and misconceived. . . .

In some ways that night never ended. She followed it, pushed herself toward it, kept the candle burning until her middle-aged body began to ache with the strain that even girlish youth can hardly endure.

Three years. Three long hard years wild and intoxicated and trying not to think of what she'd lost because she'd never found it . . .

One night the year MarySue turned thirty-nine the music grew slumberously dull, and the smoke from her filterless cigarettes came soft as air, and the gin in her glass went flavorless as water. She looked at the drunken men and women moving listlessly on the dance floor, and she heard herself speaking to no one at all. "I wish I was stupid," she said. "Stupid girls have families when they're twenty. And I'll never have a family."

She tried to get drunk that night, but it wasn't any use. No matter what she drank, the world refused to recede from her. When the bar closed, she went looking for excitement, adventure, *something*—but there was nothing to find. No life, no intrigue, no danger; even the drug dealers down in the Tenderloin had rolled up their coats and gone home to their beds. After a while there was nothing to do but go home.

She didn't end up going home.

She ended up in Denny's getting breakfast. She saw the sign as she drove by the restaurant, saw the lights on and a decent crowd of people inside, and she had to go there because anything was better than going home alone again; she hated going home alone.

So much. Hated it worst of all when she was sober.

So she went into the restaurant, because she had to, and inside it she found the last thing she expected. It grieved her when she found it, and sometimes later she regretted it, and sometimes she was glad she did. What she found inside that Denny's was the one man she'd forgotten.

The man she'd loved so many years ago in Vegas when she still had a plan and still had the world by the oysters, back when she knew where everything went and the way that everything had to be—she found the man she'd loved who'd never loved her, and she hated him for that.

He was a man she'd sworn to get even with, because he'd broken her heart and been right to do it. It felt so strange to see him there. He was at the counter as she walked in, sitting quietly before a half-empty cup of coffee and a plate he'd barely picked at. He was reading a newspaper—so absorbed by the news, reading so intently that he hardly even noticed when MarySue sat down beside him.

"I thought I'd never see you again," said MarySue.

Strictly speaking, that wasn't true. The truth was she'd barely thought about him at all these last few years, and when she did think of him it was only idle reminiscing. But underneath the literal falsehood was a fundamental truth: when she saw him sitting in the restaurant she saw a thousand possibilities never come to fruition, saw a life she'd never had that could have been, and it was a good life, a full and meaningful life so stark in contrast to the alcoholic haze that had consumed her lately.

She saw that life pass before her eyes, and she mourned it, because there was a passion there long lost to her, a fulfillment and a wholeness that she'd never come to find.

"MarySue?" he asked, looking uncertain and ill-at-ease.

"You remember my name," MarySue said.

She didn't remember his, but she saw it stamped in gold letters on the briefcase by his ankles: RAY THOMAS THOMASON.

"Of course I do," he said. "How could I ever forget . . . ?"

MarySue smiled ruefully. "Men," she said. "You've got your ways."

"I guess we do," he told her. "But I remember you."

"Good," said MarySue. She kept thinking of romance and possibility, and the life she'd planned but never lived, and God that was such a *good* life, and how did she ever end up like this?

It was his fault. It was all his fault.

She didn't know how she'd ended up the way she was, and maybe she couldn't know. She had the wrong idea, when you get right down to it, and because she did all of her analyses were flawed. Romance isn't really the point, or the destination; it's just the means. Some people need it; some people don't. All romance ever does for the ones who need it is get them involved with one another long enough for something more important to take hold. That something isn't about romance at all; it's about getting along. And nothing MarySue knew because of her brilliance made it one bit easier to get along.

Just the opposite, in fact. Her brilliance made her particular and fussy, and it sometimes made her bad company.

She was worn out and she was rich and she was totally and brilliantly lonely.

"Tell me about yourself," said MarySue. "What have you done? Where have you been?"

Ray Thomas Thomason shrugged. "Not much to tell," he said. "I ended up in sales. I make a living, but nothing spectacular. I live in the suburbs with my wife and my kids. I guess I'm happy enough, but I can't say I've got no regrets."

MarySue thought the idea of kids was totally darling.

"Do you love her?" MarySue asked. "You never loved me."

"That isn't true," he said. "I just didn't know I did."

"That's a fine thing to say," said MarySue.

Ray Thomas Thomason said, "Well," and then he just stopped.

"You said you'd wait for me," said MarySue. "You never waited!"

"You're wrong," he said. "I waited for you years and years. But you never found me."

For half a moment MarySue sat stunned, unable to answer, seeing her life slip through her fingers. And then she *knew*. "Then love me now," she said. "It's never too late for love—leave that other woman behind and marry me!"

It hurt like hell when she said that, like the words cut bullets out of her heart. She didn't know why, didn't even understand what she was saying or why, it was all a moment gone amok, taking hold and carrying her to places that she never meant to be.

"I can't," he said. "I've got a family now."

MarySue tried to stop herself from crying, but it wasn't any use.

"You couldn't love a man who left his children anyway," he said.

And he was so damn wrong, but how could she argue? She didn't argue.

She looked up at him and she knew she was going to break if he said anything else, but he didn't understand. Just like a man, he didn't get it at all. "I can't leave her," he said. "I love her."

And MarySue shattered into a thousand million pieces, scattered in kaleidoscope shards across a million miles of her life until she disappeared.

Only it didn't work out like that, because it never does. Things that bust you up inside don't kill you unless you kill yourself, or maybe if you're old and get a heart attack, and MarySue was only forty and she was too totally brilliant to kill herself anyway.

She was going to get so even with that man. She swore she would.

She sat quietly beside the one true love of her life for the longest time, waiting for the waitress to come to take her order (which she never did), waiting for her man to realize the error of his ways and change his mind, waiting for the world to stand on end and start turning in the other direction, but it never did that either.

And in that moment of broken desperation, when it'd come to her that time and possibility had run out in a life that was supposed to be full with the bounty of the gifts she'd been born to—in that moment MarySue did something utterly unlike herself.

"No, damn it," she whispered. She found her purse, pulled a fifty out and threw it on the counter to pay for her true love's breakfast.

Took him by the arm and dragged him away.

"Come on," she said. "You're mine today. God or fate or whatever it is that guides our lives didn't put you and me here today for no reason. You're coming with me, and I don't want to hear you argue with me about it. I'm not fourteen anymore, and you aren't a twenty-year-old kid with too much conscience."

He started to argue with her—he was still trying to pull away as she dragged him past the restaurant door—but she didn't let that go anywhere.

She took him to the beach first—drove south along the coast to Carmel, circuitously along the Seventeen Mile Drive, then to a cabin she owned by Carmel Town. They spent an hour there, walking along the beach.

"It's true love, damn it," she said. "You can't just ignore that. That's why I've been so miserable, isn't it? We had true love, we were meant for true love—and I forgot."

He hadn't spoken since he'd stopped arguing with her outside Denny's.

"Maybe," he said. "I don't know."

"Why didn't you find me? When I was older, I mean."

He shrugged. "Maybe I tried. You think I didn't? I still go back to Vegas every year, just that time of year. I'm always in the coffee bar downstairs at the Araby in the small hours. Waiting for you."

She blinked. Blinked again. She felt like she wanted to cry.

"Even now? Even with a wife, a family?"

He didn't answer right away. She could feel how much it bothered him to think about that question. It bothered her, too.

"Maybe."

She felt awful for no reason she could name, like, like—she felt like a homewrecker, was what it was. She *was* a homewrecker.

"I need a drink," she said. "Let's go back into town."

Town in that part of Carmel was a couple of blocks on the other side of the cabin where she'd parked—a street lined with shops that led down to the water. They walked to the liquor store, where she bought a quart of tequila, some salt, some limes.

Outside, she opened the bottle and took a long pull on it. She didn't bother with the salt or lime.

She offered him the bottle. "You want some?" she asked.

He nodded. Took the bottle gingerly, drank from it more modestly than she had.

"Thanks," he said.

"Sure. We need to find a better place for it, though— we're both too old for public drunkenness."

He laughed.

"Come on," she said. "I know the place."

She drove south again, this time through Big Sur. Most people have heard of Big Sur, but not many people have a real sense of how spectacular a place it is: miles and miles of a two-lane highway through a spectacularly beautiful area with no particular economy and nothing much for anyone to do. The highway's mostly right along the coast, and the mountains plunge directly into the sea. It isn't a drive you'd really want to take with a driver taking long pulls off a bottle of tequila.

Ray Thomas Thomason didn't complain. Maybe he was feeling suicidal and didn't care. Or maybe it was just that he was drinking, too, because he was. When they'd driven forty minutes, she pulled off the road and started up a rugged path that led along the side of one of the mountains.

When she got to the summit, she stopped the car.

Got out. Grabbed the bottle and the limes and the salt.

Walked a few feet to the very pinnacle of the mountain, and sat.

And drank, staring at the sea.

After a while, Ray got out of the car and sat beside her.

They didn't talk much.

There wasn't much to say.

After a while, they'd drunk enough that neither of them could remember when they woke the next day, sunburned and raw on the mountainside.

Even in high summer it gets cold along the Big Sur coast in the small hours of the morning. MarySue woke shivering, still drunk, somewhere between two and four. She stumbled to the car, got in, and curled up in the driver's seat.

Ray either didn't get cold or didn't care; he spent the night snoring among the rocks and weeds at the top of the mountain.

It was light when she woke again. She was in the car, and cramped, and Ray was tapping on the window.

"Ray," she said, rolling down the window. "It's morning."

He nodded.

"I've got to get back," he said. "Nobody's heard from me. People will be worried."

MarySue blinked. "What about—about us?"

"I—"

"Take me, damn you!"

"I—"

"The meaning of life is staring you in the eye, and you're stuttering! Can't you see kismet when it bites you in the ass? Fate?" Destiny? This is what was *meant* to be." She screamed, "I hate you!"

And she started her car, and drove away, leaving him alone in the middle of nowhere. Later, she was sorry about that part, but not much. He deserved it.

*   *   *

When she got home, she collapsed in her bed and slept for a time that felt like a million years.

It wasn't, of course. She only slept twelve hours or so, and then she woke and pushed herself back down into sleep, and woke a while later, and closed her eyes again. After a while she couldn't sleep anymore, but even then she didn't get out of bed—she stayed there beneath the covers, staring at the wall, closing her eyes, opening them again, hardly moving at all.

Eventually the housekeeper got to her room, intending to clean it, saw her lying in bed and slipped away.

MarySue didn't pay any attention. She didn't look up, didn't speak, didn't do anything but lie in bed, staring at the wall, and after a few hours the housekeeper came back again.

This time she was concerned.

"Miss MarySue . . . ?" she asked.

MarySue ignored her.

"Miss MarySue, should I call a doctor?"

MarySue groaned.

"Leave me alone, damn it," she said. "I don't want to talk to any doctor."

The housekeeper shivered. "Yes, ma'am," she said. "I won't call anybody you don't want. I was worried, that's all, didn't mean to be a bother."

MarySue sat for a good while longer. When the impulse to do *something* finally came to her, she pushed the covers aside, sat up, and stumbled toward the shower. When she was done, she dried and dressed and went out for a walk, not really planning to go anywhere, not meaning to see anyone, not meaning anything at all. She ended up walking through a strip-mall shopping center, the kind of shopping center that has maybe half a dozen shops all clustered 'round a grocery.

This mall had a bookstore, and through its window MarySue could see a tall triumphant display of paperback romances—beautiful men, beautiful women all over the covers, she found herself staring enraptured at the sight of them. How did people read books like that, she wondered, and then she thought, *so beautiful,* not even noticing how her thoughts contradicted one another, and then she did notice and heard Whitman in her ears: *Do I contradict myself? Very well then I contradict myself, (I am large, I contain multitudes).*

MarySue pushed through the store's revolving glass door and wandered toward the tall display. Walked 'round and 'round the mountain of it, marveling at the beauty of the women, the sinewy smooth-chested torsos of the men painted on those garish covers. Found herself at once disgusted and enthralled. How could grown women allow themselves to be seen reading novels clad in such unseemly covers?

She'd read books like that when she was younger—much younger. Thirteen? Fourteen? The last time she'd read one—was on that plane into Las Vegas.

And remembering that, she felt so sad.

She stepped close, grabbed a bulging opus decorated with the outlandish image of a pirate ravishing some poor waif, glanced around the store to be certain no one watched her.

And began to read.

It was awful stuff inside that book. She meant to put it back onto the stack she'd taken it from. Of course she did!

But something happened before she could. Something on page 197 caught her eye, and suddenly she was engrossed, reading a scene where the book's heroine rescued a child from the pirates' lair, and now she had to know the rest of it, had to start from the beginning to put the child into context, and to buy the book and read every solitary word, she just had to, it was that kind of intuition, the kind no one can ignore let alone deny, she tucked the book under her arm, grabbed three, four, five more books and secreted them, too.

Skulked to the counter like a young man mortified and embarrassed trying to purchase pornographic materials. Oh, there was nothing in those books that qualified as obscene that year in any American jurisdiction. But there were scenes . . . ! They still left MarySue feeling ashamed. They really did.

Not that she let that stop her.

She put her books and her cash on the counter, and

kept her eyes focused on the floor—didn't say a word, didn't look the cashier in the eye, didn't thank her when she pushed MarySue's change across the counter, nothing. Just shoved her change into her purse, grabbed the crinkly-thin overstuffed bag of books, and hurried out the door.

MarySue went into the fish-and-chips shop next to the bookstore, ordered the deep-fry platter, and found a dark booth in the corner where nobody could see what she was about.

Opened the book bag and started reading.

In a moment the heroine's story had consumed her. The villainous lover who would not love her; the brutality; the unkindness, intrigue, aspiration, and romance. It was everything MarySue had ever meant to live, she realized; fulfilling and meaningful, pedestrian and banal all at once. In the reverie of her reading she fantasized herself to be the woman in the book, the heroine, that was the word for a romance protagonist, wasn't it, heroine?

MarySue wanted to live inside that novel, with the pirates, the highborn serving girl who'd been reduced to servitude by the failure of her father's fortunes. The gallant young earl masquerading as a brutal pirate ensign; the well-meaning yeoman's boy who'd ended up working in the galley of the pirates' ship. . . .

The young son and daughter of the marquis, captured along with the heroine, and held for ransom. . . .

MarySue got so deep into the novel that she forgot all about the food she'd ordered. Paid for, too—they took her money at the counter when she'd ordered it, and where was it now when she was a hundred fifty pages into her novel?

She set the novel open-pages-down on the table and went to the counter where a pimply-faced girl stared at her glassy-eyed and deadpan when she asked what'd happened to her order.

"You didn't get that?" she asked. "I called you to come get it half an hour ago."

"I never heard you," said MarySue.

The girl looked around the counter, pushed aside a box of napkins not far from the second register. "There it is," she said. "Too bad you had to wait."

The manager, overhearing their exchange, made a little gasping sound. "I'm sorry, ma'am," he said. He was beet red; he looked mortified. "Your food has gotten cold—let me get you something fresh." He sounded embarrassed and apologetic. MarySue thought that was a fine thing for him to be, and she thanked him for it. Smiled, nodded, turned, and went back to her novel.

She hardly had time to get lost in it again before the manager brought her food.

"There's a cover for you," he said just after he set her platter on the table. "Is the book really that . . . explicit?"

MarySue scowled at him before she remembered to be polite. She wanted to say, *None of your damned business,* but she caught herself in time. "It's not that bad," she said. She tried to smile again, because that was the tactful thing to do, and she wanted to be mannerly. But the expression that found its way onto her face wasn't a smile, exactly; more like she was about to cry or something, she could feel that all over her face, she felt so weepy just like the heroine from the novel—oh, God, how embarrassing. What was she becoming?

"Are you all right?" the manager asked. "You look so—sad, that's what it is. You look sad, don't you?"

"Don't say that," MarySue demanded. "I'm not sad. Not a bit, no, I'm not. Really. Tired, maybe, I'm tired, it's been a day, but that's not the same as sad."

That sounded so stupid, MarySue thought. Like it was obvious that she really felt miserable and just wanted to lie about it. How could she let herself be so transparent?

"Okay," the manager said, "if you say so. But let me know if you need help, all right? We're here to help if you need us. That's our job."

MarySue wanted to laugh when she heard that. As if there was anything in a fish-and-chips shop that could salve the things that ailed her!

And then she wanted to cry, because—just because, that was all. "I'll let you know," said MarySue. "Don't worry about that."

When he was gone, she returned to her novel. Now she was at the point where the heroine of the pirate romance tried to smuggle the marquis' children away in a lifeboat.

And the romance swept her away into the hours.

She lost all touch with her surroundings, with the hour, with the restaurant around her till fifty pages from the climax the lights overhead began to flicker. When they did, she looked up blinking, somnolent, and confused, surveying her surroundings—

And saw the store manager standing a few feet from her, watching her with eyes full of something—she wasn't sure what it was, but it interested her.

"We're closing, ma'am," he said.

"Closing . . . ?"

"I don't mean to, that is—I mean, I'm sorry, but—"

"It's all right," said MarySue. "I shouldn't have stayed so long."

The manager started to say something else, something MarySue could almost hear before he said it. She knew that whatever it was, she couldn't bear to hear it.

"I don't mind," she said, heading him off. "You're right, it's time to go."

She left before the man could say another word.

MarySue drove home in a quiet daze, thinking of nothing. When she got to the townhouse she parked the car, gathered up her cache of garish novels, and wandered upstairs to her room.

Curled up in bed with the story of the pirate queen, she intended to finish the last chapter and doze away.

But she never got that far.

Before she even started reading, her eyes went out of focus, and she drifted away. She never noticed how she'd gone to sleep, and now she dreamed the reading as it was not inside the novel.

She dreamed that she was the pirate queen who once had been a highborn governess, and all the high seas were her pirate realm stretched out before her endless as the oceans, beautiful, romantic, pristine, waiting for her exploits. All the creatures in her world were Mary-Sue's children, and she was the mother of them all; she loved them and challenged them and held them to account for every deed and practice, she was Empress of the Seas, no mere pirate queen but the Mother of It All.

Her dreamworld thrilled her; she had her pick among the thick-thewed gleaming pirates and she took them as she would.

After a while that dream turned sour, filling her with emptiness.

She woke a moment later, cold and covered with fat beads of sweat.

There's nothing, she thought. *No reason to aspire; nothing to aspire to. The world is mine, but every victory is hollow of all meaning.*

She hated that so bad. She was MarySue! She was brilliant, totally brilliant! She had the answers to the world's problems, she'd taken on all the gravest ills that beset mankind and solved them in a few hard afternoons the way other girls learned calculus . . . !

And for all of that she was helpless in the center of her own crisis of purpose.

I love you, she thought, because what she wanted was love. But there was no one she loved because there was no one to respect.

I'll find you, she thought, because she was sure that she would. But deep beneath that sureness lay a starker and more certain conviction: she knew she'd never find anyone, no matter how she looked.

She let her head fall back against the pillow and stared up at the ceiling. *I need to finish the book,* she thought. *I've got to find out what really happened.*

But it didn't really matter, did it? *The Pirate Queen* was just a fiction, the fantasy of some novelist working alone in a quiet room somewhere years and miles away. There was nothing real about the story, nothing true; MarySue could devise her own ending to the tale and it'd be as real as anything on paper, whether it was true or not.

The real world was out there, waiting. She could find it. Wasn't that more sensible than hiding in the fantasies of some poor woman pounding on a keyboard?

She sighed, sat up in bed.

She waited for an inspiration to come to her—but of

course it never did. After a while she picked up the
novel and fell back into its pages.

As now the hours turned to days, and the books fell
away like leaves in the broadleaf woods as winter comes.
She went to the bookstore and bought more, many more
this time, and took the books home to horde and devour.

It went on like that for weeks, and now for months
as bit by bit the housekeeper began to look worried
again, and now MarySue was putting on weight, and she
felt fat and frumpy and unattractive. . . .

Unattractive.

The week she started feeling ugly was the week
where it finally came to her that her cycle had stopped.
She couldn't remember how long it'd been since it'd
come, in fact; all the days since the last she'd seen Ray
Thomas Thomason were a blur, somehow. Was it him,
or was it the books? Or was it alcohol? She hadn't had
a drink in weeks, months. Was this what it was like to
dry out?

Or was it menopause?

MarySue felt the novel she was reading fall out of her
hands, and she began to cry.

It's over, she thought. That was why she was so anxious and uncomfortable these last weeks—that was the
root of everything, wasn't it?

And she wailed.

When the wail trailed away, she went to the phone
and called the doctor. Made an appointment for that
afternoon, and tried to go back to her novel.

But it was impossible. She was too depressed to read,
to think, to do anything at all. She spent the morning
staring listlessly at the wall, waiting for the doctor to tell
her all the awful things she already knew.

When she got to the doctor's office, it wasn't like that
at all.

"You should have come in sooner," the doctor said.
"You're four months pregnant. I'm amazed you haven't
noticed the changes in your body all these weeks."

MarySue felt her mouth drop open, felt her breath
go still, felt, felt—something so overwhelming that she
couldn't begin to understand it.

"MarySue," the doctor asked, "are you all right? Did you hear me?"

MarySue didn't answer right away. She was too dumbstruck, too incredulous.

"That can't be," she said at last. "It just isn't possible."

The doctor shrugged. "I can run the test again, if you need me to. But I've never seen an error under this procedure."

MarySue scowled. "You're wrong, that's all. Babies don't come out of nowhere, and I've been nowhere for six months. Do you understand what I'm saying?"

The doctor licked his lips.

"If there's a problem," he said, "I can still arrange to terminate your pregnancy."

The way he couched those words was so antiseptically obscure that it took her a long moment to apprehend them.

"You'd have to sign some papers," the doctor said as MarySue realized what he was suggesting. "There are restrictions at this point, but we can work around them easily enough—"

MarySue came up out of the stirrups to grab the doctor by the collar. Grabbed him shook him, hauled back her fist to pummel the man—

"MarySue!"

"What the fuck are you saying, Mister?"

"Help!" the doctor screamed. *"Help! Help!"*

"What the hell do you think you want to do?"

As the doctor thrashed and struggled, trying to get away, and one of the nurses opened the door, MarySue lost the little bit of control she still had over her rage.

And popped the man right in the nose. But good. Blood all over the place.

The nurses surrounded her and pried the doctor from her hands.

Someone called the police while MarySue was shouting at the doctor, and they took a report and offered to arrest her, but the doctor didn't let them. Maybe he was ashamed of letting a lady beat up on him like that, or maybe he was ashamed of the offer that had prompted her to try to rip him limb from limb, or maybe he just didn't want to take the time to testify in court against her. By early evening MarySue was walking out of the doctor's office, confused and shaken, trying to figure out what had become of her life, thinking and thinking why and how and who and when, how could it have happened? But she didn't know.

Couldn't imagine.

She knew what she had to do, though. She was going to have the baby, and she was going to love it, and she was going to, to, to . . .

She was going to be a mom, was what she was going to do. She let the glow of that wash over her, and it was warm and intense, wonderful as wonderful could be.

When MarySue got home, she went straight to bed. She had to get her sleep, after all— she knew that now. Pregnant ladies need their rest, and they need their food, and they need warm pleasant happy homes that cover their children the way warm downy blankets swaddle an infant. . . .

When MarySue fell asleep, she had a dream about Ray Thomas Thomason. In her dream he was the father of her child, no matter how they could never marry; it was delivery day, and her baby was in her arms, and she called Ray Thomas Thomason from the hospital to summon him to meet his son. When they were on the phone, he reminded her that wasn't possible, and she agreed with him; but she could see the baby in her arms and the baby's eyes were just the match of Ray Thomas Thomason's.

"You've got to meet your son," she said. "I know what's possible and what isn't, but I know what I'm seeing, too—this is your child, Ray. I'd know him anywhere."

Ray Thomas Thomason didn't answer right away. Instead there was a silence on the line that stretched on and on, till now the baby's crying shattered it.

"I'm waiting for you, Ray," said MarySue. "I want you here."

Ray Thomas Thomason told her that he'd visit, and he was as good as his word. In her dream it only took a moment before he walked through the door to her hospital room.

"I knew you'd come," said MarySue, but that was a lie.

Ray Thomas Thomason frowned. "This isn't right," he said. "You need help, MarySue. I want to help you find it."

MarySue ignored him. "He's got your eyes, Ray," she said.

That was absolutely true—the infant boy's eyes, his features, all of them were Ray Thomas Thomason's writ small, as if the baby were a mirror of the man.

Ray Thomas Thomason stepped close to look the baby in the eye. When he was close enough to see, he drew a startled breath.

"So strange," he whispered. "How . . . ? Who . . . ?"

"You, Ray. I told you that."

He looked away from the baby, looked at MarySue, and she saw that he was frowning again, and his eyes were full of . . . that was pity, wasn't it? He was patronizing her, wasn't he? MarySue thought that that would make her mad, but it didn't. She wasn't sure why not.

"MarySue—"

"Hush, Ray. These things are knowable these days. Don't you realize that? You think that I would say he was your child before I was absolutely certain?"

He didn't have an answer for that, but MarySue could see him trying and trying to find one. He started to speak, and stopped; started again and stopped. Drew a breath and started to tell her that there wasn't any way, because he knew, because they both knew. . . .

MarySue held a finger to her lips.

"Hush," she said.

Ray Thomas Thomason blinked.

"Some things are meant to be," she told him. "Sometimes they happen whether we mean them to or not."

It was all the revenge that she could ever ask for: perfect, absolutely, in every way.

EVEN TEMPO

by Jody Lynn Nye

Jody Lynn Nye lists her main career activity as
"spoiling cats." She lives northwest of Chicago with
two of the above and her husband, author and pack-
ager Bill Fawcett. She has written twenty-two books,
including four contemporary fantasies, three science
fiction novels, four novels in collaboration with Anne
McCaffrey, including *The Ship Who Won,* a humorous
anthology about mothers, *Don't Forget Your Spacesuit,
Dear!* and over seventy short stories. Her latest books
are *License Invoked,* co-authored with Robert Asprin,
and *Advanced Mythology,* fourth in her Mythology
101 series.

"SING, then," the witch said, as she stirred the pot
of soup.
Derren of Bannockby paused nervously with his long
fingers curved over the strings of his harp as he sat on
the ring of stones surrounding the cooking fire, the only
source of light for at least a mile in any direction. He
was accustomed to singing for his supper, but this was
the oddest place and the oddest audience for whom he
had ever performed. Hidden in the shadows was a cozy
hut and a small garden that he could never have found
even if he was looking for them. Somewhere nearby was
a self-satisfied orange tabby cat and a snow-white owl
that answered their mistress' call like well-trained dogs.
And there was the woman herself, generous to a
stranger as though she knew she had nothing to fear in
all the world. Not that he was regretting the wrong turn
he'd taken off the forest path. At the moment it felt
like fate.
In the life of an artist, he reasoned, there were times
when the art ran true in one's veins. The rest of the time
one spent vainly trying to recapture those times, a sorrow

that made sad songs all the more poignant. This time
he'd got it right.

The witch, a woman of about fifty summers named
Vanisa Night-Eyed, picked up the ladle and took a sip.
Was that a . . . lizard's leg sticking out of the bowl? Her
bright green eyes caught the firelight and slitted like a
cat's. Derren gulped mightily, and began to sing.

The words spoke to a woman who was kind and willing to listen to the hopes and dreams of a poor wan-
derer. His poet's eye saw Vanisa as she must have been
in her youth, with black hair instead of silver, and pink
cheeks, not withered beige. He was surprised at her
beauty, and added allusions of his vision to the verses,
making the singer's journey one toward love. The lyrical,
rhythmic tune led him on a path as soft as a meadow,
taking him on staccato stepping stones that led across a
wide living river of discovery and joy. He forgot his early
fears, his inexperience, even where he was, in the glory
of the music. It knit together as nothing ever had before
in his life, giving him a glimpse of true beauty, the very
sound of the stars above.

"Who is that?" the witch shouted suddenly. Derren's
hands jangled on the strings. In the bushes outside the
circle of fire, he heard frantic rustling. Derren huddled
his long arms and legs around his instrument, hoping
Vanisa wasn't going to make him go see what the distur-
bance was. He was a musician, not a fighter. His hands
were his fortune, and if he hurt them, he would starve.
With one look at him, she guessed his thoughts.

"Don't worry," she said, as the scurrying died away.
"If it was an enemy coming for us, it would have come.
The folk around here are scared enough of me. Such a
wonderful song. I wish I were giving you a better dinner
in exchange."

"I'm sorry, my lady," Derren said, feeling ashamed of
his fear. He bowed his head so his long brown hair hid
his face. "My fingers fumbled. I . . . I could have played
it better. I'm not yet the harpist I hope someday I will
be."

She reached out to touch his hand. "You could have
played it with a hundred musicians each the finest in his

kingdom and it couldn't have been a more wonderful moment. To hear something first borning is like seeing the sun come up in glory!"

Derren looked at his feet, abashed. "It's not wholly new, lady. I've had the tune in my mind's ear for a long time. This is when it finally became a song. I believe it's the best I've ever made."

"Well, I'm proud that you made it for me," Vanisa said, lifting her hand, the one without the ladle. "A blessing on you and on your harp. May you always have good weather and a soft bed and a receptive audience."

"I hope so, indeed," Derren said, accepting a bowl of stew. The sludgy, lumpy contents were predominantly . . . green. Her eye was on him as he reached for a spoon. Would she pop him into the pot, too, if he couldn't stomach her cooking? Steeling himself he took the smallest sip he could possibly manage. To his surprise and pleasure the color had nothing to do with the flavor, which was superlative. He almost felt he could write a song about that. He scraped the bowl clean, enjoying every bite.

"What in the name of heaven is a soft-fleshed traveler like you doing wandering through the Harwood Forest?" Vanisa asked, passing him bread and cheese on a wooden platter.

"Going to Harwood," Derren admitted. "Though I lost my way. I was hoping to get to the Ribbon Road Inn by this evening. Her grace the Duchess Sofia is holding a celebration for the Womanhood of her daughter, Lady Melanda."

Vanisa let out a cluck of disbelief. "Can it be thirteen summers since the girl was born? Bless me. That will be a fine festival. Feasting! Feats of Arms! Contests!"

"If you would be so kind as to wish me success," Derren said humbly. "I am entering the Tournament of Troubadors. The prize is five golden angels. That would be enough to keep me for nearly the rest of this year. If you'll give me permission to play your song, I might be able to win."

"I'll do more than that," Vanisa said, smacking her hand down on her knee. "I'll escort you safely the rest

of the way to Harwood and root for you from the crowd.
I wouldn't miss a Womanhood celebration for all the
stars in the sky."

By popular demand, the bards assembled for the
Tournament of Troubadors had their own cobblestoned
courtyard in which to rehearse. Horses passing the open
gate shied at the ungoldly racket, and dogs howled.

Inside the red stone walls, it was much, much louder.
With a hundred pipers, flautists, lutenists, harpists, and
singers tuning up and practicing, it sounded like every
cat in the world shrieking at a dawn chorus of birds to
shut up. Shouting to be heard over the noise, Derren
found the steward who assigned him bed space in a
chamber with seven other bards, instructed him on how
to find the necessary, and told him when and where
meals were to be served. He left some of his possessions
in his room and went out to find a spot to practice. A
fellow harper of his own age, Pippa of Kown, spotted
him and bumped her way toward him through the crowd.
Like Derren, she was battling to stay upright with bags
slung over her arms and back, the typical burden of a
traveling musician.

"Have you heard the news?" she asked. "Old Scaur,
the duchess' minstrel, has decided to retire! Her grace
will be looking for a new court musician. And with a
hundred of us to choose from, well, one of us will surely
have a new job by festival's end."

Derren drew a breath. "That would be the greatest
luck that could befall us."

"And all of you will have to come and congratulate
me," said a suave baritone voice. Simman of Aldrew was
a man out of an epic poem with fine, tan skin, rose-pink
lips and cheeks and china-blue eyes set off so well by
wavy, sable-brown hair that he looked like a beautiful
boy rather than a man. He leaned in between them and
took Pippa's freckled cheek between his thumb and fore-
finger, squeezing just a little too hard. She swatted at
him, but he stepped back out of reach just in time. "If
you think any of you tone-deaf string pluckers will walk
away with either the prize or the post, you're dreaming."

He straightened his pale-blue silk tunic and strolled away without a look back.

"Chances are," Pippa said, with a sigh. "He is the best."

"He is, at that," Derren agreed, "but I think I've got something to give him an honest challenge. I've written a fine song. Simman will stand agape when I play it."

Pippa's eyes twinkled. "I'd give five golden angels to see that for myself."

So many people, Derren thought, as he sat at the side of the great hall awaiting his turn to perform. The tossing light from hundreds of torches and candles made it seem as though the multitudes of the earth were jammed into the room. Derren peered around, hoping to catch sight of Vanisa, but it was hopeless. If she was there, her face was a pale blur in the uncertain light. Upon the dais the Duchess Sofia sat on a throne covered in dark green velvet trimmed with gold. She was a handsome, silver-haired lady, dressed in a melon-colored gown that looked like a gorgeous peony nestled in the leaves of her chair. Her large bones and big hands suggested the shield-maiden she had once been. The matching throne to her right lay empty. Duke Illimor had fallen in battle four years earlier. Their three sons, all older than Melanda, defended the realm for their mother.

Melanda sat to her mother's left. She was a slim, dark lass who kept dropping her head shyly whenever someone looked at her. Derren caught her gaze upon him once. He offered her a friendly smile and a deep bow. When he rose, she was looking the other way, but she wore a tiny smile on her lips. A nice lass, and not used to being the center of attention. Beside her was a basket of roses.

The rules for the Tournament were simple. Anyone who offered him- or herself as a contestant participated in the first round. Boos and catcalls could knock a player out during this round. Everyone attending was invited to judge, except other performers, and seven of Duchess Sofia's largest and most fearsome guards stood over the waiting musicians to make sure they didn't emit a peep, under pain of expulsion. Contestants were judged on both performance and composition. Derren knew his skills as a musician were above average, not excellent, but he couldn't wait to play his beautiful journey song. He knew the audience would love it. In his mind he heard the melody ornamented by delicate glissandi, and hugged the knowledge of her certain success to himself.

A fiddler, a tiny, quick-moving woman who Derren did not know, was just finishing her piece. Amid enthusiastic applause she let the bow drop to her side and curtsied. The duchess beckoned her forward, and Lady Melanda gave her a rose, indicating that she had passed. Excellent job! Derren started to clap, too, then put his hands in his lap when the guards glared at him. This was going to be a difficult contest to win.

After a big, hearty man dressed in parti-colored leather rendered a rousing drinking song to laughter and loud applause, a hush fell over the audience. Simman strode into the open circle, his guitar slung on his back by a bright sapphire blue ribbon. He swept a cursory bow to the dais and the crowd. A few of the young girls in the audience sighed and were shushed by their neighbors. Everyone waited with pleasurable anticipation as the famous bard brought his guitar around, tightened a peg and struck a chord. Smiling, he began to sing.

Derren listened to the beautiful, warm tones giving life to the words Simman sang, but within a sentence he was on his feet, seething with outrage. The bastard was singing *his song*! How in the raging hell could he possibly know it? Derren had never practiced Vanisa's Song in front of anyone else, not even Pippa. Then he remembered the rustling in the undergrowth the night he played for the witch. Simman had to have been hidden there, listening.

"Sit down," Pippa hissed, grabbing his tunic hem and pulling. "You'll be disqualified."

"He stole my song!" Derren whispered furiously.

"There's nothing you can do."

"Oh, yes, there is!"

The other contestants began to look discontented, whispering to one another that Simman would almost certainly earn the prize. The singer finished his tune to tumultuous applause. He slung his instrument on his back and swept a hand around with a little smirk on his face. The arrogance of him!

He approached the duchess and dipped his head slightly, not even a full bow out of courtesy. The Lady Melanda had been watching him sing with her soul in her eyes. She offered the red rose to Simman like a votary giving a sacrifice to her god, but he didn't even look at her as he took it. Nose high, he returned to the group of bards. Derren glared at him.

"Derren of Bannockby!" the herald announced, Pippa picked up his harp and shoved it at him. Derren stumbled out onto the floor, hardly able to contain himself. He bowed deeply to the duchess.

"Your grace, your ladyship, I regret having to announce a case of cheating," Derren said. He pointed at Simman. "That man stole my song."

The duchess looked at him with bemusement. "Is this part of your performance, sir bard?"

Derren felt his cheeks burn as the audience tittered behind him. "No, your grace, it is the truth."

"If you have a grievance it will be investigated later. If this is your song, prove it. Play."

One of the men-at-arms brought out a stool for the harpist to sit upon. Derren sat down and tuned the bottom strings of his precious instrument, the ones most prone to going out of true. He was embarrassingly aware how anticlimactic it was to sing the same air that another man had just sung, and sung better, but Derren gave it his very best effort. He concentrated, and for a moment he was back in the forest at the witch's campfire, full of anticipation, fear and the glorious feeling of the music being made flesh through him. The room was hushed as he finished, then it erupted in applause. He glanced around. Some of those listening had been deeply touched. Perhaps they could tell. The duchess did not give him a clue as to what she was thinking as he came to bow before her.

"Well, sir, you have . . . something . . . but I am not certain it is attributable to creation, but you will continue in this contest." She gestured to her daughter, who

held up a rose. Derren dropped to one knee before
the girl.

"That was very nice," Lady Melanda whispered, giving him a shy smile.

"Thank you, gracious lady," Derren said. She colored
prettily. "Like a rose, you bloom when you smile."

He backed away, clutching his harp to his chest, and
withdrew from the circle of light as quickly as he could.
He needed to get out of the hall. Never in his life had
he felt so humiliated. Derren could *feel* Simman smirking
behind him. He wanted to clasp his hands around the
rotten bastard's neck and squeeze until those blue eyes
popped out of his rival's head. He wanted to throw all
the people laughing at him into a hole that fell straight
to hell. He wanted to run straight back to Bannockby,
put his head in his mother's lap, and cry.

A hand snaked out of the crowd as he passed. He
shook it off, but it took hold again, harder. He looked
down into cat's eyes and recoiled. It was Vanisa. The
witch was blazingly angry.

"Come with me," she said. She plowed through the
crowd toward the side door. One look at her furious
eyes, and they had a clear path.

"Who is that strutting cock of the walk?" the witch
demanded, as soon as the door was closed behind them.
She furled the edges of her dark cloak around her like
a bird preening its wings.

"Simman of Aldrew," Derren said. He couldn't hold
still. He began walking back in the direction of his chamber. The contest was already won. He might as well get
his things and leave. There was no reason to stay in
Harwood and be further humiliated. He raised his harp,
thinking for a moment to dash it down. In the next split
second he came to his senses, and hugged it to him. It
was not at fault.

"Goddess, but he needs a lesson or two!" Vanisa said,
striding alongside, her pupils mere slits in the sunshine,
which made her look even more like an angry cat. All
she needed was a tail to lash.

"A lesson!" Derren shouted, waving his arms. People
in the market stalls along the street looked up at him.

"Death is too good for him. I will get my revenge upon him if it takes my last drop of blood!"

The witch stopped and pulled him to a halt. "Don't say things like that, child. Mother Nature has a way of rebounding one's ill wishes upon oneself. To ruin her sacred balance is to have it rebound upon you threefold."

Derren's eyes showed their whites. He didn't like this talk of magic. "Then I won't, but . . . my beautiful song! I want him punished!"

Vanisa put her fingers on his lips. "As do I, but there's a price to be paid."

"I'll pay it," Derren said passionately. "All I wish is to have that self-satisfied smirk wiped from his face. He stole from me. He stole from *you!*"

The witch nodded. "I'll do it for you, then, and no more than he deserves. You wrote that song for me in exchange for a night's shelter. I gave you permission to make your fortune with it, if you can. I gave him no such permission, so he *is* stealing from me. We will do a working. Come with me."

Simman was enjoying his celebrity. Once the contest in the great hall had broken up, listeners and fellow musicians alike followed him, finding excuses to talk to him. Ladies kissed their hands to him and sent servants running to give him small tokens of their favor. He offered them nods of courtesy, and was rewarded with melting smiles. If he'd been a less moral man, well, he would not have had to sleep alone for a year at least.

Without having to bribe the stewards for a look at the standings, he new he was favored to win the Tournament. He could tell by the manner in which people made way for him. At the fairground he was bidden to sit in a pavilion with a rich silk merchant and his family. The man suggested that he might see his way to giving Simman a nearly priceless cloak if he would agree to wear it during the final round of the contest.

How lucky it was that he had lost his way in the forest that night! His three servants had complained mightily about having to set up Simman's pavilion in the middle of nowhere. In order to get them to stop fidgeting and

looking about fearfully he had had to let them stay in it
with him. And none of them had had the nerve to go
looking for water. He'd had to do it himself. That was
when he'd come upon that callow oaf, Derrydowndilly
or whatever his name was, singing that perfectly lovely
song. It had been a gift, so easy to remember that once
he'd heard it it stuck in his memory like honey. He was
gone so long his servants were beside themselves with
fear, but when he returned he knew he had the means
to win the Tournament of Troubadors—not that he'd
had any concern in the first place that he might lose.

The duchess was already beguiled by his skill and
charm. When he arrived at the hall to dine, he was escorted by the seneschal himself to a seat at the head
table beside Scaur. The elderly lutenist was polite to
him, as befit, in Simman's opinion, the man who would
replace him here at court. All the rest of his rivals were
scattered along the boards, every one of them below the
salt. And all because of a song. Simman found himself
tapping along with the rhythm of the tune in his mind.
Catchy, it was.

"Roasted swan, sir?" inquired a page, kneeling beside
him with a platter. Simman speared a piece with his belt
knife and chewed on it meditatively. Subtleties were presented to the Lady Melanda, who clapped and laughed
at each new delight. The girl was unsophisticated. She
was going to be easy to please. Simman made himself
comfortable on the padded bench and took a swig of
watered wine. *Here's to my future,* he thought.

"Sir bard," the duchess called to him, as sweets were
being served. "We were well pleased with your performance today. Will you not favor us with a song?"

Simman rose and inclined his head. "It would be my
pleasure, your grace." A page leaped to bring him his
guitar. As he tuned it, he saw people turn away from
their conversations and put down their wine glasses, the
better to listen to him. He knew a fine song that had
gone over well at a feast of the Duke of the Eastern
Marsh. He strummed a few opening chords and began
to sing.

The first words were just barely out of his mouth when
he realized that he was singing the love song. He faltered

on the strings, but he caught himself. It must simply have
been so much in his mind that his fingers had begun to
play it against his will. No matter. The duchess was tapping the slow beat on the tablecloth with her fingers. He
finished with a rolling chord that was drowned out by
the applause and cheers from the audience. Derrydown-
dillo sat among them, glaring murder at him. Simman
enjoyed the look on his face.

"Another," begged Lady Melanda, her eyes gleaming.

Simman picked out a lively chord, and launched into
the drinking song. It didn't take him long to realize that
he was singing the love song again. He felt his face burn
with embarrassment, but he had to finish it. He couldn't
not finish it, so urgently did it pound at the inside of his
brain. The applause this time was genuine, but much less
enthusiastic than before.

"Sir bard," the duchess chided him, "when I asked
you to play us a song, I meant one after another, not
the same one over and over."

"I'm so sorry, your grace," Simman said, flustered.
"I . . . I simply must have practiced that one so much it
has driven the others back a bit in my mind. I know a
thousand songs."

"Well, then, play one!"

"Of course," he said. "Here's another!" He plucked
the chords for a comic melody about a knight who fell
off his destrier, which proceeded to win a tournament
all by itself. Instead of the laughter he expected, the
faces of the audience were pained. No matter how he
started and tried again, he could sing nothing but the
stolen love song. It ran over and over again in his mind,
and he could not stop. Everyone in the hall just looked
at him. The duchess shook her head ruefully. Simman
had to escape. He clenched his fingers to prevent them
touching the strings.

"I, uh, if you will excuse me, your grace. I'm not feeling well."

Simman strode out of the hall. He glanced at Derren
as he went by. The other bard was seated next to a
woman in amber silk. He was startled to see that she
had cat's eyes. A witch! She'd put a spell on him!

Perhaps a good night's sleep, Simman thought. Girls

who had offered him favors earlier in the day swarmed
him, pleading with him, laughing, to come and stay the
night with them, but Simman could think of nothing but
his disgrace. The man of the day spent the night alone.

Derren and Pippa were sharing a breakfast of a small
loaf and some fruit between them on a bench in the
practice courtyard.

"Stop *humming,*" Pippa commanded.

"I can't help it," Derren said. "The song's running
through my head like a river."

"Yours and everyone else's," she said. "It's a good
song."

"Not like for you," Derren said. "I've got a curse on
me. So I can get even with Simman."

"So you have a curse on *you*?" Pippa asked.

"It's got to do with the balance of nature," Derren
explained, his mouth full of grapes. "Vanisa told me . . ."

At that moment, strong hands hauled Derren up off
the bench and pinned him against the wall.

"What have you done to me?" Simman demanded,
his face red with fury. "I've been up all night. The
tune! The tune is eating away at me! All I can think
of every moment is that damned song. Everything I
play turns out as that damned *song*! I can't get it out
of my head."

"I thought you wanted it there," Derren said. "Tell
everyone that I wrote it, and it will go away."

"Never!"

Derren shoved the shorter man away. "Then you'll
have to live with the consequences. Lies and theft have
a way of being found out."

Simman glared at him, then realized everyone in the
courtyard was staring at them. The guards near the door
looked at one another, then one of them left his post to
approach. Simman stepped back, straightening his tunic,
then withdrew with all the dignity he possessed.

"I'll tell them you're consorting with witches," Simman shot over his shoulder.

"Tell away," Derren said, thumbing his nose. "She's
an honored guest of her grace."

*   *   *

The second round of the Tournament of Troubadors was a test of knowledge. While playing a tune, the bards were quizzed on musical notation, tempo, the parts of instruments, anything that the judges wished to know. Derren prided himself on his memory. His master, the piper of Bannockby, had hammered all these details into his head when he was a child.

Only twenty-eight contestants were left. As the top-ranked player in the first round Simman went first. It was traditional to play a series of teaching tunes and exercises during the session. Duchess Sofia's eyebrows went up as the guitarist strummed the love song and nothing but the love song.

". . . And how many beats per measure in waltz time?" asked Scaur.

"Three in four," Simman said, playing the last bars of the fifth repetition. That was the final question for his round. With evident relief he let his hand drop.

"It seems that you're a lute with only one string, master bard," Duchess Sofia said. "I believe we're all a little tired of that melody. Will anyone else play?"

"I will, your grace," Derren said, springing up. He strode forward and went down on one knee before Melanda with his little harp propped on his thigh. He knew how Simman felt. The song was stuck in his head, wearing a rut into his consciousness like a plow into a field. He played the tune through, ripping off a sharp arpeggio with all eight fingers at the end. He bowed to the duchess. "You see, among the things I know is to stop at one repetition."

The crowd laughed. Lady Melanda giggled. Derren winked at her. Simman glowered.

That night Simman sat below the salt with the other troubadors and lower-ranking guests.

On the third day only five musicians remained. In spite of the stolen tune coloring every aspect of his conscious thought Simman was still at the top of the competition. No one there was as good as he. Scaur had been most complimentary regarding his knowledge of his art.

Surely he would be recommended to take the old bard's place, if only he could get that cursed song out of his head!

"For the final competition," the steward announced, "each performer must play a masterwork, a song in the style of her grace's choosing. To celebrate this day, on which her grace's daughter enters the sisterhood of shield-maidens, the style is a heroic epic. A tale of derring-do, and no other type will be accepted," he added, with a sharp look at Simman.

The crowd cheered and settled down to enjoy themselves.

"Sir Simman will begin!"

Derren stood against the wall, grinning. Simman grabbed the younger man by the shirtfront. "You know I cannot sing an epic. All I can hear is this Gods-cursed tune of yours! Break the spell."

"Give back what you stole," Derren said simply. "I am suffering likewise as long as you refuse to do the right thing. But I don't mind. I like the song. It's the best thing I ever did." He began to hum it. Simman let out a muffled exclamation and grabbed the harpist's fingers, squeezing. Derren turned white with pain. "All you do to me will return to you threefold," he warned. Simman let go, breathing hard. "Give it back, and all will be as it was before."

"Never!"

Heroism. Great deeds. Men on horseback. Simman called all these images to mind as he stalked into the open circle, fighting against the tune that beat inexorably in his memory, drowning out all else. He wished he'd never come to this city. He wished he'd never set foot in the Harwood Forest!

Gritting his teeth, he bowed to the duchess. Fighting the music in his head he began to play one of his finest pieces, renowned throughout the eight dukedoms. He strummed a chord, then another, hearing the wrong chording ring from the guitar. He knew what was happening. If he touched another string his fingers would play the opening note of the song, and his voice would follow, no matter what.

"All right!" he shouted, holding his hands out as far

from the guitar as possible. "I confess it. This is his song!" He pointed at Derren. "I overheard him, and I couldn't resist it. I stole it!"

As soon as he said it, his hands went limp. For the first time in three days his mind was clear, and his body was under his own control. He was so grateful he nearly wept. "I withdraw from the competition, your grace." Bowing deeply, he backed out of the circle of light. He passed Derren, who nodded to him.

"Well said," Derren told him.

"This is not the end of our dispute," Simman hissed.

"It had better be," Derren said. "Threefold, remember?" For just a moment Simman thought he saw the young man's pupils slit like a cat's. He hurried out of the great hall.

"Derren of Bannockby!"

Derren took a deep breath of relief. At the moment of Simman's confession he, too, was freed of the curse of the endlessly repeating melody. Never again would he ask the witch to cast such a spell. Revenge was too hard a burden for anyone to bear.

"Your grace, my lady, I would like to play for you a tune taught to me by my master," Derren said. "It's a tale of sacrifice and truth, of a young knight who is not the swiftest nor the most skilled, but he does the best he can to slay a dragon in the service of his lady." He bowed to Lady Melanda, who watched him avidly.

Drawing a glissando on the strings of his harp he saw approval in the eyes of not only old Scaur but the duchess. Who knew? Derren thought, as he sang the ancient lay. Perhaps he could win the prize and the job after all—most likely if he promised never to play Vanisa's song again.

NOTHING SAYS "I LOVE YOU" LIKE THE KISS OF COLD STEEL

by Von Jocks

Von Jocks believes in the magic of stories. She has written since she was five, publishing her first short story at the age of twelve in a local paper. Under the name Evelyn Vaughn she sold her first romantic suspense novel, *Waiting For The Wolf Moon,* to Silhouette Shadows in 1992. Three more books completed her "Circle Series" before the Shadows line closed. Her short fiction most recently appeared in *Dangerous Magic,* from DAW Books. The book was selected as one of the top 100 of the year by the New York City Public Library, and her story was nominated for a Sapphire Award.

Von received her master's degree at the University of Texas in Arlington, writing her thesis on the history of the romance novel. An unapologetic TV addict, she resides in Texas with her cats and her imaginary friends and teaches community college English to support her writing habit . . . or vice versa.

PLATITUDES about "the best revenge" and "a life lived well" be damned. I'd meant ne'er again to set eyes on the jewel-drenched softpalms who'd spawned me, unless it be for retribution. When the retribution I chose had the extra benefit of securing my infant son's future—by securing his inheritance, I took it from the others—what was there to stop me?

My husband, that's what. I longed to outshine the mother who had betrayed me, the aunt and uncle who had done worse . . . the father who had ignored me.

But how could I, married to . . . him?

"Cal," I whispered to the babe's father in desperation, the night before we would arrive.

"Wha'?" His response tickled the hair on my neck, since I'd of course seduced him toward compliance first. *That,* at least, we've always done well. It led to the baby, and the baby to the marriage. Simple causality.

"I'd like you to do me a favor."

"Mmhm?"

"When we're at my parents' home, I'd like you to pretend you love me."

During the ensuing silence, I held my breath for worry. Then Cal said, "Of course; why wouldn't I do something like that for you?"

For a foolish heartbeat, I even believed him. Then he added, "Darling."

Cal ne'er calls me "darling" but in mockery.

So we fought—and not even in the way we both enjoy.

" 'Tis not so big a favor," I insisted finally.

But he rolled out of bed, yanked on his breeches, boots, and blouse, then strapped on both his swords. "Pretend I love you?" he repeated bitterly. "*You?* It's a bigger favor than you realize—*darling.*"

And he left—for the night, anyway. At least I could plot ways to avenge this latest of *his* betrayals. Even if I must now fawn to the family who'd tormented me long before he took over that task.

Much of this *was* Cal's fault, after all. The baby *and* the bad impression.

Why should I be the only one to suffer?

"Mari!" greeted my mother from the second-floor landing of our echoing manor home. As small as I, Constanza Telemachus boasted hair a close imitation of the brassy color it once had been—the color mine still is— and her cheeks glowed with carefully applied excitement. From her ears and her wrists, her fingers and her throat, glittered gemstones rivaled only in dragon lairs.

And I've seen dragon lairs.

She descended the curved steps in a practiced sweep, grace personified, and I considered stabbing her right there. But in deference to my fine gown—yes, a gown— I wore no more weaponry than a dagger in my boot. And why bother to use it? The family kept expensive healing potions in the pantry to buy off even death.

When I did not lean in for a kiss, Mother bucked to an awkward stop.

"Why, darling," she gasped. "Whatever is wrong?"

"Nothing, Mother," I lied through my distaste. "But my arms are full." And I drew my brocade cloak farther back to reveal my sleeping son—

The new heir, to the old heiress.

Mother's mouth, eyes, and hands opened in feigned pleasure. "What a love!"

Raphi wriggled at the disruption.

Then she nailed me with a look of classic Telemachus wile. "Is he yours?"

As if I'd steal one? But of course were Raphi not mine—or should Father not recognize him as such—*her* inheritance remained safe. For this reason, the babe would ne'er be without me, Cal, or the walking fortress whom we call Mouse—the biggest, hairiest fighter of a nanny ever imagined.

"Mother," I said, "this is my husband, Cal Truloni."

And I braced myself.

To his credit, Cal looked good. He usually does. In honor of my homecoming, he'd even brightened his usual assassin-black leathers—the fitted doublet and high boots—with pale blue silks. The blacks matched his long raven hair, which had been tied into a queue. The blues matched his pale, predatory eyes. Perhaps he'd ne'er manage elegance, but with his lean figure, and the two Dwarven steel swords glittering from his hips, he *did* look rakish.

Yet he still has the surname of a peasant.

"Why, he's . . ." Mother tried, flustered. "He's . . . ?"

"Isn't he?" I agreed with an overly sweet smile, which I turned from my mother to my husband. He grimaced back, as disenchanted with the air here as I, and my heart lifted. Perhaps last night's teensy misunderstanding would be forgotten.

"Pleasure," he purred now, speaking at my mother's expensive sapphire necklace. "*Mari* here has told me so much about you."

He *would* make a fuss about my discarded name. He'd only known me as "Tuppence," for my brassy hair, until this moment. Did he expect *me* to say otherwise?

"And this is our son, Raphael," I continued, shifting

the babe's weight into my other arm. "Raphael *Telemachus* Truloni."

Raphi mewed a sleepy protest, groped at my breast with a baby hand, and sighed back into sleep.

"Ah," said my mother. I imagine she's pictured the scene often enough before—I arriving at her doorstep with a child and a lowlife companion.

I doubt she could have conceived how well we would be dressed.

"We would like to see Father," I told her, in hopes of shortening this ordeal. I wanted out of the gown, back into my leathers. "Cal and I will be at the Royal Arms—"

"An *inn*?" I'd told Cal as much, and felt him slipping a silver into my pocket because I'd won the bet. "After we've not seen you in years? No! You and your . . . husband? . . . must stay here!"

So we did.

Lucky us.

Father did not, of course, attend dinner. Mother did. Her sister, Aunt Lydia, did. And Lydia's husband, Rojar.

To write of Rojar makes my hand cramp for want of a sword over a quill. Though handsome enough, in an overly glamoured way, and charming enough to convince innocents that he loves them, Rojar makes Cal Truloni seem like the catch of the five kingdoms.

Know that my family did not, in fact, raise me. Though an only child, I was troublesome enough to be sent to the temple sisters, as sacrificial lamb for my parents' many sins. I still returned home often enough for Rojar to seduce me, then lie about it.

Aunt Lydia provided his alibi, and my mother accused me of spinning tales. Just thinking of that day shortens my breath—the accusations and dismissals had occurred at this very table! Aye, I do not hate so easily as some would think.

But these people, I hated.

At least when I escaped the cloister for a life of quests and adventures, I neatly robbed the Telemachus clan of the sacred indulgence I might have bought them by taking the veil. Poor nobles. And after they'd committed so many sins that needed divine forgiveness.

Yet here I sat, come home.

"So," said Aunt Lydia now, over a cut-crystal goblet of wine—her third. "You two are married? When was *this*? How old is the baby?"

As if her world did not swim in scandal without us.

"Yes," answered Cal, in a tone that asked what business it was of hers. "Over a year ago. And seven months." He was fudging on the dates . . . perhaps he'd meant to be on good behavior all along. Through the fog of angry memories, I clung to that hope with pitiful desperation. He *was* my husband, after all, and had fought beside me more often than either of us liked to admit. And he claimed to have had a real family once, long ago. Unlike me, he knew how true family supposedly acted.

"Not even weaned?" Lydia followed Rojar's gaze to my décolletage, perhaps my best proof that I'd not purchased the infant from some gypsy beggar, just to steal their inheritance. As long as I kept well padded against leaks, carrying milk complemented my figure in ways neither Lydia's nor my mother's seemed to have e'er known.

Aunt Lydia, I should mention, favors my mother. But instead of dying her hair back to the bronze of her youth, she'd simply turned it a glaring red. The color did nothing for her and, worse, she wore rubies.

Worse yet, my old sot of an uncle, from the cut of his eyes, seemed to be considering a reunion with me. Stupid, stupid man.

"Something got your attention?" demanded Cal, noticing.

Rojar smiled blandly. "Nothing untoward, I assure you."

"So how did you meet?" interrupted my mother.

"In a tavern," answered Cal, and I winced. Ah well, at least I'd have less to remember. "Tup here was broke, so I let her share my room."

"Tup?" purred Uncle Rojar.

It speaks to how Cal has worn me down, since our marriage, that I did little more than glare at his abbreviation.

"Mari." Cal sounded like he wanted to laugh, whenever he said my birth name. "I call her Tuppence, because she rarely had two pence to rub together."

I stomped on his foot. That was *not* where I'd got the nickname! But he went right on. "Still, she had her uses, and she kept hanging around me. . . ."

I smiled at their shocked faces, laughed softly as if at a clever jest, and muttered, "Stop it, you lying bastard, or I'll make you a eunuch," in his ear.

"You wouldn't cut off the supply, darling," he chided back in a return whisper.

"So why marry her?" demanded Lydia ravenously.

Cal shrugged, and now lied outright. "She begged me."

"Is that right?" I challenged, my remnant hopes of outshining my family unraveling into nothingness.

"You were pretty drunk at the time."

So I waited. As he lifted a spoonful of soup to his lips, I elbowed him in the side. He spat soup across the table, paused for a moment to reflect on his options—and lunged for me.

I skipped out of the way, well-practiced from numerous other skirmishes, and our chairs toppled in the ensuing flight. I would've made it, too, had dear Uncle Rojar not caught me around the waist as I passed.

It was being outnumbered and without allies that most enraged me.

"Tsk, tsk," Rojar chided, copping a surreptitious feel while Cal literally lifted me from him and reset me on my feet, holding tight. "These Telemachus women must be kept on a tight rein."

Cal hesitated, torn between anger at me and at Rojar. Feeling someone's hand across the back of my leg—and knowing that both of Cal's held my shoulders—I took advantage of the distraction to twist away, snatch a silver meat knife from the table, and stab it deliciously into my dear uncle's gut.

"Remind you of anything?" I snarled softly beneath his gurgle and, claiming his napkin to daintily wipe the blood from my hand, I stalked from the dining room.

Even Cal was surprised enough to give me wide berth.

Behind me, I heard my uncle whimper, my aunt gasp, and my mother call, "Marsais, healing potion!" Damn the luck—Rojar's injury would be far more fleeting than that which he'd once done me.

Welcome home.

"What was that?" demanded Cal. He'd thrown open my bedchamber door so hard that it banged against the wall and woke Raphi. "Some sort of fuckin' family tradition?"

I looked up from my seat in the thick window embrasure, which overlooked the torchlit courtyard garden. "You scared the baby."

"No shit," he muttered, stalking across the room to Raphi's cradle and lifting him. "Like he shouldn't be scared with a mother like you!" But he bounced Raphi in his arms until the baby burbled at him.

I hadn't begged to marry him. *He'd* begged . . . though for the baby, not for me, which is why I hadn't had the courage to correct him at the table. Somewhere in his murdering soul, *he'd* wanted a family.

Me, I had more family than I could stomach. I hated it here. These walls. That garden. I hated the sense that I'd lost myself simply by entering these portals.

I missed a sword on my hip . . . though steak knives do suffice.

"I know you think I'm stupid about nobility. *Mari,* but even I know you were out of line tonight."

"Lady save us," I sighed. "Tuppence got out of line."

"I thought you wanted to make a good impression."

"You made sure there wasn't a chance of that," I accused.

"I was gonna tell 'em how I made an honest woman out of you," he protested.

Sadly, I had nothing to throw.

Cal returned our baby to the cradle. Then he came to stand over me. "C'mon, Tuppence, what's wrong? It's not your flux. That was last week."

Vulgar man. I studied his shadowed, predatory features in the starlight and momentarily wished we had a true, caring marriage. I could tell him how much I hated these people, how just being near them made me feel like a foolish, trapped child. I could ask him to take me away, to find some other way to secure Raphi's future. And he, he would pet my hair, soothe my soul, promise me everything.

Yeah. Right.

Impatience sharpened his eyes. Not only wouldn't he comfort me, but at any moment now he'd stalk away to his own bedchamber. Can you imagine that? Cal and I, in separate bedchambers. Only the nobility would think of such a thing. . . .

Then I remembered his abrupt departure the night before, and the idea of separate chambers became more believable.

So I took the next best thing. I threw myself into his chest and kissed him. His arms closed around me, mainly to hold on as he staggered backward.

"Tup," he demanded with a gasp, "hold on a—"

But I was already yanking on his belt.

To my relief, he snarled something and attacked my fine gown with equal enthusiasm.

After coupling deliciously on the carpet, we lay quite still, as if stunned.

"I hope they heard us," I decided, frowning when Cal rolled off me.

"I think they did," he assured me, standing. "Dunno how the baby slept through—oh, he didn't." And he waved at the cradle.

Raphi chortled approval. He was used to us.

I sat up and stroked a torn swatch of my gown. Then I grinned up at Cal. "I know where they keep the really good wine."

Standing sleek and mostly nude beside the great curtained bed, his long black hair half out of its queue, he seemed to be considering something weightier. "How's any of this supposed to convince your father to recognize Raphi?"

"It's not," I admitted. "It's just a way of surviving until Count Telemachus deigns to notice we're here."

"And how long's that gonna take?"

"He knows we're here," I explained, "but he'll avoid us for at least a week. It reminds us of our place. Then there'll be a ball, where he may look us over from a safe distance. If he likes what he sees, he'll come to dinner sometime after that, and we can start the process of convincing him—"

"That reeks," said Cal, as annoyed as if I had something to do with it. Damn it, he was dressing again!

"Don't blame me," I protested. "*I* ran away."

"Could you at least stop *stabbing* people until we get through this hell?"

As if he had something against stabbing people.

"No promises," I said.

So he walked out again.

Oops. I must have forgotten to mention that, in the meantime, my charming relatives would all try to gain control of the only truly precious person involved in the game.

The sleeping, black-haired successor.

My mother appeared in my chambers two hellish days later, after some difficulty slithering by Mouse, who stood guard. "I'll make a deal with you, Mar . . . er, Tuppence," she said. "Something you'll appreciate."

I waited with my arms folded. Was there aught she could offer that I would want? Her head on a platter, perhaps. My childhood back.

Mother said, "I want to keep the baby."

One charming relative down.

"Don't you see what this could mean, Daughter?" she pursued. "You would be free! Because of the baby, you stay with that boorish peasant. Because of the baby, you hold yourself back from those little escapades of yours . . . indeed, force yourself to return here! Such suffering, Mari, because you're chained to an infant you ne'er wanted. No," she insisted, when I opened my mouth to protest. "You're too like me, child. You're no mother! I'll admit, I had you too young. I resented you, just as I see you resenting my grandson."

The idea intrigued me. "Then why, Mother, would you possibly want another one?"

"Reparation," she answered immediately. "I'm no longer so young or foolish. Now—now I could be a good mother. And in doing so, I can benefit you. Not that it would make up for the past, but 'twould be a start. Just think of it . . ."

"I would be free," I finished for her.

She nodded happily.

Raphi's absence *would* free me from many a concern. Speaking of which. . . .

"What about Cal?"

"What about him, dear?" How easily Mother dismissed the bane of my daily existence.

"The *peasant* is strangely fond of the child—and even if he weren't, he'd protest from sheer stubbornness."

"True. The baby is the only thing tying you to him."

"Exactly." I enjoyed the unlikely image of Cal pleading with me to stay with him in Raphi's absence. Ha!

"I'm certain we can arrange something." Mother moved to the cradle and lifted the heir in question. He was getting big. Soon, to carry him on my back would render me useless in a fight.

"Say grandmama," my mother instructed, while the baby blinked at her.

If Raphi remained here, he would have a secure, if unhappy, future. I'd gain one unfettered by previous mistakes.

A heady thought.

"Say grandmama," my mother insisted.

I lifted him out of her inexperienced arms. "He doesn't talk yet, Mother."

"Perhaps if I gave him some honey."

"He is not a pet." Although she made her mouth into an adorable moue—or perhaps because of it—I could not stem my anger. She wanted my baby? *My baby?* Look at how terribly she'd raised *me!* "The answer is no. Leave my chambers, now."

"What?" She sounded like Cal.

"I said *go away*. I am not giving you my son."

"I'll pay you gold," she lured.

"How much?" Automatic reaction.

"A thousand crowns." Her eyes glittered at that, and well they might. My own heart sped at the thought—but my arms tightened around the baby.

"No," I said.

"Two thousand." Damn, but she made things difficult.

"Mother," I managed, "If only from sheer *meanness*, I would never give you this child. So you're merely embarrassing yourself."

Her smile faded. "You really did grow into a *shit*, Mari Agne," she said.

"Thank you." I smiled, and she left.

I wasted no time discarding Raphi into his pillowed cradle—little brat cost me two thousand gold crowns! Thinking to leave him with Mouse, grab a cloak, and get out for some fresh air, I yanked back the wardrobe's heavy curtain—

And nearly screamed to see my husband.

"How much," he echoed, to assure me that he'd heard everything. *"How much?"*

"You'd have taken the first thousand." I reached around him for my cloak, but he caught my wrist.

"So why didn't *you*," he countered, still dangerously low.

"I was holding out for five—I knew you'd pout about getting a cut."

"She's right, you know."

I arched a brow.

"You really did grow into a shit."

I shrugged—did he expect me to argue?

He lifted my hand, kissed the inside of my wrist. He really shouldn't. I came near to passing out at the erotic sensation. "If you'd said yes, I would have killed you," Cal whispered, his words cooling across the dampness his mouth had trailed.

"Not—" My voice didn't work; I tried again. "Not that you've done so well at that anyway."

"I haven't really tried." He was kissing my palm again. "I mean, those were just for practice."

It passed the time.

'Twas at the ball that Lydia made her move. I know this because I saw her scheming with a handsome, auburn-haired nobleman, in the shadowy courtyard, not long before he approached me.

Please. Why *wouldn't* I be watching the shadows?

The man was as attractive as the best of bait, though

he'd likely prove no more use in a melee against, say, goblins than would Raphi. Still, in part to learn more, and in part to annoy Cal, I encouraged his advances.

Sadly, I succeeded too well at the latter to win the former. Lord Bramwell had barely intimated a glorious future together—though he *did* intimate it into my throat with nibbling kisses—before my husband spun him into a wall tapestry.

I'd forgotten Cal's already foul mood. Blame it on the ball. He knows little of dancing or etiquette, after all, and like most men, takes his ignorance out on others.

Which explains a great deal, does it not?

"Look," he hissed into Bramwell's soft, auburn hair, while the party clattered to stillness around us. "Consider this a favor. You do *not* want the bitch."

Spoilsport.

Then Bramwell said, "How dare you insult the lady so!" And I pieced together the rest of Lydia's delightful plan. "I challenge you," announced Bramwell, "to a duel!"

Oops. I must have forgotten to tell my family that Cal is a blademaster.

"You're joking," said Cal, who *did* know.

But Bramwell merely scowled at Cal's swords. "No man of *honor* would use more than one weapon."

Instead of laughing in his face—man of honor?—Cal handed me his right-hand sword. They set, *en garde*.

Then they dueled.

Have you e'er seen two masters duel? Aye, Bramwell was also skilled, or Aunt Lydia would ne'er have hired him. 'Tis glorious to watch. Lunges. Parries. Advances. Retreats. Even the occasional acrobatic leap—all to the slick, musical clack and slide of metal on metal.

Beautiful.

But Bramwell would still be of little use against goblins. He fought formally, while Cal fought to win. Despite that the partygoers cheered their own champion, the fight ended too soon with Bramwell, disarmed, standing on tiptoe and Cal's rapier against his throat.

"She's my wife to insult," Cal informed him. Pig.

Then, after the nobleman nodded cautious defeat, Cal turned on me. "What are you doing, *huh?*" he demanded, pushing me against a table hard enough that the punch sloshed out of its crystal bowl to stain the linen cloth. "You *want* me to kill these people? You *want* everyone to think you're a slut? You—"

Unimpressed, I murmured, "I *wanted* to know how Aunt Lydia thought I would be so charmed by him embarrassing you at swords that I would give him access to Raphi. But I guess I won't find out now."

Cal, furious face near mine, paused. "Oh."

Which gave me a chance to savor the heat roiling off of him. Fights can be marvelous aphrodisiacs . . . especially when one isn't a nice person.

We heard the noise at the same time. I leaned out, Cal spun, and we skewered Lord Bramwell in unison, each with one of Cal's rapiers.

Backstabbing softpalm.

Lord Bramwell crumpled to the carpet. Cal, with a grunt of disgust, slung me over his shoulder and headed from the ballroom.

Mother called, "Marsais! Healing potion!"

I considered my protest carefully—"Put me down" could land me in the punch bowl—and tried, "Cal, you're embarrassing me."

"Right," he laughed.

But the way the gentry stared at us, while my husband carried me out, compensated for both his coarseness and the waste of another clean kill, as Marsais scurried in to revive Aunt Lydia's gigolo.

Our audience was jealous—aye, *jealous* of the foreceful lout I'd paired with. And they were, I suspected, avidly imagining what would happen when we reached the bedchamber.

I could have got down myself, if I'd liked. My feet hung dangerously near a vulnerable area of Cal's anatomy, and he wouldn't take a knee in the face too happily. But that would disillusion our audience.

I waited until we were in the bedchamber to knee Cal in the face.

What truly surprised me was when Uncle Rojar made his bid toward Raphi's future. As Mouse was out with Cal and the baby, my uncle walked into my chambers as if invited. As if I could not now kill him as easily as look at him. And for perhaps the first time in my life, he truly impressed me.

"You wish to kill my husband," I repeated.

"And be appointed guardian of the baby, yes," he agreed. "Co-guardian, I mean. You, as a widow, couldn't shoulder the *entire* burden."

"Or the entire fortune?" I guessed. His scheme intrigued me. Opportunity knocking, and all that.

"Exactly!" exclaimed my uncle. "Of course, to keep the Count ignorant, we should snuff the peasant in a way that will appear blameless. I was hoping, since you know him better, you might suggest . . ."

He stopped because I'd raised a hand to silence him. Uncle Rojar grew pale as I carefully checked the closet, the doorway, the bed-drapes. I wished no repeat of the scene with my mother.

Luckily for both of us, Cal lurked nowhere near. A peek out my window revealed him in the courtyard below, near Mouse, holding Raphi by the hands so that the babe could walk a tiled garden path. I waved. He deserted one of Raphi's pudgy hands for a quick, wary wave back.

That dispensed with, I turned back into the room, amused. "You were hoping I could suggest a weakness of his, to kill him without suspicion."

"Exactly!" My uncle seemed e'en happier with my intellect than he'd been with my body, if I recall correctly.

I leaned against a bedpost, contemplating. "The usual 'accidents' would not do," I admitted. "Poisonings, misplaced arrows, that sort. Father might watch for that."

"Perhaps if we hired someone," began Rojar, but I shook my head.

"No, there's always the possibility of capture, and anyone can crack under torture. Almost anyone," I added, since I never have. "Far better to kill him outright, admit it freely, and just let the circumstances absolve you."

"What?"

I grinned, pleased to arrive at a perfect plan at last. 'Twas an artistic creation. "Of course! He laid the groundwork himself, at the ball!"

Rojar looked confused.

"You kill Cal in self-defense," I explained. "Father couldn't deny your innocence in *that!* The only suspicious thing will be that the pantry shall have no more healing potions, and we can blame that on him. Corpses make excellent scapegoats."

Like a child before a storyteller, Uncle Rojar nodded for me to continue. Dull-witted softpalm.

"Once he's mortally wounded, we'll be unable to save him."

"How do I get him to start a fight?" Rojar asked. Idiot.

"Cal has already proved himself jealous. Get overly familiar with me, and he'll attack." A distasteful image, but I supposed I'd need to make *some* sacrifices.

"I like it!" beamed Rojar—then faded. "No, I don't! Mari, your scheme sports a very large knot. He'll kill me!"

I glanced out the window again, watched how the sunshine caught in blue patches on my husband's black hair, and my son's. "That's the best part," I assured Rojar softly, then turned back. "The secret weapon," I teased.

Once he was all but quivering, I said, "Get him drunk."

Uncle Rojar's joy was visible. " You think that will work?"

"In all the time I've known him, never have I seen Cal win a duel drunk." For effect, I raised my right hand. "I swear by my Lady Goddess."

"That's what we'll do, then!" declared Uncle Rojar, swooping in for a kiss which I ducked. "I'll do it this very night," he exclaimed.

Once he left, I wandered back to the window and stared into the courtyard. When Cal noticed me, I began unlacing the front of my gown. That caught his attention—and that of several servants. The silken cords of my bodice made whisking noises as they slid loose. I leaned over and, with one extended arm, dropped the cord into the garden below.

Then, straightening, I shrugged my bodice the rest of the way off—turning at the last minute, so that all my audience could see bared was my back.

Cal made it upstairs before I'd finished removing my stockings. He'd left the babe with Mouse.

"Not that I'm complaining," he muttered huskily, running his warm hands over me. "But what has you in so good a mood?"

"Mm." That's all I could say, since he chose that moment to kiss me. It kept me occupied while he yanked his boots and breeches off. When his mouth left mine, other parts of him distracted me quite as well.

"What makes you think something—" I gasped, then purred. Hands, again. "—put me in a good mood?"

Now he had to coax the truth out of me.

"Fine," I gasped finally. "I've been scheming."

Cal pretended to gasp. "No! Not you!"

"Mmm—and if you don't start performing your husbandly duties real damned soon, I might go through with it."

"Go through with what, darling?" A gentle brush of his fingers reassured me that he was still on my side, despite the endearment.

"Kiss me, and I'll tell you."

It was a long, wet, probing kiss.

"My uncle and I have plotted to kill you," I admitted. "Kiss me again."

The funny thing is, he did. Then he asked, "Why would Rojar want to do that?"

"For Raphi, of course."

"Huh," said Cal.

I applied more pressure on his back with my nails, and to my distinct relief and pleasure, he shifted into me in all the right ways. Then he paused. "Why'd he tell *you*?"

"I'm already confessing," I protested.

"Go—" He gasped himself. "—on."

"He wants me to—mmm, like that—help him."

"Like this?" And he said something else, but I couldn't hear over my own happy whimper. "Mari, pay attention."

"I *am*."

He grinned, and things got out of control for awhile. Decisions, decisions. I would miss this, without him.

"So," he prompted, eons later. "Where'd you hide Uncle Rojar's body?"

"I did no such thing!" I protested. "He asked for help and I gave it. Rojar's going to make it look like self-defense."

Cal laughed. "He thinks he could actually beat me in a fight?"

"He thinks he can if he gets you drunk." I giggled.

He narrowed his eyes. "And what would give him that idea, Mari?"

Even when I *am* innocent, the look gives me difficulty. So I did not try. "I told him you'd never won a fight drunk."

The slow grin of admiration that lit Cal's dark face was a beautiful, gratifying thing. "You bitch," he accused lovingly. "I don't get drunk."

"Well, you might pretend you are tonight," I pointed out. "And take care how thorough a lesson you teach— he's ridding the pantry of healing potions."

"Nice touch," he admitted. "Here's what I don't get, though. If Raphi has everyone so worried, why don't they just kill *him*?"

As if *anybody* would consider assassinating a child, and not just us. Silly man. "They're afraid of divine retribution," I told him. "Their hopes of buying indulgence ran away to play with the lowlifes."

"You're good at it, too," he said.

But I wondered if he knew just *HOW* good.

Rojar invited us into the drawing room for brandies and cards after dinner, witnesses to corroborate his story of self-defense. Mother and Aunt Lydia suggested I join them in needlepoint. I, however, chose the card game.

The brandy my uncle unbottled was superb, perhaps my father's best. Yet he claimed stomach problems, and so after one snifter—to prove 'twas neither poisoned nor drugged—he only sipped on it, but generously offered refills.

Unfortunately, I accepted almost as often as Cal . . . and my tolerance for alcohol in no way nears his iron stomach. Within four glasses, I'd quite relaxed. With another, I accused the men of cheating.

Cal drew himself up proudly—he was doing a fine acting job, blinking at me and swaying *just* a little. "We do not cheat," he stated primly. "You're just stupid."

Then he laughed, turning to Rojar to share the mirth.

Knowing full well that he was sober, I stomped on his foot. After two tries.

Rojar said, "Why are you so often unkind to my niece?"

"Because she's so often unkind to *me*," Cal protested.

"Ha!" I challenged. "I've been . . . I've been kinder to you than I've ever been to anybody. Have I ever killed you? Huh?"

"You couldn't kill me if you tried," dismissed Cal.

"Ha! Wait until—" But someone stepped on my foot, and Rojar stared me into silence.

"Oh, yeah," I said. "Shhhh."

Then *CAL* stepped on my foot. I began to pout, and sipped some more brandy.

"You're confident about your fighting abilities," Rojar noted.

"Ha!" said Cal, and I realized he was using me to judge just how drunk he should pretend to be. " 'Course I am. I'm a professional snass . . . Snunass . . . I kill things."

"I'm curious about that." Rojar dispensed more of Father's best. "Does that mean you only kill for money, or would you ever kill someone you know? Like Mari here. If she ever took a lover, would you kill her?"

Cal frowned unsteadily toward me. "Not till the baby's weaned," he decided with a nod.

I narrowed my eyes in challenge. He returned it. We both laughed.

Rojar joined the laughter. "I appreciate your attitude," he admitted. "I'd worried about you finding me and Mari out. . . ."

Mother and Aunt Lydia gasped. So did the maid. I wasn't too thrilled myself. He was supposed to make advances, not imply we were already involved.

"What?" Cal was letting his drunk act slip and getting witty again.

"Mari and me," Rojar insisted, despite me kicking his chair.

I'd gone along with him till now, but no way, even in pretense, would I let everyone think I'd sleep with him. It came too close to that old pain. . . .

Suddenly, I wished I wasn't drunk so I could stab him myself.

"You're lying!" I exclaimed.

"Now, Mari, he's not going to hurt you," Rojar placated.

"Damn right he's not, because you're lying! I wouldn't sleep with you. I'd never—"

And then, to my horror, I stopped. The fact that I would have been lying *actually stopped me*! Of course I could lie. I was Tuppence!

"I've never slept with you," I finished. It came out well, but the pause preceding it had ruinous effect.

"Oh?" asked both Cal and Rojar.

"C'mon," persisted Rojar. "Admit it, Mari."

"No."

Cal was staring at me, like he wasn't sure whether to believe me or something.

"Don't feel bad," soothed Rojar to Cal. "Mari and I go back a long way. I was her first."

I wasn't even wearing a sword! What had happened to me that I wasn't even carrying a sword!

"Her first?" repeated Cal.

And from the corner my mother said, "But, Rojar—you said she was lying."

Silence. I couldn't believe my mother even remembered that long-ago accusation, the one that had set my heart against them all.

Rojar made a few "uh" noises, realizing his own slip, but I was watching Cal. I'd never told him that story, never trusted him—or me—with it, but he seemed to be piecing it together pretty quickly, and he stood.

"You are a dead man," he announced.

Rojar was too excited to notice yet the clarity of Cal's demeanor. He stood as well, drew his sword. "Don't make me fight you, Truloni," he began, to complete the scene we'd devised.

But he stopped with a squeak and a sword through his chest. Not just his chest, but his heart. Blood spurted out around the blade.

"Who said anything about fighting?" demanded Cal of my uncle's quickly fading eyes, and he twisted the sword.

Aunt Lydia screamed for Marsais to fetch healing potions, but even were there any, they couldn't come fast enough. Cal had just made a hit, the first I'd ever actually watched. He'd been fast and thorough, and now he was wiping his sword off on my uncle's velvet doublet.

"Not just for money," he sneered down at the corpse. Then he held out a hand for me. "Tup."

I blinked up at him, so he took my hands for me, pulled me up, and led me back up to the bedchamber. I should not have drunk so much. I couldn't banish the memories, the angers, the hurts.

Once in our room Cal assured Mouse that we were fine, checked on the babe, and sat me on the bed. Through a brandied distance, I watched him strip off his bloodied clothes by a washbasin. My heart hurt, my eyes burned, his image blurred. Only after watching Cal's quick, sure movements for several blurry minutes did I realize that I was crying.

Cal noticed it at the same time. "Oh, shit," he said. Dressed only in a breechcloth, he came to sit beside me. He wiped my cheeks with his thumb.

"Tup? It's okay, Tuppence. He's dead. He . . . ?" A horrible stillness came over him, a look of frantic disbelief. "You did want him dead, didn't you?"

I nodded, still crying silently.

"Then what's wrong? Huh?"

I didn't want to say it. It didn't matter anymore. But the pain wasn't mine—not Tuppence Truloni's—to silence. It was Mari Telemachus' pain, carried ever since her favorite uncle and her mother betrayed her on the same day. It was fetid and rotting, and I couldn't swallow it back, no matter how stupid. So I met Cal's worried gaze, hot tears still squeezing from my eyes.

"They didn't believe me," I whispered.

Then he had me in his arms, safe against his warm chest, petting my back, petting my hair. "He's gone," Cal kept saying. "It's all right, love. Nobody can hurt you now. He's gone."

And I cried against his bare chest. When I could breathe again, he tucked me into bed—I cannot remem-

ber ever being tucked in, though surely I was as an in
fant—and he kissed my forehead and my eyes and my
nose. I remember muttering . . . something . . . blurred
with brandy and sleepiness. It must have come out
clearly enough, though, because Cal grinned like he had
the day Raphi was born.

"You, too, Mari Agne," he smirked. "Now go to
sleep."

The next day, despite my hangover, he announced we
were leaving.

"What about Raphi's inheritance?" I demanded—
had *not* been through this hell for nothing!

Besides Uncle Rojar's death and hearing my husband
call me "love," anyway. I'd gone through this for money.

"Even *we*," insisted Cal, "have got *some* standards."

So we packed. I even put my good leathers on again,
strapped a rapier to my hip. But before we'd even sent
our trunks to the foyer, a knock on our door announced
the chamberlain.

"Marsais!" I said, surprised to see him—what with the
chaos of Rojar's death, and all.

"Miss," he greeted me. And he handed me a folded
sheet of vellum. My father had officially recognized Ra
phael Telemachus Truloni as his heir, complete with
his seal.

And we could not leave fast enough.

"Maybe we should head west," said Cal as Mouse
single-handedly loaded our gear onto the pack animals.
"I hear there's good adventure to be had, out there."

But I was hardly listening to him. I was busy noticing
the faces appearing at the upstairs windows—my aunt's
full of accusation. My mother's, full of envy.

And in one high, tower window, I saw a face that
could easily have been my father's.

I waved, and he waved back.

"Uh . . ." Cal hesitated, which surprised me, so I
turned back to him. "Tuppence?"

I waited, curious.

"What do you remember about last night?" he asked,
too casually.

We mounted our horses. I remembered him calling

me "love." And me saying something that pleased him greatly. *You, too,* he'd said.

Uh-oh.

"Not much," I lied. "But I'm sure you embarrassed yourself, as usual."

"Me?" And we rode away from the Telemachus manor for good, Raphi safely on my back, Mouse leading our packhorses. "I wasn't the one sloppy drunk."

"So you've no excuse," I said with a superior smile.

He called me a bitch. I called him a bastard. And then I surprised us both by laughing, completely *un*ladylike. Perhaps there's something, albeit minor, to that cliché about the best revenge, at that.

We raced each other out of town.

But I shan't tell you what we wagered.

LISTEN TO THE CAT

by Janet Pack

A native of Independence, Missouri, Janet Pack now resides in the village of Williams Bay, Wisconsin, in a slightly haunted farmhouse with cats Tabirika Onyx, Syrannis Moonstone, and Baron Figaro de Shannivere. Her extensive rock collection adorns her living room. Janet's two dozen plus short stories, interviews, and nonfiction articles have been published by DAW and a number of other publishers, and "At the Lake" Magazine. Her musical compositions can be found in Weis and Hickman's *The Death Gate Cycle* and in Dragonlance sourcebooks. Janet works as the manager's assistant at Shadowlawn Stoneware Pottery in Delavan, WI, and, when needed, at the University of Chicago's Yerkes Observatory in Williams Bay. During free moments she sings, reads, embroiders, walks, cooks, watches good movies, plays with her companions, and does as little housework as possible.

ELAINE stepped into her new apartment, slipped the shoulder strap of her briefcase off, and dumped the case by the door, then hoisted her cat Mithril for a hug. "How's the only guy in my life?" she whispered, nuzzling the cat's soft gray ear. "I'm so glad you're here to meet me." She was happy again, finally happy. She hadn't realized how long it had been since she'd enjoyed her life—at least, not until her husband Rob had got out of it and left her free to find joy in living again. Funny how she, a trained psychologist, had taken so long to diagnose her own problem.

The cat purred, tipping the top of his wide head against the side of hers. She rubbed her chin against his stripes and put him down, then checked her phone messages. Frowning, she listened to the last one twice, then wrote down the number. A pang went through her gut-one that was all too familiar. Her husband had caused them often—through their marriage, throughout their divorce, and—it appeared—even now, after she thought it was all over. Rob might not be out of her life as thoroughly as she'd hoped. She picked up the phone and dialed her lawyer's number.

"Elaine Marshall for Leslie Kelleher, please." She watched Mithril play as she waited for the receptionist to transfer her call. He flopped sideways on the fake Oriental rug, as gracefully as only a cat can. Why would her divorce lawyer be calling when the divorce was finished, the papers were signed, and the bills paid for?

Finally, her lawyer got on the line with the bad news.

"There's a new, um, development," Leslie told her. "Rob is insisting on a face-to-face meeting. Tomorrow at three, with you, his lawyer, and me. We have to be there. He's forcing this before he moves out of state at the end of the week."

"What?" Elaine collapsed into a chair next to the phone, feeling exhausted and besieged. Mithril thumped into her lap and settled down, his tail and hindquarters hanging off her knees. "I'll have to cancel a session with a patient. Isn't everything finished with our divorce?"

"It was as far as I was concerned, but apparently Rob's found something to holler about and is demanding reparations for it. I couldn't find out any more than that—his lawyer's being very quiet."

"Reparations?"

"We'll see tomorrow. I'm going over the details tonight. I want to make certain the divorce paperwork was all done exactly as it should have been. We'll use the partners' conference room here at the office. I've already reserved it." Leslie's voice tried to be reassuring, but fell short. "Don't worry. It's probably nothing. Let me take care of this."

"Yes, thanks. I appreciate your help." Elaine put down the phone, drained as she hadn't been since learning Rob had fallen out of love with her. She gazed at the far wall, not seeing it, dreading the coming confrontation.

Mithril brought her back to reality by standing precariously in her lap, kneading her stomach and purring. His bright adoring eyes soothed her mental anguish, and his uncharacteristically clumsy solicitation of her affection garnered a laugh.

"Thanks, Mithril," she murmured, rubbing his ears. "You're usually right about these things. Somehow we'll muddle through this. We always have; we always will."

The next afternoon, fifteen minutes late, Elaine rushed breathlessly into the meeting room where the attorneys and her impatient ex-husband waited. "I'm sorry," she said. "My last session ran long. I couldn't get away sooner. Hello, Ms. Kelleher. Good afternoon, Mr. Holt." She turned to her husband and gave him a civil (she hoped) nod. "Rob." She sat in the chair next to Leslie, trying not to let anyone see how nervous she was.

"So, you finally got here. Now we can get this thing settled," her ex began. She looked at him for the first time, then looked even closer, surprised. Rob looked uncharacteristically seedy. He was dressed carelessly in a threadbare sports jacket, worn jeans, and a cotton shirt he'd had before he married her. Beard stubble frosted his cheeks and chin, and his eyes, despite their unfriendly heat, looked reddened, tired. She'd never seen him in such condition, even when he'd come home from a camping trip with his buddies.

"Let's get on with this," Rob complained, throwing himself into a chair, his arms crossed on his chest in a gesture that managed to be defensive and threatening at the same time.

"Uh, yes, Ms. Marshall," Rob's lawyer began, settling a heavy opaque plastic garment bag at arm's length on the table. "My client claims that your cat Mithril damaged most of his clothing and some of his books yesterday."

"That's impossible," Leslie, willowy and auburn-haired, said, even before Elaine could reply. "You called me with this complaint yesterday afternoon, so the incident must have happened during the workday. The animal in question lives with Ms. Marshall, all the way across town from her ex-husband. Ms. Marshall works during the day, and her patients can vouch for her presence at the office. The cat stays indoors at her apartment while she works."

Rob's lawyer rattled the garment bag. "The evidence is undeniable."

"Neither my client nor her cat had the time or opportunity to commit such an attack. If I remember correctly, Mr. Smithson said throughout the divorce hearing that he never wanted to see his wife or that cat again. Neither the cat nor my client has been invited to Mr. Smithson's home. My client has never had a key to it." She looked pointedly at Elaine. "Mr. Smithson hasn't been to your apartment, has he?"

She shook her head. "No. When we exchanged the few things he'd overlooked, we did it in a grocery store parking lot. Neutral territory."

"Nevertheless," Holt insisted, "the damage has been done. Mr. Smithson will have to replace several business suits, eight dress shirts, a number of silk ties, two pairs of leather shoes, and some leisure clothing. Also ten hardback books, collector's items all."

"What is the nature of the damage you allege was done by my client's cat?" Leslie asked.

"Claw and tooth marks." The male lawyer reached for the garment bag and reluctantly unzipped it. The thick, pungent smell of cat urine leaped forth, permeating the room. The attorney donned disposable plastic gloves and pulled out a trouser leg and one sleeve of what had been Rob's best suit. Turning back the cuffs, he revealed shredded fabric.

"I see nothing that's conclusively a claw or tooth mark," returned Leslie, rising to inspect the suit. "That damage could easily be normal wear and tear. Let's face it, your client might have caught the hem on something as he walked. As for the smell, he could have leaned on a post that a cat had just sprayed. Or met a stray tom on the street that took a dislike to him." She didn't say it, but her look implied that it wouldn't be hard to justify such feelings. She sat down again. "From what I understand, your client's job takes him into warehouses and partially-finished buildings. Such an encounter is not inconceivable. Besides lack of opportunity, I'd like to point out that Ms. Marshall's cat was declawed soon after the marriage—at your client's insistence. The cat couldn't possibly have done damage like that."

"My client's wardrobe is currently unusable." Holt leaned forward toward the women after zipping the evidence back into its bag and divesting himself of the protective gloves. "Most of it permanently. He insists that your client's pet is responsible, and requests reparation in the form of ten thousand dollars. In addition, he is demanding that Ms. Marshall's cat be euthanized."

No! Elaine's nerves sluiced sudden ice along her veins.

Leslie's calming fingers touched Elaine's forearm beneath the table. "Your client's request is absurd, out of the question for such a spurious claim. What makes your client think Ms. Marshall's pet might be the culprit?" she asked.

Rob spoke up, his voice quivering with the depth of his anger. "Every time Elaine and I had a fight, the cat trashed my things. Once, after a really nasty argument, I went to stay with a friend for a couple of days. When I got back, the cat had shredded most of my slacks, a shirt, a belt, some pictures, and my favorite pair of exercise shoes, and sprayed them—all just like that." He pointed at the bag. "Who else would have done such a thing to me? That cat never liked me, even after I took pains to make friends with him."

"Do you have pictures of the former damage?" Leslie asked coolly. "Or better yet, did you keep the items?"

"No." Rob folded into his chair. "How could I? They reeked. I threw 'em all out."

Unflappable, Rob's attorney turned to Elaine. "you can't deny, Ms. Marshall, that your cat hated Mr. Smithson. That my client went to extreme measures to be friendly and likable to your pet. The cat is a menace and should be put down."

"Of course we can deny it. Your case is solely based on your client's word," Leslie snapped. "Mithril doesn't hate anybody. I've met the cat. He seems to be a very normal pet. He's got a great personality and, I repeat, doesn't have front claws. And I'd like to point out the lack of opportunity once more. Mithril's a house cat. My client never lets him outdoors. Even if she did, the cat doesn't even know where your client lives."

"We're back to the word of the client—that's what your client says . . ."

"Right." Leslie's tone shaded with sarcasm. "My client has not got a key to your client's abode. She was not available to provide transportation to her pet, as she was at work yesterday. Your client is claiming that the cat could get out of my client's house, run eight miles to a place he's never been before, break into Mr. Smithson's secure apartment, use his declawed paws to shred Mr. Smithson's clothing before urinating on it, and run back, all without leaving any evidence of his actions except for the ruined clothing. Sorry. It just doesn't lay. Ms. Marshall doesn't let her cat outside, Mr. Holt. Ever. Which is a fact that Mr. Smithson knows."

Leslie turned a cool professional look on Rob. "And, by the way, Mr. Smithson, what about your new girlfriend? Does she have a pet, either a dog or a cat?" Rob looked up in surprise at the smooth flanking maneuver. Perhaps he thought his new squeeze was a secret.

"My client doesn't have to answer such questions," Holt declared. "Those details have no impact on this discussion."

"Of course they do," Leslie continued. "My sources indicate that his girlfriend does have a pet—several of them, in fact—which means they could have done this damage. Even a neighborhood stray could be responsible: Your client leaves a door open, the stray runs in, does the damage, then splits. All much more plausible than pointing a finger at my client's distant and confined cat. This divorce was over several months ago. The papers are signed. We're not going to discuss reparations, and certainly no consideration will be given to euthanasia for Mithril. You and your client have no case, Mr. Holt." Leslie rose to exit. Despite trembling knees Elaine managed to follow, emulating her lawyer's regal stride as best she could.

"Your claim is absurd, Mr. Smithson," Leslie continued from the doorway. "It's founded on nothing but a

desire to create more heartbreak for my client, who's
been through quite enough already at your hands. It is
unconscionable, Mr. Holt, that your client desires retribution for a failed marriage so much that he threatens
her pet. I'll be taking this matter up with the judge—
who is an ardent cat lover. I imagine she'll have a great
deal to say about this."

"You haven't heard the last of this, you bitch . . ."
Elaine banged the thick door shut, cutting short Rob's
yell in mid-profanity.

Leslie led the way across the waiting area, down a
hall, and to her office. She closed the door behind them.
Elaine sank into a chair, feeling as though she'd
reached sanctuary.

"Coffee?" Leslie's voice was gentle.

"Yes, pl–please."

"Back shortly." The attorney returned in moments
with two steaming mugs on a tray, flanked by packets
of raw sugar and flavored creamers, which she set down
amid the papers piled on her desk. Gesturing Elaine to
pull her chair closer, Leslie stirred enough sugar into a
coffee cup to soothe a three year old's sweet tooth,
added a double dose of creamer, and plopped the cup
down on a marble coaster in front of her client.

"Drink up. You look like you could use it." She sank
down in her leather chair to doctor her own drink.

Elaine took a sip of the steaming, fragrant liquid, then
set down her mug. "Leslie, d–do you think he's got a
case against Mithril? I can't stand the thought of my cat
having to be . . ."

"Not a chance." The lawyer allowed a smile to take
over her features. "Especially since the new girlfriend
has pets. I remember Rob fussing about that once in a
deposition before your divorce. I can find the record if
I have to. You know, your ex hates animals. But, Elaine,
I have to say, he seemed convinced that Mithril had
done this to him. If he's right, he and Holt could get
DNA tests done if he wanted to be nasty about it. It
would be very expensive and time-consuming, and that's
something your ex doesn't like. He thought he could
bully you—that's cheap and easy. He failed. The testing

costs big bucks, and results take a while to get back. It would take that to be certain of his accusations, and I don't think Rob will spring for it. But, ridiculous as it seems, Rob seems to be sure of his facts." Her eyes speared Elaine's, curious. "Just between you and me, Mithril did it, didn't he?"

The two women stared at one another for a long minute, then dissolved into helpless laughter.

"I don't know for sure, and I can't figure out how he managed it, but I saw that suit. Rob's right—it looks just like Mithril's work," Elaine replied. "Mithril didn't like Rob from the beginning. He *has* done this before when Rob was particularly bad to me. You know, there have been nights after Rob moved out when I'd wake up and realize the cat wasn't on the pillow beside me, but he always came back very soon, as if he knew when I was listening for him. He's a heck of a watchcat, you know. I can always tell if a strange car pulls up or a salesman knocks on the door by his attitude. From the day I met Rob, Mithril always treated Rob like a stranger, until I decided to marry him. Then they came to an uneasy truce. But I knew Mithril was only making friends to please me. And the truce was broken every time Rob hurt me. Mithril always got even somehow."

Leslie looked at Elaine over the edge of her mug. "You can imagine what I spend on my suits, so that's one cat I'm going to stay in the good graces of, girlfriend."

"No problem there. Mithril'd never do that to you. Now, Rob, on the other hand . . . I wonder how Mithril did it? I wonder if I can help next time?" That earned a giggle from them both, then Leslie became serious again.

"You know, Rob can maybe push this matter to a hearing. If Mithril *did* do this, a DNA test will prove it. Rob's case is weak, because the divorce papers were signed a couple of months ago, and both of us know nearly all his belongings were in his possession prior to his signing. If he wanted to charge negligence, he should have done it before then. But I don't think there's a judge in this city who'll hear the case. Not even that Judge What's-'er-Name on television would take it. It's just too wacky."

"That's a relief." Elaine finished her coffee. "Hey, want to come to my place for dinner tonight? I'm going to roast a chicken with herbs."

"Mmmm, lovely. And it gives me a fine excuse to observe the suspect, see if he's exhibiting any signs of guilt."

"Six-thirty, then, and bring some of that Chardonnay you like." Elaine rose, setting down her cup. "Thanks, Leslie. I feel much better."

They walked toward the door. "My pleasure. I just wish there weren't so many men like Rob in the world; men who insist on making it difficult for the women they've hurt and abandoned, women who are just trying to put their lives back together. I'm with your cat on that—sometimes it's necessary to make those feelings known."

Elaine looked at her lawyer, her expression serious. "You know, in addition to acquiring you as a friend, there's one good lesson I've learned from going through this whole, nasty mess with Rob."

"What's that?"

She sucked in air, sighed it out, and smiled wryly at the attorney. "Next time, before I date a man seriously, I'm definitely going to listen to my cat!"

BOON COMPANION

by *Elizabeth Ann Scarborough*

Elizabeth Ann Scarborough is the Nebula Award-winning author of *The Healer's War*, as well as twenty-two other novels and numerous short stories. Her most recent books are *The Godmother's Web* and *Lady in the Loch*, as well as an anthology she edited, *Warrior Princesses*. She lives in a log cabin on the Washington coast with four lovely cats who find her useful for the inferior human DNA that granted her opposable thumbs for opening tuna cans. When she is not writing, she beads fanatically, and is also the author/designer/publisher of a bed book of fairy-tale designs called *Beadtime Stories*.

SASSAFRAS was but seven and a half weeks old when her mama finally died. Spring was cold and there were lots of other cats in the barn where Sass was born, which meant there was very little for a mama cat whose insides were not quite right anymore and an unripe kitten.

"Don't die, Mama. I been watchin' that Sally Cat and I think I can do what she does and hop us a mouse for supper. I will miss you, Mama."

Her mama had shushed her and pinned her down with a paw to wash her face one last time. "Mousin' will come soon enough, baby. But what you got to do is get yourself out of this barn. Barn cattin' ain't a good life for such as us. You know you had six brothers and sisters that perished before you and only you, with that little caul on your face, was born the right way. Did I mention that when I was born I had the same circumstance? And I have come to this barn late in my career, just long enough to deliver my younguns before I die, too.

"But you, baby girl, you are a special one, just like I

171

was, and it's up to you to play fate like a mouse and
make it feed you." She licked the long fur of Sassafras'
calico face. Sassafras bore red-and-white patches and a
black ear on the blue-eyed side, and black-and-white
patches with a red ear on the green-eyed. The effect was
lopsided but fetching, her mama had always said anyway.
The other cats hissed her and told her she was ugly.

"Who is fate? Would she really feed me? I heard old
Tom Fool say he was gonna kill me soon's you died."

"Don't give him the chance. I want you out of this
barn right away. You have to go look for your true callin' and to do that you will need help. Town help. You
have a pretty face and winnin' ways and if you're willin'
to play the handy mouse-catcher for a time, you can stay
alive in the home of some doting town-dweller while you
look for you boon companion."

"I got a boon companion, Mama? Other than you?"

"Not yet, but you will have one soon or you will likely
die. I never have told you how I come to be so low as
to be birthin' my kits in a barn, and I ain't got time to
tell you all of it now, but it was through the loss of my
own boon companion. One more thing I will say before
I gasp my last, little gal, and that is look among the
young and healthy for your own. They tend to hold up
better."

Sassafras' mama shushed her with another one of the
lullabies she purred to her all the time, but after a while
she broke off and didn't say anything else. Sassafras
licked her and tried to nurse, but it didn't do any good.
All the milk was gone, and so was the warmth, the
strength, the protection, and the tender care Mama had
given the kitten for the whole of her short life.

Presently along came ol' Tom Fool who, seeing the
situation for what it was, took a swipe at the orphaned
kitten, missed, and smacked her poor dead mama on the
her ear so hard his claws got stuck. That made Sassafras
so mad the anger inside her swelled up as big as a house
and blazed out of her eyes so it liked to fry Tom Fool.

He knew he was in trouble, too, cause he dragged
Sass' mama a little ways across the floor trying to loose
his claws, and when he did, he ran away, just as Sass
growled and pounced.

She nudged her mama back into her sleeping pose,
and lay down beside her again, but she knew this was
the end of her and the barn. Ol' Tom Fool or some
other cat would be after her now that she had no mama
to look after her. So when all the other cats were
sleepin' in the hay, Sassafras picked herself up and took
herself out of the barn and onto the long bumpy dirt
road leading off the property to another long road that
led to town. It was a far piece and a cold journey for a
little bitty kit, but fortunately, Sassafras was a longhair,
and she would curl up tight in the crook of a tree limb
and take her a little nap when she was tired.

One time (because during that period she didn't count
by days and nights but by waking and sleeping spells)
after she woke up, she heard a lot of noise and felt the
sun on the parts of her not shaded by the tree limbs.

Looking down from her perch, she saw she was outside a building and there were a lot of human kittens
playing in the yard. These were young and strong, just
like her mama had said for her to get, but they could
also be mean and cruel, as she knew from Tom Fool's
story of how he came to lose his tail to deceitful boys
with tin cans and firecrackers.

She watched those children all day long, studying
them to see if one of them might be her boon
companion.

One little gal sat off by herself reading and Sass was
drawn to her. She jumped down from the tree limb and
sat in the corner of the schoolroom window, under the
branch of a bush growing up against the building. She
watched that little girl read. And cough. She coughed
over and over, her mouth funneling into her hand, her
eyes tearing up. With her common sense as well as her
second sight, Sassafras figured that while this child might
be young, she was not strong. More than likely she'd be
gone before spring came again.

None of the others looked just right. The teacher
looked nice, but her gown was flecked with many colors
of cat fur. Sass reckoned others had a claim on the
teacher before her.

While the children were in class Sassafras hunted the
playground looking for a drop of spilled milk, a little

bite of something to tide her body over. Not much was left behind by the hungry youngsters, but she did find a dropped bite of chicken sandwich and gobbled it up.

School let out and as the children passed by her bush Sassafras stared hard at each one. This one cared more for dogs, that one was allergic to cats, another one liked cats but except for that didn't have a brain in her poor little head.

Sassafras followed after them at a safe distance. It got darker and colder, and pretty soon she was going to have to find another place to nap. But what she really needed the most was some more food. That previous morsel had filled up her little belly at the time, but it was long gone now.

As she padded along the one rutty windy road, something kept trying to lure her off it, out into the fields again, but she didn't give it any heed. She'd go hunting later on for a mouse small enough she could hop it without too much fear of bodily harm. Right now she needed to make tracks.

When it began to snow, she sat down on her haunches, curled her tail around her, and looked up at the whiteness coming down from the skies. It was pretty. It was cold. She said, "mew," in a complaining kind of way, just to let that fate gal know that she did not like the way this was going so far.

The town was a long way off. Or so she thought, until after a while when she came to a crossroads. There were no signs and if there had been, she couldn't have read them.

Since it didn't much matter which way she went, she closed her eyes, ran round widdershins following her own tail as fast as she could go and as many times as she could before she got almost too dizzy to stand, then she staggered off in the nearest direction.

She opened her eyes and stared up at the bottom of the grill of a great big old truck about to run right over her. Before she could run, the truck squealed like a rabbit and stopped and a gal in great big galoshes and a heavy coat jumped out.

A hand smelling like soap cupped Sassafras' entire body while another hand slid under her tail and back

paws and scooped her up so she was looking straight
into freckles and a pair of thick spectacles. "Little kitty,
you almost made catsup," the gal said. "What you doin'
out here in the middle of the road in the middle of the
winter anyway? You got no home, have you? Well, you
do now." And with no more ceremony than that, the
gal lowered Sassafras into one of the big pockets in the
front of the wool coat and they got back in the truck.

As soon as Sass got herself turned around, she crawled
up to the top of the pocket and looked around. The
landscape whizzed by at a speed faster than she could
run, and she mewed in dismay.

The gal lowered one finger and stroked Sass between
the ears. "Hush up, little kitty, Sophy's gonna take care
of you now. Nothin' gonna get you with Sophy here.
We'll take you home and show you to Mama. She'll be
glad to see somethin' as little and pretty as you. She
doesn't get to see much these days."

That was because Sophy's mama was not long for the
world. She was dying and that was a fact. Had there
been any question in anyone's mind at all that Sassafras
was coming to stay at the farmhouse with Sophy, Sass
put paid to it by making herself indispensable. She took
turns comforting Sophy's mama, purring her to sleep,
then comforting Sophy while she rested from her labor
of running the farm and taking care of her mama.

Sassafras plumb exhausted her own small self just
helping out. When the day came that Sophy's mama finally passed and it was time to bury her, Sass guarded
the house while Sophy went with the other relatives to
the graveyard.

It was a good thing, too. The house needed guarding.
Before Sophy had returned from her mama's grave,
there was a loudmouthed skinny woman with stiff-
looking yellow head fur and a thin sour mouth tapping
on the door and peering through the windows, then poking around outside. Pretty soon she was joined by a
heavyset gal with eyebrows that looked like they'd been
drawn on her face with one claw.

Sass just looked at them, then the heavyset one pulled
a key out of her purse and unlocked the door and
walked in, bold as brass. "I know Melinda kept it around

here somewhere," she said. "I always admired it even when we was small, and she told me a long time ago I could have it when she died. That was way back before she saddled herself with that horse of a girl."

"Well, she took the punch bowl and serving set our Granny meant to leave to me and I mean to have that back, too. And Sonny is bringing the truck later for Aunt Thea's sideboard and brass bed." But the woman didn't seem to be looking for the things she was talking about. Sass saw her pawing through the books on the shelves, especially the cookbooks up above the stove. While her back was turned, Sass skittered away down the hall. Behind her she heard the sound of doors and cabinets opening and slamming shut again.

"While he's at it, maybe he'll load up that television and home entertainment center Melinda got last year. She barely used it and I offered to buy it from her when she got sick, but she said I could just have it later. That girl won't need it when she goes back to the orphanage. No sense in it goin' to waste."

"No, indeed. And Melinda borrowed a recipe book from my Aunt Ally before the dear old soul died. I want it back for sentimental reasons."

Sass hid behind Sophy's mama's pillow and closed her eyes tight, trying to make herself invisible as the two horrible women rummaged through the house. In her mind's eye Sass saw them picking up bits and pieces wherever they went, figurines, knickknacks, a set of knives, whatever they could stuff into their pockets and purses.

They were still poking around when Sophy came home, her eyes all red and her shoulders sagging. Both of them made for the door like they were just going when Sophy came in.

"Hello, Sylvie," one of them said and Sassafras could tell the old gal knew Sophy' real name but was callin' her the wrong one out of contrariness, like she wasn't important enough to take notice of what she was called. "We just came to check the refrigerator to see what you might be needing. I know people will probably be bringing by cakes and casseroles and you can't possibly eat all of that by yourself. We'll be glad to take any of it

off your hands so you don't have to get fat or risk of-
fendin' people by lettin' their baked goods spoil," said
the woman. Her shoes, in spite of the winter weather,
were skinny little sandals on long narrow feet white as
plucked chickens with blue veins standing out on them.

"Speakin' of which," said the other one, whose puffy
feet spilled out over the tops of new black patent plastic
pumps, "Your mama borrowed an old recipe book offa
me and I want it back. You seen it? It's got a red and
white checked oilcloth cover."

Sophy shook her head and, trembling with anger,
waited silently while they left, their purses and pockets
clanking with things they'd stolen.

Sophy slammed the door behind them and plopped
herself down at the kitchen table with her head resting
on her clenched fists. Sass jumped up beside her on the
table, glad the old biddies hadn't managed to cart it off
yet. She inserted herself in the crook of Sophy's elbow
and mewed inquiringly.

"Poor little kitty, you probably haven't had a bite to
eat or a drop to drink this livelong day and for that
matter, I haven't either for all their going on about casseroles. If I was to take any casseroles to those two, I'd
lace 'em with rat p'ison first."

Once Sophy fixed Sass some supper, the girl looked
inclined to sit and cry again. Sass felt it was her bound
duty to do something cute and bewitching that would
keep her gal from foggin' up her glasses again. So,
selflessly taking no heed of her own hunger, the kitten
leaped over to the kitchen counter and stretched up to
the cup rack where she tapped a tiny paw on Sophy's
favorite mug. The one with the cat on it. Then Sassafras
walked over to sit beside the teakettle on the stovetop
and wait for Sophy to get the idea. It only took three
repeats, but Sass was patient and considerate of her
friend's fragile emotional state.

When the girl didn't pay her any mind after the third
try, Sass jumped back onto the table and gently, patiently, and considerately sank a single claw into the
hand Sophy was using to crumple the Kleenex to her
nose.

Sophy screeched, batted half a foot from where Sass

had been, and dabbed at her hand with the end of the
Kleenex. Sass, now that she had Sophy's attention, went
through her routine again, tapping the mug and sitting
by the teapot again.

"Bossy little thing, aren't you?" Sophy asked with a
sniff. "I had no idea kittens drank tea." But she filled
the kettle and put it back on the stove, stuck a teabag
that had only been used once before into her cup, and
calmed down some.

Sassafras relaxed and sprawled across the kitchen
table while Sophy drank. This was no time for her friend
to be backsliding just when she had been making so
much progress. Already Sass had taught Sophy to produce food, open doors, stroke and groom on request.
Not command. Sassafras didn't like being pushed around
and she didn't reckon anybody else did either. Besides,
Sophy could do all this with just little hints and nudges,
unless the poor girl was terribly preoccupied. Then, Sassafras had to allow that it took a little stronger language
and a slightly louder voice to produce results. Generally
speaking, though, the girl was intelligent and coopera-
tive, mostly biddable, and predisposed to be kind. But
those two old hissycats who had come to steal and pry
had none of those good qualities. Why, they would drive
an orphaned girl and an orphaned kitten from their
home and laugh about it afterward.

It was pure and simple up to Sass to help Sophy save
their home from those sneak thieves, or they'd be out
on their ears before the sun set again.

The kitten was studying on the matter when there was
a loud commotion at the door, like someone was about
to pound it in. Sophy blew her nose and went to see
who it was. A massive, sullen puppy of a boy stood in
the doorway. His boots were black and muddy and
smelled like the blood of slaughtered animals.

"What do you want here, Willie Pewterball?" Sophy
asked. Sass could tell by the girl's tone she didn't like
him.

"Come for that brass bed and sideboard my mama
wants—and the TV and stereo, too. You can help me
load 'em in the truck."

"I'll do no such thing. Those are mine. My mama left 'em to me."

"That's not what *my* mama says. She sent me to get 'em and I'm gonna get 'em. If you don't want to help, get out of my way," he said, and knocked Sophy aside when she tried to bar this entry. Sass attacked his ankles and he kicked her away.

Sophy, who was half knocked to the linoleum herself, reached down to pet Sass and make sure she was all right. Sass felt a little jolt, like someone had rubbed her fur the wrong way on a cold dry day and made sparks jump from it. Suddenly she was Sophy and Sophy was her and what they felt and who they were was the same. They were linked. This was the kind of thing Sass' mama had been talking about. What was in Sophy made what was in Sassafras bigger than ever it could have been had the kitten been her own. And if the kitten had already been in a huge snit, it was nothing compared to the bottled-up store of anger and grief that poured into her from Sophy. It was as intense and painful as the fit that came over Sass at Tom Fool when he hurt her poor dead mama's ear. Outrage and anger flooded from the girl into the cat, who had far fewer scruples about directing it back where it belonged. She growled at the boy.

"You keep that damn cat off me or I'll kill it," Willie said, but then he made the mistake of looking down at Sassafras.

He didn't have to look near as far as he thought he would. As it had with old Tom Fool, Sass' rage had made her as big as it was, and bigger, because she had Sophy's anger, too. Sass' back was up, her ears were flat, her fur was all bristly, and her tail was like a many-barbed whip of righteousness lashing behind her. She hissed and spat through fangs like the blades of pocket knives and lashed out at him with claws that looked five inches long to Willie.

He turned tail and lit out like his britches were on fire. "You're gonna get it!" he yelled back to Sophy. "You're not allowed to keep wild animals in the house!"

He jumped in his truck and roared away and Sophy, puzzled, looked down at Sass, who sat grooming her neat small self, licking the last few tufts of fur on her white right paw back into place.

"He's on drugs," Sophy said, fists on hips. "Has to be. Nothing else explains it. Somehow or other, even though he kicked you, you scared the pee-waddin' out of him and I say good riddance to bad rubbish." Then the air went out of her and she scooped Sass up and rubbed the kitten's side against her cheek. "But, oh, Sassafras, what are we going to do if he comes back with help? Other folks aren't gonna be scairt of a little pussycat like that fool. Shoot, he's likely to come back with the sheriff and try to arrest me for keepin' a dangerous animal."

Sass yeowed once and then reflected that both of them carrying on didn't do much good, so she started to purr a little song her mama used to purr to her. She purred the melody into Sophy's ear and beat time with her little tail, which was now a good four inches long, on the back of Sophy's neck.

> *"Hush, little baby, don't you cry*
> *You'll have your own place by and by.*
> *Mice in the walls and moles in the lawn*
> *Feed my kit when Mama's gone on."*

Sophy sat down and went back to her tea and stared into the cup. Sass kept on purring, and pretty soon Sophy began to run her finger around the top of the cup as she hummed. She wet the end of her finger and her cup made a whirring, chiming noise. Sass didn't like it at first, but it grew on her. It was part of the magic they were going to make between them to take care of their troubles.

They had to make them some protection. "Wards." The word came into her mind, and she knew right away that's what they needed. It wasn't like it was just a human kind of idea. Cats did it all the time when they marked their territory. They needed something to mark this house and all the things in it and all the property around it.

Sass jumped down and began racing around, rubbing her face at things and wondering why there were no tomcats around when you needed them. They had that handy tail-shaking thing they did that would be just the ticket in this situation. Sass stopped rubbing and looked up at Sophy. Sophy looked back at her. Didn't people have anything to ward off intruders? Surely they didn't expect their cats to do everything by themselves.

Sophy screwed up her face and said, "You know, kittycat, you've got a point there. What we need is something to keep people away from our property without knowing why they're doing it. Nothing you or I can say or do is going to make them go away if they know it's us doing it. But there's ways of makin' them steer clear so they think its their own idea. I don't know anything about that stuff, but old Miss Ally did, and she was a friend of my mama's. That old biddy niece of hers was awfully keen on havin' her recipe book, and I know my mama got it from Miss Ally before she died, but I'm durned if I recall what she did with it."

Sass, who had been wound tighter than a fiddle string, collapsed with relief and began grooming herself. The girl was coming along real well.

Sophy hunted high and low for the book, and at last she found it under her mama's mattress, between the ticking and the box springs.

Hugging it to herself, Sophy sat back down at the kitchen table while the kettle boiled again. Sass hopped back up to see what was in there.

"Hmmm," she said. "I was right, Sass. This is no book to make biscuits from. This is Miss Ally's witchin' book." Sophy said, and stroked her, nose to tail tip. "You know, Miss Ally had her a cat, too. She was so worried about her. Asked my mama not to let her cat nor her recipe book go to that niece of hers. Mama was fixin' to bring the cat over here when Miss Ally died and we couldn't find hide nor hair of that cat. Then Mama got sick before we could look anymore.

"Too bad Miss Ally died before Mama, or she might have been able to save her. She was wonderful with cures, Miss Ally was. Miss Ally was a witch, of course, but Mama didn't hold with witchin' so she always said Ally was a 'nature doctor.' But she was more what folks here call a white witch because she didn't do any harm.

And whatever Mama liked to think, Miss Ally had cures for more than just bodily diseases and injuries.

"She knew how to mend a broken heart or incline love in someone's direction—the girls in school talked about goin' to see her for such things. I reckon all that is in the recipe book."

Sass yawned and put her chin down on her paws. She took a nap while Sophy hunted around the house for things needed for a protection spell.

Sophy was pleased and that pleased Sass. Kittens needed a lot more sleep than she'd been getting lately, and she dozed off again while Sophy chanted happily to herself, "Iron filings—got them and some rusty nails, mountain ash berries from right out in the yard, three times three yards of red thread—why don't they just say nine?" she asked Sass and scratched her small pink tongue out from between her teeth, then blinked sleepily and rearranged herself into her compact napping posture.

Sophy continued. "Will you listen to this, Miss Sassafras? It says here we need to draw this picture of an eye here on a brown eggshell and break the egg on our doorstep. I reckon that way if someone comes that shouldn't, they'll slip on the egg and fall and break their necks. What do you think?"

Sass thought that sounded a little silly and wondered how it was supposed to do anything. It seemed to her something was missing from all this but she could hardly be expected to figure it out, young as she was, and without her sleep.

After a time during which something tangy and herbal boiled on the stove, Sophy scooped her up again, along with a sugar shaker full of stuff and the egg with the eye drawn on it, and carried her outdoors. It was growing dark later now and Sass realized with surprise that she had been here more of her life than she had been in the barn with Mama. She woke up and wriggled out of Sophy's grasp to climb up on her shoulder and watch what she did. Sophy walked around the house three times sprinkling a sugar shaker full of the herby smelling stuff and broke the egg on the doorstep. She said some words, too, but they didn't make much sense to Sass.

They both felt vaguely uneasy as Sophy carried her back inside the house, picked up the recipe book, and tied it in a plastic bag from the grocery store.

"I thought of the best place to hide this when we're not here, Sass. I'm gonna put it in the bottom of your pan and sprinkle litter over it, so don't scratch none too hard, okay? It's got oilcloth on the cover so the top and bottom will be all right."

Sass watched while Sophy did this and then went to her box and dampened the littler to add a little touch of realism to the scheme. Then she jumped up on the bed and stretched out diagonally across the middle of the bed. A few minutes later Sophy picked her up, and laid her back down against the curl of her own body.

A stinging sensation in her nose woke Sass sometime later. She opened her eyes and they began to water. The room was dark and fuzzy looking. Smoke.

Sass mewed and when Sophy didn't wake up that very minute, she hooked her hard on the hand for the good of them both, then jumped down before Sophy's reaction sent a wrathful hand to bat a cat off the bed.

Sophy opened her eyes, sniffed and cried, "Lord have mercy, what now?" She shoved her feet into her fleece-lined moccasins and staggered after Sass, who was near the door already.

The old outhouse was in flames. Before Sophy could unroll the garden hose and turn on the outside faucet, the smell was way worse than smoke. Sassafras retreated as far as she could while still keeping an eye on Sophy. She didn't want to return to the house where all the smoke was trapped inside either, so she ran up the road a ways thinking she might hop a mouse while Sophy put out the fire. That's when she saw Luly Pewterball's boy's truck. Good thing she *hadn't* returned to the house. That boy was not kind to small animals.

Still, she thought she had better warn Sophy. She sprinted back down the road to where Sophy was standing away from the soaked and smoldering ruins of the outhouse.

Sophy grunted and headed back for the house, but Sass meowed and meowed and snatched at her legs and ran away from the house and snatched again. The girl didn't have the sense God gave a goose though and went right in, even though the front door was still standing wide open.

Luly Pewterball and her boy came out of the bedroom as Sophy walked in.

"*You* set that fire!" Sophy said.

"What if he did?" the boy asked belligerently. He paused to cough. The smoke was still thick in the house. But Luly's mean little eyes narrowed up and she said, "No such thing. (*cough cough*) We saw the smoke and come to see if you were safe."

"You did (*cough*) not!" Sophy exclaimed hotly.

"That's right," the boy said, and moved menacingly toward her. "We (*cough*) did. 'Cause we figured if you were (*cough*) safe, we'd (*cough*) change that. Now, my mama really wants her (*cough, cough cough*) inheritance, and we can't (*cough*) find it (*cough*) anyway. Where'd you (*cough*) put it?"

"You better not (*cough*) hurt me," Sophy said. "I told people about you (*cough*) comin' here. I could have (*cough*) you charged with assault."

The boy had spotted Sass, and said, still coughing between all his words, "There's no law in this state against killin' feral cats, though. That one fooled me once, but I see she ain't so big now. Maybe I should open her up and see how she did that."

"Don't you touch her!" Sophy screamed and tried to catch Sass to put her out the door but only succeeded in blocking the exit. Sass scrabbled on the linoleum for half a second before rocketing in under the bed, then cursed herself for a fool. Now she was cornered.

Soon she was backed against the wall with a big ugly face looking down at her on two sides. She heard Sophy's steps and saw her feet edging toward the bedroom window. Bless her, she was going to open it and try to let Sass escape.

A long arm lashed out while Sass was watching Sophy and pulled the kitten's tail. It was a short tail, though, and the grasp was only a couple of fingers, so Sass got it back and huddled closer to the wall. Then the bed started to move.

"Let her alone! We haven't done anything to you.

Leave us be!" Sophy hollered, the effort costing her a whole long string of hard hacking coughs.

"Give me my book and we'll go," Luly told her.

Sass could hear Sophy's thoughts. She was about to break and give it to them. But Sass knew that wouldn't do any good. Luly would try to use the book then to get all of the rest that rightly belonged to Sophy, and maybe do them both harm and a good many other folks as well. She was mean. And even if Sophy did give them the book, that boy was even meaner than his mama and he was bound and determined to kill him a pussycat.

Oh, they needed help, and they needed it bad. Sass heard a cat crying and realized it was herself, bawling for her mama over and over again. Then she heard her mama's singing again in the back of her mind, the song Mama always sang when she returned to the nest whenever she head Sassafras howling from fear and worry.

"Hush, little kitten, don't you yelp
Mama's come a-runnin' here to help.
Moles in the yard and mice in the barn
Mama's gonna keep her babe from harm."

A pudgy-ringed hand sideswiped Sass and then closed around the kitten's leg.

But just then they all became aware that a siren had been blaring outside because suddenly it cut off and there was a banging on the front door, then it slammed open.

"Where's the fire?" A masculine voice yelled.

"Here!" Sophy called. "In here!"

Three young men in heavy boots stormed into the room. They started coughing, too, as soon as they came in.

Luly let go of Sass' foot and both she and her boy stood up. "We'll just be (*cough*) going now, Sophy, but you give us a call when you find that thing we were discussin'," Luly said, as if the visit had been a friendly one.

"It's nothin', boys," Willie laughed loudly to cover up what Sophy was trying to tell the firemen. "You know how hysterical these old maids get about burnin' outhouses and cats in trees."

The Pewterballs skedaddled out of there quicker than the outhouse had gone up in flames.

Sophy needed to tell the volunteer firemen, two of whom were father and son, the son being a high school classmate of Sophy's, what had happened.

Sophy began talking excitedly, trying to tell them what the horrible Pewterballs had done, but she was coughing so hard in between her words that the men, who were coughing too hard to be able to listen carefully, didn't pay much attention to her. The excitement was all over, the fire was out, and the house was still full of nasty-smelling smoke. They were in quite a hurry to get out of there. Her classmate's daddy offered to take Sophy over to their house for the night, but Sophy said she didn't want to leave her kitten alone and the daddy said that they had a big old dog who would take exception to a cat. So they left, the daddy giving Sophy his telephone number.

Sass crawled out from under the bed.

Sophy sat up the rest of the night in her mama's rocker, and Sass curled in her lap and slept a fear-exhausted sleep. The house still stank from the fire, but Sass was too played out to care.

Later in the day, when Sophy had cleared the house as best she could with electric fans and nice smelling candles, the girl told Sass, "I should just get rid of that book, kittycat. It doesn't work anyway. I did that protection spell just like it said in there, and it didn't do a darn bit of good. And if those firemen were what it brought, all I can say is that it took its time gettin' them here."

Sass jumped down and went to her box to scratch. Sophy laughed, "I know you don't think much of it either, but Miss Ally set too much store by it for you to be poopin' on it." She plucked the book from the box and shook the cat litter off it while Sass did her duty.

When Sass returned, Sophy was sitting at the table with the book open, staring at it. "You know, there's something peculiar about this book if it is the spellin' book Miss Ally used for her white witchin'. There's plenty of recipes, like it says, with funny ingredients in them and they all sound magical enough, but it doesn't seem right somehow. I thought witchin' had more to it than that. Aren't there spells or somethin' you have to say?"

Sass stepped onto the open book and lay down. Right away she knew the book *was* magic because she could feel all the magical words soaking into her right through her belly, filling her full of spells and sorcery. She felt something else, too. She felt something of her own dear mama about this book, and it confirmed what she had been reckoning ever since Sophy told her about Miss Ally's cat disappearing. Miss Ally had been mama's boon companion and this was *her* book. And now it was theirs, hers and Sophy's. She stood up and put a paw on Sophy's hunched-over shoulder and licked her cheek, backed up, sat down on the book, and mewed in a humorous tone. What was missing from the recipes was right under Sophy's nose and right behind Sass's own! It was herself. And as for the spells—her mama loved her and would not have left her all alone in the world without teaching her the magic words she needed to follow her career of controlling world events to suit herself. All those little purred nursery rhymes and lullabies *were* the magic words. The book was only to give people like Miss Ally and Sophy a list to look at so that they could do the tedious gathering of items a cat couldn't easily describe or tell them where to locate without speaking words of human language.

Excited by her new insight, Sass leaped back and forth from the kitchen counter to the table and batted at the remnants of the ingredients Sophy had used in the useless warding spell of the previous day. *Now* they could make it work.

Sophy looked at her sadly. "You poor little thing. Did all that smoke addle your brains? You act like you belong in the county asylum, though I don't believe they take kittykats."

But while Sophy was young and much burdened with cares beyond her years, she was not stupid. She followed Sass' directions and began putting together the same ingredients as the night before. Only this time, there was a difference. Instead of keeping her mama's song to herself, Sassafras sat on Sophy's shoulder as she mixed, grated, pounded, boiled, and stewed the fixins for the ward spell. And while Sophy did all the manual labor requiring the use of thumbs and fingers, Sass purred her the protection spell Mama had taught her, the one that had come into her head when Sophy mixed up the potion before.

> *"Hush little baby don't you cry*
> *You'll have your own place by and by.*
> *Mice in the walls and moles in the lawn*
> *Feed my kit when Mama's gone on."*

But that, Sass remembered as she sang to Sophy, was just the first verse.

The second was:

> *"Hush, little children, don't be afraid.*
> *Wait till you see what mama's made.*
> *Sprinkle all around like tomcat pee*
> *Keep our house safe as safe can be."*

But then she remembered a more crucial verse, one that called for an ingredient only she could provide. It came into her head just as Sophy was about to blend all the fixin's together.

Sass hopped down, went over to the doorjamb and stretched herself up as high as she would go, almost a whole entire foot, and scratched her little claws for all they were worth, till some of the casings came away with the wood splinters.

Then she mewed for Sophy to come pick them up.

Sophy had come to know that mew and had learned that it meant she needed to pay right smart attention to what was being told her.

She gathered up claws and splinters and all in the dustpan and with a look at Sass, dumped them into the brew. Sass sang her the last verse, purring triumphantly.

> *"Hush, my kit, don't flap your jaw.*
> *Put you in just a little claw.*
> *Gives your ward-juice mighty paws*
> *To smack them breakin' mama's laws."*

They worked all day long brewing up a huge batch of the magic mixture until Sophy's arms ached and Sass' purrer was worn to a frazzle.

But then it was time to sprinkle it. This time they had enough to circle the house, the drive where Sophy's truck was parked, the henhouse, and the barn even though it didn't have ary a horse or cow anymore, and the biggest trees. Sophy sprinkled the mixture onto the snow and Sass purred her spells as they circled the property, widdershins, counterclockwise, singing the spell through three times three times seven.

For a long time, they were left in peace and the Pewterballs didn't come near enough for Sophy to know of it or be troubled by it.

Sass grew in length, strength, and beauty, and she and Sophy were soon able to talk to each other right clearly with no words passing anybody's lips. She and Sophy practiced lots of the spells, as much as they could by themselves. Sophy carried potion with her whenever she left the house and farmyard and Sass was careful never to hunt outside the charmed circle. One day, Sophy took the recipe book to the town library and used the copy machine to make another book, which she put with her school things.

Then spring came, and as Sass shed much of her heavy, long coat, so the farmyard shed the snow, which melted, running away in little rivulets from the charmed circle.

Back came Luly Pewterball and her awful offspring, one sunny day while Sophy was at school.

Sassafras recalled the burping gasping noise of Willie Pewterball's truck and ran for cover when she heard it. She hid under the sofa, up inside the frame where she had pulled loose the stuffing to make herself a cozy nest. They weren't likely to find her there, she thought.

"Well, I'll be if this ain't our lucky day, Willie!" Luly cried. "There's my very book lyin' open there on the table where that careless girl must have left it! She doesn't deserve such a treasure."

"Then take it and let's go, Mama. This place gives me the creeps."

"It's not like you to be so timid, Willie."

"No, ma'am, but let's leave all the same."

When Sophy came home and found the book gone, Sass told her what had happened and she called the sheriff. Of course, the Pewterballs lied about it.

But that was all right, because Sophy had her copy and right away between them they whomped up a spell to get the book back.

> *"Hush, little children, don't you yearn*
> *Bad folks got them a lot to learn.*
> *Their luck will sour and their guts will burn*
> *Till what's not theirs is safe returned."*

The spell was not purred like the others but transmitted in a low, threatening growl. Sassafras enjoyed singing it a lot.

Once it was made, all they had to do was wait. Normally, you had to put a potion or something within range of the people that needed spellin', but in this case the recipe said, the thing that had been stolen provided the contact.

Sass made up her own verse now, which showed she was getting bigger and better at this.

> *"Luly and Willie, time to weep*
> *You won't rest and you won't sleep*
> *You won't drink and you won't eat*
> *While our spell book's in your keep."*

On the third day after the theft, Sophy found the recipe book in her mailbox with a note from Luly attached.

"Keep it. The damn thing doesn't work anyway."

Sophy giggled as she showed it to Sass, but Sass just washed her tail and smiled to herself. Of course the spell book wouldn't work without a cat to sing the words. And as mean as Willie was to animals, he was about as likely to turn into a horny toad as he was to get any cat to do charms for him and his horrible mama.

The Pewterballs picked up and left town after that and nobody heard from them again except the skinny gal who had come with Luly on the first day. She was nicer now and taking her medicine real regular these days. She came by to return what she had stolen from Sophy's house and to tell her that she had received a letter from Willie, wanting cigarette money, since the prison guards wouldn't give him any without him buying them.

Sassafras winked at Sophy and Sophy winked at Sass, but neither one of them let on about what they knew.

PUNKINELLA

by Deb Stover

As a child, Deb Stover wanted to be Lois Lane, until she discovered that Clark Kent is a fraud and there is no Superman. Stover has received over a dozen awards for her unique work, and *Publishers Weekly* once called her "clever, original, and quick-witted." Also "contorted," but she tries to ignore that part . . . Deb's tenth novel, *Mulligan Stew,* is a contemporary romantic fantasy release. For more information, visit www.debstover.com.

SHARON Detwiler stared at her reflection in the bathroom mirror. "You're fat," she muttered. "Ugly." She sniffled, wiping her nose with the back of her hand. "Hideous."

Her lower lip trembled and tears filled her eyes again. Her mousy brown hair was plastered to one side of her head, tears and snot had left streaks on her face, and splotchy red patches marred her already ruddy complexion.

In short, she looked like hell. Hadn't Larry said so?

Sharon's face contorted in rage and she shook her fist. "Congratulations, Larry. You were right. Does that make you *happy?*"

Sobs tore at her throat as she grabbed a tissue and blew her nose. After several deep breaths, she regained some semblance of control and looked at her puffy face again.

No wonder Larry had left her. What man would want a fat, ugly wife with cellulite on top of her cellulite? She sniffled again.

What had she been thinking? Of course, it made perfect sense that Larry would leave her for his new bouncing blonde secretary—named Bambi, of all things—who was young enough to be his daughter.

It didn't make sense. Nothing did anymore. Logic had

always been Sharon's friend. She'd made a career out of
numbers and logic. She lifted her chin a notch and
squared her shoulders. She was a CPA, made a decent
living, and now she had the house to herself.

Yeah, right. Accountants were boring. She was boring.
Everyone she loved had abandoned her.

The kids were grown. Larry was gone. She was alone.

Her lower lip trembled again, and she bit down on it
brutally. Pushing herself away from the bathroom
counter, she staggered into her bedroom and refilled her
brandy snifter. No little slosh of cognac for Sharon. Not
tonight. She absently glanced at the decanter, realizing
she'd consumed almost its entire contents.

"Hurray for me." She lifted her glass in a mock toast
and gulped a huge mouthful of burning liquor, coughing
as it slid down her throat.

They called this stuff liquid courage for a reason. Oh,
yes, she was definitely brave enough right now to confront her asshole of a husband. No problem. If she had
a gun, she'd drive over to his little love nest and blow
Bambi's simpering face off.

And she'd aim much lower when she took care of
Larry.

"Bastard." She drained the contents of her glass, and
her belly roiled. Placing a hand over it, she dropped the
snifter to the carpet and staggered to her bed, falling
face first atop the satin spread Larry had chosen. She
raised up and stared at the bronze spread, hating it. Hating Larry.

The tears came again, and she took solace in watching
them stain Larry's precious bedspread. She was over
forty and alone.

She balled up her fist and punched the spread. If only
she could live her life over again. If only she could go
back and make different choices. If only . . .

"All right, then, let's get to work," a grating voice
said from behind Sharon.

She opened her eyes, blinking. "Who . . . ?" Slowly,
Sharon raised up and looked over her shoulder. A
woman stood there wearing a crooked crown and holding a stick with a star on the end of it that looked as if
it had seen better days.

Her gaze settled on the woman's face and the acid level in her stomach hit a new high. "Oh. My. God."

"Not quite, punkin'."

Sharon swung herself to a sitting position, holding her head with both hands. Her mother was dead, but this strange creature standing in Sharon's bedroom could be the woman's clone.

"Not a clone." Her mother opened her arms and reached toward her. "Is this how you greet your own mother?"

"Oh, God." Sharon shook her head and closed her eyes. "Am I asleep?"

"Nope." Her mother straightened her crown and waved her wand-stick-whatever with a flourish. Sparkles filled the air in its wake. "It's magic. Ain't it a blast?"

"Mom?" Sharon pushed to her feet. "How? No, never mind. This can't be real."

" 'Course it's real." Her mother made that infernal tsking sound with her tongue. "It's your dear, departed mother. Are you ready for this?"

"No." The alcohol level in Sharon's blood must be astronomical to create such a realistic—and horrific—hallucination. "You're not real."

"I'm your fairy godmother." Her mother's husky laughter filled the room. "This should be fun."

"Fun." Sharon's head throbbed and her mouth tasted like crap. "I need some aspirin." She went into the bathroom and popped two aspirin, washing them down with plain water. No more cognac for her.

She caught a glimpse of her mother—rather, her hallucination—in the doorway and watched her float into the bathroom. "What are you doing?"

"You always were the stubborn one." She positioned herself directly behind Sharon. "Now, see for yourself." She pointed her magic wand toward the mirror.

Sharon blinked, leaning her head to one side, then the other. Her hallucination was right behind her, but there was no reflection in the mirror. "Huh. This just proves you don't really exit, so go away."

"How do you expect me to grant your wish unless you show your mother a little respect?"

Oh, now *that* really sounded like Mom. "Go away," she whispered.

"You always were an ungrateful and selfish child."

That sounded even more like her mother—the Connie O'Toole she'd loved and hated most of her life. "Mom?"

"In the flesh—er, well, not exactly." Her mother heaved a sigh. "I'm your fairy godmother. For now." The woman laughed. "I guess that makes you Punkinella."

Sharon groaned.

"Damn shame they don't allow smoking in heaven." Mom looked around the bathroom. "Got a cigarette?"

"That's what killed you, Mom." Sharon swallowed the lump in her throat and opened the medicine cabinet for the bottle of antacids and chewed three. "And you know I don't smoke."

"Boring as ever, I see."

"Lung cancer is exciting?" Sharon winced at her own words. "I'm sorry, Mom. I shouldn't—" She grabbed her forehead. "What the hell am I doing? This is nuts. I'm asleep and dreaming it all."

Her mother folded her arms beneath her ample bosom and her lips pressed into a thin line. It was the same look she'd worn when Sharon had announced her intention to major in accounting.

"I was right."

"Are you reading my mind?" Sharon asked, giving her mother's sparkly, diaphanous gown a good look. "So I'm supposed to believe that you're an angel?"

Mom coughed and laughed, then floated out of the bathroom with a befuddled Sharon close behind. "I most certainly am not an angel, though I am some kind of spirit." She shrugged. "I was sent on a mission."

"Namely me?"

"Bingo."

"What kind of mission?" Suspicion oozed through Sharon. "Mom? What kind of mission?"

"I told you already." Mom shook her head. "You never listen. If you would have listened when I—"

"What *kind* of mission?" Sharon repeated through clenched teeth.

"I'm here to fix your messed-up life, of course."

"Ah, that's where this fairy godmother gig comes into play, I suppose?" Sharon arched an eyebrow and waited. The fact that she was buying into any of this should've worried her.

No, it should've terrified her.

"All right, so let's get to work," Mom said, standing in the middle of the bedroom. "You said you want to do it over. Are you sure about that?"

"Wh . . . No, I'm not sure of anything." Sharon shoved her hair back from her face and started pacing. Then that lust for revenge hit her full force again and she froze, spinning around to face this figment of her pickled imagination. "Are you telling me you have the power to—"

"Grant your wish, or a better version of it." Her mother shook her head again. "I mean, really, Sharon, you can do better."

"Better than what?" God, she was so confused!

"You want to go back and live all the hell over again?" Mom's expression was skeptical. "I mean, all the misery? Let's face it, you may be older, but you're a whole lot smarter now than you were when you let Larry get in your panties."

"I know."

"I told you the first time you went out with that walking, living, breathing ego that he'd turn out to be an asshole."

"You were right." Sharon sighed. "Worse than an asshole."

"Back to business." Mom waved her stick or wand again. "Your wish is my command."

"Get real."

"I am. Accept it."

"This is nuts." Sharon laughed nervously. "All right. I want to be young and beautiful." She drew a shaky breath. "Most of all, I want . . ."

"Say it, Sharon."

She met her mother's gaze. "I want to get even with that son of a bitch. I want to scratch Bambi's eyes out. I want . . ."

"Revenge isn't all it's cracked up to be."

"Maybe." Sharon chewed her lower lip. "But it's all I can think about."

Her mother appeared thoughtful, then asked, "Instead of going back in time, wouldn't you prefer to look young and beautiful but with an older and wiser head on your shoulders?" Mom tapped the magic wand against the knuckles of the opposite hand. "We learn from our mistakes, after all."

"That's true." Sharon frowned. "I'm not sure."

"Yes, you are."

"No, I'm not."

"Yes, y—"

"No!" Sharon pressed her hands over her ears. "You're doing it again. Christ, you're doing it from your grave. Sometimes I'm right, Mom. Accept it."

Her mother smirked and took a step toward Sharon. "All right, what year do you want to go back and start from?"

"1976 was a good year."

"Yes, and I'll be right there at your side again." Her mother batted her lashes.

"Oh." That was a kick in the gut. "If I go back in time, then . . ."

"We all do." Connie O'Toole's smile was downright disgusting.

"I see." Sharon drew a shaky breath, then released it very slowly.

"And, frankly, I'm not sure if I want to go through menopause again." Mom shuddered visibly. "I'm dead, you're not. Let's fix your life without messing with mine. Besides menopause, there was the cancer. I'm finished. You're not."

"I'm sorry, Mom." She approached the woman and tried to hug her, but a strange electrical charge stopped her just short of contact. "What's that?"

"A barrier between your plane and mine. Nothing to worry about. It comes with the gig." Mom smiled. "All right, now. Who do you want to look like?"

"You can *do* that?" Sharon looked at the mirror over her dressing table. "Julia Roberts? Sandra Bullock? Pamela Anderson?"

"Or . . . do you want to look like Bambi?" her mother chided, batting her lashes ninety miles a minute.

"Well, damn." Sharon drew a deep breath, forcing herself to be realistic. Now *there* was a joke. Nothing about this even came close to realistic. "Okay, I want to look like me, only better."

Mom waved the magic wand and the room went dark. Breath was sucked from Sharon's lungs and a burning sensation covered her skin from head to toe.

"What the hell?"

The lights came back on and Sharon stared in awe. She blinked several times as the image became clearer. Her wrinkles were gone, her eyebrows were back up where they belonged, and the jowls she'd started to develop recently were nonexistent. She looked downward, gasping. Her breasts were high and firm again—fuller than she remembered them ever being.

She cupped her hands beneath them and turned to stare at her profile. "Amazing." And her waist was narrow, sloping gently to perfectly proportioned hips. Curious now, she lifted the edge of her flannel nightgown and looked at her smooth, cellulite-free thighs. "How'd you do that?"

"Magic, punkin." Her mother's voice was quieter now. "You said you, only better. Is this what you meant?"

Sharon blinked, staring at herself again. She nodded, swallowing the lump in her throat. "Thanks, Mom."

"You're welcome." Mom's tone seemed wistful. "It's time for me to go back now."

Sharon whirled around and faced her mother. "Wait! What am I supposed to do with the new me?" She gave a derisive laugh, seriously concerned about her mental state.

"You said you wanted revenge." Mom lifted one shoulder, but her expression was solemn. "Be careful what you wish for, Sharon. Make sure you get what you really want. Really deserve . . ."

Sharon drew a shaky breath. "I do want revenge," she said, clenching her fists. "More than anything."

"Just be sure. What about the Spring Dance at the country club?" Her mother reached out as if to cup her cheek, then began to fade. "Be very sure."

"The dance." Sharon smiled. "I'll need a new dress."

"Dress to kill." Her mother faded even more.

"Mom, don't go." Tears gathered in the corners of Sharon's eyes. Despite her mother's imperfections, she'd missed her.

"I have to."

"Will . . . will I see you again?"

"I'll check on you again." Mom smiled and blew Sharon a kiss. "You know what, punkin?"

"What?" Tears clogged her throat.

Her image faded, leaving only her voice behind. "Being your mom was the best thing I ever did."

"I love you, Mom."

A bowling ball hurtled down the lane and crashed into the pins that were Sharon's brain. A strike every time. Clutching her throbbing skull, she sat up in bed and opened one eye, then shut it immediately.

Sunshine blasted like a laser through the windows and her brain. What was left of her brain . . . *Another strike. Perfect score.*

Her stomach roiled and she recognized her headache as the lesser of two evils. She dashed to the bathroom just in time to hug the commode for several minutes, then hung over the sink while she brushed her teeth and fumbled for some aspirin, keeping her eyes closed as much as possible.

After swallowing the medication she climbed into the shower and allowed steam and warm water to revive her. By the time she reached for a towel, she felt woozy but alive. Almost human. Her head still throbbed, but more like classic rock than heavy metal with bass set to kill.

She grabbed a towel and scrubbed herself dry, glancing down at her downright perky breasts. "Mom," she whispered, lunging for the mirror to wipe away the steam.

The new Sharon stared back at her. "It wasn't a dream?" She shook her head, reaching out to touch her unwrinkled reflection. Steam encroached on the image, so she wiped the mirror clean again. Narrow waist, high breasts, no wrinkles.

It *had* happened. Her mother's weird visit had been

much, much more than a dream or a nightmare. Dumpy Sharon Detwiler's bustline rivaled Pamela Anderson's. Her butt was better than Jennifer Lopez's. She was a . . . babe.

A smile curved her lips and she remembered why she'd wanted the new look. Revenge. She would buy herself a dress that would make Larry drool, then she'd dump *him* instead of being the dump*ee*. And poor little Bambi would learn how it felt to have her man stolen out from under her.

Energy flowed through Sharon as she threw on a pair of jeans that were looser around the waist and hips than they had been last time she'd worn them. She managed to squeeze herself into an old, stretched-out bra, but all the others were too tight. *Yes!* And her sweater looked as if she'd been poured into it.

She punched in her office number and let them know she wouldn't be in today, then grabbed her purse and headed to an exclusive boutique she'd always wanted to shop in, but had never been brave enough to enter until now. Today, she strolled into the place without qualms and tried on an incredibly short black cocktail dress designed to fit like a second skin. The sales clerk informed Sharon that the one she'd chosen was too big, and returned a moment later with one in a size Sharon hadn't worn since about seventh grade.

As the sleek, shimmery fabric skimmed her body, she actually cackled with delight. She even had *cleavage,* of all things. Amazing. The clerk gave her a knowing smile.

Sharon selected stockings with a sparkly finish and a pair of dangerously high heels to complete the look. Once upon a time, she would've said she looked like a high-priced hooker, but her new daring self refused to allow her old narrow-mindedness to interfere.

She was a woman on a mission, after all.

After bribing the receptionist at the most expensive salon in town, she managed to secure an appointment with Mr. Roy. His talents were legendary, yet Sharon had never considered herself worth his exorbitant cost. But now it was all part of the whole picture that would help her achieve her goal.

After all, revenge had no price tag. . . .

Mr. Roy was a small man with dark hair and a soft voice. "What is your heart's desire?" he asked.

Sharon knew she'd come to the right place. "Make me irresistible."

Two hundred dollars poorer, she walked out of the salon with a sophisticated cut and shimmering auburn highlights. Men actually stared at her as she walked to her car. A construction worker made a suggestion that would have made her blush before, but now she simply laughed and tossed her highlighted locks over her shoulder.

Never in her forty-three years had she felt this much confidence. Larry would never be able to hurt her again. No man would. She was not only irresistible.

She was invincible.

She sashayed into the country club with the invitation that had arrived weeks earlier, addressed to Mr. and Mrs. Larry Detwiler. Well, Mrs. Detwiler had invested an obscene amount of money into her assumption that Mr. Detwiler would also attend.

With Bambi.

And they would never forget their first communal experience with the country club crowd. Sharon would see to that.

George the doorman did a double-take when she showed him the invitation.

"It's really me, George," Sharon said, laughing at his openmouthed, wide-eyed reaction to her transformation. "Honest."

"Yes, ma'am." He cleared his throat. "I hope you don't mind if I say that you look really . . . hot, Mrs. Detwiler."

Sharon laughed again and thanked George, then concentrated on the swing of her hips as she crossed the marbled foyer toward the ballroom. The staccato rhythm of her heels pounded her mantra through her mind, reinforcing her determination.

Larry and Bambi will pay.

Stodgy businessmen she'd known for decades stared with open appreciation. Once recognition registered, shock was the universal and unmistakable reaction.

Sharon danced with several men and tolerated a little groping, but she wasn't happy, because there was no sign of Larry or his bouncing, blonde Bambi. Surely they would show. She'd gambled that they would.

As she quenched her thirst on a fourth glass of champagne, a voice from behind her lasered right for her bone marrow. Deep, resonant, intimate. And definitely *not* Larry.

She spun around to face the owner of the sexy baritone and found herself staring into the greenest eyes she'd ever seen. His face was tanned, his smile deadly.

"Would you care to dance?" he asked, his appreciative gaze sweeping the length of her. Twice.

"Y–yes." Sharon the wallflower was the belle of the ball for the first time in her life. And she *liked* it.

To the rhythm of Nat King Cole's "Unforgettable," Sharon learned her admirer's name was Sam McClintock, and that he was a professional golfer. She'd never followed golf, so his name didn't register, but the rest of him certainly did.

Sam said all the right things, made all the right moves, and reminded her she was a desirable woman at every turn. He looked at her with adoration, and she made another shocking discovery.

He was actually *nice*.

She'd always assumed men like him would be first class jerks, but not this guy. He gave time and money to several charities, was active in the community, and now that he was retired from the pro circuit, he wanted to settle down.

Sam left her standing on the balcony and went to get more champagne. Sharon leaned on the rail, gulping the cool evening air.

"Sharon, is that you?" Larry said.

She whirled around to face him. Light from inside flowed around him. Now was her chance. "In the flesh," she said.

"So I see." He took a step closer. "I saw you on the dance floor."

"Hmm." She held her breath, wondering what her estranged husband thought of the changes in her. "And?"

"You . . . look fabulous." He released all the air from his lungs with a loud whoosh. "Could I come by later so we can talk?"

Now he stood so close she could smell the aftershave she'd given him last Christmas. A small tremor swept through her and she tilted her head back to meet his gaze. "Why?"

"I . . . you . . ." He raked his hand through his hair and lifted a shoulder. "I miss you."

She digested that for a few moments. This was her big chance. The anger she'd felt over his rejection whipped through her again. "What about Bambi?" she asked caustically.

"Maybe . . . I don't know." He shook his head and reached out to put his hands on her bare arms.

Sharon felt nothing from his touch. No warmth. No tingle. Not one iota of desire. Sam only had to say her name to turn her insides to gelatin.

What had Mom said? *Be careful what you wish for, Sharon. Make sure you get what you really want. Really deserve . . ."*

Did she want revenge more than she wanted a *life?*

A shadow emerged from inside. Sharon recognized Bambi's big hair immediately. The woman's eyes were round, her lower lip trembling as she stood staring at them with betrayal in her heavily made-up eyes.

Revenge was supposed to be sweet. All she felt was emptiness.

And guilt.

Why should she feel guilty? She was the wronged woman. Bambi was the enemy.

It didn't matter why. Sharon *did* feel guilty. Hell, she hadn't even done anything, though she'd certainly thought about it.

Bambi's shoulders drooped, and Sharon looked up at Larry again. "I don't want you, Larry," she whispered. "Bambi does. Go to her."

He appeared startled as she eased away and turned her back, pretending she hadn't seen Bambi at all. She sensed Larry's continued presence for a few moments, then she heard him walk away.

This time there were no tears, no self-deprecation. No, all she felt was a sense of relief and freedom. God, what incredible freedom.

"Champagne?" Sam asked, standing shoulder to

shoulder with her as she looked out across the garden below.

She half-turned and looked up at him, growing more and more aware of her sense of him and all the possibilities. The future was hers to do with as she pleased.

"Be careful what you wish for, Sharon. Make sure you get what you really want. Really deserve . . ."

"I will," she murmured, laughing at herself.

Sam smiled as he handed her the champagne flute, their hands brushing together for a brief but poignant moment. Warmth and happiness filled Sharon as she took a sip, then looked toward the open doors to the ballroom.

The faint outline of a figure stood beneath the archway, a crooked crown on her head and a magic wand in her hand. Her mother waved the wand through the air, creating a rainbow of multifaceted sparkles over her head. Then Connie O'Toole smiled, made a thumbs-up gesture, and blew her daughter a kiss.

A moment later, she was gone.

No, Mom wasn't gone—not really. A part of her would always live in Sharon's heart. She didn't need revenge, bigger boobs, or even auburn highlights to be happy. What she needed was a sense of self-worth and pride.

Her mother had shown her that.

Sharon set her champagne glass on the railing and took Sam's hand, smiling up at him and at the strength and determination that filled her. She smiled and he gave her hand a squeeze.

"Will you excuse me while I visit the powder room?" she asked, suddenly needing a minute to herself.

"Will you come back?" His appreciative gaze held hers, desire etched across his ruggedly handsome features.

"Yes," she breathed, her heart doing the "Minute Waltz" in about ten seconds.

She made her way through the crowd to the powder room and leaned against the counter for several minutes before she grew aware of someone staring at her. She looked in the mirror and saw Bambi.

"I . . . I just wanted to say thank you," the younger woman said.

The hatred Sharon had felt toward Bambi had diminished to mild resentment in less than an hour. In fact, she couldn't suppress a strong feeling of pity for Bambi. After all, Bambi had Larry.

"I appreciate you not trying to come between me and Larry," Bambi continued.

"No problem." Sharon drew a steadying breath. "Good luck." Unfortunately, the idealistic young woman would probably need it.

"Thank you. That's very sweet of you."

"Not at all."

The blonde spun around and left, leaving a cloud of perfume in her wake. Sharon drew a deep breath and squared her shoulders, then turned to face the mirror.

The face staring back at her was the same one she saw every morning. The breasts were no larger, no higher, and the crow's-feet at the corners of her eyes w ere still there. She knew without looking that the cellulite would still be present, too.

Suddenly, she recognized another truth. Her mother hadn't actually made her look different at all. She'd merely altered Sharon's perception of herself. But why had her clothes fit differently after her mother'd waved the magic wand?

"You dummy." She shook her head, remembering how Larry had always complained that she bought her clothes too big. *So true.* She'd been trying to hide all her imperfections, and succeeded only in making herself look dumpy.

"You are *not* dumpy." She smiled, realizing that everyone else's sudden appreciation had resulted from her own sense of self-worth, and not from any actual change in her appearance. She lifted her chin a notch.

That meant Sam was attracted to the *real* Sharon Detwiler, cellulite and all. Amazing. She smiled again at her reflection. At least the highlights were real.

With her newfound confidence in every step, she made her way back to the balcony where Sam stood waiting. He handed her a glass of champagne and she took a sip, though she didn't need alcohol to enhance the miraculous feelings swirling through her.

She was alive and pretty in her own way. More importantly, she had a life ahead and she intended to make it a good one.

"Would you like to dance again?" Sam asked.

"Yes." Her breath caught and she nodded. "In fact, I never plan to stop."

SMOKER

by Mel Odom

Mel Odom is an Oklahoma-based author who has
written nearly a hundred novels that span the spectrum from science fiction to gaming to young adult
to mystery. Among his recent novels are several
books in the *Buffy the Vampire Slayer* and *Sabrina the
Teenaged Witch* series, the novelization for the film
Vertical Limit, and a book on Lara Croft, of *Tomb
Raider* fame.

WHEN the Malaysian stopped heckling the young
waitress and upped the ante by grabbing her, I
tossed the pair of jacks and deuces I'd been holding onto
the ratty tablecloth and pushed my chair back. The
docks of Singapore were some of the most dangerous in
that part of the world, and if the police came at all,
they'd be too late to help the woman.

Tipper's was a sailors' bar and had a reputation as a
bad place to be. The only decor consisted of American
movie posters of Bogart, Edward G. Robinson, Errol
Flynn, Rita Hayworth, and a half dozen others on the
smoke-stained walls. Bottled beer sat at room temperature behind the scarred bar and everybody paid to drink
from the house bottle. Night draped the room and left
heavy shadows that felt cottony from tobacco smoke. I'd
stayed past the sundown curfew I'd promised myself I'd
stick to.

The sandy-haired British seaman to my left glanced at
me casually. A tattoo of an island girl in a grass skirt
with bared breasts decorated his left forearm. He spoke
in soft warning. He was fortyish and spoke softly, belying
his rough exterior and the oily smudges on his weathered
face and scarred arms. "This isn't any of your concern,
Yank. Let it go."

The young waitress struggled against her captor. I

guessed that she was sixteen or seventeen. The Malay
sailor laughed as he held the woman and ran his free
hand over her. He bumped up against his prisoner
obscenely.

"Can't," I said. Part of that decision was mine, but
a lot of it had to do with the way my old man had
raised me.

The Britisher shrugged. "Suit yourself, mate." He
checked his cards again, then tossed in another American quarter. The three other men matched his raise
grudgingly with coins from all over the world. Eventually, they'd all reach ports where the coins could be
spent. "His name's Shafeeq. Carries a bayonet hidden
along his left forearm. Bloody bastard likes usin' it on
blokes, too."

"Thanks."

"What ship you with?" The Britisher looked at me
calmly. "In case I have to tell your cap'n what's become
of you?"

"Sunfisher," I replied, watching the Malaysian. No one
else in the bar moved. Most of the bar patrons ignored
the struggling woman. It wasn't the first time something
like that had happened at Tipper's, but it had never
happened when I was there. "Flies under an American
flag out of Los Angeles. Just ask for Cap'n Zachary
Tyler."

"There's your problem, mate," the Britisher said.
"You've been watching too many of those bloody Roy
Rogers cowboy films Hollywood is putting out these
days."

Actually, I'd always liked John Wayne's pictures more
than Roy Rogers'. When I was a kid and my old man
had a little extra money—which wasn't often—we'd
spend a Saturday at a theater in Los Angeles. My old
man always got there in time to watch the news footage
of World War II even though I'd wanted to sleep in and
get there in time for the first Fleischer Superman
cartoons.

My old man usually slept through the cartoons and
the movie, so that didn't leave us much to talk about
afterward except the footage of the war effort. But when
I'd been a kid, I'd always liked knowing my old man

was there, one seat between us so none of the local
toughs would be tempted to say anything about us sitting
too close together. My old man didn't put up with that
and most of them had learned it the hard way.

Seven years ago, when I'd been fifteen and had discovered girls, I'd lost interest in going to the movies with
my old man. Or maybe he'd lost interest in going with
me. Or maybe we'd just quietly chosen up sides and
decided we'd lost interest in each other. Neither one of
us had liked each other very much over the next few
years.

Me joining up with the Merchant Marine four years
ago had given us something to talk about for six days
till I caught my first berth. It was the most we'd talked
in a long time. Still, I think we were both relieved when
I stepped on deck and sailed out past Angel's Gate
Lighthouse in Los Angeles Harbor. My old man never
seemed to know quite what to do with me, and having
to raise me by himself after my mother ran out hadn't
helped. But he'd walked me out to my ship and waved
when I left, told me not to do anything that he wouldn't
do. I knew he meant it.

It had been over a year since I'd seen my old man. I
remembered thinking that for some reason as I stood
and approached the bar. Maybe it even crossed my mind
that I wouldn't see him again after the Malaysian got
through with me. Setting out to do something and being
able to do it were two different things.

Shafeeq turned toward me, hiding behind the woman.
She squealed in fright as he grabbed her throat with his
free hand, closing off her scream. "What do you think
you're doin', Yankee?" he asked me.

For a minute, the only sound in the bar was the slow,
squeaking sweep of the ceiling fan's long blades.

Then I smiled one of those sassy, smart-alecky smiles
my old man had taught me when I was just a kid. No
matter how scared I was, or how hurt physically or emotionally, my old man had always made me smile at somebody threatening me. I always did, too, because my old
man was bigger and scarier than anyone I'd faced as
a kid.

He told me if other people saw you smiling when you

should have been scared or crying, it made them wonder just what the hell they'd got hold of—made them think you were a tough guy and maybe they should be afraid of you. I'd seen my old man grin at collections guys the bookies sent around when he was a hundred in the hole, late on the vig, and all broke up inside already from a fight the night before. And he smiled at them through the whole beating they came to give him. The bookies always sent three guys or more to take my old man.

"Getting a beer," I told Shafeeq. I held up the empty bottle from the card table. "Seems like you got the only waitress all tied up."

After a moment's hesitation, Shafeeq grinned wickedly and nodded. "Get you a beer. Get me a beer." He was a big man, bronzed dark from the sun and the sea through at least twenty years' of hard sailing. Scars crisscrossed his skin like fat gray-and-pink worms, some from nets and others from knives. His eyes glittered blackly, like a bilge rats's trapped down in a cargo hold.

Shafeeq didn't see much of a threat in me. In his eyes, I was just a skinny Irish kid with freckles and short-cropped red hair burned strawberry by the sun and the salt. He'd know I was a sailor from my stained dungarees and unbuttoned shirt over a frayed undershirt, and from the reddened skin that somehow always seemed to burn but never quite tan.

I was lean but hard from handling tons of cargo over the last four years. I'd never got my old man's broad, sloping shoulders or his height. He was a heavyweight, and I was a solid middleweight on my best days. He blamed my mother. I took his word for it because I'd never even seen pictures of her.

I crossed the uneven wooden floor to the bar, listening to the squeaking ceiling fan and knowing every eye in the place was on me. Probably most of the sailors there figured me for a poster child for stupid. Maybe some of them were generous and thought maybe I was drunk enough to want to play the hero.

They didn't know I didn't believe in heroes. Superman and Popeye were great cartoons for a kid, but my old man had raised me on the streets—the school of hard knocks, he'd called it—and I'd spent the last four years of Merchant Marines in cesspool ports all over the Pacific. You didn't find heroes in those places, only tough guys and wise guys.

I wasn't sure I knew which I was, or even which one my old man would have accused me of being. But I knew I couldn't let the Malaysian do anything to the young woman. If I'd left Tipper's when I'd promised myself I would, I might have heard about her over breakfast the next morning, said, gee, that's too bad, and gone on with my day. I'm not a hero.

A skinny old Chinese man with gray hair, a wrinkled New York Yankees baseball cap, and a cigar stub clenched in a vacant spot between crooked yellow teeth tended bar. A dirty bar towel draped one narrow shoulder. "What you want, Yank?"

"A beer for me and my new friend," I said. I saw my father's smile in the age-spotted mirror behind the bar. It looked strange on my face, but I left it there. "And a shot."

"You pick up friends fast," the bartender said as he uncapped two beers, then poured a shot in a glass.

I didn't say anything as I paid for the drinks. I picked up the shot and poured it into my mouth, holding it there. Then I lifted the two bottles by the necks in one hand. I turned and fished a pack of Lucky Strikes from my shirt pocket as I walked back toward Shafeeq. I palmed the black crackle Zippo lighter from my shirt pocket as well.

I stopped in front of Shafeeq with my hands full, just out of arm's reach.

Shafeeq's eyes narrowed, and I knew he didn't trust me. His pupils were pinpricks, and I guessed that he'd visited one of the opium dens around the city before he'd wandered into Tipper's.

I shook the cigarette pack at the Malay sailor. I only smoked occasionally, just to cut the stench of the sea every now and again. My old man didn't hold with smoking because it cut down on a guy's wind and took some snap off his punch. He'd busted my lip for me when he'd found me smoking with the guys when I was thirteen.

"Smoke." Shafeeq nodded. "Like American cigarettes."

I shook a cigarette out, still holding the whiskey in my mouth and ignoring the harsh burn.

Shafeeq took the cigarette, coming out from behind the waitress a little more. He lipped it and waited on me.

I put the pack back in my shirt pocket, then flipped open the Zippo. The click of the hinged lid sounded louder than the squeaking ceiling fan. When I thumbed the flame, I blew the whiskey from my mouth the way my old man used to for gags with his pals. He'd learned it from a broken-down old magician that played in some of the bars where he worked occasionally as a bouncer.

The whiskey spread thinly through the air and ignited into a rolling ball of gassy blue-and-yellow flame as it shot toward the Malaysian sailor. With him standing behind the waitress, I couldn't put the flame directly in his face the way I would have otherwise. Still, he cursed and dodged back. The alcohol flames brushed over the left side of his head and burned out before they got much past him.

I dropped one of the beer bottles and broke the other one across Shafeeq's face. Scared by the flames and hammered by the beer bottle, the Malaysian released the waitress and stepped back, howling in murderous rage. I stepped in and planted a jab in the middle of Shafeeq's ugly faced, snapping his head back. The beer bottle had cut him across the nose and cheeks. I stepped back and brought the waitress with me, pushing her behind me.

One thing I'll have to say, Shafeeq could take physical damage. Or maybe it was the alcohol and opium burning through his body. My jab rocked him back on his heels, but he righted himself quick enough. He snapped a bayonet from under his sleeve along his left forearm and swiped it at my face.

The blade cut the air in front of me as I pulled my head back like a turtle. Maybe if I hadn't been told he had the knife, he would have got me. With the waitress safely behind me, I stepped into a fighter's crouch, light on my toes and both hands balled before me.

Shafeeq sliced the knife at me again, but I circled to the left to avoid it and popped him in the eye with a left jab. I kept moving, staying loose and ready, just the way my old man had taught me.

The Malaysian sailor came back with the bayonet again, hacking at me and cursing. I sucked in my gut, faded back long enough to let the knife go by, then stepped in with two quick jabs to his face and buried a tight, right roundhouse into the side of his neck so hard it sounded like I was chopping wood.

He tried with the knife again, but I stepped in close, blocked his knife arm with my left, and hooked my right fist into his stomach three times as quickly as I could, so close to him now his breath whistled over my shoulder each time I hit him. He pushed himself away with his free hand, and I let him go. He stood swaying, holding the knife in front of him.

I still felt that cocky smile on my face, but I didn't fool myself. If Shafeeq put his knife into me, even if he didn't kill me, I'd be forced to lay up in Singapore till I was healthy enough to take another ship. A sailor doesn't find many friendly ports when he's broke, and I was near busted after having a few "easy" jobs turn sour lately.

Shafeeq cursed me some more, then came at me, yelling like a wild man.

I went right back at him, hooked my left arm over his swinging knife arm, and pulled him to me, leaving the knife in his hand behind me where he couldn't stick me with it. Then I head-butted him in the face, breaking his nose. He breathed his own blood as I powered an uppercut into his jaw and lifted him from his feet. He was unconscious by the time he hit the beer-stained sawdust covering the wooden floor.

I kicked the bayonet away from him and picked up the Zippo where I'd dropped it.

"You about done here, Farrell?"

I looked up at the mention of my name and saw Cap'n Tyler standing in the doorway.

Cap'n Tyler was a short man with a belly on him and a full brown beard so slick it looked like a beaver's pelt. He was closer to fifty than forty, dressed in a faded gray sweater, khaki pants that had seen better days, and a stained yachting hat one of his ex-wives had given him.

"Aye," I said.

"I need you to come with me."

I nodded, and I could tell from the cap'n's expression that whatever had brought him to me was nothing good. I followed him outside and breathed in the muggy, stale air that clung to the port.

We walked along the wooden walkway to stay out of the mud that rolled on down the hill to the ships sitting at anchorage. The working girls were out in force, dressed so they were almost undressed, talking in a half dozen different languages but quickly bringing everything down to the bottom line as the sailors came to meet them.

"That personal business back there?" Cap'n Tyler asked.

I shook my head and shoved my hands into my dungarees pockets. My hands hurt and were already swelling. "Didn't even know the guy."

"Over a girl?"

"Kind of."

The cap'n shook his head. "Stupid reason to fight."

I didn't bother to explain. My old man always taught me never to say more than I needed to about anything. But then the conversations my old man usually avoided were with legbreakers and cops.

"Got some bad news, Farrell." The cap'n stopped and handed me a telegram envelope.

My name—Terry Farrell—was scrawled across the front. I opened the envelope and read the brief message inside.

TERRY FARRELL STOP REGRET TO INFORM YOU OF YOUR FATHER'S DEATH STOP IT WAS BAD BUSINESS STOP PLEASE COME HOME STOP FATHER LIAM MCMURDY

"I'm sorry," Cap'n Tyler said.

"Yeah," I mumbled, "me, too." And I stood there in the stink of the harbor and the thin moonlight drawing gray shadows on the mud and tried to figure out how the hell I was supposed to feel about my old man being gone.

* * *

Father Liam McMurdy's church was a small stone building in the old neighborhood where my old man had lived. Sometimes, when I was younger, I wondered if my Piccolo still lived nearby. My old man never said and I never asked, because he was always angry whenever someone brought her up. He told most people we didn't know, like schoolteachers, that she was dead. Maybe he was guessing or maybe he was hoping. My old man was hard to figure when it came to personal stuff.

I guess maybe I still wondered about my mother from time to time, but I felt guilty about it that afternoon. It had taken me eighteen days to get back to Los Angeles.

I walked between the empty pews dressed in a watch cap and my peacoat, straight off *Sunfisher*. I'd walked most of three hours, hoofing it over from the harbor. There were cabs, but my money was tight and I'd wanted to walk through the old neighborhood.

It was funny seeing the places I'd gone to with my old man when I'd still been a kid. I used to think Papa Giovanni's Pizza and Bistro was the biggest, most expensive place on the planet, but that was before I saw some of the restaurants downtown where the movie stars ate. My old man had taught me to whistle, "Shave and a Haircut, Two Bits," there one night.

Ellenberg's Secondhand Shop had disappeared sometime between then and the last time I'd stopped by to see my old man. He'd taken me there as a kid, talking boxing with Mr. Ellenberg, who knew my old man from the old days, and together they'd found clothing that mostly fit me or only needed a few repairs.

My old man had remade my clothes, fixing tears, letting out or taking in, while drinking an occasional beer and sitting out on the small balcony of the fourth-story walk-up apartment where we'd lived most of the time. I asked my old man once who'd taught him to sew, and he told me his father had, that he was a tailor. I'd never met my grandfather or grandmother, or any uncles or aunts that might have existed. As long as I could remember, I'd had no blood family but me and my old man.

And then there were other places where the names had changed, but the businesses remained pretty much the same. Most of them were taverns and pool halls where my old man had tended a little bar or been a bouncer. Honest work, he called it, because he wouldn't have anything to do with legbreakers or running numbers. He saw gambling as different, though, like it was something a hard-working man was entitled to—a chance at the brass ring, or a way to be personally involved with a boxing match.

I stopped at the front of the church, aware of the bright glow of the stained-glass windows depicting the Stations of the Cross around me. I dropped my duffel on the wooden floor beside me, knelt, and genuflected. I said a short prayer for my old man, knowing the whole time that probably he wouldn't have appreciated it. He'd never leaned on nobody or nothing. I glanced back up and wasn't surprised to find Father Liam standing to one side by the black curtained confessionals.

"Hello, Terry," he said, smiling a little.

My old man had never smiled so softly. Father Liam was a short, stout man who'd finally gone gray, which was adding insult to injury, as bald as he was. He wore the black robes of the priesthood with authority, though, and nobody messed with him much.

My old man sometimes told me stories about Father Liam. The priest was a hard-drinking man, but he never let it get ahead of him—always knew when he'd had enough. And he watched over his congregation, always having a kind word for everybody and a stern word for us kids who sometimes got a little hard to handle. But Father Liam was also a man who wouldn't put up with a lazy man that wouldn't work to feed his family, or a drinking man who hit his wife or kids. The priest was known to fight those men, and mostly he won. And when he didn't win, he healed up and went back at those men again, till they gave in because Father Liam wouldn't.

"Hello, Father Liam." I stood. He glanced at my head and I remembered I was still wearing my hat. I snatched it from my head, my face turning hot with embarrassment. "Sorry." My old man had taught me better than that, and we both knew it.

"You received my telegram, then?"

"Aye, sir. You didn't say how my old . . . *father* . . . died. I'd always thought he was healthy as a horse."

"He was," Father Liam agreed. "Wasn't his health that killed him." He looked at me. "You a drinking man these days, Terry?"

"Not much of one."

"Well then, let me stand you to a good Irish pint. A man talking about his father's death ought to be somewhere other than this place." He glanced around the quiet church. "This is a place for sayin' good-byes an' such. Not for talkin' about the things me and you got to be talkin' about."

"Your old man was killed in a fight," Father Liam said.

We sat at a back table in Sweeney's, a pub that served green Irish beer on St. Paddy's Day and had a clientele that would sing together when they were deeply enough into their cups. The small room was dark with old wood, heavy with years-old smoke. A dimly lighted Wurlitzer Jukebox in the corner next to the small bar dragged a needle through a worn Glenn Miller record. "In the Mood" was one of my old man's favorites.

"The bookies?" I asked. My old man was always in hock to one bookie or another. Usually it was over the boxing matches, but occasionally it was the ponies. The old man had always been a sucker for an underdog.

The last time I'd been home, I'd asked my old man how things were going. He'd just smiled and told me the bookies were crying every time he showed up to collect his winnings. I didn't believe him, but even as a grown man, I knew he wouldn't let me into his business if he didn't want me there.

"No." Father Liam shook his head. "Your old man, sometimes he'd get behind payin' off the book, you know, like always, but everybody knew he was good for it. He never stiffed anybody."

"Then what?" I asked. I was still trying to get around the fact that my old man hadn't simply keeled over from a heart attack or got hit by a bus.

"A smoker."

I sat back in my chair then and looked down into my untouched beer. I felt confused, mostly. If my old man had been killed in a smoker, it meant someone had killed him—had *meant* to. And that didn't set well with me at all.

It wasn't unusual for my old man to fight in smokers after his career in the ring went south. Over the years I'd heard all kinds of stories about how that had happened. Most people agreed that my old man didn't like the arrangements the mob made with boxers during those days. Too much money changed hands through the bookies for the wise guys not to make sure a good piece of it went into their pockets. So the wise guys fixed the fights, or they fixed the fighters.

My old man had refused to take dives in the rings. But he'd taken money from some of the wiseguys to pay off debts to other sports books. In the end, all the fighting he'd gotten to do once he was kicked out of the circuit was with legbreakers and at smokers.

A smoker was an illegal boxing match fought in the back rooms or basements of clubs and bars. A fee was charged at the door for anyone wanting to see them, and the winning fighter took a piece of the gate while the losers got bupkis, except for bruises, broken bones, and a few days missed of work or chewing food. Sometimes smokers were fought with gloves, but more often than not they were bare-knuckle events, guaranteed to leave a fighter bloody. And that was what the audience paid to see—the blood.

They were called smokers because the back rooms and basements had little or no ventilation. Cigarette, cigar, and pipe smoke filled the air, sometimes so thick that you'd think fog had engulfed the room.

"What happened?" I asked.

"You know Tony Milano?" Father Liam asked.

"Aye." I did know Big Tony Milano. He was the wise guy my old man had told me had broken him out of the fighting circuit and ended his boxing career.

I was hanging on the priest's every word, not knowing if I wanted to cry or curse, or just walk away and try to get to my ship before it sailed the next morning. There hadn't been enough between me and my old man to do

more than hurt for a while and then get over it. And I
knew that's what my old man would tell me to do—just
get over it. But Big Tony being involved somehow made
it harder to walk away from.

"Tony's got himself a fine new fighter, he does," the
priest told me. "Goes by the name of Handsome
Piccolo."

"He's a goombah?" I asked.

"No, Terry. Handsome's only connection to the
mobbed-up guys is Milano."

"Maybe that's enough," I pointed out. "Handsome
fights in smokers?"

"Not usually. He's a circuit boy. A boxer that's bein'
brought along. There's some that say he's goin' to be
the next heavyweight."

"Then how'd he get in a fight with my old man?"

"You remember Clara Bingham?" Father Liam asked.
I nodded.

"Well, she calls herself Clara Starr these days. She's
been in a couple movies the last year, she has, as an
extra here an' there, an' likes to talk like she's rubbin'
elbows with all the greats. But she isn't. However, before
she got into those movies, she was seein' your old man."

I didn't say anything. My old man had always been a
slick operator with the women, but he'd never let any
of them stick under his skin. When I was little, he'd
always told me it was just going to be him and me. And
even when I got older and saw him hanging out with
some of the women from the neighborhood that had
questionable reputations or I knew to be married, I pretended like I didn't see him and he pretended like he
didn't see me.

Sometimes I thought it was because he didn't want
me knowing his business, but mostly I figured it was
because he was embarrassed about who he was out with.
Those women weren't good, and Clara Bingham had
been one of them then. I didn't figure being in a couple
of movies had changed her if she was still hanging
around the old neighborhood.

"My old man saw a lot of women," I replied.

Father Liam nodded. "After you left, he settled down
somewhat. Took up with Clara. I think they were good

together, an' she was good for your old man. I think he
was lonely after you left, but with him, you never could
really tell."

I couldn't imagine my old man ever being lonely. He'd
always been too complete, too sure of himself. The bets
were his only weakness. "So what happened?"

"Clara started working in pictures an' got full of herself, she did. Wasn't long before Tony Milano started
snoopin' around. You know he owns Stars and Glitter?"

"Aye." Stars and Glitter was a neighborhood club that
tried to act uptown. My old man had bounced in there
before Big Tony had bought the place and gave it a face-
lift. Word in the neighborhood was that Big Tony was
pouring a lot of his own illegitimate profits into the place
to keep it open, but the business was also good for laun-
dering money.

"After she appeared in those movies," Father Liam
went on, "Milano offered Clara a job as a singer. She
took it, then started seeing Milano instead of your old
man."

I waited. Waiting was something you learned to do
around my old man, and something you learned to do
on a ship. I waited, but I was seething inside. But I
didn't know who I was really mad at more: my old man
for getting himself in a jam, or me for caring so much.

"Your old man took it pretty hard," Father Liam said.
"Clara's leavin' busted him up more'n I've ever seen
him busted up before. An' you know yourself that your
old man had seen more'n his fair share of trouble."

I nodded.

"A few weeks later, your old man went into Stars and
Glitter. He shouldn't have been there, an' I'm sure he
knew it. But he went. He tried to talk to Clara, then
Milano interrupted. Your old man broke Milano's nose."
Father Liam shrugged. "If that had happened somewhere other than the public eye, Milano probably would
have gunned your old man down himself. But Milano
gets up an' says maybe your old man should try pickin'
on somebody else that knows how to defend himself."

"Handsome Piccolo," I said, putting it together.

"Yeah." Father Liam regarded his empty glass. "Your
old man an' Handsome Piccolo went down into the base-

ment with Milano right after that, with Milano still bleedin' like a stuck pig and honkin' like a goose."

My stomach tightened, remembering the slap of fists on flesh and the way blood poured from every cut in those places. My old man hadn't let me go to a smoker when I was a kid, but when I'd got older and been on my own, I had.

"I was there, Terry," Father Liam said hoarsely. "Your old man didn't stand a chance against Handsome Piccolo. Your old man went down an' kept goin' down. Got so that Handsome Piccolo just picked him up every time an' beat him some more."

"Someone should have stopped the fight." My voice sounded brittle even to me.

"There wasn't nobody goin' to stop that fight 'cept Milano," Father Liam said. "An' he chose not to." He shrugged. "Maybe if your old man had asked him—but he didn't."

My old man had never asked anyone for anything, and we both knew it. And if he wouldn't have asked a friend, he damned sure wouldn't have asked Big Tony.

"When Handsome Piccolo finished," Father Liam said in a toneless voice, "your old man was dead on the floor. There wasn't anything could be done for him. Milano let me take his body out of there and tell police I found him out in front of the church. They think your old man was robbed and left for dead."

"They're not looking at Big Tony for it at all?" I asked.

"No. An' them that might hear something about that fight, they're turnin' a deaf ear to it. Milano is too well connected these days. There are people in the city council who like him just where he is."

I sat there and drew in the silence of the bar for a moment, understanding what my old man got out of coming to such places. When you sit in the shadows of a bar, you can adopt a kind of still quietness inside yourself that keeps all the pressures outside at bay for a while. It's like time stops.

"What's on your mind, Terry?" Father Liam asked.

I shook my head but didn't look at him. Father Liam had learned to tell when I was lying.

"Don't go gettin' no foolish notions, boy," the priest admonished.

I looked at Father Liam then. "I just came back to settle my old man's affairs, that's all."

The priest held my eyes for a moment, but what I'd said was close enough to the truth. Still, he felt compelled to warn me a little more. "Stay away from Handsome Piccolo, Terry. He ain't right. There's a bit of the devil that clings to him."

I looked at Father Liam but didn't say anything. The priest wasn't one to go talking about religion and beliefs out of turn.

"A year or so back," he went on, "Piccolo was on a fight ticket at the Forum here in the metro area. He went up against Tommy Bluelegs. You remember Tommy Bluelegs?"

I nodded. Tommy Bluelegs was one of the old guys from the fight cards. His last name came from the unpronounceable Greek name he had. He'd been a young club fighter coming up when my old man was still stepping into the rings ten years ago. Tommy Bluelegs was a dirty fighter, and he'd taken every dive the wise guys had paid for.

"Tommy Bluelegs looked like he was going to get the worst of it at first," Father Liam said. "Handsome Piccolo had a fistful of dynamite in each hand and he kept bombing Tommy Bluelegs no matter which way he turned. Handsome Piccolo kept razzing him, working him over verbally as well as mentally. Then Tommy Bluelegs caught Handsome Piccolo in a clinch, head-butted him and looked like he beat him to death against one of the corner poles. I saw that fight, Terry. There was blood everywhere. Nothing human could have lived through that beating. Tommy Bluelegs knew he wasn't going to beat Handsome Piccolo, so he decided to kill him."

I listened quietly. My old man used to tell me similar stories. Sometimes the rage and fear a fighter kept bottled up inside himself couldn't be stopped once it was let loose. There was a thin line, my old man said, between genius and insanity, and a fighter walked it every time he stepped into the ring.

Father Liam looked at me with quiet concern. "They

told me Handsome Piccolo died three times that night durin' the ambulance ride to the hospital. I mean, his heart stopped and they had to beat on him to get it goin' again."

"People talk," I said.

Father Liam nodded. "Yes, they do. And there's some that say Handsome Piccolo is a lucky man to be up walkin' around these days." He covered my hand for a moment with his and leaned in to whisper. "There's also some that say Handsome Piccolo sold his soul to the devil that night, because he walked out of that hospital the next mornin' like a new man. The doctors who'd looked at him hadn't expected him to live."

"Maybe he wasn't hurt as badly as people thought."

"I saw Handsome Piccolo that night, Terry," Father Liam said. "I've seen hurt men before, an' I've had them die in my arms durin' the last war. I'm standin' here tellin' you that man was dead. Instead of bein' buried, he came back stronger an' meaner than he's ever been. He's not human anymore. There's a shadow on his soul, something unclean that exists just to hurt people."

Listening to the priest, I felt the nape of my neck turn cold and prickle up. I knew he believed what he was telling me, but I had a hard time believing it. "You make Piccolo sound like some kind of monster."

Father Liam nodded. "He is, Terry. My hand to God on that. I've been around Piccolo, and I know the man has changed. I got a sick stomach every time I've been around him."

I didn't know what to say, so I said nothing at all.

"Stay away from him," Father Liam advised. "Your old man, God rest his soul, would have wanted that, too."

My old man had left all his earthly possessions in Father Liam's care. The priest had held them for me, knowing that some day I'd come calling for them.

There wasn't much, and it all fit into a shoebox. There were a few folding bills, a handful of change, a simple gold wedding ring I'd never seen him wear but that he carried in his shirt pocket and hadn't gotten rid of in all those years. I kept the Zippo he'd carried for over thirty years and the moth-eaten lucky rabbit's foot that I'd always known had held no luck but had possessed a sentimental value.

There were also faded pictures of women. I didn't know them, didn't know if any of them was my mom or if they were part of my old man's family I'd never heard about. There were medals and even a trophy he'd won as an amateur boxer, keepsakes that were made out of cheap tin but had evidently meant a lot to my old man.

I found a few pictures of me from grade school, and even a few that had been taken by camera girls working at different places where my old man had bounced. I hadn't even known he'd bought them. There was also a bottle of my old man's aftershave. I remembered how he'd called it fancy toilet water, but he never went out without splashing some on.

The only thing I knew for sure was missing from my old man's possessions was the golden gloves pendant he'd won as a kid. It'd been made out of real gold, and no matter how far down he got owing the bookies, he'd never given that up. Sometimes he'd hocked it to pawnshops to get us by, but it was always to guys who respected my old man and wouldn't sell it out from under him for anything.

When I'd discovered it was missing at the church, I went to all the pawnshops but none of the brokers was holding a ticket on it. I didn't know where it had disappeared. The county had buried my old man, and Father Liam had said that the pendant hadn't been with him. It was the one thing of my old man's that I would have liked to have, but I guessed that some morgue attendant had it now.

I sat on the sagging bed in the low-rent flophouse that catered to sailors and smoked. Then I stood by the window and looked out over the downtown area as the sun sank over the Pacific and the shadows deepened and filled in the gaps between the buildings.

By nightfall, I knew what I had to do.

I took a long shower, splashed on some of my old man's aftershave, and dressed in my best dungarees and a white shirt. I slicked my hair back with hair oil and pulled it back into the ducktail my old man had hated when I was a teen. Then I gathered up the battered leather gym bag my old man had given me when I was eleven and he'd started taking me to McHale's Gym, and I headed for the door.

I kept remembering Father Liam's words concerning Handsome Piccolo. *Nothing human could have lived through that beating.* Handsome Piccolo had lived through his beating, but my old man hadn't. Maybe Piccolo had made a deal with the devil that night, but my old man had never taken any deals from anybody.

The Stars and Glitter crowd was in full swing by the time I got there. I paid the door cover and was surprised at how much Big Tony could get away with charging in the neighborhood.

I walked along the outer fringes of the crowd with my gym bag in my fist. Women stared at me, but I ignored them. Men stared at me, too, and they stepped out of my way. I pretty much ignored them in return, except for the big guys in the tuxes that looked like muscle.

The nightclub rented glitter. For the money, you could come down and live like the movie stars did on the big screen. At least, like the moviegoers thought the stars lived. And for another few bucks, a roving photographer would take a picture of you living the high life.

The band played backup to a torch singer with platinum-blonde hair and a dusky voice. She stood in a baby spotlight and sang "That Old Black Magic" pretty well. I recognized her as Clara Star at once, but she didn't see me because I was moving in the darkness that filled the place.

I found Big Tony at the back of the club near the kitchen area beside a huge fishbowl built into the wall. A dozen guys sat at the big round table with him, all of them eating his food and laughing at his jokes.

Big Tony hadn't changed much over the years, maybe got a little bigger through the middle, but his tailors hid it well in his tux. His dark hair was lacquered back from his forehead and he was clean-shaven with thick jowls. He blew a huge smoke ring from the fat cigar he smoked. A diamond ring glittered on one thick finger.

I approached him directly. Trying to get cute might have got me shot by one of the bodyguards sitting at the table. I felt their eyes on me as I got closer, as watchful as a fisher hawk waiting for a fish to get too close to the sea's surface.

I stopped in front of Big Tony just as one of the body-guards on my side of the table started to get up. Big Tony waved the guy back to his seat.

"I know you, kid?" Big Tony asked.

"Not really," I answered, surprised at how tight my voice was.

"You got business with me?"

"Personal business," I assured him. Knowing he body-guards were mostly interested in the gym bag in my hand, I dropped it to the floor. Then they turned their dead eyes onto me full-bore.

Big Tony waved expansively. "This is my family, kid. I got no business I hide from them."

"You had my old man killed in the basement of this nightclub," I accused flatly.

Big Tony's eyes got as hard as ball bearings.

"Let me bounce him, Tony," one of the bodyguards suggested. "You don't gotta listen to nothin' like that in your own place." He stood up at the table.

I looked the bodyguard in the eye. "Bouncing me is going to get messy. Probably upset people—even if you were able to do it." I'd never talked like that in my life. My old man had always been big on not doing tough-guy talk. Waste of energy and broke your concentration, he told me.

"You think you're that tough, kid?" the bodyguard asked.

I didn't say anything then; we were past the point of talking.

"Step back, Frankie," Big Tony said.

Frankie held his position, but he didn't look happy about it.

"You Mike Farrell's kid?" Big Tony asked me. "The one he used to train down at the fight club?"

I nodded, feeling the anger and fear surging through me. I was a live wire, juiced with current and ready to snap. And I knew if I made a wrong move, Big Tony's bodyguards would shoot me.

"What are you doing here?" Big Tony demanded. "Thought you was off seein' the world."

"You murdered my old man," I said.

Big Tony shook his head. "You don't know what you're talking about, kid."

"I'm talking about the smoker you set up between my old man and Handsome Piccolo," I said. "And I'm talking about the way you had Piccolo beat my old man to death."

"You heard wrong." Big Tony glanced at the bodyguard. "Bounce the kid."

The torch singer on stage finished her number and the baby spotlight winked out behind me as the bodyguard stepped toward me. The bandleader announced the name of the next song and asked the audience to turn their attention to the huge fishbowl built into the nearby wall. Spotlights swept through the audience, stirring them up as they headed for the huge fishbowl.

I kicked the bodyguard in the crotch without warning, catching him by surprise. Turning green and moaning, his legs gave out and I saw his right hand come out from under his jacket holding a .45 military Colt pistol. I caught the man with my left palm, plucked the .45 from his hand with my right, then twisted my left arm and threw my elbow into his face. His nose broke with a hollow pop, then I caught his jacket and yanked him forward again, letting him fall to the floor.

The spotlights swept over me as I pointed the .45 at Big Tony. I slid the safety off and racked the slide, thinking maybe the bodyguard left the hammer on the empty chamber. A fat bullet spun free of the action and another one slid home, the hammer back and ready to fire.

My old man hadn't taught me about pistols and rifles; Cap'n Tyler had. I'd never shot at anything living but the occasional shark, but Big Tony was staring down the barrel and didn't know that.

Big Tony waved the other bodyguard to stay put. No pistols made an appearance, and my gut unclenched a little. "What do you want, kid?" Big Tony asked.

I pasted on one of my old man's smiles although I was scared and almost sick inside. "Handsome Piccolo," I replied. "I want a shot at the title."

Big Tony cupped his hands and quietly relit his cigar, but I saw the hatred and anger in his eyes when he took in that smile.

The baby spotlights had raced over us. Even the nearby tables hadn't got a good look at what was going on. A moment later, a scantily-clad redhead splashed down into the water of the fishbowl. She wore clamshells over her breasts and a mermaid fishtail. She swam around in the water like she lived there. The band played another swing song.

"Put down the heater," Big Tony said, "and I'll let you walk outta here in one piece."

I smiled at him again and choked down the feeling that I was going to throw up. "You'd do that after I embarrassed you in front of your friends?" I shook my head. "I don't think so. Unless you've gone soft, Big Tony."

"Call it a favor outta respect for your old man."

"Why?" I asked. "He never respected you. And he wasn't afraid of you either. That's how you got your nose busted. And that's why you had him killed."

Big Tony's face darkened with rage. "You're signin' your own death warrant here, kid."

"You've got good at fixing fights," I said. "Fix this one, or you won't live to fix another one." I don't know if I meant that or not, but it came out of my smiling mouth naturally enough.

Big Tony cursed me, but it wasn't anything I hadn't heard before while crewing a ship and working the docks. He stubbed his cigar out and stood. "You want this?" he bellowed. "You got it, you dumb mick bastard."

I slipped the safety back on the .45 and lowered it. The bodyguards immediately reached for their own hardware.

"Don't," Big Tony growled, freezing them in place. "Let Handsome Piccolo do for this one." He smiled at me then. "I'm gonna enjoy watching that little exhibition." He pointed toward the kitchen area. "C'mon, kid. Let's see if you got the stones your old man had. You got the dumbness from him six ways to Sunday."

I tossed the .45 onto the big table, causing the men seated there to scatter apprehensively. Then I hoisted that battered leather gym bag and followed Big Tony.

*   *   *

Minutes later, I stood in the nightclub's basement dressed in the shorts and off-white canvas shoes I'd brought with me in the gym bag. I stretched my body, running through the routine my old man had taught me.

My breath came tight into my chest, but I tried not to show it, tried not to act like I was uncertain about myself in any way. Appearance is everything, my old man had told me. You can beat a guy before you ever step into a ring.

Our ring was an empty space in the middle of the room, framed by a few tables and chairs, and shelves of foodstuffs. Dim ceiling lights barely penetrated the heavy smoke that was already filling the room. MY eyes burned and my lungs ached from it.

If you'd asked me then why I'd gone there and insisted on confronting Handsome Piccolo, I don't think I could have really answered. Part of it was locked up in what I perceived a man was, as well as what a man would stand up for. Since the police weren't going to do anything about Handsome Piccolo and Big Tony Milano, I figured I had to. I didn't think I could live with nothing being done about my old man's death.

But another part was maybe because I wanted to try to understand my old man. He'd been there for me all my life, fed me, clothed me with things he'd had to sew himself, taught me to box, and made sure I turned out to be a man. But somewhere in my early teens, I felt like he'd abandoned me. I hadn't got to know him, and he hadn't got to know me.

While I had been out at sea, I'd often thought that maybe my old man had thought of me as if I was just another responsibility, like the beatings from the bookies' legbreakers and the nights he'd had to spend bouncing at a club to put food on the table.

I never knew if he really loved me.

Maybe we'd never have got around to having that conversation at some point. But we were all we'd had.

As I stood there warming up, I thought about him. When I'd been a kid, I'd thought he was the biggest man around. I'd thought he was the toughest guy I'd ever met. Not even Superman or Popeye could measure up to my old man. People respected him for the way he acted and what his word meant. And guys who were afraid of him, they'd got out of his way.

I remembered those Saturday morning movies with him snoring one seat over, and the occasional ice cream float we'd had afterward. And I remembered how my old man would sometimes give me a dime at the drug-store so I could buy a couple of comic books. He'd called them funny books, even when they weren't funny at all. When I was too little to read, he'd read them to me, sometimes struggling over the words because he'd never learned to read too well.

When I'd got sick as a kid, my old man had sat up with me. He'd made broth and fed me, told me stories that I think he sometimes made up then and there be-cause they were so bad and disjointed. Mostly, they'd been about fighters—real David and Goliath stuff. He'd put cold compresses on my head, given me cold baths when I ran fever. I'd never been alone.

But that had changed somehow as I started growing up. He'd got distant, or maybe he'd started realizing I was going to leave him, too. Like everyone else had maybe left him.

Maybe in all the confusion of the teenage years, I'd forgotten that I'd loved him. I didn't know where to place the blame for my confusion and pain, and having my old man get killed now only made it all worse. Now I'd never know him.

Maybe in all the confusion of the teenage years, I'd forgotten that I'd loved him. I didn't know where to place the blame for my confusion and pain, and having my old man get killed now only made it all worse. Now I'd never know him.

But I couldn't help wondering how my old man could have loved Clara Star enough to die for her—knowing she didn't love him the same way.

Or had his death been for another reason? My old man had been in his mid-forties. I couldn't have hung an actual year on it because he'd never told me, and I never even knew his birthday because he'd never told me. But he'd always celebrated mine with me.

My old man had died for a woman, yet he'd never

told me he loved me. Not even when I boarded my first ship and sailed away.

Handsome Piccolo stepped into the ring area and looked at me coldly. He was a huge man in his late twenties. He stood an inch or two over six feet, with broad, sloping shoulders, a big head with short-cropped blond hair, and a neck as thick as my thigh. He wore black boxing shorts and canvas shoes. His dark green eyes gleamed coldly, no emotion at all registering there.

He's not human anymore, Father Liam had said. *There's a shadow on his soul, something unclean that exists just to hurt people.*

"Hey, kid," Handsome Piccolo said.

And the casualness of the way he addressed me, like I was nothing, offended me. Had he talked to my old man that way, too? I had to work quickly to bottle the rage that filled me. I couldn't afford to feel that strongly during the fight. I bounced on my toes and nodded at him, wishing I could trust my voice.

"You ain't here to talk," Big Tony said from one of the chair's he'd commandeered to watch the fight. Clara Star sat beside him, and a momentary gold flicker at her neck caught my attention.

I looked at her just close enough to realize she was wearing my old man's golden gloves pendant around her neck. A pawnshow or a morgue attendant hadn't got it after all. I felt mad and hurt all over again at my old man. How could he have given it to her? Seeing the pendant was so distracting that I didn't hear Big Tony yell, "Go," until Handsome Piccolo was almost on top of me.

I barely got my hands up in front of me in time to ward off a series of jackhammer punches that left my forearms and biceps numb where they didn't hurt like hell. I ducked and circled back, getting the rhythm of his punches.

Every man has an inner beat, my old man had taught me, and all you have to do in the ring is stay alive long enough to figure it out. Then you have to work it to your advantage.

Handsome Piccolo was throwing everything at me, including the kitchen sink. Flea-flicker jabs tested my defenses occasionally, but mostly he tried to roll haymakers right through my arms to my head. If one of them landed, I didn't doubt that it would push my face to the back of my skull.

But I kept my arms up, kept circling, and moving, staying light on the balls of my feet. One thing I realized was that Handsome Piccolo wasn't as good a boxer as my old man, but he was damned big and he wouldn't stop coming. He had the same kind of steamroller technique Rocky Marciano was still using these days that caused a lot of sportswriters to call him a Neanderthal.

Even though Piccolo hadn't connected with my head, my arms were steadily turning numb and getting heavy. Once they dropped, I had no doubt that Piccolo would go after me like a shark on a blood scent.

My lungs burned from drawing in smoke-laden air, and I felt perspiration cover me. A sweaty guy was a hard guy to hit solidly. If you barely caught him and he turned at the same time, your fist would slide right along him. You'd miss, but you'd also step too far in and leave yourself exposed most of the time.

As I circled, I listened to Piccolo's breathing. It came steady as a metronome, like all the energy he was using up was nothing.

Nothing human could have lived through that beating. Father Liam's words echoed inside my head. I was beginning to believe that Handsome Piccolo was anything but human. But that didn't mean he wasn't fallible. He seemed to take it for granted that he would beat me, and his technique wasn't all that great to begin with.

How had my old man lost to this guy?

I stepped to the left again, turning Piccolo's right cross aside with my right forearm. I felt his skin slide along mine. Incredibly, he felt dry as a bone, but I was drenched with sweat and he slid more than he'd expected. When his right shoulder dropped, as I knew it was going to, I drove three rapid left hooks over the top of it. I screwed my feet down to the poured concrete floor and put all my weight behind each blow.

I caught him on the jaw, snapping his head back with each impact. I expected him to go down. I'd hit men in the past with hooks like that and they'd gone down. A lot of them hadn't got back up before the ten-count.

Instead, Piccolo pushed me back from him, worked his neck, then grinned at me like I hadn't done anything at all to him. "That the best you got, kid?" he taunted, and then he came at me again, barreling against me with his body and driving me back.

Big Tony and his crowd came alive again, shouting encouragement to Handsome Piccolo and wishing death for me.

I didn't try to stand against Piccolo. I gave way before him like a ship weathering a harsh sea. I didn't have a choice. One of Piccolo's punches drove through my defense and popped me above my right eye. The skin split over my eye and blood blurred my vision.

I tried to get away, but Piccolo was too strong, too big, and he wouldn't get off of me. He hammered me relentlessly, starting to drive more punches through my weakened arms. I covered my head with my arms, but his punches snapped the back of my skull against the cinder-block wall again and again. Then he went to work on my body, busting me up inside.

I tasted blood and I felt numbed all over, like Piccolo was beating someone else to death—not me. I wondered if that was what my old man had felt like at the end. Then I got mad at myself for just an instant for thinking of him when I was certain he probably hadn't thought of me at all. Out of sight, out of mind, that was the way my old man had treated the bookies and everything else in his life he didn't have total control over.

Piccolo hooked me in the side and drove the last of the air from my burning lungs. Maybe he didn't have technique, but he was the strongest man I'd ever been hit by.

My vision narrowed to a single long, black tunnel, and I knew that even that was about to close. I stopped feeling his punches after a time, but I stopped feeling everything else, too. I swayed drunkenly on my feet, but Piccolo propped me up against the wall behind me with a shoulder and kept pounding me.

"Get him off you, Terry!" My old man's voice cut

through the fog filling my head. "Step around this big palooka and get him off of you!"

I obeyed automatically, like I was back at McHale's Gym where my old man had trained me, drawing on whatever reserves I had left. I felt Piccolo shift against me, then I sidestepped to the right. He'd left himself open again, but I didn't have the strength to hit him.

"Backpedal, backpedal!" my old man shouted. "Get away from that big lug and get set up!"

I stepped back, keeping my balled fists in front of me out of instinct. And when I glanced over to my left, in the direction my old man's voice was coming from, I saw him there.

My old man was taller and heavier than I was, but we shared the same shock of red hair and freckles. He wore slacks and a white button-down shirt, pretty much all he'd ever worn outside the ring. He'd always looked at home in those clothes whether we were in church, or he was working, or we packed a lunch to eat in the park like we sometimes did.

Piccolo turned and came for me like a runaway locomotive.

"Get ready," my old man directed, lifting his hands in front of him like he was boxing. "This ape ain't gonna stop coming at you, see, but you can step around him and get a couple shots into his rib cage."

I stepped around Piccolo, but I forgot to punch him.

"What the hell are you doing, Terry?" my old man yelled, dropping his hands irritably. "You had a couple of shots you could have took. This guy's big. You're gonna have to wear him down." He turned and looked at Piccolo. "Now turn around and get set up again."

"I thought you were dead," I mumbled, staring at my old man.

He looked at me and smiled in that smart-aleck way of his. "I am dead, kid." He shrugged. "Found out you'd gone and got yourself set up to fight Handsome Piccolo. Not the brightest thing you've ever done, so I thought I'd drop by."

I stood with effort on trembling legs. "You came back for revenge?"

My old man hesitated then. "Yeah. Partly. This guy

Piccolo, he ain't what he seems like, Terry. He ain't human."

I wasn't paying attention to Piccolo. He was on me again before I knew it. A looping haymaker came from way back, a blow so loose and telegraphed it should never have touched me. I ducked under some of it, managed to slip a little more, but Piccolo pasted me with enough of it to send me to the floor.

"What the hell was that?" my old man roared, running over to stand by me. "Damn, why don't you just put your head on a pole and let him have target practice? He's gonna scramble your eggs for you if you keep boxing like that."

"It's not going to matter," I mumbled through split lips.

"What the hell do you mean by that?" my old man demanded.

I focused on my rage at him and at myself and managed to push myself to my feet before Piccolo reached me. "I'm here because I was stupid. I heard about you and Piccolo, and thought I should even the score with Big Tony if I could."

"I'd have done the same for you," my old man told me.

I knew he meant it, but it hurt me that he didn't get what I was driving at. And maybe I was a little mad at myself because I couldn't say what I wanted to say.

Then I concentrated on Piccolo for a minute, making sure he didn't hurt me anymore right away either. I kept my arms in close, turned his punches away with my elbows, and somehow kept dancing back out of his reach so he couldn't pin me up against a wall again.

"It's stupid," I told my old man again, concentrating on him.

Piccolo hit me while I was looking at my old man.

I left my feet and landed on the floor limp as a dishrag. Piccolo closed on me, grinning coldly, a butcher getting the knife ready and enjoying every second of it.

"Get up, Terry!" my old man yelled. "Get up or this ape'll kill you!"

But I didn't. I was weak and hurt and near exhaustion from everything I'd been through the last few days.

Maybe I'd thought facing off against Big Tony and

Handsome Piccolo would have let me off the hook for not being there with my old man when he died. Or maybe I'd just come there to die because it was the only way to truly end all the confusion of feelings. I didn't know.

My old man dropped to his hands and knees beside me, shoving his face into mine. "You get up! You get up now!"

"Can't, Pop," I mumbled, gargling blood at the back of my throat.

"I didn't raise you to quit!" my old man yelled.

"Is that all you're worried about?" I mumbled, my jaw barely moving. "Whether or not I quit before I die?"

Piccolo reached down for me. A boxer wearing gloves had a hard time helping an opponent back to his feet so he could beat on him some more. But with bare hands, Piccolo had no problem at all. He only lifted my head up high enough to drive his fist against my jaw and punch through. My head twisted violently and for a moment I thought my skull had wrenched free of my spine.

I hit the floor again, twisted over on my side this time, so dazed I could hardly see straight. I thought about my old man as he knelt there beside me. I remembered all the movies he slept through, the clothes he'd mended with his own hands, the hamburgers and fries and root beer I'd had for meals at places where he'd bounced or tended bar. I remembered watching him laugh and joke and taunt and tease, and get threatening when it came to that. I remembered the times I'd seen him fight inside the ring and out, remembered how concentrated he'd been in those moments, like nothing else had existed.

Like I hadn't existed.

I'd been around him nearly all my life, but I didn't know him. I hadn't known my mother or any other family except my father.

Piccolo towered above me, but I could hardly make him out against the dim glare of the lights struggling to make it through the smoke-filled room.

"Is that what you think, Terry?" my old man asked. "That you didn't know me? That I didn't love you?"

I watched in amazement as my old man's face crumbled in front of me. I'd seen him happy and mad, and hurting after a beating, but I'd never seen that kind of desperation or pain on his face before in my life.

"Terry," he whispered hoarsely, as if that was all his voice could do, "maybe I wasn't much of a father, but I gave you all I had. I took you away from every bad thing I'd ever done in my life that I couldn't escape. I took you away from your mom and my family, because I didn't want you to grow up the way I had, or around the people I had. I didn't want you to become the kind of man I was before you were born. I stepped away from all of that and raised you the best way I knew how. I tried to keep you away from the parts of me that I know are bad."

"Kill him, Handsome," Big Tony yelled. "Do for him like you did for his old man."

"Please," my old man pleaded, "please don't lay down and die. If I could, I'd die again for you. I love you, Terry. I've always loved you the best I knew how." He smoothed my hair out of my face. "Whatever I did to help make you, it was the best I could do, Terry. And if you lay down here and die, it's gonna be like I never did nothing right in my life." Tears glittered in his eyes. "Don't you see that?"

My vision, already blurred by the blood leaking into my eye, blurred a little more. I saw Handsome Piccolo playing up to the crowd, holding his hands clasped together above his head—the winner and still the champ.

I tried to get up, but I didn't have the strength. I looked back at my old man and tried to tell him I couldn't do it.

He wiped the tears from his face, and I heard the rasp of stubble beneath his palm. No matter how short a time had passed since he'd shaved, his chin was always rough. "Give me your hand, Terry."

I did, and I felt his callused palm against mine. He pulled me to my feet, but I still felt woozy and unsteady. Big Tony and his crowd pointed at me and warned Handsome Piccolo.

The big boxer turned around and glared at me. He hadn't liked it that I'd got back up.

"Now this time," my old man said, "we're gonna do this different."

I shook my head, listening to my breath whistle through

my throat. "Can't. I'm all used up, Pop. Piccolo busted me up inside."

"Don't you worry about it, Terry." My old man ruffled my hair like he used to do when I was eight. "You ain't gonna be alone no more. I come back for you, and I didn't come back to watch this creep hurt you."

My old man turned translucent, the way a reflection in a pane of glass was. He was there, but you could see through him. Then he stepped toward me, stepped into me, fitting himself into me like I was a glove. I watched his hands disappear into my hands. And I felt him inside me as most of the pain and hurt and fear dissolved away.

"Look at him, Terry," my old man whispered. "This is what you're fighting. This is what I fought."

My vision seemed like it was doubled for just an instant, then the images settled down to one. Handsome Piccolo suddenly wasn't handsome anymore, nor was he human.

He was tall and massive, but his hands ended with two fingers big as sausages and a thumb. His face looked like a fright mask, like one of the Tiki god face carvings I'd seen in the islands, and his nose was no longer a nose, but a jutting snout underscored by a mouthful of serrated teeth. Even in the dim, smoke-filled room I saw that his skin had taken on the deep blue hue of Concord grapes. His muscles bulged and writhed across his body.

"What is that?" I asked.

"It's whatever Handsome Piccolo sold himself out to after that fight in the Forum last year," my old man said. "Call it a devil, call it a demon. Whatever you want."

I didn't have much time to think about it. Handsome Piccolo charged us, and his three-fingered hands bunched into fists. I raised my hands almost effortlessly, surprised at how much strength I suddenly seemed to have.

Piccolo hammered at me, believing I was still defenseless and barely standing. I covered my had with my hands, kept my elbows out and low, and hunkered over a little. I took the brunt of his attack on my arms and shoulders and back.

"Just a little longer, Terry," my old man said. "He'll wear down."

Piccolo's blows came mercilessly. I didn't think he'd ever run out of gas. When he slowed down, I sidestepped, blocked a right jab with my right forearm, then delivered a left hook to the side of Piccolo's face. The skin split over his cheekbone and blood ran down his jaw.

The pain infused Piccolo with renewed fury and determination to kill me. I stepped away as he hammered at me again, keeping my head covered, then twisting and turning to protect my body as he went for my ribs and kidneys. Even then, every blow sent painful tremors through me.

"Hold on, Terry," my old man said. "Can't you feel it? He's running down."

And sure enough, even as I moved and took another painful blow, I felt that Piccolo didn't have what he'd started with. He *was* wearing down.

"Now!" my old man said. "Push him off you and go to work now!"

I twisted again, took a blow just above my right hip, then pushed Piccolo back. He stumbled back, obviously not expecting me to have the strength to do it. But even as he took his second step, I went after him.

I jabbed him with my left hand three times in a row, snapping his head back, splitting the skin over his left eye and putting a mouse below the right. Then I set myself and powered a big right hand into his face, driving him back another two steps.

Before Piccolo could regain his balance, I started hammering him with combinations. I felt my old man in me, urging me on, talking to me the way he had during sparring matches in McHale's Gym.

Piccolo tried to hold his position, but I pushed my body into his, manhandling him. When he covered his head with his arms, I punished his body with wicked hooks that threatened to break my wrists and that I felt all the way up to my shoulders and back. And despite everything Piccolo did, I drove him backward toward the wall.

Both of us breathed hard, dragging the air into our bodies only to have it hammered away again or used up. I chopped at Piccolo with everything I had. Another step back and I had him pinned against the wall. He screamed at me angrily, but he was scared, too. I saw it in the one eye that was left open.

But I had no mercy for him. I couldn't even feel the

punches he threw, so I ignored my defense and gave him everything I had, the way the Rock did when he pummeled another fighter. Blood covered both of us, but mostly it was his. When Piccolo started falling, I chased him with my fists, knocking him down even faster.

"Back off, Terry," my old man commanded in that tone of voice I knew I had to obey.

I took one more shot, catching Piccolo behind the left ear and snapping his head around.

"Back off!" my old man ordered.

Reluctantly, I did, but I kept my fists clenched at my sides. My chest ached as I breathed in and spots swam before my eyes.

Then, incredibly, the monster that had been living inside Handsome Piccolo tore free from his body. It stood before me and growled, snorting sulfurous smoke. Then it turned and walked through the wall I'd beaten it up against.

Piccolo lay stretched out and unconscious at my feet, but he was breathing.

"Let's go, Terry," my old man said as he stepped out of me and stood at my side. "You're done here."

I drew in a deep, shuddering breath, took a final look at Piccolo on the floor, then turned and started back toward my gym bag by the door. Two of Big Tony's toughs blocked the doorway, their hands under their jackets.

I took my gym bag and stared at Big Tony. Clara Star stood at his side, and the warm gleam of the golden gloves boxing pendant hung at her throat.

"You didn't think you was gonna walk out of here alive, did you, kid?" Big Tony asked.

Before I could stop myself, I smiled at him, that cocky, arrogant smile my old man had always made me smile when things started looking bad. No, I hadn't expected to walk out of the room. Some people just ran true to form. My old man had taught me that.

My old man stepped right in Big Tony's face. "Let him go, you son of a bitch," my old man snarled. "Let my boy go, or I'll drag you right down into the grave with me and kick your teeth in from now till Judgment Day."

Big Tony blanched and his eyes widened. To this day, I don't know if Big Tony heard my old man, but I know

he heard something. Big Tony stepped back away from
me like he'd been scalded. Then he waved at his men. "I
changed my mind, boys. Let him go."

The two men looked confused for a moment, but they
stepped away from the door.

I turned away from Big Tony and started for the door.

"Terry." It was Clara Star.

I turned back around to her.

Clara unhooked the necklace and shook the pendant
off. "That night Mike fought, he asked me to hold this
for you. In case anything happened to him. He said he
wanted you to have it." She put the golden gloves pendant
in my bloody palm and closed my hand over it. "He said
besides you, it was the only thing he'd ever really cared
about." She looked at him, her eyes brimming with tears.
"And he wanted me to tell you that he loved you."

"I know," I said around the lump in my throat. "I know
that." I thanked her, then somehow made it to the top of
the stairs and out the club's back entrance into the alley.

My old man walked at my side.

When we reached the alley, my old man turned to me
and said, "I got to be going, Terry. Got a lot of stuff I'm
doing now. Good stuff. You'd be proud of me."

"I already was," I told him.

He looked at me for a moment, then nodded. "You
take care of yourself. Till you see me again."

"I will."

He started to walk away, then stopped and came back
to me. He hugged me fiercely. "I've always loved you,
Terry." I held him back, hating the fact that I was going
to have to let him go.

"I got a bus to catch," my old man said after a bit. We
let each other go, then he walked to the solid wall of the
dead-end alley and stepped through the brick. I heard him
whistling, "Shave and a Haircut, Two Bits," only a little
while after he disappeared, but I couldn't help smiling.

That was my old man. And they didn't make them like
that anymore.

MATCHBOOK MAGIC
OR
HOW I SAVED THE WORLD FROM MORTIE DEMERZ

by Bill McCay

After various and sundry gigs in the publishing business, Bill McCay can testify as to the meager emolument. He also admits to living with several roommates over the years, though none were quite as exciting as Mortie DeMerz. He's written over sixty books, featuring everything from knock-knock jokes to no-knock drug raids. His Star Trek novel *Chains of Command*, written with Eloise Flood, enjoyed two weeks on the *New York Times* Paperback Bestseller List. And he's gotten his share of critical acclaim and fan letters for his five-novel series based on the movie *Stargate*.

Serious stuff. However, Bill can also be pretty silly. Case in point—"Matchbook Magic."

I ALWAYS thought Mortie DeMerz had a small soul . . . too small even for his scrawny, undersized body. Maybe that's the reason he was able to harness it in ways normal folks couldn't imagine.

Or maybe it's just a case of obsession.

He would cling to a given course long after any rational person would have bagged it. That's how he wound up with our apartment in the first place.

Mortie started out as the third guy in a dump that comfortably held two. But, because it was in the Village and we were all in college, three bodies were needed to pay the rent. Five years (and nine roommates) later, Mortie was the one who held the lease. It had only cost endless grief for anyone who lived with him and two teeth that one rather hulking roomie had knocked out during a disagreement.

I'd been around for about the last two years of this circus. Since graduation a year and a half ago, we'd managed to keep the apartment as a two-person space, although rent money was constantly precarious, given Mortie's job longevity.

Me, I'd been able to get and keep the position I wanted—editorial assistant at a large publishing company. There were days, of course . . . keeping up the monthly stream of Fizzy Farnum kid mysteries can do that to you. And, of course, the meager wage ensured I'd be staying in the roommate equation.

"Lang, I don't know why you'd want to hold on to such a punk job," Mortie often told me.

I'm Lang, by the way. Bob Lang. When Mortie started deriding my chosen profession, he had reason to condescend. He'd actually managed to get recruited before graduation, going to work in a big corporation's public-relations department. His personality being what it was, he soon found himself on the street.

Can I put this nicely? No. He had a problem hanging on to any job. Mortie moved to doing PR for a small company. Then it was fund-raising for a charity. I think the temp editing gig came after that—he got on the nerves of the accountants who were writing the training manuals. He pissed off the other temp word processors when he fell to that. Mortie even managed to aggravate the people dropping stuff off when he ran the copier. In his last career initiative, he'd been stocking shelves in the local Fair-mart.

The manager had canned him after Mortie had broken a wheel on an old lady's rolling walker.

"Bastards," he still grumbled from the couch two weeks later. "They just don't want anybody on the floor who speaks English."

He was in his usual pose. His feet, heavily callused and slightly gray, were propped on the sagging arm of the couch. Mortie didn't believe in slippers, calling them an unnecessary expense.

His right pinkie was engaged in digging the wax out of his ear. I never saw a guy for ear wax like Mortie.

He'd extract gobs of this thick brownish gunk from each ear. You'd find it rolled up in little balls all over the bathroom sink, and around all the ashtrays in the house.

Maybe what Mortie should have gone into was candle-making. Lord knows, he had the raw materials. Anyway, he knocked off excavation for the day and began fumbling at his shirt pocket. "Dammit!" he grunted. "I'da sworn I had one left."

He looked at me. "Lang, I need smokes."

"I'm not the one who smokes around here," I said.

"But you're the one who has money," Mortie pointed out. "I'll pay you back with my first unemployment check."

The guy's owed me money from the first unemployment check he drew two years ago. Sighing, I reached into my pocket. "How much?"

"Fifty cents." Mortie sat up, looking peeved at himself for answering honestly instead of hiking the amount. "Found this place in the East Village that'll sell them to me loose."

"What kind of cigarettes do you get that way?"

"Dunno." He shrugged, stuffing his feet into a pair of shoes. "Some kind of slants run the place. All they talk in is gibber-gabber. I think the only English they know is 'Fifty cent. One dallah!' "

If I thought a new nicotine fix would improve Mortie's mood, I was wrong. He returned about forty-five minutes later. The muscles of his face, usually stretched tighter than the knuckles of a fist, were twisted in a ferocious scowl.

"Screw them!" he said as he came in the door. "Screw the bastards!" From the sound of it, this was only the conclusion of a conversation he'd had with himself all the way home.

"Come to our country, and all they do is take advantage."

I looked up from the Fizzy Farnum cliff-hanger I was trying to fix. "Who?"

"Those freaking slants at the store!" He gave me one of those "weren't you listening?" looks. "I asked for matches, and they charged me."

I shook my head. Apparently, the magic of Mort's personality even transcended language barriers.

"Had to pay them a dime." Mortie continued his lament.

"I thought you were out of money."

He glared at me. "My last dime, all right?"

I shut up. Some things just weren't worth pursuing with Mortie. Other people might have skipped the matches and kept the dime. I remembered the time Mort had tried to light a butt from the kitchen range and set his hair on fire.

He dug in his pocket and thrust something under my nose. "Look at the crappy thing! And they wanted ten cents for it!"

The crumpled matchbook looked as if it had been printed by an English as a Fifth Language class. I squinted at the smudged type. "Learn power?"

"What?" Mort snatched it away. "It has advertising on it? It has advertising, and those lousy bastards made me buy it?"

He held up the cardboard cover, squinting. Then he rejoined me at the kitchen table where the light was better.

"Learn Power," I read again. "Learn to kill merely by point at enemy. Others in my secret cult kill me if they think I give away the secrets."

I looked up at him, but he leaned in, treating me to a blast of cigarette breath. "What else does it say?"

Back to deciphering. "You send five dollars to—it's a post office box downtown somewhere—and secrets of ancients revealed."

I was ready to laugh until I saw Mortie pacing back and forth. His index finger thrust through the air as if it were a stabbing weapon. "Learn to kill merely by pointing your finger at enemies," he muttered as if it were a mantra.

Lord knows, Mortie had lots of enemies, real and imagined.

He broke off, glaring at me as if I were prying into his life, and hurried off to his room.

I heard the rattle of drawers, then coins clinking against glass.

After a few minutes, Mortie came back out. He made the rounds of every upholstered piece in the living room, digging into the seams around the pillows. When he rose, more coins jingled in his hand.

I went for my pocket. "How much do you—"

"No!" He cut me off. "I'll take care of it myself."

It should have been a tip-off. Even from the beginning, he didn't want to share.

Mortie went to the hall closet and began going through the pockets of all the coats. He was probably hitting my clothes as well as his, but I didn't have the heart to call him on it.

Finally, after carefully rearranging the coins and counting them twice, Mortie looked up in triumph. "Five dollars," he announced, "and seven cents."

I still got to play bank. Mortie exchanged his piles of quarters, dimes, nickels and pennies for a crisp five dollar bill. He wrapped the bill in several layers of paper, then dug out an envelope he'd liberated from one of his former jobs. Crossing out the firm's name, he wrote in our address. Mortie triple-checked the P.O. box on the matchbook and finally wrote it in.

He brought the envelope back to his room, only to return again. "Need a stamp," he growled. "Got a couple I steamed off letters, but no stickum."

So I got to play post office for the start-up as well.

One of my household duties on coming home from work was to pick up the mail before tackling the five flights to our Sty in the Sky. Yes, Mortie was home much more than I was. You'd think he might take a couple of minutes to handle this little chore. But Mortie didn't like mail. He said it was usually trouble, and he stayed away from it . . . unless it was the day checks arrived from unemployment.

So there I was, juggling my backpack and a Fair-mart bag while I jiggled the worn key in the mailbox lock. A door opened down the hallway, and Mrs. Merson looked out. This building didn't need a doorman or even a lock on the front door. With eighty-year-old Mrs. Merson, we enjoyed round-the-clock security surveillance.

"Your friend got it—the little one," she announced, as if I still had other roommates I might confuse him with.

At least she talks to me. I don't know the history, but whenever she and Mortie meet in the halls, each pretends the other doesn't exist.

"Thanks, Mrs. M.," I said, recovering my key. Then I began the trek up the north face, the steep tenement staircase that led to the fifth floor.

The sty was its usual self. Mortie was ensconced on the couch, watching the tube. I noticed he'd tried a new arrangement to improve reception. A length of wire ran from the ball of foil wadded on the end of the antenna to one of the living room lamps. The picture was marginally better—we were down to only two ghost images. But the actors on the rerun of "Friends" still sounded like aliens from "Star Trek."

"I hear you got the mail," I said by way of greeting.

"Table," Mortie responded. "Bastard didn't send anything."

It took me a moment to switch over to his train of thought. "He probably hasn't even got your letter—or the five—yet."

"Bastards," Mortie muttered, back to the sitcom. "Screw 'em. Screw 'em all."

I got to enjoy ten days of increasing agitation over missing out on the secrets of ancients revealed. Even the arrival of Mortie's first unemployment check didn't distract him. After nixing a proposal that I call in sick and join him in a stake-out at the post office box, I decided to work late at the office.

The mailbox was empty when I got home. I made my way up the stairs and unlocked the apartment door. Silence. Mortie would usually be on the couch, abusing the contestants on "Who Wants to be a Millionaire."

"Mortie?" The kitchen was empty. So was the living room. I went to the door of his bedroom, which hung ajar.

What I saw made me gasp. Mortie was on the bed—well, half on the bed, from his legs to his butt. The rest of him hung head down. His scrawny torso was bare.

All he had on was a gray pair of briefs. All sorts of wild thoughts went through my brain. Stroke . . . auto-asphyxiation . . . I could just see the smirks on the EMS team when I'd have to let them in. . . .

The kitchen timer suddenly bonged, and Mortie opened his eyes and began sitting up.

"What the hell are you doing?" he demanded, glaring.

"That's what I was going to ask," I said.

"It came!" he announced, grabbing up a sheet of paper.

I squinted across the room at the purplish lettering. I hadn't seen something like that since grammar school.

"Mimeograph?" I said in disbelief.

"It's the ladder of mental exercises." Mortie got off the bed and headed toward me. "You start off hanging upside down and thinking of nothing."

Okay, I admit it. I read the blurry list of pidgin English. I even tried some of the exercises. All I got was a headache.

Maybe it was because I couldn't make out whether I should hang upside-down thinking of nothing for thirty or eighty minutes.

Anyway, like any sane person, I did something stupid, then I stopped. Mort kept at it. I didn't know how far he'd gone until the kitchen incident.

One of the reasons our place deserved the name Sty in the Sky was a difference of opinion on housekeeping. Myself, I believe there's clean dirt and dirty dirt. A pile of newspapers in the living room—clean dirt. Balls of ear wax in the kitchen—dirty dirt.

When I found greasy plates crawling with roaches, I called Mortie on it. He responded by complaining about clutter in the living room. When we descended to the respective disease-bearing merits of papers and roaches, Mortie offered a deal.

"I'll kill the little bastards if you pick 'em up."

Considering his slow reflexes, this was, to put it mildly, an unlikelihood. I agreed just for the entertainment value, and sent him off with our second-best spatula. (I didn't want to be turning my eggs on a roach-killing weapon, thank you very much.)

Fifteen minutes passed with Mortie merely muttering

in the distance. That was way too quiet. I'd expected my roommate to wreck the place in his bug pursuit. Instead, he emerged from the kitchen with a smug expression. "You're up."

I went in expecting to find the results of a single lucky shot. Instead, the dishes were covered with a small mound of cockroaches. Gingerly, I loaded them into a garbage bag then swept up the remaining dead from the countertop. One thing struck me. Not a one of them had been squashed.

I sniffed around. Nothing. Just that overcharged, tingly feeling you get right before you let go with a fat spark of static electricity. I stuck my head into the living room. "Okay, Mortie. What did you spray them with? We've got to eat off these plates, you know."

He was ensconced on the couch, watching the tube. "Untouched by human hands," he said. "Or chemicals." He blew across the top of his finger as if he were getting the smoke out of a gun barrel.

I washed the damned dishes until the design almost came off the plastic.

The next demonstration came a few days later. I was home early for once. The end of the day had been reserved for a farewell party for one of the older editors. I'd bailed after the first glass of cheap wine.

Mortie greeted me at the door with, "That goddamn neighbor's dog. It's been barking all day."

Edie Butler was our next door neighbor, a young lady who lived alone. She kept a big Labrador for company and protection. Mister was generally a well-behaved mutt. But every once in a while, he'd get lonely while Edie was off at work. Mister would call for her . . . and call for her. . . .

Now, most people with a free day and a barking dog next door would have gone out. Not Mortie. By the time I got home, he was positively homicidal.

"Here's what we do," he said, pushing up the window that opened onto the air shaft. "I lean out. You hold onto me."

I leaned out, doing a little mental calculation. "You'll barely reach Edie's window," I said. "What will you do?"

"I'll shut up that goddamn mutt," Mortie growled.

Don't ask me how he got his way. Soon enough, Mortie had one knee on the outside window ledge while I held onto his belt. I heard his hand slap on brick. "Mister—hey, Mister!" he called.

The dog's barks grew louder. Suddenly, I felt a quiver go through Mortie's frame. I heard the words "Screw you!" and that static-electricity tingle made the hairs on my arms stand up.

Oh—and the barking stopped.

About an hour later, a tearful Edie Butler was at our door. "I just came home from work—Mister's dead!"

Mortie didn't even turn from the sitcom he was watching. I accompanied Edie to her place. Mister lay in a heap in front of the air shaft window. I also noticed the window was closed. Mortie couldn't have passed something to the dog.

Edie just stood over us as I checked for the doggie equivalent of a pulse. There were tears in her eyes.

The tears began to fall when I confirmed her fear. "But Mister was only a couple of years old!" she protested. "This shouldn't be happening."

"Could he have got at anything he shouldn't have?" I asked. "Bug spray, or something like that?"

"I don't use that stuff because of Mister," Edie replied. "Besides, the bugs seem to have gone down recently."

I helped Edie wrap Mister up and got her the city number to call for a pickup. Then I went back to my place to confront Mortie.

"Okay," I said. "What's going on?"

"The Master's exercises have paid off," Mortie replied. The guy who'd bilked him out of five bucks had become "the Master" two days after the mimeo page arrived. Too many kung fu movies in Mortie's past, I guess.

"That—" I swallowed the word "crap," and made a more diplomatic substitution. "That paper you got?"

"You saw it," Mortie said. "The exercises to harness the will. The trigger phrase—"

" 'Screw you,' " I said.

The look he gave me was positively murderous. "How—?"

"I heard you say it just before the dog died."

He sank back on the couch. "Just keep it to yourself, Lang."

I headed for my room. "Who would believe me, anyway."

The evidence, you might say, was mounting. Still, I could dismiss it was coincidence and wishful thinking.

I was getting the mail about a week later when Mrs. Merson popped out, brimming with a hot piece of gossip. She still had the phone in her hand. "You know that nice Mr. Jessup at Fair-mart?" she asked. "He just passed away. Dropped right in the store."

Her face suddenly hardened and she disappeared into her apartment. I turned as the front door swung open. A very smug Mortie DeMerz walked in . . . carrying a Fair-mart shopping bag.

It definitely did not make sense. It defied rational logic. But people began dying. People on Mortie's enemies list.

He started buying a newspaper, an unheard-of expense for him, just so he could circle articles. Some were just obituaries—I recognized the names of temps or staff people he'd worked with. Then a corporate vice president from his first job collapsed at lunch.

Mortie laughed over that one. "Bastard had a window table, of course. Couldn't have been easier!"

Then the comedy star who'd fronted the telethon during Mortie's fund-raising stint was run over.

"Got him crossing the street against the light." Mortie jabbed out with his finger. "Perfect."

I shied away from the digit. "Careful where you point that thing."

Mortie gave me a superior look. "I wasn't primed. You have nothing to worry about."

Sure, but I got the unspoken corollary. "As long as you don't annoy me."

Week by week, the papers piled up on the kitchen table. This was clutter Mortie could appreciate. It was a record of collapses and deaths among executives, supervisors, and coworkers who'd somehow crossed Mortie. I recognized a couple of professors and college classmates. The hulking roommate who'd knocked Mortie's teeth out died in a men's room—on the pot.

"Couldn't resist it when I saw him go in," Mortie crowed. "Got into the stall next door, squatted down, and let him have it."

The papers became a bit more sporadic for a while. And the names were more unfamiliar. Teachers. People from high school and grammar school.

When Mrs. Merson passed away, Mortie didn't even mention it. But when I heard how she was discovered— found half-in, half-out of her apartment—I could fill in the details.

The outside door being unlocked . . . Mrs. M. checking to see who it was . . . making eye contact with Mortie . . . the old woman turning away, Mortie energizing himself, pointing . . . "Screw you!"

After Mrs. Merson, I figured Mortie had exhausted even his lengthy enemies list. It didn't improve his disposition, though. He paced around the apartment like a caged beast. I avoided him as much as possible, and walked on eggshells when I was around him.

Then came the night he burst into my room. "I've got it, Lang!" Mortie cried.

"What–what?" He'd woken me from a sound sleep.

"The Master gave me this power for a reason. I'm going to use it to make myself rich."

I blinked, trying to unstick my eyelids. "How are you going to do that?"

"The details will need work—Swiss bank accounts, stuff like that. But here it is. Unless I get one million dollars, the mayor will die."

I stared at him, speechless.

"He's a public figure, right? I won't put any time limit. Sooner or later he'll have to make a speech or something. And I'll be there with my finger."

"It won't work," I said, shocked awake.

"Why?" I could feel that staticky energy drawing up in the room. "Who'd tell them?"

"It's not that," I hastily explained. "The powers that be might make a connection between a threat like you're suggesting and the mayor getting shot. But people drop dead all the time. How will they know it's you and not nature?"

"I'll tell them he'll drop dead. And a time limit—say, a year. . . ."

"They'll think you're just playing the odds. If someone had threatened you that way before you saw the matchbook . . . would you have believed it?"

"I might," Mortie said grimly. "After the second or third mayor died. Then I could move up. The governor. Senators. The president."

I had to derail this train of thought. "With each of them, you'll have more people looking for you. And it will be harder to get paid. There's a lot of stuff you're not thinking of. Half of my job is crime fiction, remember."

"Little kids' mysteries," Mortie sneered. "Screw you, Lang."

But he wasn't pointing his finger, and the subject was at least tabled for the time being.

A couple of weeks later, he met me as I was leaving work. "I think I got it figured out, Lang," Mortie announced.

I didn't need to guess what the "it" was.

"C'mon" Mortie said, "let's walk for a bit."

Unwillingly, I accompanied this undersized murderer through the city streets. When we got to Fourteenth and Seventh, he brought us to a halt outside the big white-brick apartment building.

"This should be the spot," he said.

Traffic crawled by on its way to the Holland Tunnel. A bus passed. Then came another, but this one didn't continue south. It swerved out and around, preparing for a turn west.

The air grew charged, and Mortie pointed. "Screw you!" he grunted venomously.

Aboard the bus, the driver suddenly slumped over his wheel. The huge, half-turned vehicle careened across three lanes of traffic, smashing four cars and an SUV. Then it rammed into the drugstore diagonally across the intersection from us. Even as it hit, the bus slewed over onto its side. The screech of metal, shattering glass, and screams filled the air.

I stared at the carnage, appalled. Except for what had happened to Mister, I'd never seen Mortie at work.

Mortie, on the other hand, glowed with the satisfaction of a job well-done.

"I figure about three of these, and then a note to the Transit Authority asking how much they'll pay to see it stop," he gloated. "There are so many buses, so many corners where they turn. Then there are delivery trucks. FedEx would pay big, I bet. Subway motormen. Airplane pilots . . ."

Walking home, I tasted bile the whole way. I thought I'd discouraged Mortie from this extortion thing. Instead of single victims, he was setting his sights on multiple targets!

I let Mortie think I was leaving early for work the next day. Then, using a pay phone. I called in sick. I reached the address from the matchbook before the post office opened its doors.

It was a tiny substation. The good part was that you could see all the mailboxes. The bad part? Well, you're a little conspicuous standing around a closet-sized space for eight hours. The window clerk certainly gave me quizzical looks. Let me tell you something else. Eight hours without lunch or bathroom breaks is a long, long time.

And it was all for nothing. Nobody came to collect from Box 104. That was where Mortie had sent his five bucks.

"Son, we're closing," the elderly window clerk called over to me.

My shoulders slumped in defeat.

"Waiting for someone?" the old guy asked.

"I was hoping to see whoever has Box 104," I replied.

"Oh, Mr. Fung," the clerk said. "Nice little guy. Used to be in here every day collecting his mail. Damnedest bunch of little envelopes he'd get. I swear, some were addressed in crayon."

I could have kicked myself for not trying this earlier.

"Is there somewhere I could get hold of Mr. Fung?"
I asked.

" 'Fraid not," the garrulous clerk replied. "Poor little
guy keeled over just as he got his mail. What was it?
Ten days ago?"

That was it, then. There was no appealing to Mortie's
Master. Somehow, I'd have to handle this myself.

Mortie was in his usual pose, on the couch, digging
for wax. I walked over to the TV and shut it off.

"Bastard!" Mortie yelled. "I was watching that."

"We've got to talk," I said. "I spent the day trying to
get hold of your Master."

Mortie's pop-eyed look was almost comical. "You
went looking for the Master? What did he say?"

"His name was Mr. Fung," I said. "And he's not saying anything to anyone these days. He's dead. Keeled
over in the post office. Sound familiar?"

Mortie glared in outrage. "You thought I killed the
Master? What the hell do you think I am?"

"You're a guy who killed a busload of people because
you could."

Mortie wasn't listening. He was still mulling over
Fung's death. "Maybe the guys from the cult caught up
with him."

"Maybe he was opening doors that should never be
opened," I said. "When you started this, I couldn't quite
believe it. Then . . . God, I don't know. At least you
felt you had some sort of reason.

"But yesterday—none of those people had done you
any harm. You've got to stop it, Mortie."

His laugh brayed out. "And you're going to stop me?
How? You couldn't handle the exercises. What are you
going to do? Warn the cops? Approach the FBI? They
won't refer you to the X-files, ya know. They'll just put
you in a rubber room."

That was my problem in a nutshell. Laughter was the
least I could expect from informing the proper authorities. They'd think I was a nut. And if my warnings were
borne out, then I'd be a dangerous nut.

"I'll take that pile of newspapers from the kitchen to

the cops," I threatened. "I—I'll find that goddamn cult. Write letters, articles. You'll never enjoy any money you make killing people."

Even as I spoke, I could feel the electricity building up in the room. That's not supposed to happen in humid situations. And, Lord knows, I was sweating.

"I figured it out much simpler," Mortie twisted, excavating again with his pinkie. "A bag full of cash someplace deserted. If anybody's looking, I give 'em the finger."

"Just brilliant," I said. "Suppose they have cameras watching you? Or telescopes? Or a telescopic sight on a rifle?"

Mortie's face crumpled as I kicked holes in his scheme. Then it went nasty. "Screw you!" he spat at me.

He never should have said that with his pinkie in his ear.

There was a little *tzing!* like a big, fat spark leaping from a fingertip.

Mortie flopped lifeless from the couch.

And that's how I saved the world from Mortie De-Merz. I've scribbled all this down while waiting for the cops, EMS, whoever.

No, they're not going to see this. The proper authorities will just get the facts. My roomie was digging wax out of his ear and dropped dead.

These pages, Mr. Fung's mimeographed sheet, and the matchbook will all go into a manila envelope. If I had my way, I'd burn them all. I've got a bad feeling I might need this stuff, however. If Mr. Fung was killed off by the cult, they may have gotten his sucker list. And if they come calling, I want them to know exactly what happened.

One thing, though.

I just hope they don't point first and ask questions later.

SOMETIMES IT'S SWEET

by *Susan Sizemore*

Susan Sizemore lives in the Midwest and spends most of her time writing. Some of her other favorite things are coffee, dogs, travel, movies, hiking, history, farmers markets, art glass, and basketball—you'll find mention of quite a few of these things inside the pages of her stories. She works in many genres, from contemporary romance to epic fantasy and horror. She's the winner of the Romance Writers of America's Golden Heart Award, and a nominee for the Rita Award in historical romance. Her books include historical romance novels, and a dark fantasy series, *The Laws of the Blood*.

"IT'S not fair!"

"Hush, Pero," Alcinia warned. She put her hand over the imp's sharp-toothed little mouth, then looked furtively around the dark storeroom while Pero squirmed and bit and made an awful fuss. She was the only person who knew she kept such an unconventional little familiar, and she wanted to keep it that way. She didn't know why or how her family had acquired such a nasty little creature, but Pero had been passed from witch to witch on her mother's side for at least two hundred years. Mother had been most insistent and eager to send him along with her when Alcinia was accepted at the great magical college of Bantieth.

Bantieth! The very name still filled Alcinia with wonder, even though she was presently relegated to the kitchens and her sleeping quarters consisted of this musty storeroom shared with eight other scullery maids. Ah, but abovestairs was a world of velvet and gold, silk and silver, music and light and magical moving tapestries. And the books! Thousands upon thousands on shelves reaching to painted ceilings a hundred feet high. The greatest treasures

of all Bantieth were the volumes bound in gilt and leather
containing the wonders of the multiple worlds!

Bantieth was all she'd ever wanted.

"I'm lucky to still be here," she whispered to the wriggling imp pressed against her chest. She looked around
furtively, hoping no one was watching or listening, praying no one was disturbed. For she'd been warned that if
she caused the least bit of trouble or showed anything
less than perfect humility, it would all be over for her.
Though her heart ached and her pride grated, she tried
to make herself believe that a year and a day was not too
high a price to pay for the hope of someday returning to
the studies that had been so cruelly interrupted. "Do
settle down," she pleaded. *"Please."*

But Pero was on a hysterical tear, and it became obvious to Alcinia within a few wearying moments that nothing short of wringing his leathery little neck was going
to calm the imp before he had a chance to vent his
outrage. So she got up as quietly as she could and tip-
toed over the thin pallets of her fellow exhausted serv-
ingwomen. She longed for rest herself; she was not used
to manual labor and knew sleep would come easily for
her even on an uncomfortable bed in a strange place if
only Pero would settle down. Her hands were raw from
scrubbing dishes, her muscles were sore from hours of
fetching and carrying unaccustomed loads. She had a
burn on her right wrist from learning how to use an iron.
And aching calves and a blister on her left heel from
running errands up and down rough wooden and stone
servants' stairs of the great castle that she hadn't even
known existed a few days ago. She had come to Bantieth
to learn the secrets of the universe, but the secrets of
how servants made themselves invisible to their betters
were her lot in life now.

Pero was correct. It was not fair.

She could leave. She could lift her head high and walk
away. Or she could cry until she went blind from tears,
and beat her hands against the cold stones of the floor
until they were bloody. There were several things she
could do.

"You could get even," was the first thing Pero said

after she slipped into a dank privy lit only by a sliver of moonlight from a tiny window near the ceiling and took her hand from his mouth.

"No."

"You should get even," Pero declared, his little green face screwed up with sudden glee. "You will get even."

How? she wondered. "With who?" she asked.

"The prince, of course," Pero answered. "He's the one who did it. It is not right that you pay for his crime."

"What does right have to do with anything?" she asked, hating that the last few days had made her cynical beyond her years. "He is a prince, I am the daughter of a magistrate."

"A high magistrate," Pero pointed out proudly. He was quite the snob about her hedge witch mother having married into the gentry. "He's not an important prince," Pero went on. "He's a third son sent to be a wizard because there's no other place for him. He hasn't got any talent. The explosion proved that."

True enough. Alcinia nodded, but didn't say so out loud. She was not going to let herself be bitter. She would never survive the next year if she fell into the trap of being bitter and aggrieved. "Please calm down, Pero. Everything will work out all right. You'll see." She had to believe that or the next year would be endless exile in hell.

"How can I be calm?" The imp spat, the results leaving an acrid aroma and the faint sizzle of acid eating into stone.

She'd forgotten that he could excrete several sorts of poisons at will. "Please don't do that again," she requested.

"Your father should know. He will not permit—"

"He does know. Of course he knows. The Council of Elect sent him a transcript of the trial, along with the announcement of their decision."

"The decision to punish the wrong person!"

"I was in the Gray Tower when I wasn't supposed to be."

"You were lost trying to find Lady Root's rooms! You had a note! You walked in on that vicious boy botching the casting of a spell beyond his powers by mistake and everyone knows it! He lied when he claimed he walked in on you, and the Council let him get away with it!"

"He is a prince," Alcinia reminded her familiar once again. "They could have expelled me instead of imposing a year and a day as a servant to pay for the damages."

"Your father could pay for the damages—not that he should have to."

"The point is that I'm supposed to learn lessons about responsibility and duty and obedience."

"You didn't do anything!"

"It doesn't matter, Pero. *I will not* be sent away. I will give them no cause to send me away. I *will* be the first sorceress in our family. That's all I'm going to think about."

"You should think about revenge."

"I don't believe in revenge."

"Why not? It's fun."

Alcinia shook her head. "Father once told me that he's tried many cases involving people getting revenge on their enemies. All those people could think about night and day was getting even. They nursed their hate and lived for nothing else but making their enemies pay for the wrongs committed against them. He told me those people who ended up in his court for judgment were nothing but shells, their souls burned out by the desire for revenge, with nothing to live for once they had their revenge. He said, *'They let their enemies control their lives because hatred consumed their every thought and deed, so they had no lives. To seek revenge is true defeat.'* I will never be defeated." She shook her head. "Never. Besides," she added, "it isn't nice."

"Nice!" Pero was so indignant sparks shot out of his pointed ears, and noxious aromas discharged from other parts of his body.

It was enough to make Alcinia cough, and her eyes sting. She didn't see anything wrong with being nice, but Pero was a demon, albeit a small one, and very loyal to her family. It was natural for the little imp to have different views about morals even after serving several generations of white witches. Mostly white witches. There were whispered tales still in the Cragin Forest about the fates of those who crossed her great grandmother. Pero had always said great grandmother was his favorite mistress.

When Pero cackled with wicked laughter, Alcinia murmured, "Oh, dear," and held him up before her by the flappy thick skin at the back of his neck. "What are you thinking?" she demanded. It was late. She was exhausted. She wanted to retreat to her pallet and have a good cry. The last thing she wanted was a confrontation with her own personal imp.

"If you won't seek revenge for yourself, then I'll do it for you."

"You will not!"

"It is a matter of honor."

"It's a matter of your wanting to cause mischief." She shook him. Even though he turned invisible, she still had him in her grip and didn't let him go. You had to be firm with imps. "I won't have it. I forbid it. Do you understand?"

"Yes, mistress," he acknowledged after a few moments and showed himself again.

"I mean it."

"Yes, mistress."

He sounded contrite enough, but she didn't trust the red glint in his goatlike eyes. She was so dreadfully tired. She decided to accept his promise and do her best to keep an eye on him. "Come along," she said, and carried him out of the privy. "I want to go to bed."

Pero was nowhere to be found the next morning, in visible or invisible state. Alcinia hunted for him with a growing sense of dread whenever she had a free moment, but she was given very few free moments. She'd never realized how much work by how many callused hands it took to keep the great magical school of Bantieth running. The castle was ancient, huge, said to be full of more rooms than anyone had ever counted, with a population of instructors, students, researchers, and visitors that numbered close to two thousand. Not counting the servants.

She already knew she would never take servants for

granted again, and vowed to treat all menial workers
with kindness and fairness in the future. She also fer-
vently wished that she could be as invisible as her imp
as she performed her own duties abovestairs. She
dreaded the thought of drawing attention to herself, of
being stared at and teased by her former fellow students
or instructors. She hoped that to the people she served
she appeared exactly the same as every other woman in
a shapeless gray dress and head scarf who moved about
in the background of their colorful exciting world; unre-
markable, unrecognizable.

She had no such luck, of course. The duties assigned
her in her first days of punishment had kept her away
from contact with her former fellow students and teachers. She'd hoped that this would continue. Doing dishes
and working in the laundry and running errands among
the other servants had been hard and horrible, but bear-
able because she remained unseen by those who knew
her. Her luck ran out in the middle of the afternoon
when her furtive hunt for her imp was interrupted by an
under housekeeper handing her brushes, brooms, and
buckets and telling her to sweep out the ashes in the
fireplace in the Blue Tapestry Hall.

Alcinia knew the Hall very well. The walls were covered in huge tapestries depicting scenes of sea and sky,
and the hearth was huge. Large enough to roast two or
three oxen. She recalled that the mantel was covered in
giant seashells and stuffed peacocks, which she thought
an ugly and odd combination. It was used as a feast hall
during great festivals, but on ordinary days the trestle
tables were stored away and the great open space was
used for classes in magical martial and musical arts.
She'd spent several weeks learning the steps to dance
spells in a class that met very near the ugly fireplace she
was now assigned to clean out.

Of course the room was full of students when she
entered. She took a gulp of air as she stood in the doorway, and surveyed the room with her head lowered, hoping her head covering was enough to hide her shining
red hair and obscure her pale, large-eyed face. She didn't
want to look at all the colorful, bright beings that covered the room like fields of butterflies. A few days ago

she would have been among the brightly dressed throng, wearing the silver-trimmed turquoise robe of her rank. Tears stung her eyes and caught painfully in her throat when she beheld all the strange, beautiful things in their varied and vivid blue, green, purple, pink, yellow, red, and orange clothing embroidered in marvelous designs in silver, gold, and copper metallic thread. She hungered to return to this world, and already scarcely remembered what it had been like to be a creature of color with rank and privileges and purpose.

Alcinia refused to cry, but she did sigh. With drooping shoulders and her gaze turned toward the shining black-tiled floor she clutched her cleaning equipment and made her way silently and inconspicuously along the wall to the empty, gaping mouth of the huge fireplace. She stayed well out of the way of the busy classes, glad that none of them were gathered near the hearth. She set about her assigned task clumsily, but vigorously, and was delighted that her face soon bore a coating of ash as gray as her shapeless dress. A week ago, if someone had ordered her to clean away a mound of ash, she could have used a simple spell to transport the stuff to one of the castle's many refuse pits, had she known where such a place was located. Servants did not perform magic, and she was specifically forbidden to use even the most insignificant spell as part of her punishment—punishment for having been in the right place at the right time to be used as a scapegoat for a petty, selfish boy who would not own up to his own mistakes, and was that any way for a prince to behave let alone a future court wizard? And—she sighed, noticing the dark cloud of bitter ashes she'd stirred up with ever more angry sweeps of her broom. She was more distressed and angry than she thought, wasn't she? Good thing Pero wasn't here to notice.

Unfortunately—

"Well, well, look who we have here."

The prince. His name was Cardo. He had a voice like nails on a slate. And he was big, his shadow blocked out the light as he stepped in front of her. He wore an orange robe embroidered in copper, not the colors of a high-ranking student, but a gold filigree band held long

black hair off his forehead, indicating his rank in the
royal house of Ruselan. Alcinia tried not to pay any
attention, but she couldn't help but notice that he was
not alone. Elia the Fair in peacock blue and gold, slender and lovely as any half-elf should be had also approached the hearth, and Korwin of Lisedale, Prince
Cardo's constant companion, was at Cardo's side. She
noted with a certain small degree of pleasure that Korwin was dressed in lime green and silver, meaning he
was now two ranks ahead of his royal friend.

"She looks fetching in gray, don't you think?" Cardo
asked Korwin. "Good to see a jumped-up peasant put
back in her place."

Alcinia bit her lip and went on with her work, though
in truth his words struck her like a hard blow across the
back. Her first impulse was to hurl a bucket of ash in
the prince's smug face. In fact, she grasped the handle
and lifted the heavy bucket before she realized she'd
done it.

Elia said, "You're not impressing anyone."

The half-elf's words managed to distract Alcinia long
enough for her to quell the impulse for revenge. *Revenge
is bad,* she reminded herself, gritting her teeth. Really,
really bad. Only, faced with Cardo's mockery, she wasn't
quite sure why. Confusion warred with humiliation, the
reaction strong enough to make her dizzy, and start her
stomach aching. Ooh, how she wanted to say something
bright and clever and cunning to make Cardo blush with
shame. She kept her tongue behind her teeth instead,
though to her surprise the words from one of the wicked
spells from her great grandmother's grimoire appeared
bright and clear in her head.

No, no, no. She would not say a word. Especially not
those words. Though Alcinia couldn't help but smile a
little, knowing that she could make the spell work if she
wanted to, which was more than could be said for the
prince who stood there glowering at her.

"Let's go." Korwin plucked the prince's sleeve. Alcinia noticed Korwin looking around furtively. "Please."

"There are already enough people not talking to you
for letting Alcinia take your punishment," Elia said.

"I didn't do it," Cardo protested.

"Rubbish," Elia brushed his words away. "I don't know why I'm talking to you."

"Because you want to be a court sorceress," Cardo shot back. This caused Elia to lift her chin proudly and walk away. For some reason this caused Cardo to glare at Alcinia and demand, "Now look what you've done!"

Alcinia was glad she was filthy. It made it easier to get past the prince, for he stepped aside to avoid getting ashes on his robe when she took a step toward him. She held the heavy bucket full of cinders before her with both hands and moved back toward the servants' entrance to the hall. The last thing she expected was for Cardo to follow her. She heard his footsteps behind her, and Korwin's behind him, and silence sweeping the vast room with every step they took across it.

"Leave her alone!"

She pretended not to hear Korwin's whisper, though it was the only sound in the hall. By now everyone was watching their little procession. After a few excruciating moments it occurred to Alcinia that if she was being stared at, so was Cardo. He could make a fool of himself if he wanted to, but he was not going to make a fool of her. So, though she kept her gaze humbly lowered like any good servant girl, she straightened her shoulders and walked on to the servants' door with all the dignity she could muster. She looked neither to the right nor left, and paid no mind when a wave of whispering began to fill the earlier silence. She reached the door, opened it, and walked out of the bright and brilliant Blue Tapestry Hall into the bare stone corridor with her burden.

She did not know why Cardo continued to follow her down the hall, but he did. It was as though someone had attached his shadow to the hem of her skirt because he couldn't seem to make himself draw away. When he dared touch her on the shoulder, she shook him off.

Her path took her from the corridor to one of the bridges that spanned above the courtyards connecting the high towers of the castle. This bridge was suspended beneath the shadow of the retaining wall of the Great Garden. Flowering vines hung down from massive containers perched on top of the wall high overhead, and a trickle of water flowed down a moss grown path to a pool in a courtyard far below. The garden itself was beautiful, one of the wonders of the world, but Alcinia found passing beneath the wall on the narrow footbridge unexpectedly oppressive and nerve-racking. It did not help that she was being trailed by a prince and his friend.

"I want to talk to you," Cardo said when they reached the center of the span. "Stop. I command you to stop."

She could not very well ignore a direct order. So she stopped, and stood stiffly with her back to the prince for nearly a minute before she swung around. As she did so, her gaze was drawn upward as something moved at the edge of the garden wall overhead. "Hell!" she shouted, or so the young men heard, for the word "Pero" meant hell in her native dialect.

The boys looked up, just as a huge flowerpot came rushing down. Alcinia did not know what gave her the strength other than the rush of absolute terror, but she bowled into Cardo, and the next thing she knew was that she was lying on top of Prince Cardo. Korwin was sprawled beneath him, and they were all a good ten feet away from the pot when it smashed down with a spectacular, shattering boom on the spot where Cardo had been standing. A rain of dirt, pottery shards, and blossoms covered them within moments, but without doing much damage.

Alcinia's heart was still thundering in her ears when Korwin crawled out from under Cardo, helped her to her feet, held her hands in his, and said breathlessly, "You saved our lives." He turned and glared down at Cardo. "She saved *your* life."

Cardo crawled to his feet slowly, and shook his head in a dazed fashion. He looked at the remains of the pot. He looked up at the top of the garden wall. He shook his head, and looked everywhere but at Alcinia.

Korwin sniffed, and closed his eyes while he waved his hands about theatrically. Alcinia watched him with skeptical amusement, though she remembered she'd been just as dramatic when she'd been at Korwin's class level. "No magic," he said after a few moments. "Mortal mischief." His eyes came open in a shocked rush. "The Halstin assassins!"

"The vendetta's against my father," Cardo said.

"The pot was meant to crush you," Korwin shot back. "If it hadn't been for Alcinia—"

Cardo shook his head violently. "No!" he shouted. "I don't owe her anything. I don't! Don't you dare tell anyone!" he added before he turned and ran back the way they'd come.

"You saved us," Korwin said to Alcinia. "I'm grateful. I'll tell the High Wizard that—"

"Don't," she interrupted quickly. The last thing she wanted was an investigation that might lead to Pero, which would lead to her, and only make things worse. Besides, Cardo already knew she had saved him. She smiled inwardly at that. "You don't want to jeopardize your own place at court," she told Korwin. "I'm sure it was a freak accident. Let it go and leave me out of it, please."

"I don't like to, but—" Korwin leaned forward and swiftly kissed her dusty cheek. "All right, for now," he said.

Then he followed his friend, leaving Alcinia with a tingling cheek and a small glow inside her. She was so happy that she forgot she was going to have to find Pero and lock him in a spell cupboard before he could do any more damage.

"No parent likes to think they've raised a fool, and a petty one at that, but that seems to be what I've done." King Simond glared across the room at the white-clad High Wizard Vormen and added, "What you've done has only compounded the boy's foolishness."

"Sire, I thought—"

"A wizard that thinks! Please don't do that, I have quite enough problems already."

Vormen tugged on his beard and tried to look ingratiating. "The Halstin vendetta. I've heard about the threat of assassination. I'm sure we can provide you with the most powerful warding spells to—"

"I have wizards and sorcerers of my own, Vormen. Mostly I rely on my royal bodyguards to protect me while we negotiate with the Halstins. They want my attention more than they want me dead, anyway. It's all an elaborate game with them. Fortunately, I know how to play."

The king drained a jewel-encrusted gold welcoming goblet of its contents, made a face at the sweet herbs the wizards saw fit to use to ruin perfectly good wine, then banged the empty goblet down for emphasis. He noticed Vormen wince when the heavy goblet landed on the delicate painted tiles of the table. He'd arrived after a hard ride, covered in muck, and swept into the High Wizard's private quarters for a talk about his son. While wizards were not supposed to be interested in worldly possessions, the king noted that Vormen had exquisite and very expensive tastes. There was nothing austere about the High Wizard's quarters. All the luxury left Simond wondering, not for the first time, about why the school of Bantieth was exempt from paying taxes.

He took a seat in the room's best chair, a cushion-padded, carved thing more elaborate than his own throne, and said, "Explain to me what fool thing you've done."

Vormen fluttered his long, white hands. Then he tugged on his long white beard. "It was a test of character really. Not just for the boy, but for the girl, as well. Her mother's family, you see, well—"

"Did my son commit an infraction of the school rules or not?"

"Well, technically, there is no proof that—"

"You know I hate sycophants, Vormen."

"Probably," Vormen answered. "But I do not have conclusive proof. He refused to admit to it. My hope was that he would not let another take the blame for his actions. So far he has not come forward to make a confession."

"Of course not. The weasel thinks he got away with something."

"But I don't understand. Most of the other students have ostracized him. Even his best friends are angry with him. You would think peer pressure would—"

"He's the sort of prince who doesn't think he needs friends. Don't know if he'll ever learn that being a prince isn't all a man needs to be. Or being a wizard." Simond shook his head. "Don't know how he got to be so spoiled." Simond sighed. "Test of character for both of 'em, you say? Why is this girl being punished?"

"Alcinia has great talent, sire, great potential. A test—"

"So, you've decided that making this potentially great sorceress bitter against the throne and the school is a good idea?"

Vormen wrung his hands. "She seems to be taking it very well."

"Considering that she has no business being punished."

"Well, yes, but—"

"You've sent for them?"

"Yes. I—"

"Then stop talking so much and send them in."

Vormen looked more than a little relieved to open the door then retreat into the shadows. Cardo did not look at all relieved to step into the room, his father noted. The girl Alcinia, alert and intelligent looking, and pretty despite the shapeless gray clothing, stepped in behind his son. At least she had the courtesy to bow properly, while Cardo stood there like a recalcitrant lump.

"Hello, my dear," he said, with a smile.

"Father, I—"

"I wasn't talking to you. I'll have a glass of wine, Alcinia," Simond said. "And pour some for yourself, as well."

Alcinia had been nervous enough over being sent to the High Wizard. She thought surely that they'd found out what Pero had done. She'd found him, threatened to call up the spirit of her great grandmother to deal with him if he didn't behave, then locked him in a magic box with a five-day locking spell even though she was forbidden from using magic. It was a spell so tiny she didn't think anyone would notice. Then she'd been summoned by Vormen anyway. Even worse, Cardo was already waiting in the antechamber to the High Wizard's quarters when she arrived. He paced back and forth and raged at her until the door opened and they had no choice but to go into the inner chamber.

She didn't understand why the king was seated in the

High Wizard's chair, or why he told her to fetch drinks, but she hurried to obey. Behind her, Cardo continued to sputter and try to get a sentence in, but the king raged at him. She almost felt sorry for Cardo. Still, the confrontation between father and son kept the king from noticing how badly her hands shook when she picked up the wine pitcher. The handle slipped from her sweaty hands and the golden ewer banged back down on the table, hard enough to slop out some of the dark red liquid onto the lovely tiled tabletop. She quickly snatched off her head scarf to wipe up the mess, and noticed the herbs mixed in with the wine. Suspicion caused all her nervousness to flee, and she lifted her damp scarf to her nose. Then she picked up the wine container and took a deeper sniff.

"Excuse me," she said, turning around with the pitcher held between her hands. The king was shouting at Cardo by now, so she had to shout herself when she said again, "Excuse me!"

"What?" Simond snarled at the girl. He hated being interrupted. He frowned at her, and he knew how daunting his frown could be. "What?" he repeated. He waved a finger at her. "I've come here to hear your case, but if you think you can—"

"Poison."

Her interruption caught him in mid-tirade. "What?" She had his full attention now.

She held out the ewer. "Poison," she repeated. "It's a common herb, makleweed. Used to kill vermin in the country. Slow acting on humans, but effective, if enough is taken. It's been mixed in with the sweetening herbs."

"How can you tell?" Vormen spoke up.

"I can smell it." She held out the pitcher as the High Wizard came closer. "Can't you?"

"I'm no hedge witch," he protested.

"Well, I'm a hedge witch's daughter, and this is makleweed."

"What would I know about herbs?"

"Enough to poison a king, perhaps?" Simond asked, voice cold and deadly.

Vormen turned to the king. "Sire, the herbs were

mixed in this wine days ago. I had no idea you would be here before you rode in an hour ago."

Simond took the pitcher from the girl's hands. "Are you sure of the poison?" he asked her.

She nodded. "Send for Lady Root. She'll recognize the smell of the weed."

"Who could have done this?" Vormen complained. "Who would have dared?"

"Assassins!" Cardo announced.

Pero, Alcinia thought. Lord Vormen assigned her punishment; her vengeful imp might have been trying to poison the High Wizard.

"It's the Halstins!" Cardo declared. "They tried to kill me yesterday, Father. The assassin within the gates must have known you were coming. They have spies everywhere."

Alcinia recalled that she hadn't actually *seen* Pero push the pot from the wall. She'd assumed. Maybe it was the Halstins. She hoped. Of course, as long as the king was all right, what did it matter who had made the attempt? "You haven't drunk any wine have you, sire?" she questioned.

"A cup," he answered. "Is there a cure, my dear?"

He was very calm for a man who'd been poisoned. That helped Alcinia remain calm, even though his measuring gaze was firmly fixed on her. "Oh, yes," she answered. "Lady root will know what to give you."

"Send for her," the king commanded the High Wizard.

"I'll fetch her, sire," Alcinia offered.

"Vormen can do that," the king said, dismissing the High Wizard of Bantieth like the lowliest of servants. She noticed that Vormen seemed happy to go and was out the door faster than she'd thought such an old and dignified man could move. King Simond put the wine back on the table and went back to his chair.

"Now, my dear—"

"She saved both our lives," his son interrupted him. "She saved you!" He went down on his knees before his father. "Forgive me, sire," he said. "I did this lady wrong."

"I know that," the king told his son. "Why do you think I'm here?"

"I let her take the blame for my crime. I'm sorry."

"Don't tell me. Tell the girl."

The next thing Alcinia knew, Cardo was kneeling in front of her. He took her hand and kissed it, and looked her in the eyes when he said, "I've been trying to apologize for days. Really. I was trying to get you alone, but—"

"You should have told the High Wizard."

"I know. I'm sorry."

His contrition was genuine, sincere. She thought he was more grateful to her for having saved his father than for saving him. His gratitude soothed her aching spirit. Pero had wanted revenge, not her, but she had revenge anyway.

Alcinia smiled and said, "Of course I accept your gratitude."

Because the finest revenge she could think of was knowing that the man who had done her wrong was in her debt for his life. What could be sweeter than that?

THE WEDDING PRESENT

by Kristine Kathryn Rusch

Kristine Kathryn Rusch is an award-winning fiction writer. Her novella, *The Gallery of His Dreams*, won the *Locus* Award for best short fiction. Her body of fiction work won her the John W. Campbell Award, given in 1991 in Europe. She has been nominated for several dozen fiction awards, and her short work has been reprinted in six *Year's Best* collections. She has published twenty novels under her own name and has sold forty-one novels in total. Her books have been published in seven languages, and have spent several weeks on the *USA Today* Bestseller list and *The Wall Street Journal* Bestseller list. She has written a number of *Star Trek* novels with her husband, Dean Wesley Smith, including a book in the crossover series called *New Earth*. She is the former editor of *The Magazine of Fantasy and Science Fiction*, winning a Hugo for her work there. Before that, she and Dean Wesley Smith started and ran Pulphouse Publishing, a science fiction and mystery press in Eugene. She lives and works on the Oregon coast.

CHLOE thought he was a harmless old man. Every day at six, he came into the diner wearing a shapeless blue raincoat over a tattered suit which always seemed to be in need of a good press. His silver hair was cropped short, his broad face pitted with acne scars.

Some evenings he sat with the truck drivers at their corner booth, sharing cigarettes and coffee, and talking about the news of the day. Other evenings he spent with friends, all of whom were as old and as rumpled, none of whom were female. Most nights, though, he sat at the counter, nursing a cigarette and the strongest cup of coffee she could make, while he waited for his tuna on rye. Those nights, he told her stories, like the time he went

to New York City after the war and saw the Rockettes.
He blushed when he talked about their high kicks and
long legs, and she could sense what a shy and lonely
man he'd been throughout his long life.

She wasn't going to be shy and lonely. She had plans,
dreams, a future. The waitress job was a detour as she
saved money for college. Someday, she knew, she'd be
someone people talked about in diners. She wouldn't
spend her golden years on a spinning red stool, hoping
that the person standing behind the counter would find
as much meaning in her life as she did.

Chloe had been working at the diner for six months
before she learned his name, and then she'd had to ask
Angie, one of the other waitresses, during their break in
the back.

"The friendly old guy whose greatest achievement was
going to Radio City?" Angie had said. "That's Floyd
Burton. Doesn't tip well. Don't think he can afford it.
But he's harmless. He walked me out one night when
some drunk lawyer was getting grabby. Don't think he
could have done anything, but having him beside me
was nice, you know."

"I know," Chloe said, and she did. One of the draw-
backs of working the four-to-midnight shift at an all-night
diner was that lonely walk to the parking lot. Millersburg
wasn't a big city, but it was on the highway, and it had
its share of robberies, rapes, and murders, just like any
other place that people traveled through and rarely
stayed.

From then on, she took Floyd's kindness as a gift and
his stories in lieu of tips. She liked hearing about the
way the town had been in the early fifties, all full of
hope and promise—the building boom, the industry, the
families pouring in searching for a new life. He talked
as if he'd been an insider then, as if his world had been
filled with sunshine and happiness, as if he'd worked in
the processing plant, had actually owned a new ranch-
style house, and had come home every night to his dinner, lovingly prepared by his shapely wife.

But the more Chloe found out about him, the more
she knew that couldn't be true. Floyd Burton lived in a
tumbledown farmhouse near the railroad tracks. The

house had been in his family for generations, and he was the only person left. He'd closed off the upstairs, and locked the basement, living in three rooms on the main floor. The government paid his expenses every month, but whether that was disability or a veteran's pension or Social Security, Chloe never knew.

All she knew was that he was a kindly old man who was lonelier than anyone should be toward the end of his life. She felt sorry for him, and guilty for that.

Even after she started college and went part-time at the diner, she still made sure she was in at six most nights, just so she could say her customary hello to Floyd and listen to a story she'd already heard half a hundred times.

When he came to her wedding, he had five months left to live, and he looked it. His skin was a pasty gray, his eyes red-rimmed, his body unnaturally thin. He wore a suit she'd never seen before—with wide lapels and gathered pants. It had a sharp crease in the gray flannel, and it looked odd with his frayed white shirt and unshined shoes.

In the reception line he told her that he was honored to be there, and he celebrated as if she were his own daughter getting married to the richest boy in town. He ate cake and toasted her proudly. He danced with her once and proved surprisingly adept. They twirled and spun as he guided her in moves she had never been able to do.

Sometime after the bride's dances but before the throwing of the bouquet, he pulled her and her new husband aside. They went into the back of the VFW Hall where the reception was being held. The corridor was dark and smelled faintly of mold. The only light came from an exit sign above the door.

"I know this isn't customary," Floyd said, holding a square box wrapped in silver paper, "but I wanted to explain my gift."

Chloe's husband Dave glanced at her, making it clear he would follow her lead. Dave had no real idea who Floyd was. Chloe had introduced them a few times at the diner, but she knew that the introduction hadn't really made an impression on Dave. He had simply filed the strange old man under Bride's Side, and left it at that.

Floyd handed Chloe the box. "I'd like you to open it."

She took the box. It was heavier than she expected.

Dave watched. Floyd nodded to him. "You, too, son. This is a gift that has to be shared."

Dave sighed softly—Chloe could tell he wanted to go back to the reception—but he slid his hands through the wrapping paper, like a good sport.

Inside was a clear serving dish, both plain and elegant. On top of the dish was an envelope marked "Instructions."

Chloe reached for the dish, her hands brushing tissue paper. As her fingers touched the glass, she pulled back The glass was ice cold.

Floyd did not look surprised at her reaction, although Dave did. He stared into the box as if he wondered what had caused Chloe to gasp and move away so quickly.

"I don't want to darken your special day," Floyd said, "but sometimes life isn't as easy or as wonderful as we imagine. Sometimes bad things happen no matter what we do to prevent them."

Chloe found herself staring at him, at his pale gray face, at his sincere watery eyes. Dave shifted beside her, clearly not pleased.

"We can't always stop the crisis," Floyd said, "but sometimes we can get some of ours back."

"Ours?" Dave asked. His voice had an underlying tone of sarcasm. Chloe elbowed him to keep him quiet.

Floyd's gaze left Chloe and moved to Dave. "I hope you never are in the situation I'm talking about, young man."

Dave nodded, but Chloe could tell he was humoring Floyd for her.

"The day your life together hits bottom," Floyd said. "The day you think it can't get any bleaker, you take this out and follow the instructions. It won't be able to reverse the situation you find yourself in, but it should give you a measure of satisfaction, maybe even peace."

"Thank you," Chloe said, feeling confused.

"Remember," Floyd said, "I gave it to both of you.

That way it can't be used against either of you. That should give you some measure of comfort at least."

"It does," Dave said gravely, even though Chloe knew he understood even less than she did.

Floyd smiled, then he put a crabbed hand on the side of Chloe's face and kissed her on the cheek.

"I do this because you're precious to me," he said so softly that only she could hear. Then he shook hands with Dave, wished them both well, and walked down the stairs to the main floor.

"What the hell was that?" Dave whispered.

"I don't know," Chloe said, feeling unsettled. "But I'm sure some day we'll find out."

Chloe was three months into her new teaching position when Floyd died. She hadn't seen him since the wedding and she felt vaguely guilty, even though she had done what she could.

She had quit the diner two weeks before the wedding, but she had continued to go in to see old friends, and chat with the crew. She usually came in around suppertime, hoping to catch Floyd, but he was never there.

She had written him a note, thanking him for the inexplicable gift, which she kept in its original box in the back of her clothes closet. She had got no response. She hadn't really expected one, but since she couldn't see him, she had hoped to hear something.

Then, one afternoon, the day manager from the diner called her with the news of Floyd's death. The funeral was on a Saturday. She didn't ask Dave to accompany her because he had thought Floyd had been extremely strange.

The regulars from the diner were there, along with a few waitresses and some of the truckers. But no one else. The large bouquet of flowers gracing the table behind the altar came from the diner's owner. The smaller bouquet next to it had come from Chloe. No one else had bothered.

The coffin was open, and she was startled to see how he had shrunk in the last few months. He wore the gray flannel suit. It had been beautifully pressed, and someone had placed a black handkerchief in the lapel pocket. The white shirt beneath it was new, and his shoes shone.

He looked almost natty, nothing like the Floyd she
had known.

The service was short. The only speaker, the minister
at the church Floyd belonged to and never attended,
didn't seem to know the man at all. He offered platitudes that meant nothing, while Chloe stared at the
waxen face of a man who had thought she was precious,
and wondered how she could have let him die alone.

In the intervening years, Chloe thought of Floyd only
when she had to move the box. Then she'd feel that
flash of guilt mixed with the odd sense of unease she'd
had at the wedding, as if she were holding something
she didn't deserve.

It took thirteen years for her to feel that bottomless
despair that Floyd had talked about. That year, Dave's
construction business had failed, taking with it their life
savings and their half-finished home. Chloe's parents
died within a month of each other, and her only sister
nearly died in a car wreck.

She and Dave sold their manufactured home because
they couldn't make the payments, and they moved into
a one-bedroom apartment on the highway, not too far
from the diner. They had to sell most of their furniture
because it didn't fit into the tiny space. She took a second job working nights at the diner because her teacher's salary did not meet the debts and the bills. Dave
found work with the only other construction firm in
town, but payment was by the job—and there wasn't
much building going on in Millersburg in those days.

Chloe could barely get herself out of bed in the morning, barely face the kids at school, barely find a way to
smile at her customers at the diner. She never saw Dave.
The answering machine was filled with hang ups and
the flat-toned voices of creditors. The mail consisted of
dunning letters and threats of lawsuits.

When she got home from the diner at midnight, she
would sit at her grandmother's heavy oak dining room
table, crammed beneath the single-paned window and
the pass-through kitchen, and stare at the bad news of
the day. Dave's snores would waft down the narrow hall-

way, and she would wonder how he could sleep when their world was crashing in.

One night in late February, she sat at that table, head in her hands, remembering the hope she had felt on her wedding day. When she had paid her way through college, she had thought she was going to be someone. She hadn't expected to end up back where she started, with the same job in the same town, apologizing to people she had known all her life for a failure that had not been her fault.

And somehow, Floyd's words came back to her. Floyd, who had been dead so long only Chloe, Angie, and the diner's day manager remembered him. Floyd, who had stood before her rumpled and proud, and said, *Sometimes bad things happen no matter what we do to prevent them.*

Chloe got up and went to the linen closet in the dark hallway. Dave's snores were louder here, buzzing as he often did when he was completely and utterly exhausted. He was more defeated than she was—it had been his dream that had disappeared, after all. She didn't know how to comfort him, how to make things better. It felt as if they were drowning together.

Her hands found the box in the far right corner at the bottom of the closet. When she sold the furniture, she thought of selling the box as well. She'd sold many of their other wedding presents—the three place settings of expensive china, the silver candlesticks, the small kitchen appliances that had been trendy a decade ago. But she hadn't been able to part with this gift, mostly because she knew what it had cost Floyd to give her anything, and she didn't want to betray his memory by casting the gift aside.

The box was smaller than she remembered. Silver wrapping paper was still attached to its sides by yellowing Scotch tape. A tiny gift envelope with her name and Dave's written in Floyd's cramped handwriting had been jammed between the box's flaps.

She carried it into the living room and sat down on the threadbare couch. Even though she had kept the box, she hadn't opened it since her wedding day. She wondered if the plate was as elegant as she remembered, and doubted it. Her perspective had changed in thirteen years. Nothing was as shiny as it had been then, especially not her life.

The tissue paper crinkled backward as she reached inside. The plate was as cold as she remembered, and she wondered how that effect was achieved. Before she took it out, she reached for the second, larger envelope, the one marked *Instructions*.

Her hands shook as she pulled it out. Somehow she had never thought it would come to this, never thought her life could be as bleak as anything a man like Floyd could imagine. Yet here she was, reaching for something that was, at best, an old man's fancy; at worst, a joke of the most tasteless kind.

The envelope was sealed. She broke a fingernail prying it open. A faint scent of mothballs reached her. She slid her finger inside and pulled out a piece of paper so old that it was thick and brittle.

The handwriting on the paper was unfamiliar. The ink had once been black and it had faded to a yellowish brown. Chloe held the paper beneath the light because the words were hard to read.

To Avenge a Wrong

When someone has injured you in such a way as to make forgiveness impossible, this dish will serve retribution.

Make the person's favorite food and place it on the dish. Serve the person from this dish and this dish only. Do not let anyone else eat from it, although you may.

As the food is being consumed, remind the person as to the nature of his crime. Tell him you now believe the score is settled.

Remind him that revenge is a dish best served cold.

Chloe dropped the paper as if its toxicity could slip into her fingers. The paper floated through the air slowly, landing on the scuffed hardwood floor. She stared at the words, her heart pounding.

What had Floyd been thinking? She had been a newly married woman, the world open to her, everything filled with love. If she and Dave had read that on their wedding night, or even on their honeymoon, would it have tainted the relationship? Would it have changed her outlook forever?

She stood, feeling vaguely nauseous, her hand over her stomach. She did not look at the dish. Instead she went to the windows, pulled up the cheap plastic blinds, and stared into the street below.

She was angry. Furious, in fact, although she had never admitted it to herself before. She did not want to be here, in this tiny apartment, on this low-rent street, looking through the window at rusted cars and unmowed grass, at broken streetlights and cracked pavement.

When she had known Floyd, she had imagined herself escaping Millersburg, doing something grand (then why had she gone into teaching? How many famous teachers were there, after all?), and living well. She and Dave would have a fantasy romance, the kind books were written about, and they would share their love with children— children they had been too busy and too poor to have.

She had never foreseen this place. Life, she had thought, had been a staircase that went up—improving with each placement of the foot, getting better with each passing year. She had never imagined that the staircase would also take her down.

But Floyd had.

That day he had looked at her with such pride and sadness, hoping she would never have to use this gift, and fearing that she would need it.

Perhaps that was why he had avoided her in the last months of his life, because he didn't want to think about what he had done, the power he had given her.

The queasiness was passing. Chloe shook her head. She was acting as if the dish had true power, as if he had given her something magic.

But if he hadn't, how did the dish remain ice cold?

*   *   *

Try as she might, Chloe couldn't stop thinking about the gift. Not the dish, per se, or even what it could do, but how the gift made her feel about Floyd. She had thought he was a sweet, sad, and lonely old man, and instead, he had had an undercurrent of bitterness that she hadn't even seen.

She wanted to toss the dish away, but she was unable to do so. She still felt guilt whenever she looked at the box.

Two days later, when she took her students for the monthly trip to the local library, she spent her afternoon looking up magic systems and beliefs. She searched for magic dishes, and revenge spells. She found nothing about magic dishes, not in any book or even in her internet search, but the revenge spells surprised her.

They were, she soon discovered, as varied as magic's practitioners. Some black magic books told her that anything could be changed into a vessel for revenge. Others said all that she needed was the recipe—the spell itself. Still others insisted on actual participation from the victim—a lock of hair, a bit of skin, a fingernail—something.

She supposed her box had all three: the item that became a vessel for hatred, the recipe for the spell itself, and participation from the victim in the form of eating a meal served on the dish. She couldn't imagine how the victim would react to the suggested conversation.

She tried to imagine herself sitting across the table from someone she'd accidentally wronged, having them make her a nice cold treat, and then proceeding to tell her how she had harmed them. She shivered. If the person ended the conversation as suggested—telling her that revenge was a dish best served cold—she would probably believe that she had been poisoned.

But the word poison was not mentioned in the spell. It wasn't even suggested. In spite of herself, she was intrigued by all of it. She was also appalled by that; she'd always thought of herself as a sensible woman, not one prone to flights of fancy. But she found herself thinking about the dish at the oddest moments, and wondering how she could use it.

*   *   *

Two nights later, she shared a shift with Angie at the diner. Angie was the only other waitress who had worked there while Floyd was alive.

After the dinner rush, the night was slow. They bused tables, refilled condiments, and cleaned the ice machine. Someone on day shift had broken a glass in the machine, and rather than get sued, the manager wanted someone to clean the machine. The first slow shift got the job— which was, oddly enough, evening.

Chloe usually hated slow nights—less money—but this time she didn't mind.

"Ange," she said as she scooped ice out of the machine into a bucket, "do you remember Floyd Burton?"

Angie was carrying the buckets out back. She was a sturdy woman with solid legs, who'd spent the last twenty years on her feet, working for minimum wage and tips that didn't always come.

"Floyd Burton," she said as she pushed open the door with her backside. She sounded as if the name were familiar, but not one she remembered.

Angie disappeared into the darkness. Chloe heard the ice rain against the parking lot, and then Angie came back inside.

"Old guy? Used to sit at the counter?"

"Yeah," Chloe said. Her hands were red with the cold. The ice machine was half empty.

"What about him?"

"He was at my wedding. He gave me a weird gift that I just found the other day."

"Weird how?"

Chloe shoved another bucket toward her. "Unexpected, I guess. What do you know about him?"

"Besides the fact I haven't thought of him for ten years?" Angie grabbed the two full buckets and set them near the door. Then she came back to the ice machine and helped Chloe fill two more.

"He used to live near the railroad tracks. Old house, got condemned by the city."

Chloe nodded. "I remember that."

"Had all kinds of strange stuff in it, too. Books not even the library wanted. Bottles full of things that smelled like they died years ago."

Chloe stood and stretched, her back aching.

"I remember something about his grandmother being a witch."

"No kidding," Chloe said.

Angie shrugged. She scooped the last of the ice out of the machine. "I think that's just made-up stuff. You know, the spooky house at the end of the block kinda thing."

"Was the house spooky?"

"It was a rundown farmhouse with some dead trees around it. I think that qualifies as spooky."

Chloe had to agree. She made sure the machine was unplugged, then cleaned it according to the instructions on the side. Angie took the rest of the ice outside, dumping it on the pavement.

Chloe wasn't sure what made her colder, the conversation or the ice machine.

Angie came back in and started stacking the buckets. She peered through the order window to see if there were any new customers, but apparently there weren't because she helped Chloe wipe out the stainless steel.

"You remember anything else?" Chloe asked.

Angie shook her head. "He seemed nice enough to me. Lonely and harmless. Told a lot of stories about the war—cleaned up stories, I always thought, considering he'd been in the Pacific."

Chloe started. She hadn't thought of that. He had been in areas that saw a lot of action, but no matter what stories he told, he never mentioned anything bad.

"What was this gift?" Angie asked.

"Just a dish," Chloe said. "A strange old dish. It got me wondering."

Angie wiped her forehead with the back of a reddened hand. "Wish I could help you more," she said. "It's amazing how little we actually know about these people we see every day, isn't it?"

Chloe nodded. It was amazing indeed.

It was more amazing, she thought when she got home that night, tired, sore, and chilled through, that she couldn't get the letter—the recipe—out of her mind. She found herself fantasizing about it as she sat in a steaming bathtub, vanilla-scented bubbles rising around her and popping in the air.

She'd cook something for one of the faceless dunning agents, a woman with a deep smoker's voice who never seemed to believe any of Chloe's explanations for late payments. Or she'd give it to the school board, who this year decided against the teachers' cost of living raise because it cut too deeply into the annual budget. Or maybe she'd make a chiffon pie for her tart-tongued mother-in-law, who somehow saw her son's business failure as his wife's fault.

That was the danger of a thing like this—the temptation to actually use it, to believe that it, and not good hard work, would make her situation better.

But, she admitted, as the bubbles faded into a free-floating scum on the surface of the cooling water, she had felt better since she found the dish. It was as if she had found at least one way to escape the darkness that had been weighing her down.

"Hear you been asking about Floyd," Pete, one of the truckers, said three nights later.

Chloe set a pot of coffee on his table. "I just found something he'd given me, and I realized I didn't know a lot about him."

Pete nodded. He was a grizzled man of indeterminate age, whose oily black hair looked too uniform to be natural, and whose leather skin spoke of hours in the sun. He reached over the back of the booth and grabbed an ashtray off a nearby table. The diner's smoking section was larger than its nonsmoking section, something the truckers seemed to appreciate.

"Interesting guy, that Floyd," Pete said. "Always was careful to be kind to everyone. Said there were cosmic forces that balanced things out, and you never knew when one of them would turn on you."

The chill Chloe had been feeling for days ran down her spine. "What else did he say?"

"Oh, he had stories." Pete lit up and took a drag off the cigarette, its tip glowing red. "Imagine you heard all of those."

"What about his family?"

Pete leaned back in the booth, an arm spread. "Never really talked about them. Always suspected there was something back there, you know. But the guys who tell the best stories are usually the ones with the most secrets."

Behind Chloe, the bell dinged, signaling that an order was up. She glanced at the order window and saw two burgers waiting for her to pick them up.

She did, delivering them to the young couple who had clearly taken the first stop they'd seen along the highway, then got a piece of apple pie for Pete. He always ordered it, never wanted it heated and hated it when a waitress "ruined" it with ice cream.

She set the pie in front of him, and he grinned at her. "You ever ask Marvin about Floyd?" Pete asked.

"Marvin?"

"The guy who always wears the John Deere hat. He drives a refrigerator unit, usually shows up on Saturdays."

She'd waited on the man for years and never learned his name. Angie's comment about how little she knew about these people came back to her, startling her with its accuracy.

"No," she said. "Were they close?"

Pete shook his head. "Marvin hated him. They grew up together. He probably knows stuff the rest of us don't. You should ask him next time you see him."

"I will," Chloe said. "Thanks."

She gave Pete's coffeepot a test shake to make sure there was enough coffee in it before she left the table, and then she went into the break room. She leaned against the wall, needing a moment alone.

Thirteen years ago, she wouldn't have been able to imagine why anyone would have hated Floyd Burton. But now that she'd examined the gift, she thought she knew.

She wasn't sure she was going to talk to Marvin. She wasn't sure she wanted to hear his version of the truth.

That night, Dave was awake when she got home. He sat at the dining room table, in her usual post-waitressing spot, bills scattered before him, the checkbook open, and a yellow legal pad at his side. An old square calculator rested beneath his right hand, and his fingers flew across the numbers as if he were trained as a keypunch operator, not a construction worker.

Chloe closed the apartment door quietly and stared at the back of his head, balding near the crown, and wondered why she didn't blame him for the situation they were in.

She had set her dreams aside to follow his, after all. The teaching had initially been a backup position, something she could do anywhere, after she tried a few other things. She'd once thought of a modeling career—going to a big city and seeing if people there believed she was as pretty as the locals did. Then, she thought, she might segue into acting or singing, something in the arts.

But she'd put all that behind her when she met Dave. He wanted to build a life here, use his skills to make Millersburg a better place. She thought that a worthy goal, so long as she had a nice home and children to fill it. Then teaching wouldn't be so bad, and the other— well, they had just been pipe dreams, after all.

Funny, how they seemed more important now.

He looked up, saw her, and gave her a tired little smile. "I'm beginning to think these things reproduce in shoe boxes," he said, sweeping her hand over the bills.

She nodded, set her sweater on the hook behind the door, and came inside. Her uniform smelled of grease and Pete's cigarette smoke.

There were new lines on Dave's face, lines that hadn't been there the year before. "I keep thinking maybe we should take that lawyer's advice. At least if we're bankrupt, we can start over, clean some of this up."

Color flooded her face. That had been her argument in the beginning, but Dave had reminded her that they had to live in this community, and no one would treat them well if they stiffed a whole bunch of businesses.

Only it wasn't the local businesses that were dunning them and threatening them with lawsuits. It was the credit card companies, and the out-of-state suppliers, and the banks, not to mention the tax people who wouldn't go away whether there was a bankruptcy or not.

"I'm sorry," he said, just like he had a thousand times since the business folded. "I'm sorry for the mess."

In the past, she would have told him it was all right. The words were automatic. But this time, they hovered behind her lips, trapped by a feeling she'd never had before.

Fury.

All of it directed at him.

At three a.m., the apartment's pass-through kitchen was uncomfortably dark.

Chloe turned on the light above the stove, but it didn't help much. A kitchen made out of a hallway did not provide comfort the way that a kitchen should. Comfort or privacy.

She couldn't sleep. She had tried, lying down next to him as she had done every night for thirteen years. Only this time there was nothing calming about his steady breathing, nothing secure in his broad shoulders and square back.

He took all the covers as usual, and she didn't even have the fight to wrestle a few back to her side.

Instead, she took her chill into the comfortless kitchen, and thought about breakfasts that tasted good cold.

She supposed the meal really didn't matter. A chilled coffee cake would do as well as a slice of grapefruit. All that mattered was the plate, the discussion, and the parting shot.

She crossed her arms over her flannel robe, remembering the day she'd received the dish, and Floyd's instructions. If they ever needed to use the dish, he had said, they had to use it together.

It had been a subtle promise, one she had made without thinking.

One she wasn't certain she could keep.

Marvin the truck driver uttered a disgusted grunt. "Floyd Burton. Now that's a name I hoped I'd never hear again."

Chloe had just gotten off work on the Saturday afternoon shift. She was subbing for Angie, who had some sort of family emergency. Chloe had worked both jobs all week long, and she hadn't slept well the night before. She was happy to slip into Marvin's booth and share a cup of coffee at his invitation.

"You didn't like him," she said, bringing her legs up on the booth and rubbing her feet through her rubber-soled shoes.

"Almost felt sorry for him by the end." Marvin's John Deere hat was sweat-stained around the brim. The top was pilled, and the colors were faded with age. "He was so pathetic then."

"He seemed sweet enough."

"I suppose." Marvin cut into the large cinnamon roll that was a diner specialty. He was older than he looked. His face had only a few lines, but his hands were covered with tufts of hair and liver spots. "Old men can pretend at sweetness. People are predisposed to think they're harmless."

She started. "He wasn't?"

"Dunno. Never could pin anything on him."

"Pin anything. Were you a cop?"

Marvin's smile was small. "A brother-in-law. An ex-brother-in-law. Not that Myra did well by him. She didn't. She slept with everything that moved, that one did. And from the time she was sixteen. It was hell being her brother. I beat up guys for following their gonads, if you know what I mean. All she did was lead them on. But she didn't deserve what happened to her."

Chloe grabbed her sweater and pulled it tight. "What happened?"

"We warned him, long before the wedding. Even the minister did, I think." Marvin took another bite of the cinnamon roll. "But Floyd was just back from the war, and so determined to forget all the bad stuff that ever happened to him. He thought he deserved to be happy. As if people deserve anything."

Chloe wrapped her hand around her coffee mug. The ceramic was hot to the touch, but didn't soothe the chill that had moved all the way down to her fingertips.

"He does the whole postwar thing—good job, starter house, pretty wife at home. A year in, he comes home, finds her in bed with an old boyfriend. The hell of it is, he's not even home early. She meant to have him catch her—probably gave her some kind of thrill. She mighta thought it would give him a thrill, too. There was no telling with Myra."

"And?" Chloe asked, afraid of where this was going.

"He walked out. Just left her there, with the house, the payments, everything. He went back to his family house. It was out in the country then, and his folks were still alive. He never moved out after that."

"So what did he do that was so wrong?"

Marvin shook his head. "I don't know exactly. It just seemed Myra's life went into the crapper after that. Little things, important to her. One morning, she wakes up with a cut on her face. Disfigures her for life. Doesn't remember how it happened, swears she was alone in the house when it occurred, and there ain't even blood on the bed. That was the one that destroyed her. She lived for her looks, did our Myra."

"You think Floyd did it?" Chloe was trying to imagine the man she'd met cutting a woman in her sleep.

"Like I said, we couldn't prove nothing. But Myra sure thought it was him. She kept blabbing about their last meal together, about something he'd said."

Chloe froze, trying not to look too avid.

Marvin didn't seem to notice. "Told her she'd destroyed his every hope for happiness. She said he did the same to her. And it seemed like it. Any time she started to enjoy her life, something got in the way. But nothing we could prove was him."

Chloe waited. She could sense Marvin wasn't done.

Marvin tilted his hat back and scratched his bald scalp. "The hell of it was that he seemed pretty broken up by what happened to her, in the end."

Chloe wrapped her other hand around her coffee mug. The coffee was lukewarm now, but she hadn't drunk enough to top it off. "What happened?"

"Ended it. She did. One hot summer night. Booze and pills. Called me—that was before I took to the road—her voice all slurred, said he'd cursed her and she had no reason to live anymore." Marvin shoved his plate away, the roll only half eaten. He closed his eyes, shook his head. "I got there too late."

"I'm sorry," Chloe said.

He opened his eyes, shrugged. "It was a long time

ago." Even though his expression said it wasn't, at
least not for him. "I couldn't even celebrate when the
bastard kicked. He wasn't the same after she was gone.
Like he was a shell of a person, with nothing left to
live for."

Chloe shivered. "You'd think a man like that wouldn't
believe in revenge."

"Why the hell not?" Marvin frowned at her. "A man
like that, he don't take responsibility for anything. Anything goes wrong, it's someone else's fault. We told him
what she was like. He didn't have to marry her. When
he did, he had no right to punish her for being who
she was. He took her, for better or worse. He should've
remembered that."

"Oh," Chloe said softly, "I think he did. When it was
too late."

She thought about that conversation all the way, as
her car shimmied because its wheels needed to be
aligned and white smoke belched out of the tailpipe because it needed a tune-up.

She still didn't understand Floyd. He'd given her the
gift of revenge, then told her not to use it against the
person she loved the most.

Why didn't he warn her that it would backfire, no
matter how she used it? Or did he think she wouldn't
feel those effects if she didn't love the person she sought
vengeance against?

When she got to the apartment, she hurried up the
steps as fast as her tired legs would take her. The door
was locked and she struggled with her keys before letting
herself in.

The apartment smelled stale, empty, unlived in. Un-
loved. The smell of despair. Late afternoon sunlight fil-
tered in the dirty windows, revealing dust motes floating
in the breeze she had kicked up.

She pushed the door closed and hurried to the closet
without changing out of her uniform. The box was in
the back corner where she had left it.

She wasn't sure what to do with it. If she shattered
the dish, she might release a power she didn't understand. But if she kept the pieces together, someone

might use it, and then regret that use for the rest of
their life.

Chloe slid the box toward her, opened it, and pulled
out the large envelope. She'd learned enough about
black magic to know that all the elements were needed
to make a spell work. Without the letter, the dish
wouldn't work properly.

Her hands shaking, she took the envelope in the bathroom. She pulled the letter out, saw the faded words,
and then ripped the paper into tiny pieces, dropping
them into the toilet bowl.

The ink ran in the water, the letters blurring as if they
had never been. She wished she had never read them.
She wished they hadn't burrowed into her mind like a
disease, tantalizing her with a way out that was no escape at all.

The formula was so simple. She would never forget it.
No matter how she felt, no matter how she reasoned
with herself, any time anyone crossed her, the temptation would always be there.

She flushed the toilet. Then she grabbed the box with
the bowl still inside, and carried it to the dumpster
outside.

Chloe had just raised the heavy green lid when Dave's
truck pulled into the back parking lot. His face was grim,
his hands clutching the wheel as if it were a lifetime.

She glanced at the box in her hand. The dish wasn't
at fault. Her mind was, casting about for someone to
blame for the worst year of her life. Her parents died
from disease and loss of companionship, her husband's
business folded because Millersburg was dying.

They were dying, she and Dave, because they hadn't
looked for a way out. And they needed to find one.

Not just a way to pay the creditors, but a way to find
that hope they'd lost somewhere in their life together.

She tossed the box into the dumpster, heard the dish
rattle as it landed on the metal bottom, then she
slammed the lid closed. Dave had got out of his truck.
He was watching her as if she were a stranger which, in
some ways, she probably was.

She would never tell him about that dark night in the
kitchen, when she had nearly made him a meal that

would have poisoned them both. She would never tell him how close she had come to forsaking her vow, forgetting for better or for worse.

For people were responsible for their own lives, the dark times as well as the light. Life carried with it tests, like wars and loss of love. It also carried joys, the greatest being simple things, like slipping into bed after a difficult day and feeling the warmth of another human being, one you trusted more than anyone else in the world, and who trusted you.

Chloe wiped the filth from the dumpster—from Floyd's gift—on her uniform, and then went to greet her husband, a man who deserved so much more than she, up to this point, had been willing to give.

HAVE A DRINK ON ME

by Gary A. Braunbeck

Gary A. Braunbeck is the author of the acclaimed
collection *Things Left Behind*, as well as the forthcoming collection *Escaping Purgatory* (in collaboration with
Alan M. Clark) and the CD-ROM *Sorties, Cathexes,
and Human Remains*. His first solo novel, *The Indiffer-
ence of Heaven*, was recently published, as was his
Dark Matter novel, *In Hollow Houses*. He lives in Co-
lumbus, Ohio and has, to date, sold nearly 200 short
stories. His fiction, to quote *Publishers Weekly*,
". . . stirs the mind as it chills the marrow."

I AM not a happy man, but I find these days I am
happier than I was.

It's important I remember that.

I was back to drinking white wine again, which had
been my poison of choice after first arriving. In between,
I had consumed every form of alcohol on the premises,
sometimes sipping politely, other times guzzling uncon-
trollably: red wine, bourbon, Scotch, four different kinds
of vodka, three different kinds of brandy, champagne,
gin, tequila, liqueurs, several bottles of Mexican beer,
grappa, and so many cups of rum-spiked eggnog I'd lost
count. All of it on an empty stomach. I was stumbling
around, lurching and weaving, bumping into people,
apologizing in a slurred voice if I caused their drinks to
spill or their dip to dribble, and then moving on, stumbling from lamp to lamp, from plant to plant and group
to group, being loud and jovial but never obnoxious. The
past year had shown me I possessed a redoubtable talent
for affectation; still, it was no fun being an imposter. It
was bad enough having been an irresponsible alcoholic
without the necessity of now having to assume the role
like some superhero concealing his secret identity.

If approximate measurements are something that you need in order to understand exactly how much liquor I had consumed in that short time, then it would not be hyperbolic of me to say that I annihilated something in the quantity of five quarts. And this was after a two-week-long binge wherein I drank *at least* that amount of liquor every day. By any stretch of the imagination, I should have been dead from alcohol poisoning—or at the very least strapped to a stretcher inside a speeding ambulance on its way to an emergency detox center. But I wasn't. Nor was I sick.

I was stone-cold sober.

Not only was I not drunk, I wasn't even tipsy.

Nothing. *Nada.*

Point me at a straight line and I could easily walk it with eyes closed, repeatedly touching my nose with the tips of both index fingers and singing an aria from *Götterdammerung* just to be a smart-ass.

I simply cannot emphasize this enough. I was completely sober. Lucid. Totally unimpaired.

Having made a necessary bother of myself, the hostess—a charming woman in her early fifties who looked ten years younger and carried herself with a fragile grace—took my arm and led me aside.

"Alan, don't you think you've had enough?"

"I'm still seeing only one of you, so . . . no." I smiled.

She slapped my arm; half-playfully, half out of what I'm sure was genuine irritation. "You never change, do you?"

"I don't know about that."

"Still, Alan . . . this party is too important for the Art Guild, you know that."

"I do."

"If we woo these guests properly, it is quite likely that we'll raise enough money to finish the new wing for the Altman Gallery."

"I know. And if I'm embarrassing you, I can make a quick and noiseless exit." I hoped she hadn't noticed that my speech was not as slurred as before.

"Not in your condition. So—" She grabbed my shoulders and gently turned me in the direction of the stairs.

"—go upstairs to the study and have a bit of a lie-down, will you? There are three sofas up there. I'm afraid one of them's already occupied. My brother."

It was everything I could do not to smile. "Yes . . . I thought I saw him stumbling about a little earlier."

"I don't understand it, I really don't. Warren has never drunk anything more than a glass of wine with dinner. My guess is he's been drinking more since the divorce and the rest of the . . . ugly business that followed. But his health has been so precarious lately, and he doesn't seem to know why. I've never seen him get so drunk before—and the odd thing is, I honestly don't recall having seen him with a drink in his hand all night."

"First time for all of us," I said, surprised by the minor key tone that was in my voice.

She squeezed my hand. "You've been so good up until now, Alan. What was it—nearly six months sober?"

I nodded as if shamed.

"Do you mind if I ask what caused this . . . detour?"

Detour. What a tasteful way to put it, as only an elegant woman would.

"Alan?"

"Hm?—oh. Yes. What caused it, you say? I don't mean to be coarse, but if you really want to know—"

"—I do."

"Toilet paper."

Her face never changed expression, but her blinking eyes seemed to be signaling *help* in Morse Code. "Oh, you're definitely going upstairs to lie down. When the party's over, I *have* to hear the rest of this."

"Your wish . . . and all of that."

She leaned in and gave me a warm kiss on my cheek, then with a gentle push sent me on my way up the stairs.

Halfway up the resplendent winding staircase that was the centerpiece of the massive downstairs, I quit affecting my drunkard's stumble, stopping just long enough to look at the dozens of well-dressed guests who milled about downstairs. It would be a successful affair, of that I had no doubt. My display—inoffensive as it was—would do nothing more than provide all here with a lovely piece of gossip they could recount to their friends over lunch at the club tomorrow.

If everything went as planned, they'd have a great deal more to talk about.

I looked up toward the landing and continued on my way. Beneath my jacket was a bottle of whiskey I'd taken from one of the four bars.

I walked slowly down the hallway, the sound of my footsteps swallowed by the deep golden carpet. I stopped at a set of doors that were ornate slabs of burnished teak set within a bronze frame. I knew who waited on the other side, and what I was going to do.

I stood in silence, aware of the rhythm of my breathing, the sweat covering my face.

I kept my face expressionless, willing the same emptiness into my eyes.

Emptiness was easy now. I had the person on the other side of the door to thank for that.

I entered the study, making sure the door closed tightly behind me.

There was almost no light in the room, save for that from the moon which bled in from a large window across from me. Outside it was purple-gray, the night devouring the remains of the day and taking its rightful place in the world. A thin layer of snowy mist enshrouded the outside as a dispirited breeze sloughed its way through the trees. Frost glistened on every surface, shimmering at the tips of leaves.

My mother had always loved this time of night. Sometimes, she'd wake and get out of bed, then just sit in her favorite chair and patiently watch the night, just to see a moment of perfect peace. In the months since her death, I found myself on more than one occasion driving to the now-empty house of my childhood and sitting in that very chair, hoping to feel some remnant of her spirit waiting in the night for a few minutes' worth of company.

I moved toward one specific plush leather sofa.

Looking at the shuddering man who lay curled in the fetal position there, I cleared my throat and said, "Stop me if you've heard this one before: *'Vengeance is mine, so sayeth the Lord God.'* Or perhaps this Oldie-but-Moldy is more to your liking: *'If thou art struck, turn thy other cheek.'* "

He coughed—a deep, wet, racking cough—then groaned and fisted his hands against bloodshot, glass-rheumy eyes.

"I've got a million of 'em," I continued, "half of which were plagiarized or paraphrased from that grand best-seller of all time starring your favorite Savior and mine, but rather than bore you with a recitation of them all, allow me to encapsulate."

He started sobbing; softly at first, then harder, louder, and with less control. A dark stain began to spread outward from his crotch as his body spasmed with greater violence.

I looked away from the pathetic spectacle. "In a nut-shell, what these eminently-quotable tidbits of wisdom boil down to is this: *If someone wishes to stick it to you, then it's best for your soul if you simply smile a good Christian smile, walk over to the nearest corner, drop your pants, and bend over. Amen.*

"Not for me, thank you very much." I pulled a chair up beside him. "It has always been my fervent belief that if there is an Almighty Whatchamacallit overseeing us, it's too damned busy just trying to keep the Universe in one piece to be bothered with tallying all the trivial little trespasses committed against you by this weasel or that.

"If you've not yet figured it out, sir, I am not a big believer in—you'll pardon the phrase—'divine retribution;' rather, I am a strong adherent to the philosophy that one should seek retribution oneself, using any means necessary, thereby saving the Almighty Whatcha-macallit the trouble of having to deal with your griev-ances once you stand before it after the Imperial Last Call."

He pulled his fists away from his eyes and, blubbering like a child, reached toward me with a hand which trem-bled so ferociously it could've belonged to an epileptic in mid-seizure. I leaned back in the chair, taking myself out of his reach.

" . . . eeeze . . ." he managed to get out. ". . . oddsakes . . . pleee . . ."

Not blinking, I broke the seal on the bottle of Jack Daniels Black I had brought in with me.

" 'Please,' is it? For *God's* sake, you say?"

His outreached hand twitched once, twice, then dropped slowly, almost gracefully, toward the floor, fingertips brushing the expensive carpeting below.

I lifted the bottle to my lips and took three deep swallows. With each drink, his body convulsed.

Looking at him, I felt no sympathy, no pity, no remorse; only a burgeoning satisfaction.

Pardon my invoking a tired cliché, but as it turns out, revenge *is* indeed a dish best served cold. It's even better if there's a beverage included.

Wiping my mouth on the sleeve of my jacket, I continued: "Did you know that researchers studying the brains of people with a history of alcohol abuse have identified key differences that may predispose people to compulsive drinking? The problem seems to be an imbalance between two chemical signaling systems that regulate the stimulation and inhibition of brain cells. Since alcohol acts on the brain pathway involved in stimulation or 'excitability,' the findings suggest that alcoholics may drink to restore the balance in their brains. Just as the body depends on a regular heartbeat to live, the balance between the neurotransmitters that control inhibition and excitability is absolutely critical for proper brain function. Are you paying attention? There may be a quiz later."

Somehow he managed to find enough strength to glare at me.

"Glad to see there's still some comprehension swimming around in there." I set the bottle on the floor. "So I'll tell you what, Mr. Warren Parsons—I'll give us a break for a little while, how's that sound?"

His only response was to continue glaring.

"I'll take that to mean you approve." Cracking my knuckles, I looked around the room. "This is quite an impressive study, if you don't mind my saying. But of course, you always were one to demand only the finest things in life for yourself and your family. The finest homes, the finest schools, finest cars, finest mistress for yourself, and—oh, let's not forget this last: only the finest employees, be they your top litigators, mailroom staff, gardeners, or, in the case of my mother, the finest housekeeper.

"Ah—a spark in your eye! *'Housekeeper?'* Yes, sir. You might remember her—Virginia Hards? Sixties, on the short side, thin gray hair, small but very strong hands, eyes with heavy lids. Oh, come on, Mr. Parsons! A man in your position doesn't achieve the social rank you have without remembering names and faces . . . or is the name and face of a woman who cleaned your toilets and folded your linens for fifteen years of too little consequence?"

It looked for a moment as if he wanted to laugh.

A moment of weakness, then: grabbing the bottle off the floor, I had a sudden, vicious, overpowering urge to pulp his face with it, but then the Reverend's words came back to me: *You mustn't allow yourself to get emotional when the time comes, Alan. Emotions are for* before *and* after. *Letting them surface* during *will rob the experience of any lasting glory when you remember. You'll have to live with this for the rest of your life, so take care you don't revel in it while it's happening. Pretend you're dead; pretend that you are nothing; pretend you don't exist. Be nothing more than a conduit.*

"I am dead, I am nothing, I do not exist," I whispered several times, eyes closed, hand clamped around the bottle's neck. "I am dead, I am nothing, I do not exist."

How long I sat there chanting this mantra I do not know; only that when I was calm again, only when I felt removed from the world of Man and no longer existed—except in the safe, cold, uncaring state of anesthetized nothingness—only then did I release the breath I'd been holding, slowly open my eyes, look directly into Parson's gaze, and say: "I am not a happy man, but I find these days I am happier than I was. It's important I remember that."

If he understood, he gave no indication. His eyes were losing their focus. I needed to regain his full attention. This I achieved by raising the bottle to my lips but not drinking.

"Back with me now, are you? Good." I placed the bottle between my legs. "I suppose you're wondering why I've called you all here. Sorry—I realize that there's only the two of us in this room, but I've always wanted to use that line in real life.

"So stay as you are, Mr. Parsons, and I will tell you that tale, one that begins where it will also end, and—like all good drunken narratives do—occasionally wanders off the path in order to fill in details which the teller, between refills, realizes are compulsory, if not crucial. . . .

I was not a very good son to my mother during her final years. A childhood spent under the thumb of a drunken, abusive father had all but stripped me of any compassion for her tears after Father had finished any one of his thrice-weekly rampages. Looking back on it now, I find it more difficult to blame her for her inaction . . . but back then, I sometimes hated her. She should have packed a couple of suitcases and removed herself and her young son from the house the first time Father sent us both to the hospital, where I was forced to lie about how we'd come to be there. She spent forty-two years married to a man who, until he succumbed to cancer during the last two years of his life, terrified her. It didn't matter to him that she had a heart condition; all that mattered was his anger, his wants and needs; it was, after all, *his* house, and if you lived in *his* house, if you resided under *his* roof, then, by God, you lived by *his* rules. Perhaps there had been a time when they were young newlyweds that he brought her flowers, or made her breakfast in bed—perhaps even took her out for dinner and a movie or dancing, in the days when dance halls still existed in Cedar Hill—but if there were any memories of tenderness and laughter between them, I never encountered any ghost of it as a child. I saw a brutish drunk and a horse-whipped woman made old before her time. Only later, after Father's death, did I see any of my mother's true self emerge, and then only in sputtering starts and stops, as if she were becoming the person she'd always dreamed of being, only now this dreamed-of person was more intruder than guest.

By the time my father died (I did not attend his funeral), I was employed as a history teacher at Wright
State University in Dayton, some two hours' drive from
the sad little town of Cedar Hill. My drinking, though
quite heavy at times and a cause for concern to what few
friends I had, never impeded my ability in the classroom.

After Father's death, my mother, at age fifty-seven,
tired of being alone with no one to appreciate or comment on what a splendidly—almost morbidly—clean
house she kept, decided to seek out employment. This
is where you come in to the scenario, Mr. Warren Parsons, Senior Partner of Parsons, Marriot & Winter. My
mother was hired by a cleaning service—Happy Home-
makers, Merry Maids, Scullery Wenches-R-Us or some
such name—and one of their assignments was to clean
your offices. So impressed were you by their service that
you had one of your underlings make arrangements for
them to clean your offices on a permanent basis. Then
one night a few months later the housekeeper you employed at your private residence resigned two nights before you were scheduled to entertain the State Attorney
General at dinner. In a panic, you asked my mother—
who happened to be the first cleaning woman you encountered in the offices—if she would be willing to work
a few nights at your home.

"You should have heard her voice when she called to
tell me the news, sir. "Oh, hon," she said, sounding as
if she might cry at any given moment. "You should see
this house, it's a real mansion. I never seen a real mansion before. It's gonna be a lot of work, but you know
what? I don't mind. It'll be nice to get paid for doing
what I been doin' all my life."

You'd have thought she'd been given her life back to
live again. She absolutely *treasured* her time in your employ, sir. Somehow, cleaning *your* toilets, shopping for
your groceries, emptying *your* trash, washing and folding
your linens, vacuuming *your* floors . . . somehow doing
these things gave her a renewed sense of worth and purpose because not only was she *paid* to do these things,
she was *appreciated*.

It was pointless to try and tell her that, even during
those times as a child when I thought I hated her, I

always appreciated anything she did for me. An extra spoonful of mashed potatoes, a few quarters found at the bottom of her purse so I could buy some comic books, the heaviest blanket on my bed when the weather turned cold, despite my father's slapping her over it . . . I always appreciated it. I know now that she cared for and protected me as best she could, and only stayed with my father because that's what she'd been raised to do: stay with your husband through good and bad, regardless of just how horrible the bad became.

It is a terrible thing to grow old believing you never had any options.

She would call me every Sunday to tell me every excruciating detail of her week, most of which was spent in your employ. Remembering it now? How you hired her on as your full-time housekeeper after she stunned you with her talent for cleaning? Hm? Oh, well, no need to strain yourself—you'll either remember her or you won't.

The point is, *I do*.

Five years she worked in your home, sir. *Five years* she cleaned up the remnants and messes left by you and yours as you waltzed in and out of her path, offering her a few moments of human contact only so long as it was convenient, like monarchs tossing wheat to starving peasants. She never complained, nor did she ever resent it. After all, because of the job you so *generously* gave her, she was able to buy herself a comfortable chair and a nice color television. She was able to get *cable*. I think once she even went mad and bought herself some nice clothes—going-out dresses and a silk blouse of some sort—forget that her only child never bothered to come into town and take her out so she might show off her new wardrobe, so she might enter a restaurant and not worry that she wasn't properly attired, or go to mass and not think herself looking like a charity case. But even then, she wasn't bothered.

"Don't worry about it, hon," she'd say to me. "I know how busy you are, and it *is* a long drive. It's just nice to know that I got some nice clothes if I ever need them."

When I asked her if she ever had occasion to wear them, she said: "Well, I was reading this one magazine

Gary A. Braunbeck

at Mr. Parsons' house when I was having my break, and there was this article that said if you was a person who lived alone, it was good for your spirit if you made a fuss over dinner for yourself once a week, right? So I been trying that. Once a week I make myself a real nice dinner, and eat by candlelight, put on some nice music, and I dress for dinner. It's real nice, makes me feel special, you know?"

If only I could have expressed to her how special she always was. But I had inherited my father's vocabulary for compliments and expressions of affection.

Finally, I regained some sense. I called Mother and told her that I was going to come to Cedar Hill during Spring Break and spend two weeks with her, starting with her sixty-second birthday. She would finally get to wear her posh frock in public.

Don't ask me why I suddenly did this, why I suddenly realized that I wanted to make her remaining years as happy as I could. I only knew that I did. Having awakened one Sunday morning after a particularly taxing Saturday night of bar-hopping, I saw my hungover reflection in my bathroom mirror and for a moment thought Father's ghost had returned from the grave to tie one on with his offspring. "Have a drink on me, boy! Hell makes a man mighty thirsty!"

I just knew that I was shutting her out of my life as Father had shut us out of his, except of course for those times when he needed to express himself through his fists.

I called Mother and told her what I planned to do, and she was so happy she cried, and then for the first time in our lives she and I actually talked to one another. Yes, there were a lot of wounds to heal, there was a lot of detritus to be cleared from between us, but it made her happy, it gave her hope, and for once I found that I liked being in my own company. Ever since leaving town, I had done everything in my power to erase any and all traces of my childhood from my character; I had graduated college, learned to speak English that wasn't filled with slang, flensed my speech of its regional accent, and, all in all, behaved very unlike someone who was born and raised in a town which boasts the highest unemployment and lowest graduation rate of any city in the state. But that didn't matter, because I could never erase that childhood from my memory, nor what my mother endured. But I vowed she would endure it no longer. It may be a sentimentalist's dream to think that one can wipe away six decades of misery in a few short years, but I was going to try.

I arrived in Cedar Hill the day before her sixty-second birthday. Mother looked pale and thin to me, and I asked her if she was still taking her medication and not straining herself. She told me not to worry, she was fine and so glad to see me. She had to work that night but had cleared it with you or your wife—I forget which—so she could have the following evening free.

Anything starting to ring a bell yet, sir?

That was the same night your wife discovered you had a mistress and informed you that she was filing for divorce. As Mother told it, she caused quite a scene in front of one of your partners before she stormed out the door. But you couldn't be bothered with that—oh, no: you had the Governor himself coming for dinner the following night. Having never met you or your wife before, he would have no way of knowing that the woman hosting the affair was your mistress, a woman twenty years your junior and whom you intended to marry as soon as your divorce was final. So you called her, she came over that same night, and immediately told my mother that she absolutely *could not* have that evening off.

When I picked Mother up that night (she would not be taking the bus while I was there), she was very upset. Not only because she would have to work on her birthday, but because she was disappointed in you, sir. She thought the world of you until that night. I tried to convince her that she didn't have to work any longer, that we would go over the finances and I would help her arrange things. She would hear none of it. "All a person has is their word, hon, and I won't leave anyone in the lurch. He hired me to do a job, and I'm gonna do it. Just not showin' up, that wouldn't be right. Too many people do that today, think a job is beneath them and so just don't show up. I never done that in my life and

I'm not gonna start now. It'll be okay. I got the weekend off. We can celebrate my birthday then."

Back home—back in the house where my childhood was spent, I should say—I fixed her some tea and she sat in her chair, the lights low, and looked out the window.

"I like sitting here like this at night," she said, a wistful smile on her tired, lined, sad face. "The day's over, your work's done, and you can relax with the quiet. It's nice. I don't need to worry."

And so I sat there with her until it was time for bed. She seemed so much more tired than she should have been. I tried to convince her to go to bed, but she waved me away. "You always was a worrier," she said. "You go to bed, hon. I'm just gonna sit here and have another cup of this delicious tea you made me, then I'll sack out. Go on, I'll see you in the morning."

She looked even more tired and pale the next day. Once again I tried to convince her to quit, to not go in, but she cut the discussion off at the knees. I drove her to your home that afternoon, picked her up at eleven-thirty that evening, we once again had tea in the living room while she sat in her chair, I went to bed before her, and when I woke up the next morning she was still sitting there, quite dead. Still holding the tea cup and saucer in her lap.

Happy birthday, Mother.

I'll give the short version of the rest: I buried her, found out from her doctor that her heart problem had got worse lately *and* that she had told you about it. I took a leave of absence from my position at the university, locked myself up in the home of my childhood, and proceeded to stay as stinking drunk as I could for as long as possible.

I have no idea how long I remained in this state. It might have been only a few days, it might have been a few weeks. I didn't care. A good woman was dead and shouldn't have been; a woman who deserved *some* happiness in her life, some sense of being loved and needed and appreciated, was six feet under and hosting worms in her shell. I would never be able to tell her how much I loved her, how much I understood why she did what she did when I was a child, how brave I thought she was.

Knowledge of a wasted life—especially a life that was wasted *waiting* for life to begin—is a form of bad wisdom which I'm certain the likes of you has been spared.

I found myself in an all-night market at four in the morning. I came back to myself, came back into some semblance of awareness, in the toilet paper aisle. I was standing in front of a Cottonelle display, a plastic basket of snack foods hanging from my arm, and I was weeping like a baby.

I remember being very frightened. I could feel myself slipping over that unofficial border that separates the anxiety of the problem drinker from the hallucinations of the full-blown alcoholic, and I wasn't sure if I wanted to stop myself. I *could have* made things better for her and for myself a long time ago—two hours' drive isn't really all that long in the grander scheme of things, after all—but I chose not to. Because I was a coward. Because I didn't know if I could look at her face and see the ruins of her life chiseled in every wrinkle, line, and tiny scar. Her keepsakes, her souvenirs, my father's legacy. I didn't know if I could be with her and not feel like I had been a victim—what a trendy affliction that is. Blame Mom, blame Dad. "Oh, I'm in soooo much pain, I'm spirit-weary and emotionally dead because they screwed me up!" To hell with that. *She* was the victim, she always had been. I *knew* this, but I did not want to accept it. My legacy, my cowardice. So I stayed away far too long and learned not to treasure her. I invested too much in moments that didn't matter a damn and not enough in those moments that were *diamonds.* I think about all those little, misused pieces of time that I'll never get back—ten idle minutes here, a half hour there, the moments adding up and slipping away and all the time my mother sitting in Cedar Hill alone, *waiting* for her son to come back, *waiting* for her life to begin. I'll bet if I did the math, I've wasted years during which I could have made her happier, and myself as well. Standing there in front of a wall of toilet paper at four in the morning, I wished I could be given back just *one* of those misused days. I would have taken it, and I would have divided it up so carefully; then I'd look every second over like a diamond cutter with a jeweler's glass and say, "This moment will be for kissing her good night and giving her a hug so she'll know she sleeps under this roof with someone who loves her in the house," or, "This hour will be for a nice dinner at a fine restaurant, where I will sit proudly with her and let all the world know that this woman sacrificed so much to protect me, to enable me to pursue a better life than the one she's had."

I began weeping all the harder. Then I felt a hand on my shoulder.

I wiped my eyes and turned to look into the face of Grigori Rasputin.

That was my immediate thought. Before the break, my classes had been examining in detail the events which led to the death of Tsar Nicholas II and his family. My students all seemed fixated on Rasputin and his supposed powers of "second sight."

I stared into this face, stunned and speechless. Finally this man—who was not Rasputin but nonetheless bore a frightening resemblance to him, excepting of course for the priest's collar around his neck—asked: "What is it?"

I pointed to the Cottonelle display. "I was just thinking about toilet paper. I mean, yes, it can be used for several different things—blowing one's nose, absorbing blood from a shaving cut, applying acne medication—but its main purpose is what it's almost always used for. I was looking at this display and thinking about my mother. How she would always carefully go through the newspaper or the flyers that came in the mail, cutting out coupons and arranging them by expiration date, comparing the prices of the various brands so she could get the best possible price on the kind her family preferred to use because it was comfortable and absorbent and had the most sheets per roll so it would last as long as possible, always keeping an eye out for unadvertised sales—those always delighted her, a special surprise—and then finding the brand, selecting the package with the right number of rolls that she could afford with her coupon before it expired . . . and then, bringing it home with the rest of the groceries and putting fresh rolls in each bathroom. She would always start the roll for us so my father and I wouldn't have to bother. Do you see what I'm talking about? Toilet paper is one of the invisible things in life, something whose presence and function goes unnoticed until it's not there. but my mother made sure that never happened. Because she clipped her coupons. Because she arranged them by expiration date. Because she took the time to price the items and make the best possible purchase for what little money she had. All of the time she spent concentrating on all of the invisible things, all the time she spent on them . . . so her family wouldn't have to be troubled with it. Invisible things eat away your time, devour your days and years. God! How much of her life did she spend thinking about *toilet paper?* Being so careful to get it right just so her family could wipe—"

"—easy," said Rasputin's stand-in. "Easy now, there, there. Do you need to talk? Would you like some coffee?"

"I think so, yes."

"Then come on. Leave your basket and come with me."

I followed him over the East Main Street Bridge until we reached the homeless shelter. Inside, he poured us some coffee and made a sandwich for me. He sat in silence as I ate and drank enough coffee to qualify as a wide-awake drunk.

He offered his hand. "They call me the Reverend."

I shook his hand and introduced myself, and before I was even aware of it I had told him everything. *Everything.* My father and yourself included, Mr. Parsons.

He sat staring at me for a few moments, then— scratching at his beard—he cleared his throat and said: "Funny you mentioned Rasputin earlier. I've been thinking about him a lot lately—the last few years, in fact.

"There's a lot to be said for his gift of supposed 'second sight.' In 1911 he was in Kiev when a carriage carrying a politician by the name of Stolypin passed by. Rasputin ran up to the carriage and shouted, 'Death is for you. Death is approaching.' The next night Stolypin was shot by a revolutionary while at the theater. He died a few days later. Pity Rasputin couldn't use that gift to foresee his own assassination.

"The thing is, I have come to believe that his gift wasn't second sight, but the ability to convince himself that he had power over others to such an extent that he could convince them of his power—and not just power of the mind, Alan, but powers of the mind over cells, over genetic predispositions, over not just a person's mind but the connection between their mind and biology, as well. Prince Yussoupov's written account gives testament to this. When Rasputin applied this ability on Alexis, he in fact cast a spell over this boy who was overwhelmed by pain. Alexis' capillary blood flow declined and the strength of his vascular walls increased because Rasputin—who may have been a victim of his own delusions—made the boy part of those delusions and taught him how to unconsciously heal himself. The bleeding slowed, the boy drifted off to sleep, and eventually the bleeding stopped altogether. Because Rasputin possessed a singular ability which the church didn't acknowledge then and still doesn't: he recognized that God's power doesn't come from without, but from within. It's encoded somewhere deep in our cells and race memory from a time before we had legs and could walk upright. God's power is buried inside our chromosomes, encoded in our cellular structure. He knew this.

"I no longer have a church—my views offended too many people. What I have now is this shelter. That's fine by me. This is where God's love and power is needed most . . . when it chooses to show itself. Look at me: I am a man of God who has lost all hope but not his faith. That's a killer combination, by the way. But I'm going to tell you something now, something that I haven't told many people.

"Rasputin was right. The power of God that is encoded deep in our cells can affect not only the body and mind, but the outer world, as well. It's there to be manipulated, Alan, if you're willing to accept its presence and take the time to learn how to harness it.

"And nothing done with God's power is ever evil. You must remember that."

"Why?" I asked.

"Because I'm going to teach you. You need it worse than anyone I've seen in years."

*   *   *

I lifted the bottle from my lap and took another drink.

"Odd, isn't it? To think that God's power exists in our genetic codes and can be harnessed to manipulate the forces surrounding us. I have to confess, I thought he was crazy, but he insisted on teaching me." I shrugged. "I was sick with anger and grief and had no direction, no one to turn to, so I indulged him.

"Do you recall the study I spoke of earlier? In it, the investigators measured the electrical activity in the brains of three groups, one composed of nonalcoholics, the second of recovering alcoholics, the last of those who had been diagnosed as 'high risk.' They were all given books, and while the patients were reading, they listened through headphones to a series of tones. During the exercise, the tones were occasionally changed slightly. Through electrodes attached to the participants' heads, the researchers were able to measure the brain's electrical activity when the tones changed. The changes in tone produced a negative response in the brain's electrical activity. This response, called mismatched negativity, is a measure of brain excitability.

"The study found that mismatched negativity tended to be larger in both the recovering alcoholics and those people at high risk for alcoholism. Do you understand what that means? It means, arguably, that they have proved an excess of excitability exists in the brains of alcoholics. They've proved that lushes such as myself drink to self-medicate the imbalance, thus restoring balance to the brain since it acts directly on a neurotransmitter involved in excitability. Isn't that fascinating?

"But as they build up a tolerance to the effects of alcohol, however, alcoholics may have to drink more and more to get the same effect. Ah, well . . . behind every silver lining is a dark cloud, eh?

"I am convinced, now more than ever, that the 'mismatched negativity' they spoke of is actually the result of the worldly mind fighting the emerging power of the cellular mind; ignoring the presence of God's power in our genetic makeup. And I think that—just as God's son is rumored to have turned wine into His own blood, that our blood now struggles to turn itself back into wine. So some of us drink in order to speed up the process. But I know what you're thinking: blood is, after all, blood, and if you put your mind to it and make certain that the alcohol content in your blood exceeds fivefold, all known standards for drunkenness, you should be able to get drunk. Anybody should. It's a matter of biology. And not just human biology either. *Spiritual* biology. 'Take this cup and drinketh, and know that it is now my blood.' Damn good stuff, when you think about it.

"But after leaving the Reverend and the lessons of his shelter, I could not get drunk again no matter how hard I tried. And I *did* try, on that you have my word. I only knew that something was terribly wrong with me. Something had snapped off or screwed off or come undone inside of me. How was I to know that my cells were simply releasing God's power into my system bit by bit? I thought it was something solely physiological or psychological or neurological, something brought on by grief or a form of madness accompanying it. Perhaps some little blood vessel somewhere had burst or clogged, some brain synapse had blown, some major chemical change had taken place in the dark interior of my body or mind. I really had no clue. I only knew that getting drunk was gone forever from my life.

"I might have become immune to alcohol but not to hope. So I continued drinking in the hope that I might set things back in their proper place and somehow, miraculously, be able to become drunk again. It would make my anger and self-loathing so much easier to live with.

"But—no such luck. So, after a while, I had no choice but to consider the possibility that the Reverend's looney lessons might be true. I went over in my mind everything he had taught me— but don't worry, I won't waste any more of our precious time with describing the lessons; suffice to say that, in the end, I proved to be a rather apt pupil."

I lifted the bottle to my lips again and downed a full one third of it.

On the sofa, Parsons began to jerk and shiver. Sweat drenched his face and neck, staining his shirt. His skin had the gray pallor of a corpse. His eyes were wide and sunken, seemingly held in place only by the black circles underneath them. He stank of foulness, both his bladder and his bowels having emptied themselves at some point. He groaned wetly. His cough was the sound of an ancient crypt door being wrenched open to welcome another tenant.

"I went to a bar one night, having purposefully not taken a drink in several days. I sat at a booth and ordered a double whiskey, then—applying the methods taught me by the Reverend—chose a patron upon whom I would test my ability to manipulate God's cellular power. Within forty minutes I had consumed five drinks. I was steady and sober . . . but the patron I had selected, a man who'd had only one beer, was falling-down drunk.

"It was at that moment I became, cellularly-speaking, a Born Again."

I leaned forward to get a better look at him. His eyes were open wide as if frozen, and for a moment I feared he might be dead. I touched his throat to feel for a pulse and he immediately went into another series of seizures.

"Still with me. That's good. I wanted you to know that I was terribly sorry to hear of the death of your mistress. Your wedding was scheduled for June. I'll bet it would have been a breathtaking affair. But then, tragedy. So sad. She was so young, had so much to look forward to. To die so young and beautiful, with the promise of a world bowing down before her, the promise of so many servants to threaten." I lifted the bottle to my lips again. "Alcohol poisoning was the medical examiner's official conclusion, wasn't it?" I drank deeply.

He spasmed again, his breath sputtering out in painful wheezes.

I put the bottle down.

"What you're experiencing right now, Mr. Parsons, is something that's known as Korsakov's Syndrome. There is now an equal amount of alcohol and blood in your system. You're sweating alcohol, as a matter of fact. You are what is known by the layman as a 'wetbrain.' I was going to sit up here and drink the rest of this bottle and watch you die, but I think I like you better this way. If what researchers say is true, then buried somewhere deep in your brain is a tiny, nearly immeasurable remnant of awareness and memory. Your body is now little more than an organic keg of liquor. And for the rest of your life, Mr. Parsons—however long or short it may be—you will be trapped in there, and part of you will be forever aware of your imprisonment in an alcoholic haze. I hope you'll remember our little talk this evening—in fact, I've manipulated God's cellular power to make certain of it. And when you think of this night and the sick, pathetic sponge of your body, I want you to remember my mother's face, because I'll be damned if I'll be the only one who mourns her."

I rose, wiped clean the bottle and arranged his fingers around its neck, then said: "Have a drink on me, Mr. Parsons. Compliments of my mother, Mary Virginia Hards."

And with that, I left.

No one noticed my exit from the fund-raiser. I got in my car and drove downtown to the grocery store where my mother had done all of her shopping. I could feel the love of God's power humming in my blood, in my brain, flowing through my system.

In the store, I purchased that week's groceries—along with a goodly supply of liquor—and was loading everything into the trunk of my car when I saw three people leave the store; a man, a woman, and a small girl. The man carried a sack filled with canned beer. The woman carried two heavy-looking sacks filled with food and wore a very impressive black eye. The little girl—no more than five—carried two gallon containers of milk and looked as if she were straining herself not to drop them. She was pale and far too thin. Her face wore an expression that seemed quite familiar to me for some reason.

The woman stopped for a moment to get a better grip on her bags, and in the process dropped one. The man whirled around, loudly cursing at her, then looked to make sure there was no one around before kicking her in the ribs. The little girl began to cry, then set down her burdens and, on hands and knees, just like her mother, frantically gathered the groceries, stuffing them back into the torn bag while the man, looking ashamed of and embarrassed by them, stood over them, glowering.

I reached into the back seat and took a bottle of Scotch from one of the bags. Cracking the seal, I unscrewed the lid and downed the entire bottle.

By the time I was finished, the man was barely able to stand. Taking the keys from his hand, the woman walked toward their car, followed by her little girl.

Nothing done with God's power is ever evil.

Indeed.

I decided to follow them home. It was a nice winter's night. Perhaps I would play TV detective, go on a stakeout across the street from their house.

I had sufficient supplies, after all.

It was good to know that God's power had a purpose.

I am not a happy man, but I find these days I am happier than I was.

It's important I remember that.

EXITS AND ENTRANCES

by Tim Waggoner

Tim Waggoner has published more than sixty stories of fantasy and horror. His most current stories can be found in the anthologies *Civil War Fantastic, Single White Vampire Seeks Same,* and *Bruce Coville's UFOs.* His first novel, *The Harmony Society,* will soon be published. He teaches creative writing at Sinclair Community College in Dayton, Ohio.

"IT'S your fault I'm dead."

Morgan looked up from his pad, where he'd been jotting down notes for a review of a new production of *Waiting for Godot* that he'd had the misfortune of suffering through that evening.

Tall, blonde hair cut short with a bit of a curl around the edges, thin but not unattractively so, green dress that left her arms bare, hem above the knees. A bit on the plain side. She'd look better in black, he decided, with a neckline that revealed a hint of cleavage. Cobalt blue eyes, the flesh beneath puffy and tinged purple. Nose a bit crooked. *Gives her a bit of character,* he thought. Lips thin, a bit dry. Two words: lip balm.

He had no idea who she was.

"I don't suppose you're a waitress. I really could use another pot of hot tea." It had been his custom during the last fifteen years to dine at the Purple Pagoda after seeing a play. And in all that time, the service hadn't improved a jot. If anything, it had got worse. Oh, the food was good enough. His kung pao chicken—

"I'm not a waitress, I'm Claire. Didn't you hear what I said?"

"Hmm? Oh, yes. It's my fault you're dead. Please accept my sincerest apologies." He turned away from the woman and scooped up a forkful of chicken, vegetables, and rice—he didn't eat with chopsticks, considered them an affectation when used by anyone not raised with them—and returned his attention to his notes. He was trying to decide on a headline for his review. Right now, it was a toss-up between DON'T BOTHER GODOT—ING TO SEE THIS ONE, FOLKS and WAITING FOR A GOOD PERFORMANCE.

Out of the corner of his eyes, he saw the woman reach for his glass of water. He turned, starting to get angry now. He'd been a theater critic for two decades, and he was used to being confronted by no-talent actors and incompetent directors who felt they'd been done grievous injury by his critic's poison pen—or in his case, poison keyboard. Usually, he enjoyed the confrontations, fed on them the same way a football player or a boxer feeds on the fury and energy of an opponent. But he was on deadline tonight; he needed to finish this review, go home, type it up, and e-mail it to the paper before midnight so it could be printed in tomorrow's edition. He didn't have time to play games with this woman, whoever she was.

He intended to grab her wrist, prevent her from getting hold of the glass which, he knew from experience, she would no doubt empty onto his lap or perhaps over his head. After informing her that he'd just stopped her from committing a terrible cliché, he would tell her she'd made her point and ask her to leave him alone or else he'd be forced to summon the manager.

But he didn't do any of that. His hand froze in mid-reach, his fingertips only inches away from her flesh—flesh scarred by a trio of long, deep gashes that started just below the heel of her hand and extended halfway to the crook of her elbow. As he looked closer, he saw that the cuts were open, bloodless wounds, more like gill slits, really. As her fingers closed around his water glass and lifted it off the table, the gill-wounds parted a little, almost as if they were gasping for air. He expected to see strands of raw, red glistening muscle inside. But all he saw was blackness, as if she were filled with ink and shadows and things much, much darker, and much, much worse.

She brought the water glass toward him, obviously intending to fulfill Morgan's expectation and dump it on him. As she came nearer to completing her maneuver, the water grew cloudy, and crimson threads began to appear. A second later, the water had turned blood-red. No, had *become* blood, he was sure of it, sensed it instinctively. Thick, red so dark it was almost black. What else could it be?

And then she was upending the glass, not over his lap or head, but rather onto his notepad. He expected the contents to fall in heavy gouts, hit the paper with sickening wet plaps, splatter onto the tablecloth and his plate, blood staining white rice. But it was just water after all, though it did splatter and run and drip, and people were turning to look now, but he didn't care because it was only water, thank Christ.

The woman dropped the empty glass onto the table. Morgan looked at her wrist; the wounds were gone.

"Jerk." She turned, actually pivoted as if she were a soldier who'd just received a command to "about face," and walked off. She didn't storm, didn't stalk or stamp—she just walked.

Whatever the hell had just happened, Morgan was relieved it was over. He picked up his napkin, intending to blot his notepad dry.

And there, smack dab in the middle of the page, right over one of the O's in Godot, was a single, small dot of blood.

He typed the last phrase—which was "irredeemable dreck"—saved his file, and opened his e-mail program. He wrote a quick message to the typesetting department (*Please try not to mangle my prose too much this time*), attached the review, and clicked on SEND. He was about to log off— after all, the time display in the lower right-hand corner of his screen said it was closing in on one A.M. He'd missed his deadline, but not by too much—when he noticed a tiny envelope icon at the bottom of the e-mail window. The envelope sported a red flag that waved back and forth, back and forth, like a virtual metronome. He had mail.

Unlike some folks, Morgan wasn't particularly thrilled to receive e-mail. He had few living relatives and even

fewer people that could be called friends, even if one
were to grant the broadest and most liberal interpreta-
tion of the term. Junk mail, most likely. Someone wanting to tell him how he could make 10 K a month from
the privacy of his own home.

He gripped the mouse, intending to delete the message sight unseen, but then he hesitated. It could be
from someone in typesetting. There might have been
some problem with the file he'd sent. There was even
an outside chance it was from his ex-wife. A small
chance—she communicated with him only when strictly
necessary, and then usually by phone. But it could be
from her.

He hesitated a few more moments, then said to hell
with it and clicked on the envelope. The message
opened.

TO: MORGAN MCCLAIN
FROM: CLAIRE
SUBJECT: YOUR FAULT

There was no text with the message, only a small icon
of a paperclip. A file was attached. He knew better than
to open files that came from an unknown source, but he
was too busy trying to figure out how the woman from
the restaurant—how *Claire*—had gotten his home e-mail
address to be overly concerned with viruses. Had someone at the paper given out his home e-dress? He didn't
exactly have a lot of friends on the staff; still, it didn't
seem likely. But then how . . . ?

A thought drifted into his mind, then. A wild thought,
a crazy thought, a thought he'd dearly have loved to
*un*think, if only such a thing were possible. It was no
surprise she had his home e-mail address. After all,
hadn't she said she was dead? She was a ghost—a badly
dressed, puffy-eyed, crooked-nosed ghost—and nothing
was beyond the scope of her supernatural powers.

"Horseshit," he muttered, but the word didn't sound
convincing, even to his own ears.

She was probably just some actress he'd given a bad
review to years ago . . . God knew there were enough
of them. Hundreds, perhaps even thousands, as long as
he'd been writing. When she'd said she was dead and it

was his fault, she'd been speaking metaphorically. Her career (such as it was) was finished, and she blamed him for giving her a bad notice. It wouldn't be the first time.

Yeah, a shivery little voice inside him said, *but it's the first goddamned time you've been confronted by someone with gill slits on the underside of their forearm, not to mention who can perform a nifty parlor trick like turning water into blood, then back into water.*

She wasn't a spirit returned from the grave to exact revenge against the mean old theater critic who'd ruined her. That was the stuff of bad melodrama. Whatever he'd seen, not seen, or merely *thought* he'd seen, it had some form of rational explanation, no matter that said explanation escaped him at the moment. And to prove it, he clicked on the attachment.

The hard drive whirred as the computer went to work. An OPENING FILE message appeared on the screen, along with a horizontal series of white boxes. One by one, from left to right, the boxes turned blue as the file was opened. Twenty percent open. Thirty-five. Fifty-five. Eight. Ninety-five . . . then a new window appeared on the screen. It was a color picture of Claire. She was younger in the image, but it was clearly the same woman. In the background, plastic plants and ferns; in the foreground, Claire naked, on all fours. Behind her . . .

Morgan had been divorced for several years, and he didn't date much. He didn't have the sort of personality that worked and played well with others. But he still had normal biological urges and, occasionally, he'd surf the Net, searching for images that, if they didn't completely fulfill those needs, at least took the edge off them a bit.

But in all his prurient wanderings through cyberspace, he'd never seen anything like *this.*

There was a man behind Claire, well-muscled, tattooed, with washboard abs. He wore a black leather mask with slits for his eyes and mouth. In his hands he held the coiled length of a large, mottled-hided snake. A boa, or perhaps a python. The snake's tail was wrapped around the man's left wrist. Its head . . . Morgan couldn't see its head, but he had a good idea where it was.

He quickly closed the picture and deleted the file. He exited the e-mail program and sat staring at the screen, forcing himself to breathe evenly. But as hard as he tried, he couldn't keep himself from trembling.

"Is that the way I taught you to sit at the table?"

Morgan stopped bouncing, though he remained crouching on the dining room chair.

"No, Mother."

She bustled into the dining room, makeup and hair perfect, all perfume and nervous energy. She placed a serving bowl of peas onto a trivet—there was always a trivet; she would never allow a hot bowl to come into contact with the surface of the table. The peas were perfectly green, not too light, not too dark, and their skin wasn't puckered from overcooking or too hard from undercooking. Like Goldilocks' third choice, they were just right. But in the McClain household, Just Right was the first and only choice as far as his mother was concerned.

"Sit properly; rear on the seat, feet pointed toward the floor."

"Yes, ma'am." It was hard to make his body obey. He was five years old, and it seemed every part of him wanted to wiggle, squirm, and bounce. But he did it.

"Good boy." She patted him on the head, and he smiled as she began dishing peas onto his plate. She didn't drop any between the serving bowl and his plate; she never dropped any.

The front door opened, shut. Almost a slam, but not quite.

"You could be quieter coming in, you know," Mother called.

Morgan listened to the sounds of his father setting (not tossing) his keys onto the coffee table, moving to the front closet, the jingling of hangers (not too loud) as he hung up his coat.

"And would it hurt you to be on time for a change?"

Father walked into the dining room, a small man with a pot belly that always preceded him, and a dour, beaten expression. He sat at the table without saying a word, without looking at either of them. Morgan understood. Father hoped to avoid drawing any more of Mother's criticism.

She stood at the table, looking at him. Finally, she asked, "Did you stop at the bank on the way home?"

He stared down at his empty plate, and Morgan knew what the answer was.

Mother took in a breath of air, held it for a count of three, and then released it slowly, letting it fill the air with her disapproval.

"Do you know what makes us different from the animals, Phillip? They have no choice in how they act, what they eat, where they live, who they mate with—but we do. We can aspire to something higher. We can choose excellence, Phillip, excellence in all things . . . if only we have the courage."

Father continued to sit, continued to stare at his plate. But his jaw muscles bunched and bulged, and Morgan could hear his teeth grinding.

Mother just waited.

"I'll go to the bank tomorrow, during my lunch hour," Father said at last in a small, defeated voice.

Mother smiled. "That's nice, dear." She turned and headed back to the kitchen to fetch the next dish.

Morgan started to draw his feet up, unconsciously preparing to crouch and begin bouncing on his seat again.

Excellence, in all things, he heard Mother's voice, a whisper deep in his five-year-old mind.

He looked at Father. The man was dishing himself some peas, but he still couldn't bring himself to meet his son's gaze. And he had dropped three peas onto the tablecloth, too. Morgan *tcch*-ed and pressed his rear firmly against the seat, pointed his feet toward the floor.

I have the courage, he thought. *I do.*

The next morning, Morgan planned to head downtown and stop in at the paper. Since he often worked nights attending performances, he didn't *have* to go in until the afternoon, but he didn't have anything better to do. Besides, he knew if he stayed here he'd just keep thinking about Claire, and that picture of her . . . the man with the mask, the snake. . . .

As he headed for the door, he glanced at the glass-and-chrome end table next to the sofa and saw the message light on his answering machine blinking. Odd, he hadn't heard the phone ring. Maybe someone had called when he'd been in the shower. Probably just a sales call, though it might be his ex-wife. Either way, there was no great hurry to listen to the message. Still, he went over to the machine and hit the playback button.

Silence for several seconds. He'd been right the first time: a sales call. He didn't know what it was, the salespeople themselves or their computerized calling systems, but they often left blank messages. It was quite an annoyance coming home to a half dozen or more empty messages, all of which needed to be erased. He stabbed a finger toward the delete button, was about to press it when a voice finally came on.

"We need to talk. I'll be on the quad at the community college. Come as soon as you can." A few more seconds of silence, then the click of her disconnecting.

Claire.

He stood staring at the answering machine for several long moments. He felt compelled to replay the message, to make certain it really was her. But he didn't need to. There was no mistaking her voice. He pressed a trembling finger to the delete button and erased the message, but he sensed that he wouldn't be able to remove Claire from his life so easily. Whoever she was (not a ghost, damn it!), he knew that she wouldn't stop hounding him until she'd got whatever it was she wanted.

Besides, he was beginning to feel the first stirrings of anger within, the first hint of anticipation, of need for a confrontation. By Christ, if the bitch wanted to meet with him, then they'd meet, and he'd let Little Miss Stalker have it with both barrels. He headed for the door, and by the time he'd gone downstairs, outside, and got into his car, he was feeling downright cheerful.

Claire hadn't needed to tell him what community college to meet at; there was only one in the city. His alma mater, or one of them as he'd gone on to a four-year college and then to graduate school. But this was where he'd begun his college career, and aside from a less than

well-received speaking engagement several years ago
(the chair of the theater department had stood up in
the middle of Morgan's talk and called him a "pompous
asshole" and had gone on to call him much worse), he
hadn't been back since he'd graduated.

He parked his Lexus in the visitors lot, and strolled
down a tree-lined walkway toward the quad. The buildings
were ugly as sin; huge, blocky things without any scrap of
personality. Hell, they didn't even have names—no Mitch-
ner Halls or Davis Auditoriums—just large metal numbers
bolted to the brick. Building 1, Building 2 . . . talk about
a complete and utter lack of imagination.

The quad wasn't much better. It wasn't even square,
for God's sake, but round. How hard would it have been
to call the damn thing The Circle? In the middle was a
fountain, which during Morgan's tenure as a student had
always been filled with styrofoam cups and cigarette
butts. These days, it probably contained soiled condoms
and empty syringes. It was a warm, if breezy day in
early April, and normally this time of day, the "quad"
should've been filled with students heading from one
class to another, or just standing around gabbing, laughing, smoking. But it was empty. Was it some sort of
holiday? If so, Morgan wasn't aware of it. Maybe it was
an in-service day and classes were canceled. Whatever
the reason, the quad was deserted. No students, no faculty, and certainly no Claire.

He wondered if he'd been stood up, or if she had
never intended to meet with him, had just been playing
a prank. He was almost disappointed. He'd worked up
a good head of steam on his way over here, and now it
looked like he wasn't going to get a chance to unload
on Claire. He considered turning around and heading
back to his car. He checked his watch. Still early. Well,
he was here; he might as well give her a few minutes.

He walked over to the fountain, intending to sit on
the edge while he waited. But as he drew near the water,
he stopped. Floating facedown in the fountain amid the
debris left by students was a woman dressed in a
medieval-looking gown of green and white. A *blonde*
woman. Morgan took a step forward, intending to do
whatever he could to help, but then he stopped.

"Your tableau displays a certain amount of imagination, but it's a more than a little over the top, don't you think?"

The woman continued to float for a moment or two more, then she pushed herself to a sitting position and turned to look at him, an expression of extreme irritation on her face.

"You're not funny."

Her skin was bluish white, her face bloated as if she'd been in the water for days. Her lips were so swollen she could barely get words past them. *'Or 'ot hunny.* The sleeves of her gown were split at the elbows and hung down, their ends floating on the water. He glanced at her arms, and, as if obliging him, she turned her hands palm up so he could see the gashes, three on each forearm.

He felt an insane urge to go to her and help her out of the fountain, but he couldn't bring himself to step forward, couldn't bear the thought of touching her wet and undoubtedly cold flesh.

She pulled herself out and sat on the edge of the fountain, water dripping off her, beginning to form a puddle at her feet. She patted the concrete next to her, indicating he should sit. Her hand left dark, moist prints.

"If it's all the same to you, I think I'll stand." His voice sounded far away to his own ears, and he felt a trifle dizzy. He wondered if he might faint; he wondered if he cared.

"Suit yourself." *Shhuit yer'efhh.* She lifted her arms, the wet ends of her sleeves dangling. "Recognize the costume? My little dip in the fountain is a clue."

Her voice was still distorted, but for some reason he had no trouble understanding her. "I don't—" and then it came to him. "Ophelia!"

She clapped her hands softly, the wounds on her forearms opening and closing along with the action. "Bravo, Mr. Critic! Hamlet's girlfriend who, after her love has killed her father, descends into madness and commits suicide by throwing herself into a stream and drowning. A fountain's a poor substitute, but a girl has to work with what she's given."

A memory tickled at Morgan's mind. There was something about this school, Ophelia, an actress named Claire . . . then he remembered.

"Omigod."

She smiled, and Morgan saw black-shelled water beetles wriggling behind her teeth.

"Terribly miscast?"

"You're a good actress—" he'd almost said *competent*, "—it's just . . ." He trailed off, afraid to say anything more. His words had got him in enough trouble as it was.

They stood in the hall on the third floor of Building 6, outside his modern American literature class. People walked by, heads turned toward them, some frowning in puzzlement, others smirking knowingly.

Claire brandished the rolled-up student newspaper at him as if he were a bad puppy she intended to swat on the nose. Tears glistened in her eyes, and she blinked furiously, fighting to hold them back.

"Good actress? Not according to this!" She opened the paper, began to read. " 'Claire Ashton, as Ophelia, is terribly miscast. Her idea of portraying the character's madness is to stare off into the distance as if she were merely waiting for a bus. One hesitates to use the expression *all wet* when referring to her performance, but if the cliché fits . . .' All wet? God, what a lame joke!" A sob erupted from her throat then, a strange, unfeminine sound, almost like a frog's croak. She slapped the paper against his chest and let go of it. It fell to the floor, and Morgan almost bent down to pick it up, not wishing to see his writing discarded like so much litter. But he sensed that would be a bad move right now, so he left it alone.

"I didn't mean anything by the joke," he said. "It was just something to spice up the review, make it more interesting to read. It's nothing personal."

"Not personal?" She was almost shrieking now. "How could it be any more personal, you sonofabitch!" Tears rolled down her cheeks now.

He should've said he was sorry, that he had tried to be clever at the expense of her feelings, and it was wrong, and more than that, it was downright nasty. He started to, got as far as opening his mouth when she said, "You're nothing but a hack, you know that? Mr. Student Newspaper Critic. After you graduate—assuming they let you graduate, that is—you'll be lucky to get a job writing copy for the back of cereal boxes!"

He knew she was lashing out because he had hurt her so, but his own anger welled up now, liberally mixed with bile. It surged into his throat, poured over his tongue, and shot out of his mouth before he could stop it.

"You know, if you'd invested your Ophelia with half as much passion, we wouldn't be having this conversation right now."

Claire's eyes widened in shock and her hand twitched. For a moment, he thought she was going to slap him. But instead she turned around and ran off, and she didn't look back.

"You remember now." It wasn't a question.

He nodded. "You didn't come back to school the next quarter. The rumor around the theater department was that you'd transferred to another college."

"No. I decided that I'd had enough of school, so I moved to L.A., determined to get into movies and become famous, all so I could come back to Ohio one day and shove my Oscar up your ass." She shook her head, seeming almost embarrassed.

"Luckily for me, it doesn't look like you're concealing any golden statuettes on your person." It seemed insane, standing here and chatting with a woman he'd hurt over twenty years ago, a woman who, according to her own words was . . . "Are you really, you know . . . dead?"

She showed her arm wounds again. "These aren't exactly a fashion statement. I was smart about it, made sure to cut long-ways instead of across the wrist, and I made three cuts on each arm. That way, even if anyone found me before I died, they wouldn't be able to save me." She gave a little *hmph*. "Not that there was anyone to find me."

"When?"

"Last night, not long before you sat down at the Purple Pagoda."

Morgan looked at her for a moment then, despite

himself, walked over and sat down next to her. But not
too close. "Why did you do it?"

She clasped her hands in her lap and kicked her feet
back and forth slowly, the way a little girl might do.
"Did you open that picture file I sent you?"

"Yes."

"After I got to L.A., I auditioned my butt off, but all
I managed to get were parts in a few commercials. But
I was pretty, if not gorgeous, and more importantly, my
boobs were big enough to draw the attention of a man
who made what he said were 'alternative films.' "

"Oh."

"Uh-huh. Before I knew it, I had changed my name
to Cherry Wylde and I was making an *alternative film*
every two weeks. It wasn't so bad at first. I was paid
well enough, and while I wasn't so young and stupid that
I thought I was a real actress, I kept auditioning for
parts in legitimate movies whenever I could. But eventually, the lifestyle caught up with me. Drugs were everywhere, and I avoided them as long as I could, which
turned out to not be all that long. Age took its toll as
well, especially since my breasts were real and not store-
bought. Eventually, I began to lose the war with gravity.
If I wanted to keep working, I had to make movies of
a more . . . extreme nature. Stuff younger, firmer-bodied
actresses refused to do. That still I sent you was from
my last picture, *Jane of the Jungle*. And it was one of
the tamer shots. Once filming was completed . . ." She
trailed off, fingered the bloodless wounds on her left
arm. "You know what my last thought was as the darkness reached out for me?" She turned to him, her eyes
filled with smoldering fury. "You."

Morgan felt a cold fluttering in his bowels.

"There's a moment when you're perfectly balanced
between life and death. And during that moment, you
can *see* things. *Know* things. I knew the exact instant
when my life began to head straight for the toilet. Do I
have to give you three guesses?"

"My review of your Ophelia."

"Bingo."

Morgan felt a wave of guilt mixed with burgeoning

terror. "I admit I went too far, but I was just a kid still trying to learn how to write. And I had to be honest—it's the critic's job to serve his readers, as well as the field he writes about. Honest criticism helps actors and directors realize how their work impacts an audience, it helps them—"

"Strive for excellence," Claire said, but not in her voice; his mother's. "After all that's what makes us different from the animals, right?"

Frost formed on his spine, cold needles jabbed into his gut and stirred around in his organs. He wanted to get up, wanted to run like hell, but his body refused to obey.

"I told you I knew things." Claire's voice was once again her own.

"What . . . what do you want from me?"

Claire blinked, surprised. "I don't want anything *from* you, Morgan. I've come to *give* you something."

Cat-quick, she grabbed the back of his head, held him in an iron grip. He glanced left, right, into her gill-slit wounds, saw the darkness therein, saw that it was moving. He knew then that the black insects he'd seen weren't just behind her teeth; they filled her completely. Claire leaned forward, opened her mouth, and he saw beetles scuttling on her tongue, scampering over one another, excited.

He tried to stop himself, knew what would happen if he couldn't, but no matter how much he tried not to, he opened his mouth to scream.

She fastened her water-bloated lips to his, and a flood of dark insects rushed forth.

"You really should get your hair cut."

Morgan opened his eyes, saw a twentysomething boy with a lip ring looking down at him, framed by blue sky and clouds.

"Excuse me?" Not particularly witty, but it was all Morgan could think to say.

"Your hair—it's too long." The boy's lips formed a half sneer, making his ring twitch.

"I think he should dye it." This from a black-haired girl in a cutoff white T-shirt that exposed her pale, taut belly. "Too much gray, don't you think? If he had more, it might look distinguished, but there really isn't enough. It just looks—"

"Dingy," finished the boy. "I agree completely. And what about that shirt?"

Morgan sat up, looked around. He was still on the quad, a few feet from the fountain. But now, far from being deserted, the quad was full of students and faculty. No one was walking or talking, though. They all stood still, heads turned toward him, all of them with (was he imagining it?) disapproving expressions on their faces.

He felt feverish, dizzy. The memory of Claire—and of her kiss—hit him like a sledgehammer, and he thought he might faint again. But he managed to maintain his hold on consciousness, if only just.

"I'm . . . sick. Could you help me up?" He extended his hand toward Lip Ring.

The youth eyed his hand suspiciously. "There's no way I'm touching that sweaty, flabby thing. I'd sooner touch an octopus slathered with toxic waste."

Morgan looked to Bare Midriff who wrinkled her nose in disgust. "It would be like shaking hands with my grandfather, and he died ten years ago."

"Fine." Morgan struggled to his feet, swayed, took a stagger-step forward but didn't fall.

"Nice," called out someone in the crowd. "Where'd you learn to walk, detox?"

His stomach clenched and roiled, and he fancied he felt dozens, no hundreds, *thousands* of insects swimming in a sea of gastric juice. He started forward, pushing his way through the crowd, ignoring their taunts. He wanted to get to his car, told himself that everything would be fine if he could just get behind the wheel, hit the gas, and get the hell out of here.

Several minutes later, he reached the visitors' lot, saw a uniformed woman standing next to his Lexus, notepad in hand. Behind her, a compact blue-and-white vehicle with a rectangular cab was parked perpendicular to his car. When Morgan had been a kid, the woman would've been called a meter maid. Now, in this more enlightened time, she was a . . . what? Parking patrol officer? Something like that.

As he approached, he attempted to compose himself, checked to make sure his shirt was tucked in properly, wiped the sweat from his brow. Not that the latter action helped much; he was dripping as if he'd just stepped out of a shower.

"Is there a problem, officer?" His voice sounded too high, strained, but at least he'd got the words out.

The woman looked up at him, eyes narrowed, lips pursed. "I'll say. This is one of the worst parking jobs I've ever seen. Your driver's side tires are *on* the yellow line; they're supposed to be *inside* it." She pointed at his tires with her pen for emphasis. "and your rear end is sticking out too far by at least six inches. That creates a hazard; someone else could drive by and accidentally clip your car." She tcched and shook her head. "There's really no excuse for parking like this. If you'd just taken the time—"

"Thank you for the feedback," Morgan interrupted. A spasm of pain racked his gut, and he nearly doubled over. He finished through gritted teeth. "If you'll just give me my ticket, I'll be on my way."

The woman scowled, but she ripped a piece of paper from her pad and jammed it into his hand. "Have a nice day," she said, obviously wishing him anything but, and she got into her cart and drove off.

Morgan looked down at what he expected to be a citation. Instead, it was a ticket of a far different sort.

FOR ONE DAY ONLY, A SPECIAL COMMAND PERFORMANCE! MORGAN McCLAIN, THEATER CRITIC AND ALL-AROUND MISERABLE HUMAN BEING, STARS IN *PAYBACKS ARE HELL!* ADMIT ONE.

The ticket said nothing about where and when the performance was scheduled, but it didn't need to. Morgan knew. It was here, at the campus theater where he had watched Claire Ashton play Ophelia so many years ago. And the time was now.

Screw that! Morgan tore the ticket in half once, twice, again and again, until he'd reduced it to confetti. Then he hurled the pieces skyward, where they were caught by the wind and borne away, tumbling and dancing through the air.

"I'm not going to play your game, Claire!" he

shouted. "Do you hear me? So tie on a toe tag, shuffle back to the morgue, and leave me the hell alone!"

He felt something sharp prick the space between his shoulder blades. He yelped and spun around. Standing there, dressed in a white tunic, golden breastplate, and sandals, and holding a wooden spear tipped with a sharp black metal head, was the leather-masked snake handler Morgan had seen in the picture Claire had sent him via e-mail. Her costar from *Jane of the Jungle*.

"Let me guess," Morgan said as he felt a trickle of blood run down his spine. "You're a spear carrier, right?"

The man didn't say anything, but now that Morgan looked closely at the mask's eye slits, he saw the man had a reptile's eyes. He blinked, and a clear, moist membrane slid across his eyes then receded. The man gestured with the spear, and Morgan got the message. He started walking, the masked man following behind, the spear's metal tip pressed against Morgan's back.

Morgan stood on a bare stage, dead center, sweating in the harsh glare of a spotlight. Though he couldn't see them well, he knew he had an audience. The house was packed; there wasn't an empty seat to be had. Sitting in the front row, middle seat, was Claire. No longer decked out like Ophelia and no longer wet, she wore the simple green dress she'd had on when he'd first encountered her at the Purple Pagoda. He wondered if it were the same dress she'd been wearing when she killed herself. He decided it was. On her right, still clutching his spear, sat Snake Eyes. The Morgan McClain he had been only a couple of days ago might've made a joke about the porn actor being so attached to his "weapon," but not now. There was nothing funny about this, nothing at all.

"How does it feel, Morgan?" Claire called out. "Being on a stage, I mean. It's your first time, right?"

It was. Morgan had never so much as set foot upon a stage, let alone been in a play, not even in grade school. He felt very exposed, and very alone. But as frightened as he was—and *frightened* didn't nearly do justice to what he was feeling; he wasn't sure there was a word in any human language that could encapsulate the depth of

his terror—he was determined not to show it. He would
fight back with the only weapon he had, the only one
he'd ever had: words.

He put a hand up to shield his eyes from the spotlight. "It
would be an understatement to say you have me at a disad-
vantage, Claire. You all can see me, but I can't see you."

"Fair enough." Claire raised her voice. "House
lights, please!"

The spot switched off and the theater lights came on.
Morgan blinked for a moment as his eyes adjusted. He
looked upon the audience that had gathered to witness
his "command performance," and as he did, he decided
he had been better off when he couldn't see them. They
were shadowy creatures, vaguely humanlike in shape,
but they were indistinct, edges blurry, with no discern-
ible features. Darkness given form.

Morgan felt a stab of pain in his gut, ignored it. Even
though the spotlight was off, he was still sweating, still
felt feverish. He looked at Claire and gestured at the
audience. "Friends of yours from the great beyond?"

"Not exactly. These aren't spirits of people, though
they are ghosts of a sort. They're echoes of possibilities."

"I don't understand." The shades seemed to stir and
roil as if they were made out of smoke, and he thought
he could hear a soft undercurrent of sound, like the hush
of waves breaking on a not-too-distant shore. Were the
shades talking to one another—or were they trying to
say something to him?

Claire stood and walked to the edge of the stage.
"Each one of them represents a wrong choice, a missed
opportunity, a 'road not taken.' All because of your
words." She turned and pointed to the shade that had
been sitting on her left. "That's the newest addition. Remember your review of *Godot*? One of the leads read
your article today, and after seeing how you savaged
his performance, decided not to continue pursuing his
master's degree in theater. He was supposed to go on
to get his doctorate, and eventually he would've become
dean of fine and performing arts at a large university.
He would've, directly and indirectly, helped hundreds of
students go on to realize their dreams of having a life

in the arts. But now he's going to end up just another IT worker, clicking away on a mouse while he rots away in a cube farm."

She turned back to face Morgan. "I could tell you a similar story for every one of them. Careers derailed, families that were never started, substance abuse problems where before there were none. On and on. Every single incidence attributable to one cause: your *criticism.*"

Morgan looked out upon the dark things sitting in the theater, watching him, though they had no visible eyes, speaking in shadowy whispers, though they had no mouths. He didn't want to believe it, but he felt the truth of Claire's words deep in the core of his being.

Another lance of agony pierced his stomach. He gritted his teeth, rode the pain out until it passed. "Maybe it's true, but you can't lay the blame solely at my feet. We all make choices, and our actions all have effects, most of which we're never aware of. All we can do is the best we can. I wrote my reviews in good faith. I saw plays, and then I spoke my mind about them on the printed page. I did it for my readers, and ultimately, for theater itself. I can't be faulted for that."

"True—if indeed your motives were as pure as you say. But remember how I said that in the moment between life and death, I saw things? One of the things I saw and understood was that existence is a delicate karmic balance, a cosmic game of jackstraws. And if during your life you draw the wrong straws, tilt the balance too much one way or another, you must restore that balance after you die." She seemed to look past him, at something very far away. "And if you think paybacks are bad here, they're nothing compared to over *there.*" She focused her gaze on him once more and smiled. "Believe it or not, Morgan, I've come to do you a favor. I'm giving you a chance to pay here and now, when it won't cost you so much." She grinned. "Kind of a spiritual super-saver bargain."

"So you're playing Marley's ghost in this little production, eh?" He took a deep breath, felt his gut twist into another knot. "All right, what do I have to do? And please don't tell me I'm going to be visited by three spirits this night."

"Nothing so elaborate." She stepped back, turned, and took her seat in the audience of shadows once more. She settled back and crossed her legs. You have only to answer one question, but you must answer it truthfully: Did you write your reviews to fulfill your readers' needs—or your own? Were you truly trying to perform a public service, or were you merely passing your self-loathing on to others?"

"That's two questions," Morgan said. Claire didn't respond; she just sat, watching and waiting. The shades were quiet now, too, and though they had no expressions to read, Morgan knew they were watching him with rapt attention.

Sweat rolled off him, his stomach clenched and unclenched. He heard his mother's voice whisper in his mind. *Excellence, in all things.* He had tried to live his life according to that standard, had told himself never to settle for anything less. But now here, faced by the revenant of a woman who'd committed suicide and a theater full of aborted possibilities, he wasn't so certain of his motives. He thought of all the actors and directors who had confronted him over the years, thought of the way his colleagues at the paper always seemed distant—when they would talk to him at all, that is. Thought of his ex-wife, who'd left because, in the end, she couldn't take his endless criticism. It was so hard to think; he was so hot, and his stomach felt as if it might explode at any moment . . .

No, he decided. Excellence was excellence. People were just lazy; if they worked harder, *tried* harder, they wouldn't have to settle for mediocrity. It was the greatest life lesson his mother had ever taught him, and he refused to gainsay it now.

"Every word I wrote was for my readers, for theater. None were for myself."

Claire smiled sadly. "I knew you were going to say that. But I had to give you a chance."

Morgan stood, waiting. Seconds ticked by, but nothing happened.

"So is that it? Is it over? I—" It felt as if a giant hand grabbed him around the middle and squeezed as hard as it could. He grunted and doubled over in agony. Something small and skittery came rushing up his throat, over his tongue, shoved against his gritted teeth. Morgan spat, and a small, hard object fell to the stage floor with a tiny clack.

It was a beetle, one of the flood that Claire had passed to him with her kiss on the quad. But it was no longer black; it was white. And on its back were two words, spelled out in Times New Roman letters.

Irredeemable Dreck. The last two words of his *Godot* review. Words, he was forced to admit, he had written solely and completely for his own selfish pleasure.

"You know the expression, 'forced to eat his words'?" Claire said.

Fire blossomed in Morgan's stomach, agony beyond anything he had ever known.

"In your case, it's backward."

Morgan screamed as the beetles began their work and the audience applauded with dark, shadowy hands.

When it was finished, his white, polished bones lay on the stage floor. Claire stepped up to the skeleton, regarded it for a moment before reaching down and taking the skull in her hands, and with a single, savage jerk, tore it free from the spinal column. She held the skull to her face, looked into its smooth, empty sockets.

"Almost paid in full, Morgan. Just one more bit to go."

"Alas, poor Yorick! I knew him, Horatio: a fellow of infinite jest, of most excellent fancy."

Morgan sat nestled in the actor's palm, gazing at him with eyeless eyes. He sensed the audience out there beyond the stage, listening in the dark, hanging on every word. And why not? They were among the best words—the purest words—ever written in the English language.

"He hath borne me on his back a thousand times; and now, how abhorred in my imagination it is! My gorge rims at it."

The actor was young and spoke the lines a bit too self-consciously, but overall, he wasn't bad. Not bad at all. Morgan hoped the reviews would be good, especially considering that this was his first role. It wasn't much, but as they say in the theater, there are no small parts, only small actors.